THE SALEM LEGACY

A HORROR NOVEL

PAUL CARRO

TETHER FALLS PRESS

To Meghan,
The true Horror Babe!,

Paul Carro

TETHER FALLS PRESS

To Dad, the original Paul Carro, for hooking me on comic books and monster movies at a young age. Life is ninety-nine percent psychological and one percent of what you know...

In the quest for true evil, look no further than in the heart of man...

CHAPTER 1

SALEM 1692

WATER BUBBLED OVER ROCKS in a creek bed. In normal times, Althea Goode would rest along the bank, eyes closed, and succumb to the soothing sounds even as her children played nearby, living out childhood fantasies. But now the same serene scene brought nothing but unease. Something about the night was off. An energy lingered in the air riding a gentle wind, carrying with it a sense of danger. Never would she allow her children to play near the water at night. Oh no. But Althea had occasionally done so herself. Even in darkness, the vista usually brought comfort. Not tonight.

Splash!

Althea dipped a wooden bucket into the water against the current, allowing it to fill. The puritan woman in her twenties was once upon a time lovely, before hardship descended on her life and features. Evening clothes would have been appropriate for the hour, but the woman remained fully (and modestly) dressed head to toe in her daytime garments. Her hands trembled violently, and she struggled to hold on to the bucket as it grew heavy with liquid.

Despite spring's early arrival, some snow patches remained, though most of the ground had already thawed. The nighttime temperature had not dropped precipitously from the unseasonably warm New England day. That meant Althea's tremors were unrelated to chilly weather.

It was that danger, riding on that wind that unnerved the woman, who continued struggling with her load. Danger. Althea fought not to laugh in the face of irony, for she knew full well where danger lurked. A horrific scene played out from where she came. Yet something else was with her in the woods, something predatory. Heavily forested on one side, the brook opened into a hilly field along its opposite bank, rising into a prominent ridge. It was there the danger revealed itself. From atop the ridge, something growled. Throaty, guttural, hungry.

Althea searched the ridge for the source. The awful sound joined the wind and soon the aggressive din emitted from seemingly every direction. Occasionally, a twig snapped somewhere in the forest. Dense trees lined the bank on which she crouched. The thick foliage supplied cover to anything that wished to use it. She fought the urge to turn with every snap. Althea understood if faced with danger, she would bolt. Yet she could not afford to. Closing her eyes, she tried to focus on the serenity of the stream.

Water filled the container with minimal spill. Her full-length apron (tucked laboriously into her petticoat) absorbed stray splashes. Althea faced more dampness in her daily kitchen routine. Sweat was another thing. Water dripped from Althea's brow and joined the eddy.

Heat. She was flush with it as if the death's fever knocked on the door of her soul, announcing an invitation to visit God's realm. Yet, she was not the one sick. There were others. The thought caused her to turn back, instinctively eyeing the winding path leading to her two-story home. An owl hooted, watching from somewhere in the dark. Althea pulled her waistcoat tight, modesty in all things, even beasts. Especially beasts.

So far was she from her home, from her church, from the nearest bible. Vulnerable and alone in the night, her coif atop her hair was not enough to provide cover from evil's reach. Something opposite the creak drew her gaze. The thing danced under starlight high on the ridge.

A dog. Massive, black, fangs bared, teeth glistening even in the darkness, growling deeply. (Were that it was the only thing growling that night!) It raised itself on its haunches, eyes reflecting red as if under a hunter's moon despite there being merely a crescent visible in the sky. It was as if another beast burned within an innocent (though frighteningly large) animal, using it merely as a vessel to observe the surroundings. The distance should have been too great to even spot such details, but Althea did. The eyes haunted her. Red. Burning. Large. The dog barked.

Althea raced for the house, bucket in hand. The rear of her home revealed itself by the glow of an upper window. The flickering interior light eerily matched that of the dog's eyes. A lower window offered a more certain glow. Warm, stable. *God*, she thought. That room contained her Bible, the one she wished she currently carried but did not.

How could she have brought it along? So heavy was the filled bucket she struggled to move. Her initial flight of fear provided her strength beyond her norm, but the distance to the home stole stamina from her body. Her limbs ached nearly as much as her heart. The upper room, (a once inviting space) flickered an unholy red. *Was God there in that room*? *He who was everywhere*? Althea wondered, only to determine God must have a blind spot, for how else could he allow his flock to suffer so?

A bark. In her ear. The beast upon her? She turned, splashing in a circle, droplets ringing her in an involuntary Pagan ritual. Nothing there. No beast on the ridge. Maybe there never was. For Althea knew well the beast's location—behind that upper window. She shook off her fear and focused on the task at hand, staggering under the weight. She burst through the door.

"You do my job, Mum?" Haddy asked as Althea stumbled into the kitchen.

Haddy, a youthful and sturdy black woman, stirred a large boiling pot which sat atop the wood stove. The heat curled what little of the woman's hair showed beneath her tightly wrapped headscarf. Damp spots covered portions of the woman's attire, but the thrice wrapped garment from her country allowed for modesty even while wet. A full apron hanging from Haddy's waist took the brunt of spillage.

The servant rushed to relieve Althea of her burden, taking ownership of the water bucket. Althea fell against the wall and glanced through the open door, past the foyer, into the living room. The lit fireplace and lanterns in the distant room illuminated the space well enough for her to spot the bible resting atop a small table. Althea took comfort in the sight, wiping her brow with a cinched sleeve, clearing away sweat brought on as much by worry as her activity.

Thump! A loud disturbance sounded overhead. Althea eyed the ceiling. Haddy glanced at her employer while stirring more vigorously. With a forced smile, Haddy raised her stir spoon to the air.

"Oh, how children can play," Haddy said.

"Were it so. I would welcome such rambunctiousness, would tolerate their insubordination of house rules were things only so simple," Althea said.

"Do not bring lies into the home, missus. Never a day would you tolerate such a scandalous bout of play, nor will you in days to come, for surely after the ceremony, life will return. The old ways will return."

"Do you believe that?" Althea asked.

Wham! Did someone drop a new house top their existing one? How else to account for such a deafening noise? Althea attempted to smile at her charge, offer a reassuring agreement, but fell short. Her mouth crimped into further worry. Neither could muster a reassuring false façade.

"I have been called a fool. I prefer the term resilient missus. Do I believe doors opened can be closed? My frailty of character deems it so."

"You bring me strength, Haddy. For that I thank you," Althea rubbed the woman's arm.

Haddy poured the bucket of fresh water into the pot. Steam exploded into the air, the vapor enveloping the two women until they vanished from one another's view. Althea waved away the cloud above her. The swirling mist took on the form of a demon chasing its tail, one circling Althea in a bemused fashion, enjoying the distraught woman's plight. The reappearance of Haddy drew a gasp from Althea.

The foreign worker appeared as if melted under the remnants of the steam bath. Haddy deftly used tongs to pick up one rag, then another, dropping both into the boiling vat. She stirred with the utensil several times before pulling the rags back out one at a time, placing them in tight bunches atop an ornate silver platter. She then handed the tray to Althea.

Wham!

More chaos overhead. Althea exited the kitchen to the base of stairs in the foyer. Heavy breathing sounded from somewhere above. Althea climbed the stairs. Tremors returned to her hands as she fought to maintain a grip on the tray of steaming rags.

Althea crested the stairs to a hallway with three rooms. One each on either side of the hall, and one facing out at the end. All doors were closed. Candles flickering from wall mounted holders cast oversized shadows of Althea's form.

A boom sounded from behind the last door. Althea jerked in fright. The animalistic cries were as if from a beast not of this earth. Grunts and growls from behind the first door answered the calls of those coming from the last. Combined, they formed a symphony of raspy abhorrence. The unnatural cacophony represented violations of flesh truncated with thunderous booms of rage, all playing out through the instruments of shaking walls and furniture.

"As the Lord is with me, I beg thee for strength. I beg thee for clarity of sight, to allow me to witness the true nature of these lost souls. Through me show mercy, in my presence offer the afflicted comfort, allow those who gaze upon me to return to mindfulness of God's power and love."

Althea balanced the tray and approached the first door. She touched the knob, and the door glided open as if on its own. She stepped into the room. Unable to hold it back any longer, Althea screamed. On the bed, something inhuman screamed back.

CHAPTER 2

CALIFORNIA PRESENT DAY

T HE CHILD RAN WIDE-EYED, terrified, desperate to escape. Escape what? Something struck her at high velocity. She dropped. First to her knees, then onto her back, eyes closed. The little girl appeared angelic in repose until she leaped to her feet, laughing hysterically. Collecting the loose ball that hit her, she exited the interior of a chalk outlined playing field. Two large squares, side by side, a variation of dodgeball.

The game involved multiple balls and many children. Chaos reigned. Blood was the game's official name. None dared call it that under the shadow of an ever-present cross anchored high atop St. Mary's orphanage and school. Elimination was the accepted title of the game, which often ironically drew blood.

Andrew Williams, a crunchy granola type with bushy dark hair and an amiable smile that quickly gave way to dimples, oversaw the chaos. Lean, athletic, and in his twenties, Andrew easily kept up with the young crowd and soon found himself in possession of a ball with an easy shot at a slow classmate standing in center chalk. The heavyset boy eyed his teacher with resignation, wearing the look of one used to losing in sports. Andrew hurled the ball. And missed. The boy smiled unaccustomed to such charity.

"Move, move, move, you've got this," Andrew said.

The boy did, narrowly missing another ball. He ran inside the chalk with a newfound sense of hope. Andrew chased after his overthrown ball, which rolled farther down the playground, catching an incline, and picking up speed.

Two women sat at a nearby picnic table, lunching and watching from a safe distance. Linda Hunt sat stiffly upright despite no chair-back to support her. Linda's hair rose into an impossibly tight bun. She took measured bites from a wheat bread sandwich, occasionally dabbing at her chin with a cloth napkin, a clean sky-blue lunch tote and reusable water container at her side. Roughly Andrew's age, Linda watched her fellow teacher in the distance. A hint of longing in her gaze?

Her lunch buddy, Heather Parson, older by a decade, picked up on the look before picking on her friend. "It's supposed to be the children getting crushes, not the teachers."

"It's not a crush," Linda replied.

Heather shrugged before leaning back against both hands, taking in the scene. Despite her age, Heather wore an old-fashioned Catholic schoolgirl style outfit with long hair that reached her middle back. Andrew smiled and waved from a distance. Linda flashed red. Heather turned to her friend and smirked.

"Hot flashes in yer' twenties?" Heather slipped into her natural southern drawl while also slipping into a fit of laughter.

"Leave me alone, you schoolyard bully." Linda finished her sandwich, folding her wrapper down and placing it in her bag. Everything in its place. "Besides, he chose my best friend, not me." Linda sipped her water.

"That's because Ruby is a slut, darling."

"Don't talk about her like that, even though it's true. No crush. I just wish there were more teachers like Andrew when I used to live here."

"As opposed to what?"

"Sister Kelly and the ruler of death!" Linda made a swatting motion.

Both women startled when a ball smashed into the table between them. It bounced to the ground, but Heather caught it underfoot in a practiced motion. Andrew ran up to the women.

"Sorry ladies, can I get my ball back?"

"You know, my husband says that in the plural all the time," Heather said.

Linda bent to retrieve the ball. Heather lifted her foot while Linda remained low, looking up at Andrew. From the position, cleavage revealed itself from within her white blouse. Linda pouted sexually.

"Andrew, do you ever wonder what life might have been like if you and I hooked up that night instead of Ruby?" Andrew's turn to flush. He went silent, unable to look away. "I still think about you sometimes. What do you say?"

"Well, I'm faithful to Ruby, and I..." Andrew stiffened, realizing. "You're setting me up, aren't you?"

Linda nodded. Andrew turned to find a group of children gathered behind him, balls at the ready. They fired. He went down in a barrage, exaggerating his death under their blows. The children and women laughed at his antics. Andrew winked at Linda from his death throes.

Everyone scrambled for the school at the sound of a bell. Heather responded as if busted, rushing away from her friend. Linda, meanwhile, took time to pack everything away just so. She watched as Andrew escorted kids back inside. Linda found herself suddenly alone. A large cross loomed high over the school's entrance. The bell finally ceased by the time Linda entered the building.

Inside perfectly behaved children vanished into various classrooms. Linda stood alone in a corridor designed long ago for pomp, not paupers, certainly not children already feeling vulnerable even before entering such an opulent space. Her footfalls echoed in the absence of children moving en masse. A second set of footsteps echoed elsewhere, the acoustics making it hard to isolate where they came from.

Behind her? Linda spun. No one was there, only more space, more emptiness. It wasn't only mysterious footsteps that unnerved her. For a moment Linda was small again, a child roaming the same hallways while dreaming about a family she never met. Eventually Linda graduated, but not just as a student. Linda made the leap from student to teacher after a brief college stint elsewhere. And even during college, she worked as an assistant at the orphanage as if she could not leave, could never leave the only place she ever knew as home. Another footfall sounded somewhere down the corridor.

"Hello?"

A hand fell on Linda's shoulder. She shrieked. Ruby, twenties, with Red Bull in her veins, bounced in place. The woman wore her own Catholic schoolgirl outfit too tight and too short. Ruby pulled her friend into a hug.

"Lin Lin, last week of school and we haven't chosen our summer getaway yet!"

Linda kicked the toe of her Mary Janes against the tile and averted a guilty gaze. "You mean I haven't chosen."

"Yes, it's your turn. So, will it be kayaking in Colorado, Margaritas in Mexico, or stripping in Seattle? I'm up for some pole work. Or any alliteration vacations you can come up with."

"Ruby, stop, I can't do this anymore. It's you and Andrew plus Heather and Tom. I'm always a fifth wheel."

"Lin, no, you're not. You're more like a spare."

"Lovely. That's so much better."

Ruby gripped Linda's arm, yanking her off balance. "Oh, come on, I love our summer trips. You must go. We'll find you a boy when we get there. It will be the summer of love. I promise!"

Linda smiled at her friend's unbridled enthusiasm, reluctantly giving into the puppy dog look. "I'll think about it."

Ruby departed, walking backward down the hall vigorously while placing a button on the conversation. "Oh, it's on. Your voice box says no, but your eyes say bikinis in Belize!"

Linda shook her head and entered a classroom. She proceeded straight to the board and wrote with chalk in a practiced fluid motion. Once finished, she gestured to the three words.

"Nature. Nurture. Family. Okay students, what do these words all have in common?"

Linda pointed to one of the many raised hands, calling on Tony, a chipper kid who beamed at being chosen first.

"They each have six letters?"

"Nurture has seven," Nelly, she of the perfect braids, said with an accompanying eye roll.

"Yeah, but seven comes after six, so both words have six letters in them," Tony argued.

"By that logic Copernicus, they all have two letters in them."

"Coppertone? Did you just call me suntan lotion?"

Linda raised her hand and voice to retake control of the conversation. "Never mind. While you are both technically correct, we are straying from my point. These words mean something to all of us. What makes a family? Are we products of who we come from or more where we come from? Can we change who we are in our DNA or are we destined to..."

She eyed the bored students, then turned to the board and erased the words along with the thoughts behind it. She swiped the chalk in large swipes until one word took over the board. The word was dreams.

"Summer is almost here, so no more lectures. Let's talk about dreams. Dreams we have had or dreams for the future."

"I dreamed I laughed so hard milk came out of my nose," Scotty, a third-row student, said.

"That wasn't a dream. It happened at lunch today," said Wendy, his desk neighbor.

"Oh yeah," Scotty said, remembering. The class laughed.

"I dreamed I had a pony, but he pooped a lot!" Marnie, the lone redhead in the room, said to gales of laughter from her peers.

Linda noticed Kenny, a pale, timid boy, always sitting in the back, always seemingly friendless. She planned to bring him into the conversation despite his looking at the floor for avoidance. There was no way to embarrass the child with an incorrect answer based on the topic.

"Kenny? What about you?" He segued from the floor to the window. Must be something nice out there. Linda did not relent. "Everyone has dreams. What are yours, Kenny?"

He looked straight at her and answered. "I dreamed you died. Somebody killed you. There was blood. Lots and lots of blood."

Linda froze, shocked, and angered but postured normalcy for the children. She softened her voice, responding reassuringly to the oddball child. One appearing even more odd after such a response. He held her gaze.

"Kenny, that's what we call a nightmare, not a dream. We're not here to talk about those today."

Cassie, a girl near the back, raised her hand nervously. Linda pointed, happy for the intervention.

"I had the same dream," Cassie said, her face flushing red with guilt.

Other hands went up. Tony, Scotty, Allison, Nelly, and others not yet called on. A collective "me too" accompanied every freshly raised hand. Linda stepped back, startling herself as she bumped into her desk.

"Children, this is not funny, not funny at all..."

A shadow cast itself into Linda's peripheral. She turned and found herself face to face with a nun. "Jesu..." Linda started, catching herself before cursing before the assembled children. Linda eyed the unexpected visitor questioningly.

"Ms. Hunt, you have been summoned. I will take over the class."

Linda exited the room, all heads turning as if one to watch her leave.

CHAPTER 3

THE STERILE HEADMASTER'S OFFICE was quiet as a library. Or a morgue. Tiny chairs designed for younger visitors lined the wall just inside the door while a varnished wooden desk centered the small waiting area. A placard hanging on the lone office in the room read: Headmaster Bennett. A nun admin behind the desk shuffled paperwork so silently it was as if a cone of silence covered the workspace.

Linda sat quietly, trying to match the ambience. She smiled at the nun, who did not return the favor. The woman offered a 'tsk' when Linda nervously chewed at a nail before pressing her hands firmly in her lap, clasped as if in prayer. Linda leaned back and unexpectedly bonked her head against the wall, interrupting the fragile silence. The nun looked up, displeased. Linda frowned.

"I feel like I'm back in the headmaster's office."

"You are," the admin replied.

"I mean..."

A corded phone on the desk rang, startling Linda. The nun answered, nodding to the person on the other end as if they could somehow hear. The nun placed a hand over the receiver despite never once speaking and gestured for Linda to enter the office. Linda rose, straightened her skirt, then did so.

Father Bennet, elderly, statesman like, greeted Linda by gesturing for her to sit while taking her in.

"My pardons, I do not get to the school very many of my days any longer. Look how you've grown. I remember when you were but a student."

"I remember when you had hair." Linda winced under the slip.

They sat, absorbing the awkwardness. The priest steepled his hands. "When someone left you on our doorstep, it was with more information than most of our wards ever received."

Linda scoffed aloud, squirming in her seat. "A simple note?"

"One confirming your father was deceased. Perhaps that information informed the mother's decision to leave you behind. As an adult woman now, surely you can understand the difficulties of raising a child alone? Or will understand if ever you have your own."

Already heated from the revisiting her past, Linda let the childless comment go. "Left behind? She dumped me on a school's doorstep on a weekend. Not even given the courtesy of being dropped at a fire station or hospital."

"A school easily mistaken for a church, and by a frightened young mother who cared enough to leave at least some information."

"Forgive me Father. You expect me to think of my birth mother as altruistic? I will not. That's an area where I am sorely lacking in faith. She tells us in a note my father passed? Well, how about throwing his name out? How about giving me some breadcrumbs to follow so I could trail it back to the world's worst mother?"

"I understand your feelings. Too many of the children in our care feel as you do, but not that many women can be unfit. They all can, however, be frightened. It is our job here to do that which your mother could not."

Never a word mentioned about the fathers from a father of the cloth, Linda thought, but kept it in check. Another conversation for another time. The man had a point, as one-sided as it was. Still, her anger simmered on the surface. She rose from her chair and placed her hands on his desk, almost accusatory.

"Detectives I hired on a teacher's salary searched high and low. You know what they found? Not only did my caring mother not leave a trail back to her door, but the woman covered her tracks. It's a modern world. It is possible to find everyone. The detectives told me that for her to remain a mystery required great stealth and effort on her part. It's as if she never existed."

"She exists, my child. We have found her."

Linda fell onto her ass into the chair.

THE PAVEMENT AHEAD AND behind appeared equidistant, stretching so far it vanished in both directions. There were no other cars in sight. Linda gripped the wheel tight. Leaving school days before summer break was disconcerting. She disliked chaos. In all aspects of her life, Linda was a planner. She and her friends even meticulously planned their annual summer getaways. Collectively, they understood without details locked down, Linda would not enjoy herself. *Life rewarded the prepared,* she often told herself, though where she learned such a lesson eluded her. Certainly, it was not from her mother.

Her mother. Linda looked to the trees flanking the road and noted their beauty. Such a remote place could itself be a vacation destination under normal circumstances. Unfortunately, it was a road of sorrow. The conversation from the day before replayed itself in her mind.

"My Mother? Where? How?"

"Understand the Lord works in mysterious ways. She was living close. Only hours north, but I'm afraid your mother has passed," the headmaster said.

"I uh, oh Father, no..." Linda pounded the steering wheel in a frustrated sorrow she could not display in front of her employer.

"The rest home made the connection. They called us. Sister Mary will take over your last week of classes."

"Pray for me?"

"I will. And in her death, may you find answers to your life."

The remote wilderness cleared by the time Linda's tears did. She mocked herself for the show of emotion over a woman who meant nothing to her. She struggled to understand the anguish behind the news of the death.

"Because probably never meeting her became definitely never meeting her," Linda said to her reflection in the rear-view mirror.

Any hopes of a reunion during her lifetime ended. Linda ignored the binging texts that kept sprouting on her cell in the passenger seat. Her friends were worried. While appreciative of them, Linda did not wish to speak to anyone until she finished absorbing the weight of discovering her mother was alive until recently. The knowledge opened scars that were on their way to healing. If the woman lived so close, it meant she made a conscious choice to have nothing to do with her daughter.

And what about siblings? Were there any brothers and sisters floating out there as lost as she was? Linda's mind raced, as did her engine. Speeding through an open stretch of country road was one thing, but the forest receded as she drove into a small township. Linda slowed her vehicle.

Quaint, Linda thought when she reached the town center, but she wondered whether her mother lived there for years or only spent her last days in the retirement home. And retired from what? Hiding from relatives? That could be a full-time job as the woman clearly fooled detectives. Did dear ole ma frequent Del's Delicacies Diner off to her right? The small eatery had a large dirt parking lot with only a few cars parked. The restaurant looked fuller through the windows than the number of vehicles suggested. Perhaps locals walked a lot.

The town had no traffic signals, only stop signs. Despite being eager to get to the retirement home, road rules would not allow a quick trip. She had to hard stop at every intersection. Once past the town's center, thick forests reclaimed most of the roadside real estate. Middle-class homes gave way to ramshackle trailers dotting tiny lots as she drove past the initial quaintness heading into the town's outskirts.

An older man in a pickup truck stared her down at the intersection closest to the retirement home. He drove the opposite direction, so they faced one another at the stop sign. The man appeared old enough to be in the home himself. His bushy gray eyebrows pointed in all directions at once and appeared hard as porcupine quills. The brows gave him a permanent look of surprise.

There was nothing "city" about her, Linda thought, but maybe he saw it in her all the same. Outsider at least. She waved, hoping to end the awkward standoff, but the man only scrunched his face before peeling dirt. Show off. His truck quickly vanished from view as she rolled up on the home.

A large manor sat atop a hill, its paint peeling like sunburnt skin. The moment Linda stepped free of the air-conditioned vehicle and broke out into a sweat under the oppressive heat. A sign announcing the name of the home had long since faded under the same overbearing sun, leaving only every third letter legible.

She hoped the interior proved superior to the exterior. *Were there no loved ones to protest conditions?* Raising her cell to take a picture, Linda startled when it rang. An unknown number flashed on the screen. Surely the scourge of robo-callers, but since it was not one of her friends calling to console her, she answered. Loud static burst from the phone.

"Hello?"

Unintelligible words blasted through the speaker. Only the word Salem cut through. She killed the connection because of the intense volume of the call. Linda sighed and wiped her brow. The parking lot was far from the building, surely an inconvenience for the elderly residents. A wraparound porch surrounded the home, adding the inconvenience of steps into the equation.

It wasn't until Linda was halfway up the stairs that she noticed a wheelchair ramp leading into a section of the porch. The wood under her feet creaked with every step. An old woman sat in a wheelchair near the door. With one eye covered in a thick cataract, the woman watched Linda's approach with the other.

"Carol? Is that you?"

Linda shook her head, trying to slide past and into the home. The woman gripped Linda's arm hard enough to jerk her to a full stop. Linda looked down in surprise at the show of strength. The woman pointed to her clear orb.

"This eye does not lie. My daughter."

Linda staggered at the suggestion. She examined the woman's features, searching for signs of an error in the death announcement. Could this woman be her actual mother? A cursory exam suggested otherwise. There was nothing similar in her features, nothing to suggest any relation. The woman was a stranger, a confused old one at that.

"You can't be my mother. My mother is..."

As Linda leaned down to talk, the woman gasped. Standing over Linda's shoulder was a young dead girl with a strange square mark covering her face. Linda noticed the elderly woman's frightened gaze and looked back. Seeing nothing, she turned back, surprised to find a caretaker standing there, one nearing resident age. The wheelchair woman went slack-jawed quiet.

"Ms. Hunt? Welcome."

The caretaker led Linda into the building. They passed several residents so frail they could be specters, already passed and no one noticed the change. None seemed to take notice of the traveling pair. Linda covered her nose as they went, dismayed over the odors of decay and sewage. A lingering hint of industrial cleaning chemicals could not hide the offensive smells.

They entered a cramped room containing a bed with a thin mattress molded over time to match someone's sleeping position. A TV from another era rested on a rickety stand near the foot of the bed, tinfoil wrapped strategically over sections of the rabbit ears. A fabric chair worn down to the underlying canvas rounded out the depressing space. No place for anyone to spend their last days. Flies buzzed from somewhere.

"I never knew my mother was here. Never even knew she was alive," Linda said.

"Then you should not take her death too hard."

Linda shot the caretaker a look, suggesting otherwise. The woman shrugged before pulling a box from under the bed and setting it on the chair.

"For sanitary reasons, we burned all her clothes. This is what's left," the caretaker said.

Linda opened the box, which contained dozens of newspaper clippings. Most were older, yellowed, and showcased horrific accidents of various types. A photo of a decapitated person caused Linda to drop the pages back into the box.

"Why would she have this?"

"You would prefer a stamp collection? You would question that too. I have been at this for too long not to recognize that no one ever leaves behind more answers than questions."

"I was thinking of speaking to residents in town, check to see if she lived there. Knew people," Linda said, waiting for a reaction.

The caretaker shook her head. "Do not bother. Your mother came to us late stage. Refused to say from where, but clearly, she was not a local. Bingo on Saturday nights, hair salon twice a month, and dining once a month in town after payday. I would have seen her out and about. Same with the others on staff. Not much to do around here, so we do it together. Small town, this place."

"What was she like?"

Instinctively, the caretaker looked to the bed where an image flashed of an elderly woman, spindly, her head on the pillow moving in a blur. Unnatural, uncanny. Shadowy figures flanked the bed. The caretaker folded her arms with a shiver.

"Over the years, you've had thoughts of who she might be?" Linda nodded. "Stick with those."

In the sudden silence, the source of the flies became clear, buzzing as they were over a puddle of water in a corner. Mold grew on the wall above the puddle. Linda grimaced.

"How can you allow people to live like this?"

"We see they eat and sleep. The rest is up to the family."

Before Linda could protest further, the caretaker produced a manilla envelope. Reaching inside, Linda pulled out a group picture showing members of the home gathered on the front lawn. The blurred face of one woman stood out.

The caretaker pointed to the unrecognizable woman in the photo. "Every picture we ever took of her came out that way. Strange, huh?"

Linda tilted the envelope. A house key and an old yellow paper fell into her hands.

"It is a deed to a house in Salem. For, you know, all your years of dedication."

Linda looked at the bed. When she turned back, the caretaker was gone. Something rattled in the envelope. Linda tilted further and a key on a necklace came out. She looked inside the envelope for any more surprises before placing the empty sleeve in the box with the horrible articles.

The object on the chain resembled an intricate key. A red crescent jewel filled the interior of a bow, which gave way to an elaborate shank covered in carved lines and raised nubs. The object culminated at the tip into a quad bit with various wards cut from the bits. Linda could not fathom what such a key would open, but mostly figured it was no key at all. The chain itself appeared old, possibly valuable, so more likely the entire thing was a piece of handed down jewelry.

The buzzing grew closer. Linda looked at the puddle. The flies vanished, but she still heard their buzz. Linda eyed the closed box. She opened the top and a swarm of flies flew out of the box. Some remained inside, walking around on the faces of those pictured in the horrible articles.

Linda used the box top to wave away the horde. (Were there even more than moments ago?) She then closed the box and exited the room. She saw no staff on her way out, only sad people sitting in chairs along the way, all staring. They turned their heads to follow her movements, so she picked up the pace and made her way to the exit. The original old woman remained on the porch. Linda hurried to pass her. But as she stepped on the first stair of the porch, the woman's words gave Linda pause.

"Don't go to Salem." The woman appeared suddenly lucid, authoritarian. "The curse. If you go, you die."

"How did you know about that? Did you know my Mother?" Linda asked, stepping closer to the woman.

The woman looked up, face shifting, all smiles and unbridled enthusiasm. "Carol!"

"No. Please, you were talking about Salem."

Linda leaned in and the image of the child appeared again, her face suddenly spinning furiously as if an old TV trying to lock in on a station. The child's clothes appeared to be from another time. The old woman went wild-eyed with terror.

"Please leave, Carol."

"I'm not her."

"Leave now, you bitch! Bitch!"

Linda followed the woman's gaze and spotted a child with raised arms. The girl rushed forward. The old woman, bewildered for a moment, finally responded as her grandchild reached the hug zone.

"Grandma!" the child yelled.

The child's mother stood nearby smoking a cigarette, wearing a look of the defeated. Too skinny, too broken, too poor, with even this place likely too expensive. The mother nodded to Linda. Before Linda could respond, her phone rang. Linda answered and heard the same static as before. One word made it through.

"Salem."

CHAPTER 4

A GATE SQUEAKED OPEN on hinges overdue for oil. Linda struggled through the opening, cradling a bag under her arm. She circled around to the backyard. A large deck extended from the rear of the home prepped for communal dining with plentiful seating flanking a long metal table. Propped open French doors gave easy access to the two-story cedar shingled home. A lack of child detritus confirmed no babies on board. The place was an adult entertaining spot.

Linda brightened upon spotting the familiar faces as she crossed the lawn. Manning the grill just off the deck was Heather's husband, Tom, a congenial-looking man with salt and pepper hair. He flipped burgers and wore an apron over his *dad* body that read, 'kiss the cook's wife, but pay the cook in cash.' Andrew stood alongside the man and nursed a craft beer. Tom yelled into the house.

"Honey? We need to fix the gate. All kinds of things are getting in the yard!"

Linda kissed the man on the cheek. Tom grew flustered, but it could have been from the grill flare up. Linda stepped away from the heat. Andrew pulled her into a hug as Ruby and Heather emerged from the house, setting side dishes on the table. Andrew helped Linda pull her housewarming gift from the paper grocery bag. A large box of alcohol.

"Last Tuesday's vintage. I hear it was a wonderful week for cardboard." Andrew nodded as if he were an aficionado.

"It was a wise teacher, or maybe an alcoholic one, who said when the kids whine..." Linda started.

"We wine," the group finished in unison.

Andrew handed off the wine to Ruby, who placed it on a mini bar crammed into one side of the deck. Heather and Ruby joined the others on the lawn and passed out paper plates.

Heather hugged Linda, whispering into her ear. "You okay, kiddo?"

Linda nodded, mouthing a thanks. Andrew lined up first as Tom handed him a grilled bun and burger. Andrew smiled that mischievous smile at the women lining up.

"Eat quick. We have about an hour before the food poisoning sets in," Andrew said.

"Hey!" Tom stopped flipping. "Only half an hour at best. I'm a pro."

Linda shoved Tom playfully. He captured her hand and a smile, holding both for a little too long before sliding a burger onto her plate. She met his gaze, suddenly curious.

"Hey, do you know anything about Salem?"

"I am offended you would even ask," he said.

"Is that yes?"

"Affirmative inquisitive one."

Tom nodded past her, drawing her attention to the line. He mouthed, 'later' as she took her burger and stepped away. Heather kissed her husband on the cheek and thanked him for grilling as she received hers. Ruby took her last step in the line as a jump, landing directly in front of Tom. She extended her plate.

"Twin patties for me. I'm eating for two, as you know."

"That is vernacular for pregnancy. Are you pregnant, Ruby?" Tom asked, surprised.

"God no. How could you even say such a thing? You're a heartless monster."

"Because I asked if you were pregnant?" Tom asked.

"Because you suggested it," she said. "Besides, I can't have children."

"Oh, Ruby, I'm sorry. I didn't know. Why can't you have children?" Tom asked.

"Because I don't want to!"

"Honey, you are correct. I do not and never will understand women," Tom said to his departing wife.

"Own it, buttercup," Heather said over her shoulder, heading back to the deck.

Andrew bumped his girlfriend on the hip as Tom loaded a double burger onto Ruby's plate. "She eats extra meat to make up for my eating none. Cancels out my vote every election as well."

"What can I say? I am a contrarian. Besides, I need my strength to keep up with you." Ruby squeezed Andrew's butt and fluttered away with all the grace of a moth.

"Veggie please," Andrew said.

"Top grill so meat does not drip into yours, and separate spatula." Tom said, sliding the veggie patty onto Andrew's plate.

"If you weren't already married, Tom..."

Andrew started off. Tom looked after him.

"If I was not married, what?"

Andrew left him hanging, everyone looking to Heather, who shrugged. She gave her friends an exasperated look, showing she dealt with it daily. Everyone laughed while Tom tried to catch up. He served his own burger and joined the group.

"Oh. Humor," he said simply, then sat next to his wife as everyone dug in and passed around the sides.

Soon everyone had finished their food. They continued with alcohol while trading horror stories about various unruly students. As the conversation died, all eyes fell on Linda, who at one end of the table suddenly appeared to be the dreaded fifth wheel she feared. Gulping her wine, she raised a finger, then gulped again. Finally, she set her glass down and answered their unanswered questions.

"Thank you all for being there for me since I returned. I have kept silent about it all because I'm still processing everything. What I struggle with the most is the fact I never got to see my mother's body. They had already burned her."

"You mean cremated. Big difference, witches and all," Tom said.

Heather slapped her husband's arm. "Tom, Jesus, Lord, and Mary! Why bring up such a thing?"

"She mentioned..." Tom started, trying to justify the train of thought, but his wife stepped over his words.

"But you got pictures of yer ma?" Heather asked.

Linda shook her head. "All blurry. Even her name eludes me. They checked her in at the home a little more than a year ago under the name Jane Doe."

Ruby reached over and gripped her friend's arm, massaging it in sympathy. Linda looked around the table, taking in the group, the setting. All eyes on her. She raised her glass and others did the same.

"To never knowing who you are but understanding how lucky you are to have the family you have."

Everyone clinked glasses. Andrew gripped Linda's shoulder, holding her toast, completing the triangle between the couple and their longtime companion.

"Yeah, you are our family because we adopted you. We only adopt the best. But turns out Kristen Stewart is not an orphan and her agent asked us to stop contacting her," Ruby said.

"Shut the front door! I love Kristen Stewart. Did you see that child as Princess Diana?" Heather gushed and covered her heart at the memory.

"Oh my God, yes!" Ruby shouted back. A cough from Andrew refocused her. "Since the greatest actress who ever lived was unavailable for adoption, we settled on you."

"Now it comes out. Not your top choice?" Linda asked.

"Top five-ish," Andrew agreed.

"Ish?" Linda asked.

"That is not a very accurate numerical representation. I declare someone is failing at math, Andrew. Good thing you don't teach. Oh, wait..." Heather chimed in over a high five from Ruby.

Linda laughed and gulped more red. She looked around and felt a peace not felt since her trip to the retirement home. This was what she needed, good food and good friends. And alcohol, lots of alcohol. As the warmth settled in, her phone rang, interrupting the mood. She answered, pulling the phone away again, allowing everyone in on the torturous static before hanging up.

"I've been getting these weird calls," she said.

"I'm sure it's your students. One year they put my car on sale on Craigslist for only four hundred dollars," Andrew said to laughter from the crew. "In fact, out of the insane amount of calls I received, guess who was one of them? Tom."

Everyone suddenly noticed Tom's absence. They caught glimpses of him inside the open doors, fluttering about the bookshelves lining the living room walls. Andrew yelled inside.

"Isn't that right, Tom?"

Tom answered while still rummaging through titles. "Yeah. I saw a new car on sale for four hundred dollars. I called, and it was Andrew." Tom rejoined the group, book in hand.

"Did you buy the car?" Ruby asked.

"Huh? No, it was a joke." Tom opened the book, running fingers through pages until finding that which he searched for. He looked up at the others.

"Ruby? What would it take for you to kill Linda? What if Linda slept with Andrew? Would that be enough?"

The trio who had been touching in comfort and support all released their grips on one another. Linda shot Andrew a look. (Guilt?) Ruby scoffed and gestured for Heather to control her madman.

Heather rolled her eyes. "Honey? Stop this nonsense. It's about three bus stops short of Cute Street."

"I am making a point. Of course, they would not. But it is the exact question one could ask of a certain group of Puritans. Our group would never hurt one another, especially after partaking in my superior cooking skills." He beamed at the self-compliment, but the others were deep into the subject now, waiting. He continued. "Why cannot the same be said for residents of Salem in 1692?"

Tom turned the book toward the others. The gang rose and circled around the pages. The book showed a black and white artist's rendition of a crowd gathered around the gallows. In the background, a man lay on a makeshift altar, stones piled atop his chest. While in the foreground, a 'witch' stood on tippy toes, her head held taut in a noose, awaiting an ominous fate. A gleeful insanity appeared in the faces of the assembled crowd. With a few brush strokes, the artist captured the intensity of townsfolk pointing, leering, and making lewd gestures. Their evil grins approximating the stereotypes of witches themselves. A gruesome scene playing out in a single work of art.

"Scholars studied the witch trials for generations, yet not one person has explained how people who knew each other as well as we know one another could do this to their neighbors. These people attended the same church together."

Tom flipped the page to one on which two young girls pointed menacingly. Linda instinctively leaned away as though the kids were singling her out. As she moved, the fingers seem to follow her like eyes in a painting.

"From the mouths of babes. These children were the very ones who sealed the fate of so many."

Andrew scoffed. "Seriously Tom, school is out for the summer. Aren't you ever off the clock?"

"Oh, sure, like I am the only individual who listens to historical podcasts on his off days?"

Andrew arched an eyebrow no. Tom searched the other faces for solidarity. The group left him hanging.

"You are weird Tom, and that is why we love you. But enough of the spook show. It's time for summer fun. Let's plan our itinerary. Where to? We've never gone this late in the season without planning before," Ruby said.

"I say sun and surf. Brighten things up around here. I really need it," Heather said.

"Water sounds great," Andrew said.

Linda pulled at a chain around her neck which held the key from the envelope. She touched the object through her blouse. She considered telling them about it, but changed her mind. It helped her decide though, so she turned to her friends.

"I've waited my whole life for answers to who I am. Even if the house does not hold solid answers, there must be clues in the town's records of who originally owned the property. There is only one trip I'm taking this summer. I'm going to Salem."

"Salem it is," Andrew chimed in.

Linda looked up, surprised. Andrew smiled his winning smile, offering it as a silent declaration of a foregone decision. Ruby smiled as well. Linda breathed deep, feeling a calm overtake her at the support. She loved her friends so much and it was reasons like this. Out of them all, Tom brightened the most, suddenly pacing in excitement.

"I can give tours. The museums there are rich with history. I believe I could write some of it off for work," Tom said.

Heather wandered away from the group, found a half-filled glass of wine and chugged it down, not caring whose it was. She placed the empty glass under the box wine spout and attempted to pour. Empty. Linda caught sight of Heather and grew concerned until Ruby snapped her back to attention.

"You didn't think you could go without us, did you?" Ruby asked.

"Summer in Salem. Not a hog in a trough style vacation but should be fun," Heather crossed her arms, dangling the empty glass in one hand.

Linda rubbed the key through her blouse even harder, gripping it tight even as she refocused on the book. The two children on the page continued staring at her. Linda leaped in fright as Tom slammed the book closed.

CHAPTER 5
1692

A LTHEA GOODE ENTERED THE room, tray in hand, rags steaming atop the silver platter. Reverend Goode stood over their daughter Rose. The child lay tethered to the bed, bucking ferociously against restraints. The violent motions twisted the poor girl into positions usually unattainable by the human body. Althea winced as something in the girl popped. A bone? A tendon? The girl fell suddenly still. Had she broken for real?

The respite proved brief. Rose's eyes closed while her body stiffened as solidly as rigor mortis. Her head lifted toward her mother, every inch of movement generating a snap, crackle, and pop of neck vertebrae. With a sudden jerk, her head settled in place before turning to face Althea. Even with her eyes still closed, the child somehow found her mother. When the eyes popped open, Althea screamed. The child's gaze was absent pupils, her eyes gone white, milky. Whatever was on the bed was no longer Althea's child.

Present Day

L INDA SCREAMED, LASHING OUT while simultaneously waking, uncertain of where she was. Andrew fought back, trying to corral her. Images of an old home filled with strange people, and a horrific child quickly faded from Linda's memory, which was a relief. She disliked the awful nightmare and wished no more to do with it. Despite rejoining the waking world, she remained confused about her location.

Until she spotted her sparring partner driving the van. She sat in the passenger seat of their rented van. It was night outside the vehicle, but she could see huge stretches of forest on all sides encroaching on the road, threatening to swallow the pavement whole. They traveled in a curtain of rain. The headlights vanished a few feet ahead of the van as they drove into the night.

Andrew's free hand, the one not holding the steering wheel, maintained a grip on her shoulder, waiting for Linda to regain control. Linda caught her breath, then her reflection, in the rear-view mirror. It showed a woman frenzied enough to be one of those in the crowd on the pages Tom shared with them back at the barbecue days earlier. She slipped a lock of hair over one ear, digging deep for dignity before turning back to her friend. Andrew eyed her with concern.

"You okay?"

She nodded. "Nightmare. Bad one."

"A hell of a left hook you have. I'd say you could have taken care of anything that came your way, including carpool drivers."

"Oh, did I hit you? I'm sorry."

"No worries. I like it rough." Both blanched over the inadvertent slip. Andrew realigned his posture and changed the subject. "Wasn't enough to stir the crew back there."

Linda looked back to where Ruby slept sprawled out, taking every inch available in the first-row seat. Heather and Tom slept in the next seat but facing away from one another, leaning into windows like air passengers. Someone snored. Linda turned back to the driver.

"So sorry. I was supposed to keep you awake."

"Mission accomplished. You understand you can do so without fisticuffs, right?"

Linda smiled, happy to find things back to normal. Andrew shared his infectious grin, but a sudden flash of lightning added an air of mischievousness to his face. Linda startled at the bright burst. Andrew searched the road for signs of their destination. The wipers worked overtime, but the dancing arms did little to clear the view obscured by a cascade of water.

As the storm intensified, even the yellow lane divider lines faded from view. Jagged rips of lightning provided occasional illumination, enough to assure them they were not heading into oncoming traffic. Not that there was any. Only fools would be out in such a storm. The van of fools continued on their journey.

"We should be there by now. Can you check the GPS?" Linda asked.

Andrew looked in the rear-view mirror. "Kept the volume down for our sleeping beauties back there, but if they can sleep through this maelstrom, then I guess I can turn it back on."

He pressed a button and a dashboard GPS lit up. A red dot representing them almost sat on the blue dot representing their destination. A pleasant voice urged them to continue straight. Another bump shook the vehicle. Andrew fought not to curse in Linda's presence. Linda braced herself against the dashboard as if prepping for a crash.

"*Continue straight,*" the computer's voice chimed.

"For how long?" Linda asked.

"It's not Siri. You can't talk to it. Old school, but it works fine."

"*Continue straight. Continue straight.*"

"Thank you for going with me. Even with everyone here, I'm still frightened of what I might find."

"*Continue straight. Continue straight.*"

"Least we could do. I will say you are lucky it wasn't Heather's turn to choose our destination," Andrew said.

"You noticed too? Yeah, I think there' are plenty of other places she wants to be."

"And miss this beautiful Salem weather? That's crazy talk.

"*Continue straight. Continue straight. Continue straigh*t." The GPS voice suddenly sped up, repeating the phrase until it fell into a deep baritone voice. "*Continue straight!*"

Thunder rumbled simultaneously with the altered tone of the GPS, leaving room to wonder if the voice ever changed. Another lightning strike lit the road. The van barreled toward a massive object. A tree? Andrew hit the brakes. They skidded across the slick surface toward imminent impact. They finally stopped with the bumper, kissing the object as close as two lovers in the rain. The sudden stop threw everyone from their seats.

"What is going on up there?" Tom leaned forward and fumbled with his glasses.

Ruby rose from the floor, cursing. "Shit!"

"Language, Ruby," Heather said.

Lightning struck and illuminated the massive witch's face. It stared through the front windshield.

"Shit!" Heather yelled.

"Really?" Ruby replied in response to the black kettle hypocrisy.

Rain dripped down the statue's face, distorting its features, making it appear almost animated. Then it disappeared back into the dark, awaiting the next lightning strike. Thunder boomed. The headlights stood too close to the statue to illuminate it properly, instead casting a shadow of a witch body against a distant sheet of rain. The GPS kept up with its directions.

"*Continue straight.*"

Andrew pounded on the device. It responded by changing its instructions.

"*Back up*," it said.

"You think?" Andrew turned it off. "Lightning must have messed it up. No GPS to get us the rest of the way unless anyone's cellphones are finally getting a decent signal."

"I'll check mine," Linda said, pulling it out of her pocket and tapped the screen. "Signal, and I entered the address, but the app is thinking. Thinking. Thinking."

"That is what maps are for," Tom said.

"I didn't bring a map," Andrew replied.

Tom reached into his backpack and pulled out a folded gas station version. "But I did." He spread it open, one more object placed between himself and Heather. "First thing you are going to want to do is back up."

Heather scoffed, then spoke. "My husband, everybody."

"Lifesaver," Andrew said, backing up.

Once back on the road, the group drove, with Tom navigating. He squinted in frustration at the map, tracing a finger, following something, then starting over. "You must have the wrong address, Linda."

"I have the one they gave me."

"Which is not on the map. It is curious how far apart houses are from the next out here."

"Country livin' dahlin.' That's how it was where I grew up," Heather said, reminiscing. "Glorious thought, the idea of staying out of your neighbor's business. A girl could use more of that in the city."

"Not me. Love the city, and all the tea," Ruby said.

"We are at least on the correct road. The street itself exists, so there is that." Tom used his cell phone flashlight to trace a path. "Country living or not, it has been a long drive since we passed the last house. Maybe we missed the place. I say we turn around in the next driveway we see."

As if on cue, a lightning flash briefly lit up a driveway that would have otherwise remained hidden by the rain. Andrew stopped and asked if they should turn around. Lightning stuck perilously close to the house, revealing the Goode home seemingly untouched since its original construction. Linda leaped when her phone unexpectedly dinged.

"This is it. App finally worked," Linda said.

Thomas frowned, confused but expertly folded the document, pulling tight at the creases once compacted. He stored it in a pouch in his backpack. "I will call the map company tomorrow to inform them of the discrepancy.'

"I'm certain you will, cowboy," Ruby said.

"I would appreciate the correction were I the mapmaker. Common courtesy," Tom said.

Linda kept her gaze fixed on the house as they drove up the lengthy driveway. The house sat far off the road on property much larger than that of Heather and Tom's house. Almost all their group gatherings took place at Heather's home because it was the largest in their friend group. Until now. Linda had only been a renter her whole life, so the immense yard was her first. They parked as close as possible to the door.

Andrew turned to the group. "Luggage later. No sense soaking everything until we have access."

They exited the van and raced through the downpour to the front door, everyone huddling around Linda. Through the material of her top, she touched the elaborate key dangling from her neck, but the door's lock was a traditional deadbolt. As she retrieved the house key from her pocket, she further assumed the chained one to be nothing than an heirloom, not functional but familial. Who did it belong to and what did it signify? Linda wondered. Before inserting the key, she bumped into the door, which opened on its own. Unlocked.

Despite the surprise, the storm made everyone rush inside, stepping into a foyer. Jaundiced light from wall-mounted candleholders lit the entrance and surrounding hallway. They appeared to be genuine antique candleholders which someone at some point converted to electric. Each contained transparent bulbs that were like those adorning Christmas trees.

"Why are the lights on?" Linda asked.

"No weirder than the door being left open," Tom answered.

"Hello?" Linda yelled.

No answer. Linda looked around nervously. Andrew noticed her hesitancy and tried to put the group at ease.

"Come on, guys. Motion sensors, most likely. Place only looks old, but it has electricity. I'm sure they turned on as we entered, not before. As for the door, it means our favorite new homeowner lives in a friendly neighborhood if people leave their homes unlocked."

"Yeah, but who else besides us has ever wandered in?" Ruby said, more to herself than anyone else.

Heather coughed and scooped up Linda in her arms, spinning her friend around the space, while giving Ruby the stink eye over the creepiness commentary. Ruby took the hint and got in on the hug from the other side. They escorted their friend on a tour.

A corridor ran straight through to the rear of the house to a backdoor with a large pane window. A stairway rose from the foyer to the second floor. The stair railing continued along the right side atop the stairs, creating a small balcony overlooking the foyer and hall. The railing only ran a few feet before merging with a wall where rooms began on that side of the hall.

To the foyer's left stood a sizeable kitchen, and to the right, a large open-faced archway fed into a living room. The living space contained furniture covered with dusty drop cloths. While the home's layout appeared quite traditional, the decorations hinted at the true age of the place. Paisley patterned wallpaper in the foyer and hallway looked as thick as carpet. The same wallpaper yellowed around the fringes where it bled into wood molding lining the upper and lower corners of the home.

Tom ran his hand across a section of the elaborate molding. "Whoa, someone call Antiques Roadshow. At least we know we did not stumble into someone else's home. No one leaves furniture covered. This is your place, Linda. Congratulations."

Linda smiled, still under the grip of her female companions. Andrew slapped Tom, who squared off as if ready to fight until he registered it to be a friendly gesture.

"Let's check out the kitchen. See how they did it in the old days," Andrew said.

Tom placed his hands at his sides as if gripping pistols and spoke in a western drawl. "Sure thing, pilgrim." Off Andrew's confused look, Tom raised his hands. "John Wayne."

"Wayne who?" Andrew did not wait for an answer. He headed toward the kitchen, a deflated Tom following.

The women moved down the hall, examining pictures hanging on the wall. The images showed people on the streets of Salem and some around the home. One image was that of a stern woman standing at the end of the same hall they stood in. Linda looked up nervously, expecting to see the individual in person, but only darkness greeted her.

In all the pictures, the subjects appeared sickly, gaunt, each fighting to outdo the next in their displays of misery on film. A sad, broken lot of people. Linda stopped at one picture that showed a woman strikingly like herself through the prism of another time. Based on the pictures, a harder time. Linda lifted the frame and checked the back, hoping for a note or name scrawled on the back but found it only bare. Ruby noticed the melancholy overcoming her friend and led her away.

"Lively bunch. Come on, if we want to get lost in black and white photos, we can use a filter on our phones. Let's go. We have a house to explore!"

The women moved to the living room. Heather found a light switch which brought an overhead chandelier to life along with a couple of uncovered desk lamps. Linda found that strange when the balance of the furniture remained covered. Motion lights were one thing. Uncovered table lamps were another. Heather's excitement drew her attention away from the oddity.

"Fireplace. Real one, not the electric fake claptrap like at my place. You're the fancy one in our circle now, darling," Heather said.

Linda smiled at the thought, overwhelmed by the thought of home ownership. She examined the fireplace, noted a canvas tray of kindling, and a set of pokers all stationed at the ready. Not that she knew what to do with any of it. The women went to work pulling sheets off the furniture, revealing nearly pristine antiquated pieces of a time gone. The trio whistled with every newly exposed piece. Linda stepped back, taking in the big picture.

"Is this really mine?"

"You betcha girly. Hey what about..." Heather began.

"Bedrooms," they announced in unison.

The women trampled upstairs like teenagers. Three doorways lined the hall. Two staggered on either side and one anchored the end of the hall. The first room sat immediately to the left of the stair landing. Opposite that door rose the small balcony overlooking the hallway below and a partial view of the living room. The second doorway picked up a few feet along the hallway from where the balcony railing ended. The last doorway loomed in the distance.

It relieved Linda to find the rooms spread out. She had no desire to overhear any bedtime shenanigans her guests might partake in. Grabbing the railing to check the view, she found herself suddenly overcome with Déjà vu. Overcome with dizziness, Linda worried she might fall. Images from her nightmare in the van resurfaced. She released her grip, hoping it might make the images go away. (Was this the same view in her dream?) Linda shook it off as her friends inventoried the number of rooms.

"Wow, three bedrooms. Do you know how much a three-bedroom home goes for in Salem?" The two women turned to Ruby expectantly. Ruby shrugged. "I'm asking."

The women smiled at their incorrigible friend and entered the first bedroom, one possessed of quaint elegance. They dispersed to check out the small room. Ruby lifted a curtain, peeking out into the rain and saw a swing hanging from a shade tree on the sizeable side lawn. The swing whipped in the wind. Heather looked through a corner doorway and yelped, startling the others.

Heather clasped her hands over her chest as if something just warmed her heart. "No outhouses. We have bathrooms, thank God. That country livin' I mentioned? Let's just say I'm over my days of squatting in outhouses."

"Gross. All kinds of gross," Ruby said.

Ruby joined Linda who examined an elaborate vanity. An oversized mirror rose from the backside of the desk, an oval shape nestled in an elegant wooden frame. A small music box rested on the desktop. Linda was about to open it when Ruby noticed something.

"Why are there no drop cloths covering the furniture in here?"

Linda stiffened, realizing the same and noticing how the room appeared too pristine for a seemingly long abandoned home. The comforter on the bed was a modern brand, Lauren possibly. Heather gave Ruby the same scolding look as earlier, then grabbed Linda's hand, leading her into the corridor. Ruby followed. Something bumped behind the door at the far end of the corridor.

"Did you hear that?" Linda asked.

"No. Come on, what's behind door number two?" Heather entered to answer her own question.

The second room looked much like the first. Ruby forgot her earlier concerns, too excited to test the bed. She bounced on its edge, shimmying in place, testing her weight.

"Functional," she said.

"Minimal squeaking. I hereby declare this one yours, Ruby, so we do not have to hear you two lovebirds going at it every night," Heather said.

"How dare you! I didn't even know you knew about Linda and me!"

Ruby dramatically swept Linda up in her arms and feigned passion. Linda pushed Ruby away under a gale of laughter. All mirth ceased when they spotted an oddity on the far side of the room. A drop cloth rose from the floor in the shape of a person, like a cheap ghost costume. Whoever was under the covering seemed faced the women directly.

Linda gingerly approached the 'person' and grabbed the sheet at shoulder height. She yanked it free and screamed. A woman screamed back, but it was only her reflection. The oblong shape of the mirror would have approximated a person's physique when covered.

Still on edge, she leaped in fright when blood flowed down her forehead in the reflection. She grabbed her head, searching for the source, which poured quickly, dark, deeper than crimson. Linda's students mentioned blood and there it was, pouring down her face. Heather shoved Linda aside and set a bedpan below the mirror to catch the flow.

"We have a leak," Heather said.

Linda recovered, relieved to find the runoff simply a byproduct of the storm. The water mixed with grime on the mirror's surface, which gave it the dark appearance. Linda eyed the ceiling estimating repair costs in her head, a thought which made her smile. It meant home ownership. She never thought of that as a possibility, resigned to a life of renting. Ruby tapped the bedpan with her foot.

"Don't even want to know why that is here," Ruby said.

Something thumped loudly in the distance. They turned toward the noise and one by one poked their heads out to the hall. Nothing was there. Another loud thump. The source came from behind the last door.

"Now that I heard, let's go," Ruby said.

The women grouped together and continued down the hall.

T HE MEN MADE A cursory search of the kitchen. A modern toaster stood out in the old-fashioned space. A microwave drew their attention based on its incongruent presence. The refrigerator at least had the dignity to be from the fifties. Overall, the look came together as a mish-mosh of time periods. The wallpaper displayed roosters in a repeating pattern, alternating between one standing proudly, cock of the walk, followed by one pecking grain. Up, down, up, down. The meeting of wallpaper and corner moldings halved and quartered some of the poor birds.

A large window overlooked a backyard which extended downhill toward a creek. The darkness made it difficult to see far, but occasional lightning strikes reflected off the water and revealed a rising ridge beyond the water line. With nothing much to see in the rain-soaked night, they returned to examining the kitchen itself.

The two men spoke in the universal language of grunting curiosity and communal shrugs until finding what they searched for. A closed door anchored the far end of the kitchen. Andrew reached for the slightly rusted door handle.

"Basement. Best stuff is always in the basement," Andrew said, pulling the knob. The door refused to open. "It's locked."

"That is not possible. There is no lock."

Andrew stepped aside and gestured for the powerful man to give it a shot. Tom gripped and pulled with no better luck.

"What the hell?" Tom asked. He examined his hands covered in orange stains.

Andrew moved on to architecture patrol, tracing a hand across the molding lining the ceiling's edge. Tom kept on the door. He pressed a leg against the wall and pulled the knob with both hands, grunting. Andrew chuckled over the display but quickly refocused on the interior.

"Molding like this is crazy expensive per foot. Linda might want to think about stripping this place for parts, selling it off that way, might be worth more than the house itself."

Tom huffed and placed his hands on his knees while trying to catch his breath. "Or not. There may be serious water damage."

"You think so?"

"You have another explanation why I can't open the door? It must have warped in place."

"That's the reason Hercules," Andrew smiled and flexed his biceps.

"You didn't do any better, smartass."

"Because I'm not the one that is going to break off an antique knob in my friend's new old house. She wants me to give it the big effort, then I get her permission first. The molding feels as dry as kindling. It still has value. I don't see any warping. I see your theory and raise you another. Lead paint."

"What?" Tom asked, trying one more time before finally giving up. "What about the paint?"

As Tom turned away from the door, a mist fluttered through a gap along the bottom. The lower section of the door frosted over. Neither noticed. Andrew caressed the rooster wallpaper. Tom joined him.

"The thickness of this wallpaper and how it yellows where it meets molding suggests it has been here a very long time. That means any paint is roughly the same age. The basement's door jamb is painted. Old paint contains lead. The thickness of that over time without being opened frequently could explain the door being stuck."

The mist receded by the time the men turned their attention back to the spot, but the frost crept further up the door. It would be hard to miss soon. Tom nodded, suggesting the theory was sound. He ran a hand along the painted wood.

"Ah, fuck!" Tom yanked his hand away, gripping it with his other.

"What happened? Did it bite you?"

Tom brushed past and turned on the faucet. The pipes coming to life shook like clanking skeleton bones. Air hissed for a time before water finally gushed. Tom placed his hand under the flow carrying redness down into the sink basin. Andrew grew concerned.

"Seriously, are you okay?" Andrew asked.

"It didn't bite me, you twat. It's a splinter."

"Oh, is that all?"

"Yeah, that's all!"

Tom raised his index finger, revealing a sliver of wood almost the length of his finger, just under the skin. The large splinter at first glance looked almost stuck on the skin's surface by some combination of baking sweeteners. Molasses perhaps, or marshmallow remnants. As Tom pulled the splinter out, the nature of the wound grew clear. The oversized sliver pulled free like a sword from a sheath.

Andrew searched cabinets and drawers, finding pots, plates, and other items until finding what he looked for in a drawer nearest the basement door. His breath crystalized in the air, but he moved too quickly to notice the chill. He retrieved a dish cloth and handed it to his friend.

Sniffing the linen, Andrew reacted in surprise. "I think that's Downey. Was that around in puritan days?"

"Do not care right now," Tom said, taking the cloth. He ran it under water before wrapping his hand with it.

Andrew retrieved a second cloth and sniffed. "This cloth smells freshly laundered. How can that be?"

"I'll let you know once I'm done saving the finger."

"Please. Nasty, but still just a splinter."

Andrew handed off the dry towel and examined the area that Tom touched. "I don't see how that happened to you. Everything looks smooth."

After dabbing the wound dry, Tom bent the finger. All clear. A red line marked the entrance point to the wound, but the bleeding had already stopped. Tom flexed the entire hand while daring his friend.

"Run your hand along it. Let's see what happens."

Andrew reached for the knob again. The metal went white with frost, crystalizing over even the rusty spots. Before Andrew touched it, the women screamed from upstairs.

CHAPTER 6

L INDA PRESSED HER EAR against the door at the end of the hall. Nothing. Not that she could have heard much over her friends' frantic whispering. They leaned on her shoulders, making Linda more nervous. She grabbed the knob, twisted, and thrust open the door. Something white fluttered in her face. (A ghost?) The women screamed.

A fluffed sheet flitted toward the women before drooping flaccid in the hands of a bespectacled man in his thirties wearing a three-piece suit. The man carried a professorial air about him but appeared flustered at the unexpected appearance of houseguests. He raised his hands less in surrender than apology.

"Who are you? What are you doing in my house?" Linda asked.

"Walter Fournier, Professor of American Studies, Berkshire England, on loan to Salem Historical society," the man said, battling to tamp down a British accent. "Your house? Then that makes you Linda."

Walter extended a hand. Linda refused it.

"That answers who you are. Not why you are here," Linda said, as her friends chimed in with affirmations.

"Prepping your house for your arrival, of course. The nature of the linens was unsuitable for anyone, I must say. Stocked the pantry, and the kitchen, all the restrooms. Removed a dreadful number of spiders and their webbing, though it tugged at my conscience as they are formidable pest control..."

Linda cut him off. "Why? Why would you do this?"

"Oh dear. I left several messages and hoped one made it through, though you never returned my calls. I connected several times with someone purporting to be you, but the individual used colorful language and hung up on me each time."

"That was you making those calls?"

"Yes. Unsuccessfully. I apologize if I frightened anyone."

Ruby shoved Linda closer to the man and spoke up as a wing-woman. "No problem. Linda is not used to finding a man in her bedroom, is all."

"Ruby!" Linda scolded.

Walter pushed his glasses further up his nose. "Oh well, that's..."

"I mean a long time. Like dog years long. Isn't that right, Heather?" Ruby asked.

"You have no idea, sugar," Heather said, trying not to slip into sugah' territory in front of their guest.

"Oh my," Walter said, trying to avoid looking directly at Linda, whose cheeks could suddenly light up a room.

Andrew and Tom rushed in.

"Is everyone okay?" Tom asked.

"Next time we're facing a possible axe murderer, how about moving a little faster?" Heather said in a biting manner.

Ruby looked at the empty-handed men. "Screaming loved ones and you run from a kitchen with no knives? Epic fail."

Walter extended his look of shame to the gentlemen he had yet to meet.

A FTER INTRODUCTIONS, THE REST of the group brought in bags while Linda and Walter retreated to the rear of the house in the first-floor hall. Linda gazed out the large window in the back door while Walter further explained the reasons for his attending to her home. An unknown donor left funds in an account to spruce up the place before the return of any living relatives. Because the home was to be designated as a historic landmark that made things tricky. Only so much prep work could be done. Walter was the best to shop and fill the home with items he understood could modernize the place just enough to make it habitable. From there, he would work closely with the homeowner to discuss any changes they hoped to make.

Linda half listened as she pressed her face against the glass. Rain continued to fall, but the heavy winds of earlier had ceased, making the storm less severe. The moon broke through cloud cover enough for Linda to glimpse a forest abutting her property line and a brook in the distance. She did not see any other houses from her vantage point and none nearby upon arrival. Her new home appeared fairly isolated.

Walter studied Linda as she looked out the window, only to turn quickly away when she caught his gaze in the glass's reflection. He shifted to examining photos, all of which shared a common theme. Misery. He spoke over his shoulder.

"I have been here in the light of day. A generous amount of property outside. The child's swing offers a bit of whimsy."

"And a bit of curiosity. What child was it for if not for me? I do not see any children in these pictures, only adults. Do you know of my family?"

"Not at all, which intrigues me." He stopped at one picture and gestured Linda over. "See the resemblance? She could be your sister." Linda frowned. "I mean your grandmother, great grandmother even. You are not that old."

"It's not that. You're older than I am," Linda said matter of fact. Now Walter's cheeks could light the room. Linda continued, unaware of the awkward slam. "I assumed if you called me and were here now, you would know about the previous owners."

"I'm afraid not. I've been here for months studying the Salem trials and their relation to similar trials in England, but somehow, I missed this house entirely during my initial canvassing of the city. It's as if it magically appeared on its own. Magic. Salem, you see. Witches?" Walter slipped into the flop sweat of a failed comedian.

Linda was a tough crowd. Only interested in one thing. Her family name. "No one in town knows anything?"

"Possibly the church. Certainly, the church, but there are—roadblocks there. Meanwhile, I submitted a request for property records through all the normal channels. Small town with not much to do, but they came up empty. I sent them back for a round two and will inform you when I hear more. Also, I visited your nearest neighbors on either side. They live quite far and so you know, the land across the street from your home is undeveloped. There are no homes on that side along this entire street. Despite my failures, I will continue probing the populace."

Linda rolled her eyes at his words. "Thank God Ruby wasn't here to hear that."

"A faux pas? An Americanism?"

"No, an anachronism. Pay it no mind." She leaned into his obliviousness and innocence. "I'm grateful for what you have done to the place. I understand why you're involved. But the payments and contact, how did that happen?"

"Someone placed an anonymous call to the Historical Society. They contacted me with instructions to make the home habitable."

The two stood in silence, waiting for the other to talk. The strangers were both done, too awkward to make small talk. Linda finally coughed, breaking the silence. She gestured toward the exit. Walter took the hint and nodded as he headed in that direction.

He talked as they walked, suddenly remembering an undiscussed topic. "City officials, sadly, will be keen on visiting, often I would imagine. I will do my best to act as a buffer."

"Why? Are they worried I might turn it into a bed-and-breakfast?"

Walter winced and looked at her over his glasses. "You are not planning such a thing, are you?"

"No. It was just a question."

Walter sighed in relief. "That is precisely the type of thing they fear. This city thrives on tourism but the proper type of tourism. Tourists and people who respect the historical significance of such a place. They tasked me with limiting any unexpected changes to the property until permits clear. Much like inhibiting an infection. Oh, not that you're infected, simply talking from a historical perspective. Heaven forbid that Ikea is your life's philosophy."

Linda took a step and sank slightly. A floorboard creaked as she pulled her foot away. Walter looked down concerned.

"Then there are the safety issues." Walter stepped in the same spot. It held but appeared questionable. "Not my expertise but there are good contractors in town. I already know of several in my short time here. I will connect one of them with you for an inspection. Might be wise in the meantime to note any questionable spots in the home. And perhaps avoid this hallway where possible for the meantime."

"Do not set up my bedroom in the hallway. Got it." Linda smiled at Walter, who seemed confused by the joke. She let it drop as something else crossed her mind. "The caller knew me well enough to expect my stay, yet they spoke anonymously?"

"Not much of a mystery there, likely a living family member who is aware of your lineage. Possibly your mother?"

"If so, you spoke to her more than I ever did."

"What are you saying?"

"I never knew my mother. She left me at an orphanage. The very one I teach at. The one my friends teach at. What did she sound like?"

"Apologies. As I mentioned, I did not take the call. It went to someone in the historical society. Were I aware of the circumstances, I would have asked more questions. While inheritance typically comes at the cost of a life, I did not know a stranger of sorts passed it on to you. Quite peculiar, that."

"I saw where she spent her last days, but it was too late. She had passed. If she made such arrangements, it meant she knew about me. If so, why stay hidden and destitute for so long? I could have afforded better care for her. She lived in the squalor of a poorly run retirement home. She was gone before I ever knew she was there."

"This is all intriguing and distressing. I will make inquiries with the office that took the call to see what more I can learn, but I fear your contact information and funds for care of the house were the only information provided during the call."

"It makes no sense to me. Any of this."

"Then it appears you and I share certain needs."

Waler stopped suddenly. Linda bumped into him. Linda flustered over the proximity and suggestion. Walter caught on.

"Er, what I meant was my search for the history of this house and your search for your family name might be the same mission."

"It appears so."

"You mentioned where the unfortunate housing your mother spent her last days in. Did you receive anything from there? The smallest thing might inform my investigation."

Linda instinctively grasped the key around her neck through her clothing, but did not mention it. One of her bags sat on the floor in the foyer. Linda unzipped the carryon and pulled a manila envelope out, handing it to Walter. The historian leafed through the articles, more excited than shocked at the contents.

"I don't know why she would have those," Linda said.

"Names, dates and pictures. This a historian's trifecta. If I can borrow this, it may be of some help."

"Certainly."

Walter raised the folder in victory and waved it from his forehead like a salute. "Well, then I have fresh work to do while you settle in. I have already determined certain parts of the home to be from the earliest settlements based on design elements and certain furnishings. But someone made upgrades. Indoor plumbing, for example. That would require permits. There is a paper record to be found somewhere. I will be in touch. If you curse me out when I call, that is how I will know I have reached you."

Linda smiled and opened the door. The man stepped out into the rain, producing an umbrella as if from nowhere before dashing out into the night. Linda cocked her head. It was subtle, but somewhere within the drumbeat of rain, she heard growling. Forest enveloped the property on multiple sides. Wildlife would be plentiful. Not wishing to let anything in, she slammed the door and yelped at the sight of Ruby standing next to her.

Ruby tackled Linda in a hug. "See, first day here and you've found a man. Too rainy to go out but we looked through all the windows plenty. There's a child's swing. Maybe that's a sign you and the egg can work on children."

"The egg?" Linda asked.

"The egg. The brain. The nerd. The hot dude in glasses. Come on, wait until you see your room!"

Ruby grabbed Linda's hand and led her upstairs to the first room. Linda's bags were waiting at the foot of the bed minus her carryon, which remained at the foot of the stairs. Linda leaned in nervously, eyeing the strange place where she would spend the night alone. Ruby picked up on it.

"You okay? Want me to check the room. See if Walter snuck back in, minus any clothing?"

"You're scandalous Ruby."

"I'd say you know me so well, except you say that like you're just now finding out. Seriously, would you rather I stay with you tonight?"

Linda blocked the doorway, taking charge of her room, her space, her house. She smiled gratefully at her friend. "No. I'll be fine. I am fine. Seriously, I'll be fine."

Ruby wiped her brow. "Oh, good, because I had every intention of abusing my man's body tonight. You hear noises in your new house pay no mind. It's just me stocking up on my confession booth material for when we return home."

"They do not pay the priests enough."

"I think they do, and I intend for them to earn their keep. Ta-ta sweets."

Ruby bounced down the hall full of energy, somehow unaffected by the long drive and time zone change. Linda smiled, entered her room, then yelled over her shoulder.

"Ruby!"

"One of mine. You have a man in your life now," Ruby replied from somewhere down the hall before closing the door for her planned night of passion with Andrew.

A black sexy negligee lay sprawled out on Linda's bed. The comforter showed through much of the garment designed to show skin. Linda brought the lingerie to the closet. Empty hangers lined the interior rod. Another thing to thank Walter for.

She winced. Thinking about Walter while holding the garment felt scandalous. She loved Ruby, but the joke did not make Linda feel anymore welcome in her home. Such a garment was not in her wheelhouse. Linda was not anti-sex. She liked it. Okay, loved it, and sadly missed it. No ships had passed hers in the night for quite some time. But sex was best body on body. Accoutrements like Ruby's negligee did little for Linda.

It felt weird to baptize her new closet with such an item, but she shrugged and hung it inside. Why not? An unfamiliar environment deserved a different type of clothing than Linda normally wore. She hung the garment where it could excite the warped pine planks lining the closet.

She turned back to her bed. It was a new start, time for things to be different. Time for a new attitude, Linda told herself. It would start with her bag. The old Linda would have immediately unpacked, unable to sleep unless everything was in place. It was late, and she was weary. Why not slack off? Why not for once leave it until morning?

Linda had packed sleepwear in bag number two, a Delsey twenty-nine-inch suitcase with leather trim. She tipped the bag over onto the floor and unzipped the front. Her sleepwear, flannel Lauren nightgown, designed for the cooler east coast weather, took up space alongside the wet bag compartment.

Everything packed just so. Linda had a system and could find items even with her eyes closed. Proper packing eliminated some of the chaotic nature of travel. She disrobed and placed her day clothes on top of the downed bag instead of putting them away, something she never would have done in the past. Yes, it was time for a new Linda. The old version would have shuddered at the thought of leaving clothes strewn about, but it was her home. She could do as she pleased.

Linda draped her nightgown over her head and further examined the room. She gravitated toward the vanity. Elaborate carvings circumnavigated the mirror in a singular piece. At least the frame appeared to be one piece. If there were seams, she failed to spot them. Impressive either way. The look resembled a Bas-relief, where the mirrored portion served as the recessed portion of the sculpture. The design comprised an elaborate wreath of ivy intermingled with the faces of two preteen girls.

A sculpted leaf jutted at an angle high along one side of the vanity. Linda hung her necklace on the obtrusion. A music box sat on the desk. Linda lifted the lid. The box played a warped, haunting melody on gears as old as the song. The music box stopped on its own. Linda tipped it closed and walked over to her bed.

The sight of the suitcases bothered her immensely, yet she pulled the covers aside. *I am quite tired and would like to sleep now, thank you very much*, she thought as she climbed into bed, her bed. Her place. She could be anyone now. Someone new, less rigid.

The mattress had to be newer than the house, another Walter special. The odor of plastic wrapping lingered, the sign of a recent delivery. It was soft, better than her bed back west truthfully, at least based on first impressions. Certainly, better than her poor mother suffered.

Linda shook off the thought. If she went down that road, she would never sleep. She settled in under the covers, pulling them to her chin. All she had to do was douse the light. She closed her eyes as a test run, but they quickly shot open wide as if she saw a ghost. She leaped from the bed.

"Nope. Can't do it."

Linda lifted her larger suitcase onto the bed and began unpacking both bags. Occasionally, she moved some items from one spot to a second, deciding where everything should go. When finished, she finally placed the empty suitcases in the closet, realizing how small the space was. But at least everything was in its place. She turned back to the room, even more tired than earlier. The trip fatigued her despite pockets of sleep.

Underneath the bed in the two-foot gap from box-spring to floor laid a scraggly haired dead woman facing out toward the room on her stomach as if in mid pushup. Linda's feet cross mere inches away and the dead woman's eyes shot open. Lightning flashed across the dead grey skin of the horrific face.

Linda rushed to the side of the bed as the rumbling outside lit up her nerves. She lifted the covers and climbed underneath. The storm outside grew, howling winds driving the rain against the window like shrapnel. The window shook.

Lightning flashed again, revealing the dead woman repositioned under the bed facing up and extended just past the foot of the bed. Her arthritic bony white hands topped with yellowed chipped nails gripped the foot of the bedframe as if the bed itself were her covers for the night. The Dead Woman opened her mouth in what could not be called a smile, showing decayed black teeth. She lay in wait. For what?

Atop the bed, Linda matched the pose of the woman under the bed, minus the wicked smile. Lightning struck and cast shadows of two women in the room. Linda turned on her side toward the dark images, but the shadows bled into the night before she spotted them. Linda turned off the bedside lamp, rolled onto her back once again, and finally closed her eyes.

She failed to see the shadow of the woman now standing over her bed in the silhouette of a double lightning strike. The woman's head dangled low as if observing the sleeping beauty.

Downstairs in the kitchen, a slow creek sounded as the basement door opened on its own.

In the backyard, the swing moved. Not in the haphazard motion of the wind, but swinging under the weight of an invisible rider. Slow at first before building up steam. Something unseen hummed the song from the music box.

O UTSIDE, WALTER REMAINED PARKED in his Volvo alongside the house. New England was rife with grass parking, since driveways were often too small to accommodate guests. That was not the case with Linda's drive. Walter yard parked to bring supplies in through the backdoor. It sat at ground level while the front of the house had stairs. Back door was easier. He did not realize parking there meant the occupants would be unaware anyone was home. Had he known to expect them, he would have moved the car to the front after unloading everything. Or met them properly at the door at an agreed upon time. Their meeting was not under best circumstances but collectively they proved to be very warm people. Exceptionally so in Linda's case, Walter thought.

He flipped through the disturbing clippings from the folder. Collectively, they portrayed a series of horrific events seemingly unrelated save for their gruesome nature. He lifted his cell and snapped pictures of each all while maintaining a view of the house. Particularly one dark room on the second floor, which finally lit up.

A shadow cast across the curtain. Linda's silhouette played out against the curtain as she disrobed and then dressed. Her naked form cast a perfect shadow. Walter nodded, clinically impressed, but turned away to continue examining the articles. None of the articles listed any names, instead designating the victims as unknown subject or John and Jane Doe. A reporting flaw or something more sinister? Either way, unless a batch of the articles he had not read yet provided more detail, it left him little to go on in researching the home, if the poor deceased souls even had anything to do with the property or Linda's family.

Once the light finally turned off in Linda's room, Walter reached for the key. But then her light turned on again. He looked up, curious, saw her form flutter by the window several times.

(Was she unpacking? And at this hour?) He released his hold on the key.

When Walter received the assignment, he was less than thrilled. The process for permits in a historically rich town was daunting in the best of circumstances. Contractors were quick to offer cash under the table as bribes. Not every line of work had the same interest in history that Walter did. He could not fault the hard-working men and women, but he also could not find his way to break the rules, much to the consternation of local developers.

In Walter, the town found a person qualified for designating the historical status of properties and buildings. A woman who left Salem for the swamps of Florida formerly held the job. The town employee mentioned weather as the reason for leaving, but Walter suspected otherwise. The woman likey had grown tired of climbing under porches or crawling through attics, things Walter quite enjoyed. Towns like Salem were unique in that it was possible to still discover unknown historical locations even after hundreds of years of cataloging such things. The only thing absent in the historically relevant town was dinosaur bones.

If Walter deemed a place as a historical landmark, local officials took over. Walter served as a contracted employee only. He was not a city employee. Town leaders were happy they no longer had to go through Boston whenever a local farmer or new business owner began a dig that almost inevitably turned up something needing study.

Linda's property came under scrutiny for two reasons: one routine and one highly unusual. An anonymous call provided certain information, as Walter mentioned to Linda. The details included an owner's plans to file a quitclaim deed intending to pass the property over to an adult child. Where the common practice became unusual was when local officials checked the address on a map.

Town records listed the spot as an undeveloped lot. They assigned Walter to investigate a house where the town did not believe there was one. Such poor record keeping in such an important community worried Walter. What else did they miss? As for the surprise homestead, Walter dated it to at least to the very century he came to town to investigate. The structure existed during the witch trials.

It also appeared abandoned for quite some time based on the condition of the interior. The same call arranging the transfer of ownership supplied funds to have the place freshened up. None of that seemed odd initially. But Linda's circumstances proved unique and sad. Walter had already shopped and spruced up the place, studying it as he went, having the luxury of doing so without an owner interfering. The portraits were of great interest, and the house contained significant antiquities.

He hoped to learn more from the owner, but Linda knew less about the place than he did. Linda's desire to learn more about the house's history ensured he could continue his research. Perhaps he could even turn the place into a case study. His university employers still expected him to publish regularly. Or perish. Was not that the saying? He did not wish to perish, so he planned to turn the new discovery into a paper.

Bonus that the homeowner's goals lined up with his own. Her being so lovely was also a bonus. With lights out again, Walter finally started the car. The engine refused to turn, cranking out a horrible sound. His second attempt timed itself with a lightning strike. So concerned was he about the engine, he failed to notice what the flash of light revealed in the rear seat. A child.

Dead Sadie sat in his back seat, eyes sunken, face blanched grey, wearing clothes from a puritan era. An upturned cross covered her forehead, the child's hair parted near the center, allowing a perfect view of the knotted, scarred skin that made up the cross. Walter yelped in delight at the car starting and he drove into the sea of rain. The child went along for the ride.

The rain danced a tune atop his roof and through the pitter patter something else sounded, a melody distinct from the pattern of drops keeping time above his head. Subtle at first, but slowly growing more noticeable. Another flash lit up Sadie, who hummed the song from the music box.

Walter adjusted the rearview mirror to check the back. Nothing. The song vanished if a melody ever existed at all. The rain took over the tune again. He turned back to the road and slammed the brakes! A massive black dog with red eyes blocked the road. He swerved to avoid it and hydroplaned off the road. The car came to a hard stop against a tree. Glass shattered, blasting transparent shrapnel through the vehicle, ripping into airbag and flesh.

The airbag caught the accident victim in its wide cushion and quickly deflated, leaving Walter propped against the steering wheel, battling to remain conscious. He cast a hazy gaze toward the road, no dog in sight. Though able to blink away some of the blood pouring down his scalp, he could not find the strength to lift his arms to check the wound on his head. The steering wheel kept him propped up, where he otherwise would have slipped back in the seat, ready to sleep.

His eyes traveled where they could and he noticed the clippings scattered about the front seat, one of which appeared to bleed itself. A morose man stood covered in blood below a headline announcing his violent demise. Silly, Walter thought, momentarily laughing, until he grimaced in pain. Okay, no laughing in his condition. Check. No moving either. He still could not find strength in arms or legs.

Walter understood the man in the picture was not bleeding. It was his own blood making the rounds. His vision fading, Walter saw himself as the subject of one of the many headlines scattered near his feet. *'Religious gadfly seeks firsthand experimentation into the true nature of an afterlife,'* would be an appropriate headline, Walter thought. Would Linda add his news clipping to the others, he wondered and felt the sorrow that he would likely never see her again.

As he grew even weaker from the bloodletting, the world faded. He squinted in confusion as he heard a child giggle in the back seat. His confusion grew as a child's hand reached over the seat and stroked his hair. Walter's eyes finally closed, and he fell into unconsciousness on the steering column. The Volvo's horn screamed in protest in the night.

CHAPTER 7
1692

A VOICE SPOKE FROM somewhere within the Goode house. The growing storm battered the exterior into submission. A shutter flapped incessantly open and closed on one side of the building, ready to take flight with the wind at any moment. The voice trembled between childish uncertainty and masculine authority, sometimes shifting during the same word.

"Forgive me reverend for... (*inaudible). Forgive me reverend, for I... (*inaudible)."

Inside, tethers of rope held Rose in place on the bed, spread eagle, fighting her bonds. The child writhed and thrashed, shifting between agony and joy, laughing uncontrollably one moment before growling the next.

Althea screamed at the sight. The poor thing tied to the bed did not seem human, and yet it was. Rose was her daughter, her youngest, the most innocent, and yet now the child wore the mask of a beast. Rose was precocious. Althea never believed her child to be fully pious. Was any daughter of any reverend? But she was a good girl. And so pretty. Rose's smile always produced an adorable set of dimples. Her curly locks were the envy of many a child, and Althea frequently fought with her husband over how long it should grow.

That was once upon a time, as the child's beauty had since vanished under a visage full of rage and spittle. Sweat plastered her hair across her forehead. The child slipped back into the dimples when she occasionally laughed, though there was menace behind the laughter. Reverend Goode noticed his wife and gestured her forward. Althea moved in on jelly legs, frightened to get closer to the thing in the bed. Rose continued speaking in the up and down voice.

"Forgive me, reverend, for..." Rose bowed her body upward into such a curve against the binds it suggested levitation. She reached a height arced high enough to snap a spine. The child's gaze remained focused on her father. "I AM sin!"

Reverend Goode used tongs to lift a cloth from the tray and raised it over the child. Then he draped it over her face. Steam flushed into the air upon contact.

"In the name of the Lord, leave this child!"

The cloth clung to the girl's face, displaying the tortured child's agony as she writhed under the burn. The material molded to Rose's features as she screamed through the burn. Goode studied the image of his child with a detached curiosity.

Once the steam subsided, Reverend Goode lifted the cloth, taking some of the girl's skin with it. A massive blotch in the shape of a square covered the child's face. Drops of hot water remained on her face, continuing to burn. Rose stuck her tongue out then sucked it back in, trying to swallow it in the attempt to end that which used to be a girl.

Riddled with guilt over her part in the child's torture, Althea reminded herself that the true Rose was somewhere else, somewhere where good girls play. There was only the beast now. A tear rolled from one of Althea's eyes, tracking the curve of her cheek. Her lips quivered, holding in the desperate need to scream, to beg for God's mercy. Reverend Goode lifted one more cloth before barking at his wife.

"Go. Check on our other child."

Althea remained long enough to watch her husband apply the second cloth. The thin fabric sucked in and blew out over the open space that was her little girl's mouth. An underlying growl accompanied each staggered breath. Unable to take anymore, Althea moved on.

Moving toward the door at the end of the hall, Althea's vision blurred, the hallway stretched out, slipping away from her, the door as far away as her children were from their old selves. Where were they? Because neither was present in the home. Only shells remained, mimicking once upon a time sweet children. She shook her head until the hallway righted itself.

Bed legs pounding against floorboards sounded through the closed door. As she neared the room, the violent noises drowned out the horrific sounds at her rear. Then the howls began, sounding unrelated to anything remotely human.

Althea entered Sadie's room, leaping when the door slammed behind her of its own accord. Reverend Ramses, a church elder with facial features so severe the underlying bones threatened to rupture skin, stood over Althea's oldest daughter. Sadie was once upon a time studious and pretty, though awkwardly shy.

A daddy's girl, that one. Oh, how she loved her father's sermons and the respect that their family commanded. Though boys often noticed Sadie with her long dark hair and large expressive eyes, Sadie showed little interest, saving herself for the Lord. (Though where was he now?) Sadie always doted on her younger sister, and loved to brush out the girl's hair, as well as her own, but Althea had recently fallen ill, and her hair was losing its luster.

Now that happy child of thirteen writhed against restraints with eyes rolled back in her head. Reverend Ramses stood alongside the bed hovering over a nightstand holding a large copper bowl burning whale oil. The flames rose high above the container. Ramses produced a metal cross from somewhere in his elaborate religious garb. The stem of the cross was long, and the priest held of it what he could while thrusting the bulk of the cross into the flame.

In their church, the Bible ruled as the word of the Lord. Symbols such as the cross, revered back in England, were not commonplace in their colonies, which was why Althea's Bible provided her comfort. But the cross held some powers, and if Ramses saw fit to use one, Althea would not question him. The metal version glowed with intense heat. Althea worried about how the man intended to use it on Sadie.

Ramses grimaced under the heat of the flame as he turned to the girl. "Who has bewitched you, child?" Ramses demanded more than asked.

Sadie tilted her head to one side. The vertebrae in her neck crackled. "In infernis arderet! Na kaeís stin kólasi! Lleh ni nrub!" The child rumbled a threat in between growls.

"No. You burn in hell!"

Ramses lifted the cross from the fire and thrust it against the child's forehead at an upturned angle. Skin sizzled and burned. The girl tremored and shook as her mother stifled sobs.

The child finally slumped, and the reverend tossed the cross aside. He clenched and unclenched his own burning hand. At one point the hand made a fist, and he looked at the girl as if tempted to use it. But the fevered girl had fallen unconscious from the pain with a permanent upside down cross on her forehead.

The priest slumped, believing the fight was over. The innocence of a young child had returned to the world of the Lord. Ramses brushed the girl's hair aside, taking in her now angelic face. Sadie opened her eyes and smiled innocently.

"I'll tell you now, Reverend... (*inaudible)," Sadie said, softly, almost too weak to speak. She whispered, "Revol ym si natas."

"I cannot hear you, child."

"Closer."

He leaned in and she bit a chunk off his ear, spitting it into the burning whale oil. It sizzled into blackness, filling the room with the odor of burning flesh. Althea covered her face, trying not to gag. Ramses screamed and thrust a hand against the gushing stream of red that used to be his ear.

Sadie giggled as blood dribbled down her chin.

CHAPTER 8

L INDA TOSSED IN HER sleep, murmuring back to the voices speaking in her mind. Whatever called to her in dreams soon took hold in her house as well. A voice spoke somewhere beyond her bedroom door, one trembling between childish uncertainty and masculine authority. What started as distant and muffled grew closer, clearer.

"Forgive me Father for... (*inaudible). Forgive me Father for I... (*inaudible)."

Linda turned in her sleep and suddenly the voices vanished, as did the sound of the storm. The outside world dripped away, melting from reality as Linda finally slipped fully into a dream. In it she walked through a house, hers, but not hers. There were signs of a different time in play. Candles and lanterns provided light, electricity nowhere to be found. Linda did not see herself in the dream, instead, she interacted in the dream as if there. A tiny portion of her brain wondered whether she was sleepwalking in her new home. It was not something she had ever done, but she read somewhere that drastic changes in one's environment could instigate such a thing.

If she were not sleepwalking, then she considered it strange to dream about the very hallway near which she slept. She moved to the first bedroom and opened the door. An animalistic growl drew her attention to the bed. Linda cried out in fright at the sight of a young child tied spread eagle to the bed, her features as twisted as the sheets. A stern man wearing what appeared to be religious garb turned toward the doorway.

The man looked at Linda with familiarity, though she had never seen the man before. He reached out for something. Linda glanced down and noticed she held a platter of rags. An exposed portion of the tray reflected an image of a woman in puritan clothes.

Grabbing a cloth, the man shook it out. It fluttered loudly like a fluffed bedsheet. The swish of fabric woke Linda. She opened her eyes to a blinding light. The dream slipped from her memory as the waking world overtook her. A figure stood above her bed. The nature of the fluttering fabric became clear. Drapes yanked open. Linda threw a pillow at the offender.

"Close the curtains, it's too bright."

Ruby caught the pillow. "The fact it's so bright out is the indicator that it's late. You are in vacation mode for sure. Not like you to sleep in so long."

"If you could call it sleep."

"Up all-night thinking of your new boyfriend, were you?"

"I wish."

"So, he is your boyfriend!"

"Please, it's too early for you to bask in my relationship inadequacies. I meant I had bad dreams."

"I hear ya sister. I dreamt last night I went to bed peen free. But know what? Didn't go to bed peen free. Had the peen! Can't trust dreams."

"Oh God, is morning sickness without being pregnant a thing? Because you are single-handedly making me want to morning puke."

Ruby grabbed her friend's hands, pulling her from the bed. "Come on, the rain stopped. It's beautiful outside. Get up sleepyhead."

Linda rose from bed, careful not to disturb the sheeting too much. She noticed something odd, an imprint as if someone had sat on the foot of the bed. "Hey, did you camp out on my bed before rudely waking me?"

"Not guilty as charged. On the creepy sitting thing, only guilty on the waking rudeness."

Linda reached to fluff out the area, intending to make the bed, but Ruby pushed her friend toward the door.

"Let's go. I have something to show you. Come on."

The women left the room. The moment they exited, the impression on the bed vanished as something unseen stepped away from the bed.

Ruby led Linda to the kitchen where her other friends waited with pancakes. They presented her a plate with 'welcome home Linda' spelled out in fruit and syrup atop her short stack. Linda gushed, taking in the rustic New England charm of the bright kitchen, all creepiness gone.

"Aw thanks guys. This is so sweet."

"Too sweet. Those calories in the syrup combined with the fruit, I mean..." Tom started.

"Tom, please," Heather scolded.

Tom plated his own, adding only a dab of butter. He waved his free hand and stepped away as if to suggest *your diabetes funeral*. He leaned near a window box overlooking the backyard. The women sat at the table and ate. Andrew approached Tom and threatened to pour syrup over the man's breakfast. The two scuffled playfully. At least Andrew did. Tom appeared aggrieved at the gesture. Heather looked away from her husband, took a breath, then grasped Linda's hand.

"Have you thought about what you want to do?" Heather asked.

"What? No, I mean, this house is mine, but live in Salem? Leave the kids behind? I know they're not mine, but they need someone like I needed someone when I attended. Could this ever be my home?"

"Linda, please, you're becoming like my husband. When did you get so serious?"

Linda instinctively looked at Tom to see if the slam registered. It did not. He shrugged.

"Accurate assessment," Tom said.

Heather continued. "I meant activities. Have you thought about what you want to do? This is our summer."

Linda choked down a bite, placed her hands on the table to steady herself. "I'm sorry. Hi, I'm Linda, your recently overwhelmed friend. Nice to meet you. The old Linda will be back right after these delicious pancakes."

"Cut her a break, huh? This is a big change. There will be plenty of time for us to plan the summer of fun," Ruby said.

Andrew leaned over Ruby and kissed her head while taking her empty plate. "Seconds?"

She shook him off with a wink, refocusing on Linda. Heather walked her own empty plate to the sink, but Tom was blocking it. Andrew circled around and took Heather's from her, then forced Tom aside without a second thought. Heather sat back down.

"Sorry to be so pushy, sugar," Heather said. "I love the kids at school too, but tell me you ain't as ready for a break from all that as I am?"

"You mean would we rather be in a classroom right now battling all the demons who refuse to put away their damn cell phones for two seconds?" Ruby asked.

"Hell no," the three women chimed in together and clinked their coffee mugs in a toast.

Andrew searched cabinets. "Apparently, your friend Walter, who stocked the pantry, has an aversion to alcohol." He explored the fridge. "And kale. Who doesn't keep kale handy?'

Heather shivered. "Oh, darlin' please. I know greens and kale ain't one."

Andrew laughed. "Still, we should make a run to the store."

"I would love to see the sights, the museums, the educational centers, maybe some historical monuments." Tom lit up for the first time.

"It's on the internet sweetie. Google it. No homework, please. Does Salem have a spa?" Heather asked.

Linda finished and brought her own plate to the sink. Andrew cut her off at the pass and took it from her. Their hands brushed against one another's. She blushed over the contact, and they shared a look before she turned back toward Ruby, who gabbed with Heather about spa possibilities.

Wham!

A bird hit the window and dropped out of view. Andrew dropped the plate in the sink and ducked with instinct. Linda had her back turned but covered her head and screamed, uncertain about what had just happened. Tom charged over while the other two women rose from their seats.

Andrew rose and cautiously peered outside. "Whoa. Poor thing, he hit that good."

Wham! Another bird struck. Wham, wham, wham! Thunderous strikes as large birds, one after another, hit the glass as if being shot from a bird Uzi. Everyone scrambled away as the glass shattered. A bird flopped in through the window on a broken wing and thumped on the floor before going still. The flurry of feathers and ferocity finally ceased.

"Everyone okay?" Andrew asked.

"What the hell was that?" Tom asked.

Linda and Andrew converged at the defeated window and peered out as the others urged caution. They screamed when a face popped up in the window. A military fit officer in a state trooper's uniform stood just outside the window, looking at the carnage and the occupants in the house.

"Now that's the second strangest thing I have ever seen," the man said. Noticing the look on everyone's face, he answered their

unasked question. "Sergeant Ron Taylor. I'm here because there
was an accident last night."

T HE TROOPER DROVE DOWN a country road, sirens
blaring, lights flashing. Using the rearview mirror, he kept
his eyes on Linda in the back seat. (Accusatory?) Linda fidgeted
under the glare, nervous as if back in the headmaster's office.

"How long did you say you were here again?" Linda gestured
to her ears. The officer killed the siren but kept the lights flashing.
"Pardon. Do not find the chance to use that often. I asked how
long you have been here in Salem."

"One day."

"One day and he's asking for you after an accident?" Linda
nodded, looking out the rear window, taking in the view of her
new town. "He must like the silent type."

"I'm sorry, I just lost my mother, just got the house, then this.
Things are a little..." Linda faded off in thought.

Taylor softened. "Don't worry. Talking is overrated. Don't
mind me no how. Occupational hazard, my work brain often
leapfrogs well past my manners." The sergeant stopped the car
and turned around in his seat. "I was approaching your front
door when I heard the birds hit. That's why I came around the
back, thought someone was attacking your place. Only birds,
though. Darndest thing, that. I'll send someone to board up that
window for you."

"Thank you." Linda looked outside, confused. "This isn't a
hospital."

"No, it is not. Funny thing. All this time on the job and I
never encountered your house before. This part of the country

has back roads for days. Don't want you thinking it's a patrol problem on my part."

"I considered no such thing."

"Thank you then. Enjoy your stay in Salem."

Linda stepped out, and the trooper killed the flash-bar lights. The car drove away, leaving Linda standing before a massive building with an ornate hand-painted wooden sign designating the building as the Salem Historical Society.

The building appeared lost in its own shadow, fully enveloped in darkness. Linda looked out across the nearby courtyard and noticed a woman watching her. The woman sat deathly still on a metal bench, angled to face the building. There was no sign of a walker or a caretaker in sight. The elderly female sat so still that Linda wondered if the woman was still breathing. When Linda took a step to check, the woman followed, subtly moving her head.

That was enough. Old woman alive. Check. Old woman watching like a creep? Also check. Linda moved back to the building and used the cast iron knocker to tap on the door, which creaked slowly open. Linda stuck her head inside. Finding no one, she entered, closing the door behind her.

The door opened into a large office. A massive mahogany desk sat directly ahead, behind which rose floor to ceiling shelves loaded with hardcover books. A massive globe nested on a circular tripod abutted one side of the desk. The land masses seemed off from the globe in her classroom. A cursory glance offered the names of a few countries she never heard of before.

Tiny, recessed coves in multiple sections of the room housed prairie lanterns which emulated candlelight. The place was eerily silent. Then a flutter, subtle at first but growing in intensity, like the fluttering bird on her kitchen floor. She followed the sound to the next room.

If the front facing office served as a study, the next room approximated a museum. The room housed far more books.

Shelves lined every wall and a large glass case displayed yellowed newspapers. A doorless entry on one side of the room looked out into more of the same. A desk sat positioned off to one side of the windowless room.

She discovered the source of fluttering. A fan swept the room at a languorous pace atop an anchored pole. When it faced the desk, it ruffled a stack of papers held in place by the bust of a historical figure she did not recognize. Something else crinkled behind her. She turned and yelped as a paper thrust toward her face. Walter stood there holding an oversized map. He looked over the top, surprised to find her there.

"Scared you again? I don't seem to have much luck around you."

Linda noticed his bandaged head. "Are you okay? Shouldn't you be in a hospital?"

"Checked myself out. Bit of a concussion. Doctors say it will fit right in with my personality. Are we expecting your friends?"

"No, I thought I was making a hospital visit, so they went out sightseeing."

Walter crinkled his face, struggling to understand their apathy. Linda raised her hands.

"Please. They are not so callous. They do not know you. It does not mean they don't wish you well," she said.

"But you did not go sightseeing?"

"I planned to join them if you were okay. And it appears you are, thankfully. Tom might regret not joining me. He would lose his mind to be here."

"Bring him by sometime. I appreciate your concern. Quite kind since we are strangers as well, I suppose. I hope to change that."

Linda smiled, and Walter followed suit. Another accidental insinuation. He made a show of putting the map away as an excuse to change the conversation. Once finished, he cleared his throat and turned back to her.

"I meant since we are working together. Please follow me. I have something to show you."

Walter escorted Linda through the building until they arrived at a well-equipped computer room. The modern systems and monitors appeared out of place in the otherwise historical surroundings. Walter gestured Linda to a turn of the century desk housing a computer with a forty-inch screen displaying a map of Salem.

"This is called a cadastral map. They had various designations over time, such as surveyor maps, but cities have always used a form of these to identify borders and property lines. Currently on screen is a digitized version of one of the earliest such maps of Salem." Walter pointed to a spot on the screen. "This location is…"

"My mother's property?"

"YOUR property. Yes." Walter hit a button and an overlay of yellow spots dotted the screen. "Yellow represents homes in Salem."

"My mother's…" Linda caught herself. "Mine is yellow. So, it is an original home?"

"Indeed. They updated maps at different intervals over time, but five-year increments served as the norm. Watch as I layer a succession of updated maps over the original. Here is the same map half a decade later." Walter hit a key on his computer and the yellow dots turned red except for Linda's home, which remained yellow. He swept a finger along the outer edge of the town. "As expected, there is population growth, a large influx of families on the southern edge of the city. You might have noticed something else."

"My property didn't change color."

Walter nodded. "Now let's add the next, shall we?" Another tap and the dots on the map increased and were all purple. Walter placed his hand on a random spot. "Pay note to this spot as I post the next map."

Walter held one finger on a purple dot and hit the enter key with his other hand. The purple dot under his finger vanished and the others besides Linda's now turned sky blue.

"Why did that one stay purple?"

"Fire. They record this property as having burned to the ground, but within the next half decade mapping..." He kept the finger in place and hit enter again. Dots turned burgundy, including the spot under his finger. "Rebuilt so made it back on the survey maps."

"Then why is mine still the original yellow?"

He raised a finger without answering before bringing his finger down in an exaggerated move. He stepped back, arms crossed. The program took over, overlaying map over map at a furious pace. Colors danced, morphed, changed, and occasionally vanished. Through it all, her property remained yellow. The computer eventually pinged, announcing the pixilated dance to be over.

"Now we are current though last year."

"I don't understand," Linda said.

"Nor do I, all things being equal. Not only does this confirm your house was one of the earliest in Salem, but it somehow has remained off the radar of the local government. Even if it burned and someone rebuilt it, why would it not eventually reappear? My initial assessment of your home suggests it was an original colony home. That means it never burned down at all, at least not fully. Many places had fires of some sort over the years."

"The trooper who gave me a ride mentioned he never noticed the home. How is that possible?"

Linda pushed her face closer on the screen, studying the image as if it held answers. Walter noted her discomfort and turned to her.

"Scaring you in another manner, I am afraid. Do not be frightened. It serves as an oddity and is intriguing, but please do not attribute Salem folklore to your thoughts. As for the trooper, they cover the state. A bit of difference from a local sheriff. I would expect none of them to know every spot in town."

"Okay, fine, law enforcement could miss it, but record keepers?"

"Maybe we should call that trooper back. I believe there is a nefarious reason for this discrepancy, but it has nothing to do with the town but with its residents."

"Tell me."

"You noticed you have the luxury of electricity, indoor plumbing, heat, and other modern trappings. I mentioned I would investigate that avenue. I did and found nothing. Impossible to keep such work off official records unless foul play was afoot."

Linda nodded as it hit her. "They paid someone off to avoid permits? But my house disappears after the first map. Were there even permits back then?"

Walter shook his head. "No. But deviousness stands the test of time well. If people wanted the information hidden, it would serve them well to vanish all decades affected. It would make it harder to identify the year the crime occurred. No matter the reasons, it will make things harder if you ever choose to make changes of your own. Any new permits would take forever to clear, as they would first wish to research previous work already done on the home."

"Walter, please. I have no thoughts on what I want to do with the place other than use it to trace my history. Forgetting the strangeness of the situation, is there anything the map can tell me about my history?"

"What it reveals is that your house does not exist as far as the town of Salem is concerned. More research should provide answers, but as things stand, time forgot your house, or at least the record keepers did. If it is not the result of human malfeasance, then it is a ghost."

CHAPTER 9

C OLT WARREN NEVER TIRED of banging his child's former babysitter, Nell. Nell bounced across the top of his work desk to the rhythm of his thrusts as he took her from behind. She moaned appreciatively (unlike his wife, Colt thought). Nell's arms had long since given out, leaving her torso pressed flat across the surface of the furniture. Her lying flat while he went to town bothered him immensely, not because of how her movements scattered papers, but because the position shielded him from the bounty of her tits.

Nell was what one would call petite, while Colt was what one might call a *big fella*. That meant doing it from behind limited his reach in the best of circumstances (and his massive gut between him and his lover was not the best of circumstances). He had thirty years and pounds over Nell. At his age, Colt was a one and doner, so he dared not ask her to turn over to accommodate his desire to play whack a mole with those bouncing beauties. There was always the chance the change in movement alone might set him off. *Ah well, save those things for a rainy day. Plenty enough of those around here,* he thought.

He settled for slapping her ass and pulling her hair. She liked that plenty and it kept him worked up too (though the gas station penis pills didn't hurt either). Besides, if he interrupted their rhythm, it might give the girl time to think. She might want to try some crazy position she learned from Pornhub, which they often played in the background on the work computers. *Pegging? Christ almighty, isn't anything sacred?* Before he could finish his thought, a phone rang. Probably his wife.

Colt kept three phones. One for family, one for Nell, and one for work. Nell kept her own phone and a second for her boyfriend. The preponderance of phones threw them off their game. Nell reached out instinctively first. Instead of a phone, her hand found the crystal bowl filled with Circus Peanuts. She grabbed one and brought it to her mouth before reaching back out for the cellphones.

"Hells bells, Nell. You can't have sex without a peanut?"

"Not sure you want to talk peanuts while you're parked inside me now, do you? Why can't I have it all? Married stick and Circus Peanuts?"

As Nell reached for the phone, Colt inadvertently hit something right because Nell moaned through the marshmallow candy and knocked all but one phone to the floor. Colt groaned differently than his partner.

"Shit, Nell, you never grabbed a phone before? Now we got to pick them up from the floor."

"For fuck's sake, don't stop. I'm almost there," she protested.

Colt pulled out and pulled up his pants. "Might be my wife. She already suspects something with us."

"The Hell you stopping for? Who cares what the old bat thinks? She was mean to me when I watched your kid, and she's mean to me to this day." Nell said, putting herself back together as each scrambled for a phone.

"Well, if you didn't dress so provocative maybe she'd come around," Colt said, breathing in relief at discovering it was not his family phone. He grabbed another.

"Are you serious? You giving me grief over my clothes? Did you or did you not just have me bent over your office desk?" She breathed in relief herself, not the boyfriend. She grabbed the next one.

"Panties are different, lose em or wear the fancy stuff, but on the outside, wouldn't hurt you to prude it up a bit."

"These ain't pilgrim times no more and I'll wear what I damn well please. Now watch yourself, or maybe these provocatively clad legs stay closed to a certain ding-dong forever, and I mean that word both ways! Colt Warren construction. How may I direct your call?" She segued from dressing him down to answering his work phone like a pro. "Sergeant Taylor? To what do I owe the pleasure?"

"The cops?" Colt asked, reaching for the phone.

She gave him a finger, the index, and turned into the conversation. "Sergeant, while I have you, are any of those strong troopers of yours single?"

"Nell!"

"I prefer the big muscular boy toy types, maybe thin on the belly, unlike some people. No, I am not totally opposed to female troopers as I appear to be in the market. I have a certain position that might need filling," she said as Colt burned red.

"Christ Nell, I said I was sorry!"

"No. You did not." She slapped the phone into his chest.

Colt fumbled the handoff, bobbled the phone before pulling it to his ear where he greeted the officer. "Hello?" He looked at Nell when there was no response.

"He put me on hold, had another call."

"Jesus, you had me going. An opening that needs filling. Really?"

"Why not? Apparently, I dress like a slut."

"Honey, you are a slut, but the best kind..." Colt stumbled when the sergeant unexpectedly came back on the line. "Sorry, ignore what I just said." Nell grinned like she won the lottery. Colt went in for the save with the client on the phone. "Sure, a board up? No problem. What's the address?"

He pulled a carpenter's pencil from behind his ear that somehow held on during his dalliance. He snapped fingers in search of paper. Nell gave him another finger, the one in the center. Colt reached down for a stray sheet launched from the desk earlier and started writing. With that, Colt left his office. Nell yelled after him as she reached for another marshmallow peanut.

"Say you're sorry!"

T HE WARREN CONSTRUCTION TRUCK drove at a snail's pace along a side road with no other cars in sight. Despite the slow speed at which Colt drove, the paper with the address fluttered wildly in the wind. He finally gave up on the idea of fresh air and hit the button to close the window. He picked up his cell and dialed his office.

"Nell? A little help? I'm looking for Gallows Way. Damn Salem, and their cockamamy names. Can you fire up the computer? Yes, I understand I have a cellphone. I'm talking to you, aren't I? It doesn't mean I know how to work the damn thing. What? Apologize? Are you still on that?"

The truck passed an offshoot road and Colt leaned into it, hoping to be recused from the phone call. The green street marker read Good Hope Lane. Colt needed some of that, he figured. His destination remained elusive.

"Fine. You dress as if angels themselves were attending a rake."

She asked what the hell he was talking about.

"You know. The music places you used to go to, with the happy pills and all the hippies. Rave? Okay, you dress like an angel at a rave. Fine, now help me out. This is where I grew up. I know

Gallows Hill Road and Gallows Circle, but Gallows Way? I just passed Good Hope Lane. Another quarter mile? I might be out of Salem by then. Fine."

Colt stepped on the gas, happy to be moving again. He sped down the barren road, kicking up dust. He rounded a blind corner and slammed the brakes. A massive black dog stood center of the road, not moving. Colt swerved, and the truck launched into a ditch. A two by four in the truck bed launched through the rear window, shooting like a missile before exploding through the front windshield, missing his head by mere inches.

"Mother of Christ!"

Colt stepped from the vehicle and realized the truck was not going anywhere. He also noticed a green street marker for Gallows Way.

"Colt? You okay? What happened?" Nell asked over the phone loud enough for Colt to hear, even as the device dangled by his waist as he reconnoitered his surroundings.

He placed the phone into the cradle of his neck while he wrestled a sheet of plywood out of the back of the truck. "I'm fine. Should have pancaked a dog is all. Do me a favor. Call Charlie for a tow. I found the street. I'd abandon the stupid board up, but I was hoping we get a renovation job out of it. You know the money we make on these old places."

Colt disconnected the call, threw a tool bag over his shoulder, and dragged the plywood up the hill, grumbling the whole while. A house stood high in the distance. He hoped it was the place. It was.

"Damn, should have left a note for Charlie."

Charlie ran the local tow and garage. He regularly serviced Colt's company vehicles, so the account was in place. The man would do the job without worrying about payment, but that was not the reason Colt wished to leave a note. He wanted a ride back with the man. He looked back, trying to decide whether to go forth and board or go back and leave the note.

Figuring it might take Charlie a while, Colt got on with the board up job, quickly growing fatigued while hauling the large unwieldy piece of lumber. He cursed when he noticed an absence of vehicles in the driveway. While it did not mean no one was home, it narrowed the chances they were. That was unfortunate. His future livelihood depended on meeting the owner in person so he could turn on the charm. People appreciated his charm, well, except for his wife, and maybe his girlfriend.

He dropped the plywood in the yard, then knocked on the door. No answer. Of course. He peered in a window and got excited. The furniture confirmed what he hoped about the place. It was old enough to be considered a historic landmark. Those jobs paid well as there were only a handful of local contractors licensed for such work. He was one. Colt was questionable where it came to relationships, but he was damn fine at his job.

It was always costly fixing up such a place. *Refurbishing,* he called it. The town would designate landmark status if they had not already, so the only modernization allowed would be refurbishing. That word was the magic one which allowed work to proceed where City Hall was concerned. Someone from the town would also visit the site regularly. The pain in the ass process kept plans fluid. In Colt's line of work, a fluid situation meant two words: mo ney!

Colt prayed someone would answer the door. They did not, so he grabbed the plywood once again and headed toward the back, where the officer informed him the damage was. Feathers fluttered about on the ground, with several stuck along creases in the window frame. The state trooper mentioned something about a bird, and that animal control already came to the home and did their thing.

He only half listened to that part of the conversation as he was still fuming, thinking Nell had made an actual dick request of the trooper. Looking at the damage, Colt thought it must have been one hell of a bird. The window frame itself was fine, though he would not mention that to anyone. The glass was another story. Modern glass was better than the old stuff. Colt could either match the exact glass, a costly venture, or, even better, replace all the windows in the home with insulated glass.

There was one problem. The damaged box window was much smaller than the plywood, and the tool needed to cut it down was in his truck. No way was he hoofing back. And he was uncertain whether the circular saw inside even held a charge. He spotted a nearby bulkhead and investigated, hoping it might be open. If so, he could check the basement for tools. (And he could examine the foundation.) Colt bet it needed shoring up. Rains were harsh this time of year.

A rusty chain and an equally rusty lock the size of a human heart secured the bulkhead. It was like the locks on stocks around Salem, the ones all the goofy tourists took pictures with. Colt imagined if someone observed him right in that moment, they might see dollar signs in place of his eyes, like in the cartoons. The reason was that if a simple exterior lock was that antiquated, then there would be no end to such things inside the home. Crashing the truck was worth it. Things were looking up.

He worried what the homeowner might think about his using a full sheet on the window, but he had no choice. Colt would explain the truck accident, while touting his professionalism for completing the job despite unfortunate circumstances. And he would use the excuse of returning to replace the initial board-up as a reason to finally meet the homeowner.

Colt pressed the base of the plywood sheet into the ground, then placed its body flush against the damaged window. Choosing touch points carefully so as not to damage the window in any noticeable way, he pounded nails to secure the plywood. While pounding the last nail, a child giggled from the other side of the board.

It caught him so off guard he smashed his thumb and cursed until remembering there was a child involved. He let loose a tamer "cheese and crackers" as he did around his own kid before slipping into a mumble of more adult words. He shook off the throbbing pain. Where there was a kid, there was a parent. There was a backdoor nearby, but he felt it appropriate to enter through the front for introductions.

He strapped his tool belt on to look all official like, then strode toward the front of the house. The previously closed front door now stood open, but still no vehicle was in sight. It meant little because the family likely used a ride service.

"Hello?"

Colt knocked on the door for good measure. A curtain fell closed in a window off to one side. Someone checked him out but dropped the curtains too fast for him to see who it was. He knocked again. Nothing. He entered and called out once inside.

"Hello? Don't want to startle anyone. I'm the contractor. Sergeant Taylor sent me. Boarded your window. Need to talk to you about it."

The place smelled fresh for such an old place. Weren't many old homes in town in half as good condition, Colt thought, worrying someone already beat him to the job. Probably Yvette Stanton and her crew. She did that one makeover show and everyone started flocking to her. Colt's thumb flared at the thought as his blood pressure rose. If she wasn't so good at her job and didn't throw him some mercy work from time to time, he'd hate her. As it was, she got a rise out of him whenever he thought in her direction.

The giggle again.

Colt entered. As soon as he did, the door drifted shut, leaving him in a surprising amount of darkness. He struggled to adjust and glanced at the windows, wondering why they weren't helping much. Multi-layer curtains, he realized. Like buying two-ply toilet paper, it meant these folks had money, whoever these folks were. They had a kid, that much he knew.

To the right, he saw the living room, and to the left he saw signs of the kitchen. Standard layout. He knew the kitchen, already looked through the window. A hall ran straight ahead, one wall serving as the base of a stairwell. Figuring it was roughly nap time, that meant someone could be upstairs and not hear him. Maybe they were never gone at all. The kid woke early from her own nap as kids are wont to do. He leaned on the banister and yelled up.

"Hello! Contractor! Need to talk to you about your window, and maybe some other opportunities. Hello?"

The pitter patter of tiny feet sounded behind him. He spun and spotted movement. Whoever the child was, she dashed from the living room behind him into the kitchen (he knew it to be female based on the earlier giggling). Colt followed.

"Hey kid? Are your parents at home?"

Colt stepped into the kitchen where he spotted his handiwork, but no child. Another door lay partially open. Likely the cellar. He opened it, revealing stairs. Basement for certain.

"Come on out, kid. Don't make me come down there."

The only response was another giggle. Colt started down the steps. Weak lighting greeted him from a source he could not identify. Most likely basement windows. He had noticed none from the exterior, but hadn't looked for them.

"Come on, kid. I need to talk to your mother. Stop messing around!"

He lost his footing and stumbled down, landing in a running motion as his weight carried him forward. His outstretched arms finally met a wall that saved him from hitting the floor in a face plant. Colt grunted in pain as he turned away from the wall, feeling an ache in various joints from dancing an unexpected jig.

"That's it, kid. You could have hurt someone. Show yourself. Now!"

Something showed itself, but it was no child. An adult arm extended into a point from behind him. The limb was bony, covered in skin so thin it threatened to flutter away at the slightest breeze. Black fabric covered part of the outstretched arm, the cloth torn and dangling in tatters at the elbow joint. The hand culminated in a pointed finger. The index finger tapered to talon sharpness on its way past a marble sized knuckle.

Colt felt the cool wall of the basement on his back. How was it possible for someone to stand behind him and he not feel her? Not a breath on his neck, nothing. How could someone fit behind him within an almost non-existent space? Maybe he blocked an alcove. One containing a woman? It was the only thing that made sense, but still made none.

Stepping forward, Colt turned and gasped. A woman stood with her back against the same wall. No alcove. They had occupied the same space. Impossible! The woman from under Linda's bed now stood pointing directly at Colt. *Who was this Pointing Woman* Colt wondered? He wondered further where the child went, thinking he might need to rescue the kid from a dementia afflicted aunt. (The woman, as dastardly as she seemed, appeared too young to be a grandmother.)

As his eyes adjusted to the darkness, he took a better look at the woman. She took a step forward, and he realized something was wrong with the woman beyond dementia. The Pointing Woman moved awkwardly on twisted legs and her neck dangled to one side. Her hair, steel wool wild, jutted in multiple directions above a face of sick gray pallor. Despite being ambulatory, the woman appeared dead.

Colt had enough. He turned to run but found fresh terror waiting. The stairs leading back up were open-faced so he could see through the gaps between steps. The girl from earlier stared through one such gap. It did not take a genius to spot that she was not exactly alive either. Dead Rose's face showed the permanent square scarring of the burning rags. The shape meant nothing to Colt except more otherworldliness, a frightful stamp over the face of what should have been an innocent child.

With no other option, Colt bolted for the stairs. He made three steps before tiny child hands reached through with a strength belying their size and yanked his legs from underneath him. He flailed his arms as he fell, but it failed to stop the inevitable. His head cracked down on the dirt floor. Stars sparkled in the perimeter of his vision.

A fall. That was the answer. None of this was real. He tumbled earlier but never caught himself, smacked his head is all. That made sense. More sense than two dead women lying in wait in a basement. That explained everything, the result of scrambling the eggs that were his noggin. He would see a doctor, and all would be fine.

Except the Pointing Woman remained.

She stepped further into his peripheral with her finger still fixed on him. Her body pivoted around until she stood directly over him. Her new position masked her face in shadows, no features visible, a sea of black where a face should be. Until she opened her eyes! Wide whites served as a beacon in the darkness.

Before Colt could react to the new circumstance, something tugged at his legs, which remained elevated on the stairs. The tug was violent, far too powerful for a child. He looked away from the Pointing Woman to find Dead Rose grinning at him, her arms wrapped around each of his legs. The gleeful look on her face suggested her intentions. Colt eyed the foot-wide gap between stares and thought a man of his size would never fit through.

Dead Rose proved him wrong.

She yanked him through. The crackle of bones and the squish of flesh echoed in the basement. The stairs held, but the man did not. Colt had one thought before an explosion of pain thrust his world into darkness forever. *What do you know? I do fit.*

CHAPTER 10

C ROWDS ROAMED MAIN STREET. Ruby leaned into
Andrew's shoulder as they walked beside Heather, who
investigated a brochure. Tom lagged while snapping pictures. A
witch darted from a storefront, scaring a group of children. Tom
flustered as the kids flooded past him in their escape. The group
laughed at Tom's discomfort and awkwardness as he attempted
to scold a group that was gone before they could register the
old angry man was angry. Andrew approached the witch and
asked for directions while Tom gathered himself. Ruby spoke to
Heather as the last of the children departed.

"It's okay to miss the students. I do," Ruby said.

"Not him." Heather shook her head at her husband's antics.
"You two ever want any of your own?"

"A day in the classroom and my mind says no, but a night in
the sheets with Andrew and my body says oh yes, Daddy!"

"Ah, the good ole' days. What is sex like again?" The women
walked on, leaving the men behind.

"Please, Heather. You're my barometer for marriage."

Heather laughed hysterically until realizing Ruby was serious.
"Oh, sugar, look away. I set a mighty low bar."

"Speaking of bars." Ruby pointed to a wooden sign hanging above a door which read *The Witch's Teat*. "Hey boysos! We're going to suck on the teat. Come on!"

Andrew rushed over. "The witch, nice lady by the way, mentioned there's a bar, right..."

Ruby gestured up. Andrew smiled, and they entered. Heather remained outside and called to her husband, who focused his camera on a signpost.

"Tom? Shots?"

"Nah. Going to take some different kind of shots for a while. Go ahead!" Tom yelled, waving her off.

Heather entered the bar. Already seated at a table, Ruby called out to her friend. As Heather sat, Ruby glanced toward the bar's entrance for the other half.

"You forget someone?" Ruby asked.

"He forgot me," Heather grumbled from her chair.

Andrew stepped up with three margaritas from the bar, a tiny broom stuck out of each. Ruby kissed him.

"I knew I loved you, sweetheart."

"Witch's brew. Pre-made from a dispenser so probably gross, but hey when in Rome, get drunk like Romans do."

"You knew to only order three?" Heather asked.

"Please, this place is Tom's Disneyland. I'm surprised he kept up with us for this long."

T OM STUMBLED PAST THE bar, drunk on the promise of history unfolding before him. So far, Salem proved disappointing, much of it too gentrified. The surroundings mimicked the landscape of the South Bay in California minus the sun. Even the witch who chased the children earlier wore the stereotypical garb of a certain Oz movie. But some historical places appeared the further he wandered. The map he studied earlier suggested he was closing in on the good stuff.

The streets underfoot offered some hint of history, cobblestones built originally to accommodate horse and buggy. The difference of a few blocks in many cities could determine whether an area was safe or unsafe, and it was wise to know which when traveling. Salem itself had no safety problem based on his research, (and he did plenty before they departed) but the same concept held regarding old versus new. A few more blocks and he would hopefully find himself on a more historical footing.

He turned down an alley and crossed another block, sought a second alley, and did the same. Soon he found himself headed in the right direction. The crowds thinned, which he found sad. It meant tourists flocked to the kitschy versus historic. Some of the oldest known buildings in the country stood on these grounds. A church hovered in the distance, and he wondered what part that played in the long-ago mass hysteria.

Then Tom located his holy grail, or one of them. Stocks. The pillory stood firmly anchored street side, a device from history used to display, shame, and torture criminals in public. Here, witches. A group of teens had their fun (so some people still had taste) snapping multiple pictures, with each taking their turn in the device. Tom gripped his phone, eager for his turn. A mother and child also waited.

Tom felt a sense of being watched and looked down a nearby alleyway. He spotted a woman wearing a cloak and a witch mask. Seeing such disguises did not surprise him, but something about the woman felt off. She wore an old school Halloween mask version of a witch, the type children would wear trick-or-treating. Cheap drugstore costumes, plastic mold held in place by an elastic stretched so thin it lasted one season if the tiny staples held that long.

The woman stood ramrod straight and stared at him. He stepped forward slightly, wanting to examine her further but not wanting to lose his place in the queue. He looked away momentarily when he thought the teens were leaving. A false alarm. They merely changed positions for more pics. When he looked back to the alley, the woman not only still stared, but had moved closer, repositioned in shadows so the mask appeared to hover minus a body. Unsettling. He turned back and leaped in fright at the sight of a different woman. Nothing unsettling about her other than her proximity. The woman raised her cellphone.

"Trade? Picture for picture? I'll take yours next. You are waiting in line, aren't you?" the middle-aged woman wearing a bright pink fanny pack asked.

"He's too old. People his age don't have social media. Duh, Mom!"

"Honey? Rude much? The man has every right to want a picture. I'm sorry. Do we have a deal?"

Tom nodded and took their phone from them. Children. He had no interest in any of his own. Teaching cured him of that. The insult never even registered. When he first taught after college, students considered him old and he was only five years older than they were. Tom was young then but getting older, so all children looked at him as a grumpy old man. He wanted his pictures though, thank you very much.

Glancing back at the alley, it relieved Tom to find the strange floating head had vanished. He snapped multiple pictures as the mother and daughter each took turns in the stock while the other pretended to mete out punishment. Tom considered it strange how such a thing could inspire mirth when one considered the utter misery the torture device represented.

There were no locks to keep people truly trapped any longer, just holes to stick one's head and hands through. It would have been different for those in an earlier century. The woman and child stepped away from the device and quickly zipped through their photos, giggling over some and thanking Tom for the great shots.

"Your turn," the woman said.

Tom handed her the phone and pointed to the screen. "You just push..."

"Oh please. We have the same cellphone," she said.

Tom sauntered to the device, touching it to inspect the craftmanship, excited to see a piece of history up close. The child grumbled about him taking too long, so he stepped behind the device and placed his hands through the openings, followed by his head. A bit of a snug fit. Raising his face for the picture, he jerked in surprise. Standing next to the mother was the plastic-faced witch. The witch held a broom with a handle made of a gnarled tree branch veined with striations of uneven bark. The accessory culminated in a wild tuft of straw. While the mask was an obviously mass-produced commercial item, the broom offered a touch of aged authenticity.

The witch stood still, watching him as the oblivious mother snapped pictures. The tourist eventually noticed his stare and followed the direction of his gaze. She lit up at the sight of her new neighbor.

"Oh, you must get in the frame," the woman said to the witch.

"No, that's okay," Tom protested from a distance.

"Please, it will make for a splendid picture."

Without a word, the masked figure walked over to Tom. Bent over and posed in the stock, Tom had a strangled view of the witch's approach. From his vantage point, it was as if the woman floated to him. Once she stood alongside him, Tom struggled for a better view, but saw nothing of the real woman behind the mask. Her black scraggly hair pressed flush against the plastic. Tom could see the broom resting below his face. The child in the distance yelled for the woman to do various witch type things. If the witch did any, Tom was not privy. The broom never moved, which suggested the mask figure did not either.

Then something dripped.

A single drop first quickly followed by more. Tom ceased smiling for the camera after identifying the drops as blood. They splashed onto the broom's straw sweeper. Tom attempted to pull out from the old device but found both his head and hands stuck. He could almost hear the chains clinking as he fought against them. (But what chains?) Blood pounded in his ears as he struggled. The throbbing pulse in his temples sounded like a crowd haranguing him, mocking him.

He struggled against invisible bonds as blood poured down. The masked witch appeared suddenly in his face, glaring. *Was that idiotic grin always on the mask?* Tom wondered before his world went dark.

W ALTER POURED A CUP of tea for Linda, then the pair retook their seats in front of microfiche machines. The documents on the screens listed addresses and property records. Linda scrolled at a relatively quick place while Walter tapped through his version slowly. Tap, Tap. Tap. Linda stopped to grip the space between her eyes.

"This is mind numbing," she said.

"Welcome to my world. Think of all the man-hours that it took to get from paper to this obsolete format. Anything prior to the nineties related to property they recorded here. These have yet to be digitized, so microfiche it is for now. The historical society will eventually assign me interns from the University to convert these to digital. It is mind numbing work. I can see you reaching your limit in this brief time."

"Sorry, the travel and then last night I was up all night having dreams. Vivid."

"Natural. Stress induces such dreams. In times of pandemics across centuries, dreams enveloped dreamers with such clarity people needed time to sort out actual memories versus artificial. It is a coping mechanism designed to help one navigate through uncertain times. While you are not dealing with such a thing, you are suffering a variant. Beyond issues of relocation, you are eager to learn about your family. So bad dreams I am afraid are likely in the queue for a bit. Thankfully, the dream realm breeds forgetfulness. Soon enough, the nightmare fragments will vanish when you curl awake in your sheets. And if that fails? More tea."

Walter refilled her cup. She smiled, turning away from her screen.

"It's odd that I even consider my family has ties to Salem's dark past. Anyone can move anywhere, anytime. So what if they had a house here? If I discover I have family in Cape Canaveral, should I assume they are astronauts? I live in California. Is everyone there a movie star?"

"Wisely put, but misguided. A home of this historical importance does not change hands easily and without subsequent records, which means there is every chance your family has owned the place for generations. In England, there are many politicians and celebrities with ties to our country's witch trials. Many women brought to gallows already sired children. Bloodlines would endure. It is not unthinkable there is a connection."

"It's all too horrible to comprehend. Though my friend Tom is certainly traipsing about somewhere, enjoying every minute. He raised a good question last week. How could so many have acted in such a way?"

Walter turned off her screen then invited her to stand. "I will share my thoughts with you about that, but enough of this. You are not on the payroll. Why don't you join your friends and leave the research to me?"

"I did not expect answers immediately. Learning about the questionable record keeping for my home was reason enough for the visit. That, and discovering that you are okay."

"Well then, let me send you on your way, knowing mission accomplished for one day. There will be more to come. The missing records are a mere roadblock. It is my job to find out about it. Literally. They will fire me if I do not properly identify the history of the property. While I explore the house's history, why don't you go explore its future? It is yours, after all."

Linda smiled at the thought of being a homeowner, like Heather and Tom. She thought maybe she would make a stop somewhere to check for a gas grill. No reason they couldn't fire up a grill to break-in the place. She warmed to the thought of home ownership. She did like Walter. He kept things in perspective. In her nervousness, she almost forgot it was okay to enjoy the idea that she now had a house and she was on track to finally discovering her family roots after years of knowing nothing about her past.

As the pair walked through room after room of the historical society, she occasionally glanced Walter's way and considered whether to invite him to a drink. A date? Maybe. Perhaps it was time. Summer of love and all that. As if sensing he turned to her and smiled warmly. She wondered if he would ask her out. Then he popped a question. Not the question, but a question nonetheless.

"Are you familiar with quantum physics?"

"I am a middle grade American teacher," Linda said.

"So yes?"

"So no," she shook her head.

"Mostly irrelevant other than one distinct theory. That being that nothing exists until viewed. A tree falling in a forest would actually make no sound if no one were there because it never fell if someone were not there to witness it."

"Okay?"

"Evil, or what we define as evil, has stubbornly accompanied us ever since our birth as a species. There are no recorded times in history where unspeakable acts have not occurred in some fashion. It causes one to question whether there is any mechanism to end evil. Maybe the only way is to stop it at the point of conception or inception."

"Because once someone views it, evil then exists."

They arrived at the front entrance. Walter turned to her, pleased at the deduction.

"Correct. If evil remains hidden in shadows long enough, it might expire. There is every chance evil can wither on a vine and die. Something in the seventeenth century caused young children to see evil and, through their eyes, it was born and somehow metastasized. With every pointed finger, citizens witnessed evil which kept it alive." Walter grabbed the door handle, pausing in the doorway. "Now we live on the same grounds where tragedy struck, but understand by going about our day with blinders on ordering our Venti drinks and frequenting cookie cutter buildings identical to others across the globe, we can remain blissfully unaware of evil underfoot. We can ignore ills that remain in shadows with the hopes they will die under the foot of our neglect if we simply refuse to look evil in the eye."

He looked into hers and opened the door. The sun after time indoors caused her to squint.

"Interesting conversation. Let me know if you discover anything, no matter how slight?"

"And I ask the same from you. Shall I call you a cab?"

"NO thank you. Lovely day for a walk. Nice talking to you, Walter. I'm relieved that you are okay."

"Sturdy British stock," Walter said, but winced when he touched his bandage.

Linda stepped outside. The woman from earlier still sat on the bench, hands clasped as if she had never moved. Linda passed and the woman burst to life, pointing a finger and laughing hysterically. The woman's laughter grew into a cackle as Linda rushed away into the streets of Salem.

CHAPTER 11

A NDREW HELD HIS CELL to his ear because he had no
earbuds handy. He walked while speaking, trying to put
some distance between himself and the noisiness of the bustling
crowd outside the bar. He held a finger in his free ear, a poor
man's noise cancelling. "Linda, are you still at the hospital? I told
you we would go with you. Call back." Andrew disconnected
and huffed in frustration. "Probably didn't even bring her phone
with her."

He pocketed his cell and looked out onto the street. Salem was
not that large, so it surprised him he had yet to spot the hospital.
While the ladies worked on round two of drinks, they grew
increasingly worried about their missing friend. When Linda
failed to answer anyone's texts, the women tasked Andrew with
making an actual call to Linda. With the street nearly as loud as
the bar, Andrew had stepped into an adjacent alley to call.

That was how he missed Ruby and Heather rushing past and
breaking into a run. The two women looked around but did not
see Andrew, so kept going. Andrew left Linda a message. He was
about to reenter the bar when he received a text from Ruby that
read, 'It's Tom.'

Andrew frantically texted back for details and waited until
they gave him the location. By the time Andrew found them,

he saw Tom sitting on a bench, his head tilted back with an ice pack on his face. A teen in a green polo shirt emblazoned with a city logo on the sleeve stood nearby with a first aid kit. A young woman dressed as a witch, mask lifted above her face, argued with Ruby. Heather rubbed Tom's back and took over ice pack duty from the townie.

Andrew rushed over. "What happened?"

"Bloody nose," Tom said.

"I told you to eat more this morning," Heather said.

"Do you know how much this broom costs?" The witch asked.

"Educate me," Ruby replied to the witch's question.

"Nine ninety-five. Not to mention I charge five dollars a picture and he took like a bunch of them."

"I was unaware you charge, and I did not invite you. The woman and her child did," Tom said.

"You shush," Heather said, pressing the pack hard enough to wince him into silence.

Ruby handed the woman a bill. "Here's twenty, let's call it even. Club soda will wash that thing out."

"Fine." The woman snatched the money, then dropped her mask back into place before leaving.

Andrew turned to the teen employee. "High blood pressure. He gets these. He will be fine."

The worker picked up his kit and handed one more pack to Andrew. "Okay then. I'm with the tourism center and hope, despite all this drama, you rate us five stars." The kid climbed on a mountain bike and rode away down the street.

Ruby pulled out a pack of tissues from her purse. For all their squabbles, she leaned into attending to her husband. Tom balled the tissues, pressed them to his nose, and stood. He gestured to Heather that he was fine. She scrunched her face, unconvinced, but gave him his space.

"Okay, I'm good," he said with a wad jammed in one nostril.

"I'm thinking maybe Linda made it home by now. Probably should get him back too," Andrew said.

"No. He needs food. That's why he fainted," Heather said.

"Not to mention I left my credit card at the bar. I say more drinks," Ruby said.

Andrew eyed a nearby cab. "Well, I'll go check on her and call you all. How's that?"

Ruby pulled back from Andrew as Heather led Tom away. "Really?"

"Just, you know, she shouldn't be alone."

"But me, alcohol, a bar full of men with bad intentions?"

"Tom will look out. Anyone gets out of line he'll blow his nose tissue in the guy's face."

Ruby laughed and kissed him. "Okay but call the second you find her. Bring Linda back, let's party. I need it. She really needs it."

The cab pulled away from the curb. Andrew chased after it, flagging it down while Ruby rushed to catch up with her friends.

L INDA WALKED UP THE hill toward her home. She dripped with sweat from the walk, which was longer than expected. The van was missing, which meant she was home alone for the first time since inheriting the place. Rather than enter, she crossed the lawn and circled the house, pleased to find someone had taken care of the bird carnage. She crossed back over to the swing, taking a seat, and rocking gently as she searched the sky for some answer to the flock's earlier behavior.

She assumed it related to migration patterns somehow. Tom suggested as much before she left with the police earlier. Tom was likely correct. The animals simply got their signals crossed. Suddenly, one side of the swing caught, shifting the swing from gentle to chaotic movement. Children at the schoolyard occasionally did the same, grabbing the chain on someone's backswing. If the move knocked an unsuspecting child off, the perpetrator then claimed the ride as their own. Linda stepped off and turned but saw nothing. No naughty child. It had to be something else. She looked up to where the rope tied off at the tree branch.

Then she saw it.

In a window on the second story, a curtain fluttered. Movement within HER house! No Walter this time because she knew exactly where she left him. She suddenly wished he were there now. Then a figure passed by the window. Someone there for sure. Linda rushed to the front of the house.

Opening the front door slowly so as not to announce her presence, she gripped the stair rail and listened. Nothing sounded from above. But something did off to her left. The kitchen! Linda stepped up next to the door frame and peeked around the corner. Someone moved past the doorway. She threw herself back against the door frame. More footsteps, then a rustling. She poked her head in again and glimpsed someone crouched, back turned. A broom leaned against the sink, making her think of witches.

"What are you doing in my house?"

Andrew rose in fright and sent the dustpan of glass shards flying back all over the floor. "Shit Linda! Give me a heart attack."

Linda finally breathed. "Andrew? What are you doing here? I didn't see the van."

"Well, my day was going swell, but I figured I haven't had the life nearly scared from me since you dreamed yourself awake in the van. So, here I am for my daily Linda adrenaline spike."

"Serious."

"I am. Why are you sneaking around like that?"

"I saw someone in the window upstairs."

Andrew walked toward her and scooped up a cell from the table on the way and handed it to her.

"Me. Looking for you. I found this upstairs instead. Next time you leave, bring it, please. We were worried when we could not reach you. Hence the gracing of my presence."

Linda flustered, both over his proximity and her forgetfulness. She raised the phone. "Just got your text. And hers, and hers, and more of yours."

Andrew smiled, all forgiven. He went back to work on cleaning up the mess. "After the weird bird thing, everyone was ready to get out. We waited for animal control and left them to do their thing while we went into town for a drink. Had to since your home is sorely lacking in alcohol."

"Stock the bar," I got the hint, Linda said. "I checked out back. They cleaned up."

"I forgot about the glass inside until now. But this is the last. Your place is like brand new."

"Brand new?"

"Well, newish. Like eighteenth century instead of seventeenth."

"Yeah, instead of a screening room, I think I have a theater in the round somewhere in the back."

Andrew laughed and set the dustpan down to grab some garbage bags. He fluffed two open and inserted one into the other, creating a double bag into which he poured the glass shards. The bags poked out where some sharp edges threatened to cut through, but the two-ply worked. Linda opened a side cabinet and lifted the cover to the garbage can inside. Andrew dropped the bag into the can and set the broom and pan next to it, then closed the cabinet door.

"Thank you," Linda said.

"My pleasure. How is Walter?"

"A little head thing, but fine. How was downtown Salem?" Linda asked.

"Well, the margaritas were green. I'll give them that. Our friends are drunk and still drinking. As the sober holdout, I took a cab, left them with the van. Probably should have thought that out." He noticed Linda fidgeting. "Hey are you okay?"

"I don't know. I've been on edge since we arrived. Foolish really."

"You lost a mother you never met. Your first home is in a state you've never set foot in. I'd say you've earned the right to freak out a bit."

"Thanks. You've always been so good with the kids."

"In case you haven't noticed, you're anything but a kid."

Andrew moved in on her. His scent caused her to flush with excitement. He moved closer still, almost on top of her.

"Andrew," she said in an inviting tone,

"Are you thinking what I'm thinking?" Before she could answer, he reached behind her and lifted a bottle of red off the counter and waved it in front of her face. "Walter may not have stocked the bar up, but I made the cab driver stop by a liquor store on the way home. You game?"

Linda stepped away, almost embarrassed by her eagerness. She opened a cupboard and produced two wine glasses. Andrew danced toward the doorway and urged her to follow with a crooked finger. As he exited, she pushed a hand to her chest, calmed herself, then took the glasses and followed.

The two settled on the couch. Andrew opened the bottle like a seasoned pro and poured well past the single serving point. She waved for him to stop. He playfully offered the bottle up straight to her. She laughed, sipped, and settled in as he poured his own.

"What's up with you and this Walter guy?" Andrew asked.

"Nothing really."

"You know your eyebrows arch when you lie?"

She instinctively grabbed for them.

"They do?"

He shook his head. "No, but if you weren't lying, then you would not have grabbed them. I am nothing if not a human lie detecting machine."

"Nicely played. Well, since I never knew my family, I must look at every date as, well, a potential family member." Andrew almost spit out his wine. She laughed. "Seriously, I could be dating my brother. Therefore, I have developed a radar."

"And what does your radar say about Walter?"

"That he's smart, intriguing, probably the very stability I need in my life and—he gives me that brotherly feeling. "

"Rough times for you. How do you ever date at all?" He leaned in and poured some more, despite her glass being half full.

"Sometimes there is a distinct feeling, one I can't explain other than to say it's different. It feels like..." Linda looked into Andrew's eyes. "...destiny."

His breath hitched. Just a breath away. He clunked the bottle down on the table. "Let's start a fire."

Linda rocked her head in frustration, as if suggesting they already were, but Andrew bolted away. She gulped from her glass and wondered. Was she flirting? Obviously, she was. Was it the wine, or just related to a long-held attraction? Either way, Linda deemed her actions inappropriate. She tried to refocus, suddenly interested in his task.

"What are you doing?" Linda asked.

Andrew lay on his side and reached up into the fireplace. "Gotta make sure the flue is open. Don't want to burn your place down or smoke us out."

Andrew's arm waved around in the tight space leading into the chimney. Dead Sadie hung upside down, just out of reach of Andrew's outstretched arm, squeezed into the tight confines. She wormed her way toward his arm; her inverted cross appearing upright based on her positioning. The dead child moved in unnatural stops and starts.

Andrew smiled at Linda as if to signal he found it, but when he pulled his arm, it remained stuck. He grimaced in confusion before pulling again. It did not move. Then his arm shook violently, trapped inside the chimney. He screamed.

"Ah!"

Linda rose to her feet and rushed toward him. He laughed and pulled the hand free, waving her to sit back down. She did, but not before throwing a pillow at him. He caught it and set it aside, still laughing. A metal container hung above the nearby fire poker set. Andrew opened it and retrieved a long match, lit it, and touched the flame to the kindling.

The fire caught, knocking Andrew back as a fireball erupted into the living room. Linda yelped at the conflagration and shielded her own face as it shot toward her. A face appeared visible in the flames but vanished as quickly as it appeared. The fire settled into a normal flicker.

"What the Hell was that? I worried I would have to light kindling for an hour to get it going. Guess the wood is super dry."

Before either could question it any further, their friends returned with bags in hand. Ruby rushed over to drop a witch hat on Linda's head. Then she moved to Andrew and kissed him. A different fire lit. Linda tried not to watch them but failed.

"We come bearing gifts, sugar," Heather said and handed a shirt to Linda.

Linda raised it to examine the front, which showed a witch hanging from the gallows and read, 'I fought the law and the law won.'

"You guys are terrible. Thank you for thinking of me, though. How was your day trip?" Linda asked.

"We almost followed you to the hospital with a victim of our own," Ruby said, crawling down from her boyfriend's arms.

"I never went to the hospital. Walter is fine. But what are you talking about? Andrew, you never mentioned anything," Linda said, surprised.

"You didn't tell her?" Ruby back-smacked Andrew before jumping onto the arm of the couch. "Our friend Tom here had low blood sugar and high blood pressure and passed out."

"Tom?" Linda asked.

"I passed out," Tom said, sitting in a nearby chair. Heather stood alongside him, hand on his back.

"He hit his head on the wooden stock after getting a nosebleed," Heather said.

"Pillory. Actually," Tom said.

"You can tell by the words he is using that it was no big thing. He's fine," Andrew said.

"Says you Mr. Left Us All behind," Ruby said.

"It happens to him all the time when we play basketball. He's fine," Andrew protested.

"Correct," Heather said. "Didn't stop him from having some beers."

"Pumpkin Ale actually. Nice hops," Tom said.

"I'm sorry, guys. I know it's our group trip and we haven't grouped yet. Tomorrow?" Linda asked by way of apology.

"Sure. I've got a new book to read before drifting off tonight, so I'm ready for bed." Tom lifted a handle bag from a local bookstore.

"Oh, my stars, someone stop the ride. My life is too exciting. Will the adventures never cease?" Heather draped an arm across her forehead, Norma Desmond style.

Her friends laughed as Heather nudged her husband out of the chair and up the stairs. Ruby grabbed Andrew's hand and attempted to lead him away when she finally noticed the wine.

"Did I interrupt anything?" Ruby asked.

"A toast to christening the fireplace is all," Andrew said.

"Is that what we're calling it?" Linda asked, bursting into laughter.

Andrew joined in. Ruby eyed the fire. Story checked out. She lifted her hand in a feigned toast to play along. Ruby then

grabbed Andrew's crotch to establish ownership. He yelped
and pulled away as the two whispered through disagreement
regarding the mixed company. Ruby let go of both the argument
and Andrew's junk. She kissed Linda's forehead, then led
Andrew up the stairs.

Linda watched the couple interlace fingers and rush up the
stairs. This time Ruby went for the butt, drawing no protest
from Andrew. Once the couple crested the stairs and vanished
from sight, Linda raised her glass to the fireplace in a fresh toast.

"Fifth wheel."

A NDREW BRUSHED HIS TEETH in the bathroom, door
open, while Ruby undressed. She paced in between
removing garments. She walked toward the bathroom, passing
the full-length mirror on the way. Ruby's image filled the glass.
Once she stepped clear of the reflection, the Pointing Woman
appeared deep within the mirror, as if at a great distance. Ruby
did not notice, too busy leaning toward the bathroom to be heard
over the running water.

"You two seemed cozy tonight."

Andrew spoke through paste. "I was making her feel at home."

Ruby walked back toward the bed, her body momentarily
blocking the mirror again. Once clear, the Pointing Woman
reappeared, closer than before. Ruby spoke over her shoulder.

"With wine and candlelight?"

"There were no candles," Andrew said, fighting back a choke
of paste before giving up and spitting.

Ruby tossed her pants aside and fluffed out the blouse she
wore, which hung just low enough to cover her panties. She

crossed back to the bathroom, her reflection momentarily taking over the mirror again. Once clear, the Pointing Woman grew closer still. With each pass, the Pointing Woman never moved position, but her image grew ever closer to the glass' surface each time.

Ruby leaned in playfully, tugging at her top buttons to reveal cleavage. "That's right, just a fireplace. Silly me." She unbuttoned another button, nearing the point where the girls were ready to come out to play.

She crossed back to the bed. In a quick motion, her reflection flashed past and then the Pointing Woman was right there, filling the entire mirror, so close to the surface that the dead woman's hand reached out into the bedroom.

"Linda is nervous," Andrew said before rinsing his mouth.

"About?"

"Says she hears weird noises."

Ruby removed the blouse and bra altogether and pulled a silky slip over her head. Ruby jumped in front of the mirror and spun, checking out her outfit. She failed to notice the lock of black hair draped over the top of the mirror's wooden frame. As she straightened the silky surface of her outfit, something launched itself in her reflection. She laughed as Andrew scooped her up and carried her to bed.

He dropped her. When she bounced back, he leaned in, trapping her against the mattress until she rolled him over and straddled him. He succumbed willingly. She raised his hands above her head, their fingers intertwined. She pressed her face close to his, foreheads touching, eyes locked.

"So, my best friend is afraid of weird noises?" Andrew nodded below her. "Well then, we're about to scare the hell out of her."

Ruby released his hands and grabbed his cheeks, kissing him. Andrew explored her body before flipping her back over him on top. Neither noticed the door open slightly. Andrew reached down, pulled her panties aside and thrust against her, sliding right in. Ruby moaned, more than ready. She gripped his shoulders. He rose higher and thrust deeper into her. She groaned in pleasure.

OUTSIDE THE HOUSE, HIGH on the ridge, the black dog whined, pacing on the crest of the hill overlooking Linda's home. The enormous creature, head and tail hanging low, huffed air as it bounced on legs filled with nervous energy. As if watching, waiting. (For what?)

One by one, all the lights in the house turned off. The faint light of the moon trailed the pattern of cloud cover, clearing in spurts long enough to illuminate the backyard swing, which moved.

Inside, Linda slept on her side, facing the en suite bathroom, the door of which remained open. Suddenly, Dead Rose swung into the bedroom via the bathroom door. The dead child swung high into the bedroom with her head turned to watch Linda sleep. The dead child vanished back into the bathroom, then back into the bedroom, back and forth in time with the swing. Rose watched Linda on every upswing into the room. The child pumped her legs to move faster, swinging in and out of the bathroom. In and out. In and out.

Linda twitched in her sleep, opening her eyes just as Rose receded from view. She closed her eyes again before Rose swung back, the child almost touching the ceiling with her feet. Linda turned away from the bathroom. Dead Rose swung back out of view into the bathroom. When the swing moved back into the bedroom, it was riderless. Somewhere in the room, a child giggled.

The black dog continued pacing outside, huffing in excitement while rumbling near a growl. Below, outside the house, the swing finally came to a stop. A chill filled the air and steam rose from the dog's snout. The dog grew frantic, pacing wildly though never taking its eyes off the house.

Inside, Heather lay turned away from Tom, who hogged most of the bedding, leaving Heather mostly uncovered. She wore a sleeveless jersey style nightshirt. Heather breathed in shallow rasps, her breath crystalized on every exhale, steam rising as if it were a frigid winter day. Her frigid breath danced pirouettes into the night. Dead Sadie stood bedside, gripping one of Heather's forearms. Heather's arm turned blue at the point of contact.

Outside, the dog abandoned its whine for a deep growl as it simultaneously ceased its frantic jumping and pacing. It leaned in on its haunches and growled furiously at sights unseen down at the house.

Inside Andrew's bedroom, something growled, animalistic, wild. Ruby. She ground atop Andrew, who thrust upward to meet her halfway. She leaned her face into his chest, head splayed to one side, gasping as she neared climax. Ruby maintained the motion designed to deliver her there, the journey nearly over, the destination in sight.

She begged Andrew not to stop, not to move even, announcing "right there" as the 'just right' Goldilocks' spot. Andrew complied while fighting his own train rushing toward the station. She was too exciting, too lovely, so he looked away, trying to delay the inevitable. And that's when he saw it.

An eye.

Someone watched through the gap in the door. Andrew shoved Ruby aside. Confused, she whined in protest. The eye vanished. Andrew pointed at the door.

"Did you see that?"

Ruby flopped onto her back, frustrated. "Honey? I was close. So close..."

"Unacceptable!"

She lifted her head. "I'm sorry. What are you talking about?" Andrew grabbed a sheet and wrapped it around his waist and stormed from the room. Ruby knew the look. "Oh shit," she said, throwing on a tee and following.

Andrew burst into Tom's room. Tom leaped awake at the sound of the invasion. Tom sat up. Andrew grabbed him by his pajama top and dragged him out of bed.

"You get a good look, did you?" Andrew snarled.

Tom shoved Andrew back, and the two faced off. "What are you going on about?" Tom asked.

Ruby leaped into the fray, begging Andrew to back off, but he waved her off. "No. Leering. He's always leering at you. And now he watches us have sex?"

"What?" Tom asked, suddenly raging.

Tom rammed Andrew into a nearby wall. The sheet fell, leaving Andrew naked, but Tom didn't care. He got in Andrew's face.

"Say that again." Tom dared the man.

"You heard me," Andrew said, and the two tangled, falling to the floor in a wrestle.

"Guys. Guys. Stop. Guys!" Ruby yelled.

The two men continued battling until they noticed the impossible. They remained locked on the ground, but looked up at the same thing Ruby did. Heather continued sleeping, never once tossing during the raucous fight. Ruby touched her.

"How has none of this woken her? I don't think she's okay. She's freezing cold."

The commotion roused Linda, who arrived at the room just as Tom lifted Heather and carried her out into the hall. Linda stepped aside only to flush and turn away upon spotting Andrew naked, his muscles still tensed and flexed from the battle, a sinewy sexual display. Ruby handed her boyfriend a sheet.

"Nice job," Ruby said and stormed out.

Ruby grabbed Linda on the way and led her downstairs. Andrew rushed to his bedroom, threw on sweats, and joined them. Heather continued sleeping but did so from the couch, facing the fireplace. Andrew avoided the group and tended to the fire.

"How can she be so cold? I don't feel a fever," Ruby said, touching the woman's forehead.

Heather stirred. "So cold," she murmured before falling back into a snooze.

"It's an old house. There are drafts aplenty. I sometimes steal the blankets, but this? Yeah, this is extreme," Tom said.

Linda looked on, heavy with guilt. "I shouldn't have brought you all here. I just wanted to share it. You know my home with my family."

"Linda. Draft or no draft, your house didn't make her sick," Ruby said.

Andrew stepped closer to check on her, but Tom's look held him at bay. Tom sat on the corner of the couch, stroking his wife's hair. Looking longingly at her as she slept. The others postulated nearby.

"How can she be that cold without a fever?" Andrew asked.

"I'm going by touch. We should probably use a thermometer," Ruby said.

"She was fine. When you were all in town together earlier, she was fine, right?" Linda touched her sleeping friend's shoulder gently. "Maybe we should get her to a hospital."

"Stop. Everyone, please stop. I'm sure this is because of the stress, all the stress related to..." Tom faded off.

"Tom?" Linda asked.

"To our divorce. Heather and I are getting divorced." Everyone gasped. "We were going to make one last go of it. One last summer trip. A beach, or Europe, or..."

"Salem. Tom, I didn't know, or I wouldn't have dragged you two along. I can't believe Heather never said anything to me."

"We didn't want you to know Linda," Tom said.

"Why?"

"Heather and I are... We're, family, and as much as you want to be and as much as these two may say you are, we are not. She never told you because this was between family."

"Watch it there, cowboy," Ruby said, giving him enough room to step off eggshells.

"Hell, we're not even friends. Not really. Now that Heather and I are splitting up, who are you going to stay in contact with? Me or her?" Silence greeted him. "I thought so."

"I always thought of you as a..."

"A brother? I know. Linda, make no mistake, if I had the chance to screw you, I would."

"Hey!" Andrew protested.

"Like you haven't thought about it."

Ruby eyed Andrew accusatory. Andrew shook his head, then refocused on Tom.

"Don't make this about me. I've never said such a thing."

"You don't have to. When I told you in secret about what I thought of Linda, you never ratted me out. You did not say you would sleep with her, but you never said you would not. It is all the same thing, man. You want to fight over me sharing this secret, too?"

Andrew raged, looking like the answer was yes, but he shook his head. Then he looked at Linda and Ruby, both of whom glanced away, unable to face him at the moment. Tom sighed and looked up at the host.

"Look, Linda, life dealt you a hand. Either find what you're looking for here and play that hand or move on. Now, if you don't mind, Heather is still my wife for now and I'd like to be alone with her."

Ruby flinched away from Andrew as he reached out. She instead rubbed Linda's back and led her friend up the stairs. Andrew followed, taking one last look back at old friendships.

CHAPTER 12

M ULTIPLE SCREENS FILLED WALTER'S workspace. The scholar hovered over the devices, seeking different information from each one while occasionally jotting notes. The room was otherwise dark besides the glow of the monitors, leaving Walter lost in thoughts and shadows. He startled himself when he finally moved enough to trigger the motion light sensors, which had shut off at some point. The room came to life in a bright burst of LED. He noted the difference and shrugged.

"Well, that is much better."

Walter moved his laptop and each monitor he passed showed his laptop screen. Each returned to their previous screens once he moved past. His laptop linked to them all but only displayed on one at a time. He set his laptop in front of the largest screen in the room and dialed an overseas number.

The miniature screen came to life, showing a torso moving about. The torso wore a shirt and tie. Eventually, the individual dropped into a chair behind a desk. The man readjusted his laptop camera until the angle looked framed for a TV interview. A placard in the foreground read: Professor Robert Hopkins. The affable man in his fifties sported close cropped hair, a salt and pepper goatee and, strangely enough, cat ears.

"Robert. I take it the surgery went well. How was your first flea bath?"

The Professor moved his head. The ears followed his movements. He finally gave up trying to spot them.

"My granddaughter. I cannot figure out how to turn them off. I thought I fixed it already because none of the students in my last class bothered to let me know the ears were still in place."

"Why bother with perfection?"

"We are raising a generation of geniuses, Walter. The things these children can do. So, what do I owe the pleasure? How goes the great American experiment? Are you off tea yet?" Robert lifted a teacup for show and took a sip. A cat tongue lapped away.

Walter raised a Starbuck's cup in reply. "Don't know what I would do without my morning caffeine. Their custom is to write one's name on the cup, but you are welcome to supply any name. I suggested R. Buckminster Fuller for this cup and all they wrote was Buck Fuller. Not a scientific lot those baristas, but early risers, and hard workers they are."

"Speaking of. What bloody time is it there? Aren't you at the witching hour if I am not mistaken?" Robert checked his watch as if it held the answer.

"I suppose. Look, Robert, the reason I called is I need your help with something. What do you know about genealogy tests?"

"Without knowing specifics of your inquiry, I would offer they fall under the general guideline of hogwash."

"How so?"

"For starters, it is safe to consider an individual has a genetic link to Genghis Khan, not to mention Neanderthal ancestors. Almost certainly one could identify a link tracing back to migration from Africa. As for the celebrity versions of such shows, producers take great liberties to link current celebrities to past famous figures. Is that what this inquiry is about? Please tell me Hollywood is not calling, that you are not consulting for some dreadful reality show."

"No. More an inquiry about familial lines. Tracing a history."

"There is none of that without already knowing the history. DNA testing is useless unless one understands what they are comparing the DNA too. Most people fall into one of two camps. Criminals and non-criminals. Home testing kits have led to a spike in closing cold cases. If an individual's DNA is on file, then one can match to it, but who has theirs on file? Criminals. Sperm donors perhaps. What exactly is your business there? Have you uncovered a historical graveyard? Please tell me more."

"Nothing like that. Simply tracing the familial line of an individual. A woman."

"Well, no Y chromosome tests there. That leaves you autosomal or an MT DNA test for mitochondria. As I've mentioned, however, if you used a commercially available vendor, they are going to sex up any results, not to mention there are ethical questions related to their reporting of health marker indications in the DNA. No one can say for sure for what malady an individual may eventually succumb to, but they will damn well try to sell you on a cure for an illness yet to surface. What is all this, then?"

Walter smiled wistfully. "Chasing a dead end. You have confirmed my thoughts. A private investigator ran the tests for her, and she supplied the results to me. As you mentioned, without knowing who on the food chain we need to look for, I have nothing to go on. I have new clippings that might point in certain directions, but even then, their DNA needs to be in a public database. We are not cops; that limits our access. Which brings me to my real reason for calling."

"Get to it then. Class begins soon and if I am not there at the start, I will never sever their connection to their cellphones. Run amok technology there, I must say. Earlier, I mentioned geniuses being born, but a daft twin accompanies each one."

"Facial recognition."

Robert raised his hands and eyebrows. "Is that your ask, or is that a joke?"

"I am serious. The digitization of records here is woefully inadequate and the records I am searching for has links back to Britain. I have a better chance in your database than anything here. All I need is remote access and a password."

"And our government, who closely monitors the use of the technology, which they freely use but claim not too, will have no issues with my loaning access to America, of all places. That is heavy sarcasm in case you were wondering."

"I have need of seventeenth century records. Population sizes were smaller, so the database cannot be that large. Also, pictures were non-existent, but artwork and drawings were plentiful, as were images from trials. I am not requesting a search for current citizens. That should mean something. If I find a link that certainly must exist in Salem, then I can properly use DNA from there."

"You put me in a tough spot, my friend."

"Were that I could do otherwise, but it is important."

"She must be lovely." Off Walter's look. "The woman."

"Indeed," Walter replied simply.

"What do you think would happen to me if I chased every lovely coed? Place me in a pillory, perhaps? I urge caution in that regard."

"The request is purely for scientific purposes and relates to my studies abroad."

"Yes, well, I'll share that with my superior when I ask the request of her."

"Timeliness is important."

"As is sleep. Get some, my friend. You will hear from me soon enough. I urge you not to raise your hopes too high."

The screen went blue. Walter checked the time. Three AM. The professor was right. Walter typed Linda's address into a street-view website.

The screen offered only, 'not found.'

"How can that be? Let me try this building's address."

Walter typed in the historical society information. An image of the building appeared and offered a street view. A quick toggle of arrow keys and he verified the site worked fine. He tried Linda's address once more. Nothing.

Walter closed the website and clicked on a desktop folder. It opened to show dozens of jpg icons. He clicked on the first and a large image of Linda's home filled his screen. He clicked through the series at a leisurely pace. Walter continued the professor's conversation, but with the image of the house on the screen.

"Fine. Linda is lovely, yes. It does not mean I am any less curious as to your background, my historical friend. How have you remained incognito all these years? A house sized glasses and mustache disguise?"

Walter laughed at his own joke, then turned to ensure there were no witnesses to the outburst, the sign of a man prone to embarrassment even when alone. He touched his head bandage then took a sip of coffee. Too cold now, he grimaced and set it down.

"Must be the accident that has given me over to talking to myself."

Then he spotted something in an upper window. An image of a person. Despite the crispness of the overall picture, the resident in the window appeared blurry (filtered through curtains perhaps?). Walter advanced to the next picture, someone there for sure.

Impossible, he thought. The picture set he looked at was a series taken prior to Linda's arrival. He took them on the first day of the assignment to restock the house. Each time he brought fresh goods, he examined another part of the home and took more pictures. The pictures he looked at now were snapshots he took with his own tablet. He was certain no one was present in the home. One could chalk up the visual oddity to many things if the shots originated on a film camera. (And who used those anymore?) But the shots on his screen were digital.

He pulled his glasses off in a practiced motion and wiped them clean with the front of his shirt. The figure remained visible. Or at least a blur remained distinguishable. Something felt off about the shape. The angle near the head of the shape stood out most prominently as crooked.

With a tap, he returned to the first picture in the series. If he remembered correctly from that day, he stepped straight from the car and started snapping. Were someone home, it would have taken them time to notice his presence and get to the window. Yet there, in the very first image he snapped that day, was the blur.

Only a blur. Certainly not a person. There had to be another explanation. He leaned in for a better look, despite the size of the screen. As he did so, he bumped the keyboard. Whatever he hit started a slideshow of the pictures. One displayed after another at a relatively quick speed. The effect gave the stills a sense of motion.

At the start, the blur appeared deep in the room. But the blur quickly took shape as an actual figure when it approached the window in herky-jerky steps. Walter chalked up the strange movements to his lackadaisical picture taking. Only his past failures as a photographer even caused him to take so many shots of the same picture.

When visiting certain historical sites in the past, he unknowingly took some poor pictures (had his thumb over the lens once even). He since learned to take ten of everything he needed and select the best from the group.

He snapped dozens of the home that day. Because of that habit, a slideshow now played out. Soon it would change to a different angle, (he moved in and took foyer pictures after this series) but until then he watched whatever was occurring in the window play out. A chill overtook him as the image proved to be a person. He saw a woman, head hung low off to one side, with frazzled hair covering any semblance of a face.

With each step, the woman not only moved closer to the window but raised hand and head. She moved more quickly as she neared the glass, almost lunging for the pane near the end of the images. The last picture in the series showed the woman pointing, and the hair fell away enough to reveal a horrific countenance. The woman's eyes appeared to glow red, likely red eye from the Walter's flash. (Did digital do that though?)

The room went dark.

"Christ!" Walter yelled. He waved his arms in the air and the motion sensors turned the lights back on. The screen had also defaulted to a black screensaver at the same time because of inactivity on the keyboard. The slideshow had vanished. Walter banged the keys. "Double Christ!"

He tapped repeatedly on the space bar until the image returned, showing a still of the last picture in the series. There was no woman in the window. Something blurry, yes, but nothing approximating the image he thought he saw. He restarted the slideshow from the first picture and manually advanced the frames. There appeared to be a movement in the window.

A curtain.

Walter shook his head, feeling absurd. The motion revealed a curtain fluttering in the wind. Walter himself had found the window open in the room that day, surprised to see it so. Any abandoned building found itself at the mercy of squatters. Though why any squatters did not loot the place was a mystery. He gave no further thought to it after he closed the window that day. Now the memory meant something else.

There was no doubt he saw the flutter of curtains in the images and nothing more. Strange what a brain could attribute to something else. He restarted the slideshow once more for good measure and set it on an auto slow speed. A window, that was all. What might make him imagine more?

Sleep.

He needed it. A head wound and long hours of poring over documents left him in a miserable state. His good friend placed the idea of the three AM witching hour into his head. One of the reading rooms in the building housed a velvet loveseat. It would do for a night's rest. He turned off the computers and left the room.

"Witching hour? Robert, my friend, every hour in Salem is the Witching hour, is it not?"

Walter laughed at his fresh joke, followed by a renewed check for witnesses. With none on his tail, Walter exited the room to go get some sleep. The moment he left the room, the laptop hummed as it turned on by itself. The monitor burst to life and the picture of the house filled the screen. Within the image, the Pointing Woman stood clearly at the window.

T OM SAT ON THE floor alongside the couch, caressing one of his wife's arms while she dozed. He absentmindedly loosened her wedding ring and pulled it off. He held it up where it sparkled in the light of the flames from the fireplace. Tears welled in his eyes. He took her hand gingerly and was about to place it back on, a second proposal of sorts, when he noticed two sets of legs standing nearby.

He freed his hands to wipe the tears from his eyes so no one would see. Once he cleared the moisture away, he cleared his throat of a sob, posing as gruff to announce his displeasure over unwanted guests.

"What part of be alone with my wife do you not under..."

He turned and choked on the words. The dead sisters stood together, looking down at Tom. They each pointed a finger at him and screamed an unholy scream. He launched himself to his feet, shaking his head to clear the obvious nightmare. Had he too fallen asleep? The girls continued pointing while bellowing a torturous cry.

He backed further away, stopping only when he felt the heat of the flames at his back. Something rumbled within the chute, a scrabble along brick from inside. Two hands extended from the fire and grabbed his ankles. The burning arms lit his pants. He finally screamed and shouted to Heather for her to wake, trying to warn her even as the flames spread over his body. He looked back at Heather only to spot the two girls standing mere inches from his face, each with a shush finger over their lips.

The hands at his feet yanked Tom violently into the flames. He opened his mouth to scream but the flames sucking into his chest extinguished his voice, which gargled into a melt. He twisted and turned, kicking in agony, but the hands never let go. They were not done. With one more swift pull, Tom vanished up the chimney. Heather's wedding ring dropped from somewhere high in the chute and landed in the burning kindling.

With Tom gone, the dead girls turned their attention back to Heather. They approached the couch, and each clasped hands over one of Heather's arms. Heather's arm went blue at the point of contact, and the woman shivered in her sleep. Heather's breath crystalized despite the warmth of the fire nearby.

CHAPTER 13

FEET THUDDED, DRAGGING ON the floor like rotten meat slapping on a butcher's block. Thump, thump, drag. Repetitive. The sound fed into Linda's already horrific nightmare. The disturbing visions of a strange past visited her in sleep, accompanied by the incessant slapping of flesh in the background. In the dream world, a prone dead body, with an outstretched arm locked in rigor mortis, seemed to point at her. An accusation from beyond the grave.

Unable to recognize the deceased, Linda leaned closer. It was someone she knew. She screamed. And woke.

Thump, thump, drag.

The nightmare vanished from her mind immediately, leaving only a lingering sorrow behind. Who was it she saw? The identity slipped away, but even as the nightmare vanished, the disturbing sound continued. Downstairs. She rushed into the hall, colliding with Andrew and Ruby.

Andrew wore only boxers and Ruby one of Andrew's tees. Linda stumbled as much from spotting her friends scantily clad as she did from the collision itself. They were all friends, but since arriving in Salem, Linda experienced several risqué encounters with either half of the couple. Andrew flopped in half hardness in the loose cloth while flashes of Ruby's nether regions popped into view with every step she took. It was obvious what the two had been up to despite their argument earlier.

Linda grew more concerned with what lay below. If it was loud enough to disturb her friends' lovemaking, then the heavy thudding steps were no illusion. Something was on the move through the house. Andrew pressed against Linda to pass and take point. The feel of his body momentarily excited her, a ridiculous thing to consider in such a moment. Ruby at least remained focused on the situation, not the state of anyone's undress.

"What is it?" Ruby asked.

"I don't know, but it's my house. I go first." Linda said, shoving Andrew aside.

They descended the stairs. Once in the foyer, she checked the living room from a distance. No sign of her other friends. She assumed the married couple went to investigate themselves as they were closer to the noises to begin with. All the same, she did not call out to them, not until she knew it was safe to do so. (Could it be an intruder? A burglar?) Thump, thump, scrape. Ruby tapped Linda's shoulder and pointed. Linda nodded. The kitchen. They entered to find an open basement door.

"That was stuck before. No idea how someone could open it," Andrew said.

"Wrong. We had a contractor at the house to fix the window. Maybe Walter had him repair the door as well," Linda whispered, not sure why she kept her voice so low.

Linda remembered Andrew and Tom mentioned the stuck door the first day they arrived. She planned to call someone to fix it. Unnecessary now. Linda leaned toward the unknown part of the building.

"Hello?" she whispered.

The footsteps had stopped, overtaken by another strange sound. Scraping. Scrape. Scrape. Scrape. Not fingers on a chalkboard, but close. Whatever was causing it was methodical, determined. Possibly a trapped animal desperate to get out. She expected to hear an accompanying whine, but no, there was only scraping.

"Linda, let me go first."

Linda ignored Andrew and reached inside to toggle on a light switch. A single bulb lit up at the base of the stairs, which provided a narrow cone of visibility at ground level. The light revealed a dirt floor, common for the area. The stairs leading down appeared rickety. Linda descended with caution, the others close behind. A web fluttered near her face. Someone had halved the previously elaborate design at human height, so the intruder was not an animal.

"Hello?" Linda called out again.

Still no answer. Whomever the scraper was, they appeared on a mission, determined to achieve some unfathomable goal in Linda's basement, of all places. Linda faltered for a moment, feeling a pull in her side, a growing nervousness that twanged internally, a runner's stitch without having run.

The nightmare. Had she not woken from one? Mere moments ago, but it felt so long ago as time stretched out into the darkness, each new step closer to answers. But did she want to know? The basement felt familiar. It brought back images from the nightmare. Hadn't there been a body? Yes, in her nightmare, a body. So hard to remember. She finally stepped off the steps and onto the basement floor.

Yes. She recognized the place despite only now entering it. Maybe she was wrong. Maybe the nightmare was some other basement, but even that coincidence was mind numbing. She tried to remember the details, but it was too hard with all the scraping. Why wouldn't it stop?

Shadows absconded with any ancillary light beyond the cone. Linda stepped into the light, her skin cascading yellow under a bulb of low wattage. Even her friends vanished, melded with the shadows as they too called out, searching the surroundings for signs of movement. The scraping while incessant also seemed to come from every direction at once.

There. More light. Faint. A basement window perhaps. It provided a mere sliver of light, but it did so in the right direction. The moonlit beam cut through dancing dust motes and settled on something. A hand? If it was, it glistened in the light. Wet? Linda approached, her eyes adjusting to the darkness.

"Who are you?"

Linda walked alone, the world fell away, her other friends eaten by shadows, gone back to the waking world while she remained in the nightmare. For this was the nightmare from earlier. Linda remembered now. She moved closer as something came into view. A woman.

The female clawed at a brick wall, desperate to reach something. What? Hair jutted in all directions, but the woman's face remained hidden, turned away. Bony hands with unnaturally pale skin glistened in spots where they dripped with something wet.

Linda grabbed the woman by the shoulder and pulled her away from the wall, away from the relentless scraping mission. Linda gasped, staggering back in fright. Hair dangled across the woman's face, covering all but one eye rolled white up into the skull. Part of the webbing from the stairs covered the woman's hair in the front. Linda took a better look at the hands. Oh God, the hands! They dripped blood from scratching relentlessly at brick that refused to give.

Heather. It was Heather!

Heather hissed at the intrusion, frigid air escaping her mouth. As Linda fell back, Heather returned to the wall and continued clawing. It was Ruby and Andrew who finally went to the woman's aid, crying out in shock as they dragged Heather to her feet and up the stairs. Linda gazed at the dripping crimson on the wall.

The nightmare flooded back. Linda knew then who the body on the floor belonged to in her nightmare. It belonged to Heather. Her friends struggled to get Heather up the stairs, crying out in concern, yelling for Linda to help, but Linda could only stand there and stare at the blood, wondering when the nightmare would end so she could finally wake up.

T HE SALEM MEDICAL CENTER provided state-of-the-art equipment in a modern setting. In a town known for historical buildings, the hospital felt alien, an outlier, like an alien civilization visiting the original colonies. The vast building rose six stories high. Each level offered specialty services along with per floor waiting rooms, which minimized the assembly of too much misery in one central location. The hollow eyes of the forlorn could suffer silently if they desired. The waiting rooms offered spread seating by design along with floor to ceiling glass looking out onto the town.

Andrew did just that, looking out on the unfamiliar part of town while simultaneously watching Ruby and Linda in the reflection. The two women sat huddled together under a sign reminding them they were on the fourth floor. Andrew remembered a medical professional friend once telling him the higher the number, the worse the scenario in a hospital. Anything above two was troubling. They were already worried about Heather, so knowing such information did not help.

An elderly woman with a younger woman sat on the other side of the waiting room. The younger woman whispered soothing words into the old woman's ear. The older lady nodded as if in agreement with every utterance, yet tears filled her eyes anyway, belying any message of hope.

They had not called an ambulance for Heather, did not know if one could find them in a timely manner and their friend was so cold and bloody. They rushed her to the van and used the GPS, which thankfully operated properly, delivering them to the hospital rather than the town's witch statue. The medical staff that greeted them took their frantic efforts in stride, a normal workday where they were concerned.

Heather's unresponsiveness did alert staff to something more serious. Once her catatonic condition became apparent, the professional strangers switched into a different gear, producing transport and medical equipment as if pulled from a magician's cape. Staff wheeled their friend away, calling out Heather's name the entire way and asking her if she knew what happened. Never once did Heather respond.

The group waited in the first level lobby where other poor victims arrived occasionally, but compared to Los Angeles, the hospital was relatively quiet. The trio randomly blurted out words of concern to one another. Whenever one broke, the other two would step forward with assurances. Linda worried the situation was dire when even Ruby stopped joking. There were so many targets for her friend, cute doctors and nurses, hospital gowns showing ass crack. Yes, the environment was ripe for levity, but her ever joking friend had run out of material.

A nurse eventually arrived to inform them their friend was stable, and they could wait on the fourth floor for an update from the doctor. They still waited when Andrew finally pulled himself away from the window and approached the women who were mid conversation. They finally addressed the elephant in the room.

"I'm shocked Tom would just leave like that," Linda said.

"That's what divorce does. It separates the women from the assholes," Ruby said.

"Sure, lump us all together," Andrew said with a bite.

"I'm just saying eventually men have a way of..." Ruby started.

"Go ahead, finish the thought."

"Disappointing."

"We always knew Tom was a mutt, it doesn't mean we all are," Andrew replied.

"We did not all know that. I loved Tom. Love. God, this is so weird," Linda said.

"You are still defending him even after he said he wanted to bang you?" Ruby asked.

Linda looked away, focusing on the old woman before turning back to Ruby. "Yes. It was disappointing."

"Disappointing. See?" Ruby shrugged at Andrew.

Andrew eyed Linda. She held his gaze momentarily, speaking in a silent shorthand they always shared. Any minute of any day, any of them in their group could have crossed a line with one another. There was so much love between them all. And attraction. Linda often saw Andrew in a certain light, usually holding a beer with a smile so wide it was like he was celebrating the existence of all existence. He loved life. Linda loved that about him as much as she loved his abs, and his cheekbones, and his... She let the thought drop. Why could she drool occasionally for a friend and not allow Tom to do the same?

Marriage. That was the difference. And timing. Tom made his surprise proclamation while his wife was in a condition that eventually led to hospitalization. Yes, that made him a cad, or cold, or clueless. Linda could not decide which negative attributes to assign to her friend whom she still loved dearly. She would have to attribute a definition to her feelings later because, as Andrew broke their gaze, she noticed him about to engage with his other half. Linda cut them off at the pass.

"Guys, please stop. No more fighting. We're here for Heather," Linda said as the couple simmered.

Doctor Tammy Baldwin entered the waiting room. The black woman had warm eyes and an affable demeanor, but after a quick glance at the paperwork in her hand, she grimaced involuntarily before quickly falling back on her warm smile.

"Hello everyone. My name is Dr. Baldwin, and I have some questions," the doctor said.

Linda leaped to the forefront. Ruby leaned into Andrew for support as they waited for the news.

"Is Heather okay?" Linda asked.

"Physically, she appears fine. The abrasions on her fingers and knees from…" The woman consulted the chart. "Scratching?"

"Yes," Linda replied.

"How did that come about? Was she trapped somewhere?"

"In my house," Linda said.

"Trapped inside your house?"

"No, nothing like that. She was in the basement. She was free to leave," Ruby said.

The doctor shot them a strange look but continued. "The abrasions to her knees and the cuts on her finger proved superficial. We treated and bandaged them. Mentally, however, I am concerned. Has heather suffered any tragedies in her life recently?'

"She is getting divorced," Ruby said.

"From an asshole," Andrew chimed in sarcastically.

"Not that all men are," Ruby said. The couple gripped hands. Apology accepted.

Doctor Baldwin lit up and wrote on the chart in her hand. "That is good news."

"A divorce? Why don't we have a funeral and really cheer you up," Andrew said, still in sarcasm mode.

The doctor smiled to imply no offense. "Sorry, poorly spoken. I need to determine the need for a wellness case or not."

"You mean psyche ward stuff? No. look, we don't know how long she planned the divorce. She only let us know yesterday.

When we brought her in, we noticed her wedding ring was missing. We think they had a fight last night, and he stormed out with the ring. Maybe she threw it at him in anger. Who knows? But a psyche ward? Please," Ruby said.

"Do not worry. Your friend is in no trouble even were I to suggest such a course of action. Your information is enough for me not to recommend it at this point. There was nothing in her file about any such issues."

"Good. She's not crazy," Ruby said.

"Exactly. A traumatic event, such as a divorce, coupled with unfamiliar surroundings, can trigger severe episodes of sleepwalking."

"But she was so cold," Linda said.

"Walking around a basement near naked will do that. She's not in California anymore. Nighttime temperatures drop significantly."

"Wait. You haven't explained why you were so concerned. What prompted even a consideration of a psyche evaluation?" Andrew asked.

"Your friend said some things," the doctor said.

"Things? What things?" Linda asked.

"Sorry, that falls under HIPPA rules. She was unconscious, we medicated her. If she had a nightmare while sleepwalking, it would explain the horrible things she mentioned. And based on that same information, I could imagine her trying desperately to escape her situation. I recommend she spend the night for observation. You can see her tomorrow."

"Wait, doctor. It all happened in my house. I deserve to know. There have been a few... strange things," Linda said.

"Like what?" Ruby protested.

Linda raised her hands and voice to her friend. "Birds for a start."

"Oh yeah, some strange shit. I forgot," Ruby said.

The doctor's eyes widened in recognition. "Look, there are no borders for nightmares. They happen anywhere. In Heather's case, they happened here, but beyond your concern for your friend, do not let that influence any of you. Salem is a pleasant town, a great place to raise a family."

Andrew and Ruby gripped hands without thinking at the mention of family. Linda noticed, but pivoted her attention back to the doctor. The doctor's words calmed Linda, who wanted desperately to find some normalcy regarding her new home.

The doctor smiled warmly and continued. "Practically Halloween year-round here. Kids love it. But there are those who let imaginations run wild. Some hospitals have contests over x-rays, revealing items mysteriously placed in rectums. Our Salem variation is the worst injuries sustained from amateur ghost hunters who traipse about at night in old structures or even graveyards. News flash. We get frost around here. That makes the grass slick, and when you fall in such a place, a tombstone will gladly catch your head as you fall. You can ask Heather more about her nightmares when you pick her up tomorrow. My guess is, she will not even remember. You know how dreams are."

The doctor departed. During their conversation, the women in the waiting room received news of their own. A gray-haired doctor looked on sadly as the older woman sobbed raggedly into the arms of the younger family member. Linda and her friends departed in somber fashion past other people's pain.

Outside the hospital, thunder rumbled, the sky darkened. Rain blanketed the sky. No sprinkle of raindrop scouts to warn the populace of the coming torrent. The sky simply gave way to a downpour. A metal awning stretched from the hospital exit to the curb. The metal covering amplified the sound of the drops, each a cacophonous explosion showcasing the power behind the inclement weather.

"Wasn't raining when we were upstairs. Didn't expect it either. Umbrella and gear are in the van," Andrew said.

The trio gathered under the shelter. Ruby tippy toed up to Andrew, kissed him with the briefest of pecks.

"Dear sweet beloved, protector of mine..."

He shoved her off playfully and lifted his shirt over his head. "Fine. Let's file this sacrifice for when you talk about the whole men are creeps thing."

He raced into the rain. Linda stepped out from under cover, looking up. Ruby pulled her back.

"What are you doing? Andrew's getting the van."

"Heather's room is on this side. I think. Just wanted to see..."

"See what? In a storm?"

Linda nodded, good point. "First Heather and Tom, and now you two?"

"Please. We always fight. It's our thing. If it bothers you..."

"It bothers me."

"Fine, I will try to tone it down around you. But realize there's a reason he hasn't put a ring on it."

Ruby extended her hand, mimicking the reception of a proposal while gesturing Linda to play along. Linda made a gesture of getting down on one knee without going all the way. Then she roleplayed placing the ring on Ruby's finger. Once Linda moved in close with the invisible ring, Ruby curled her fingers inward into her down facing palm. She then turned the hand upright, her digits retracted into a claw.

"See how quickly I go from 'I will' to I'm a witch? Witch hands. A Salem joke. Get it?" Ruby released the claw and burst into laughter.

Linda rolled her eyes and smiled despite herself. "You're terrible. All kinds of terrible."

"Sweetie, I'm just saying don't overthink it. Relationships are complicated. If you ascribe things to it from the outside, it will never live up to those expectations. Don't over analyze everything. Look where it got Heather and Tom."

"I know we're supposed to be collectively mad at him, but the thing is, I still love Tom very much. He was wrong when he said we wouldn't be friends."

"Agreed. But going forward, when we're in Heather's presence, we only refer to Tom as the shit show. Agreed?"

"Agreed."

Andrew pulled up in the van. Ruby slid into the middle seat, leaving shot gun for Linda. The moment Linda buckled her seatbelt, someone slammed into her passenger window, face against the glass. Dr. Baldwin, holding a plastic gown over her head as she gestured for Linda to roll down the window. Linda did.

"One last question Heather mentioned several times something about a child. I did not notice any children accompanying you. There is nothing in her records about giving birth. Did she adopt?"

"I wish," Linda said.

"Excuse me?"

"Sorry. I teach at an orphanage. Just mean any kid would be lucky to be adopted by her. No, she is not a mother."

"Asked and answered. Well, thank you. We'll look after her." The Doctor motioned to the sky. "You know what they say about New England. If you dislike the weather, wait a minute." The Doctor rushed away.

"We need to come back tomorrow and see what all this is about. The doctor is concerned about something with Heather," Linda said.

"Listen, can we open the can of elephants in the room?" Ruby asked.

The others nodded, gesturing for her to continue, neither questioning the botched idiom, chalking it up to a Rubyism.

"She was in a damn cellar scratching until her hands bled. WTF! Why are we questioning a psyche counsel? You find me doing the same call in the straitjacket police. Why are we pretending any of this is normal?"

"Not pretending, but like the doctor said, she doesn't know where she is, in a strange house. We made it worse by moving her to the couch. She wakes up, half asleep, half dreaming. Who knows what dream she was acting out?" Andrew shrugged, looking for agreement.

"Or nightmare. I've been having them since we arrived."

"I know we are all tight, but with the age difference, those two have been around the block longer than we have known them. They had a good run. But maybe she did not see it coming. We literally only heard from Tom about the breakup, not from Heather because she was so sick," Ruby said.

"We should have taken her to the hospital when she didn't wake up initially," Andrew said.

"Except her husband shooed us away, and frankly, I was eager to get you away from him. We didn't take her when we should have, so she got sicker and that's all. The doctor is right. The poor girl needs a good night's sleep and then when we get the okay, we will be on her so hard she will forget she was ever married."

An ambulance pulled in behind the van, the lights dazzling in the rain. It sparked Andrew to start the vehicle. They drove away with Linda looking up for Heather's location, but the angle of the van was off. None of them noticed Dead Rose looking down on them from Heather's hospital room.

NELL LEANED INTO THE windshield and her cellphone, speaking as fast as the windshield wipers that worked overtime. The storm stunted the visibility of the road. Nell watched for red trains or white trains like leaving a bar at night. Except there were no headlight or taillights in sight. She seemed to be the only one foolish enough to be out in the storm. She wished to be anywhere but driving in such a squall.

"Colt, you son of a bitch! What kind of service are you providing to that woman at the board up? Are you two banging more than nails? Where are you? Your wife has been blowing up my phone because you didn't come home last night. She thinks you were with me. I know you weren't with me. Why? Because someone sexually satisfied me last night, that's why!"

Nell disconnected and threw the cell down on the passenger's seat of one of the company-owned trucks. She wore a white puffy jacket (not waterproof) over one of her company logo white polos. Colt ordered them on purpose in slim because it showed off certain things when she wore them, and if the light was just right, clients got a show and offered more work.

She never much minded the leering as Nell was deep down a flirt, but she was particular with who she slept with, and she had made one hell of a poor choice with her boss. Once she was in, she was in, though, unwilling to admit defeat. She pulled the sleeve over one hand and used it to wipe away condensation from the window to better see. She never could figure out dashboard vents on any car other than her own.

"Well piss my fanny," she cursed at the sight of a sleeve gone black with grime after wiping what she assumed was a clean window.

A white wedding would be out of the question for Nell, so she figured it was fine to wear at work, where she could use it to her benefit. But dirt (like the window washing proved) was a constant issue. Their clients dragged much construction site gobbledygook into their office. She appreciated the roughshod way the men (and some women, but not enough, Nell often thought) trounced through their office without a care as to the damage they might create. That meant they did not care about their appearances. It also meant they did not care what she thought of them, no matter whether they wanted to take a tumble with her or not. Most claimed to want a go, but she was never certain what was talk, and what was intent.

While considering herself discerning, she slept with a few that came through. Only the married ones, though. Nell was not fond of the younger ones, the idiots pretending they knew everything when they just now started on the job, growing out peach fuzz on chins so slight they likely only had to shave once a year. The self-anointed studs announced themselves via too much cologne, or dreaded body sprays. That artificial scent lingering in their wake whenever they appeared meant they didn't work hard enough to break a sweat.

Most of those younger ones wouldn't last in the job, and most wouldn't in her bed. She had a thing for older men, always. Since a young age with no drama, no creepiness from relatives, her family leaned on the well-adjusted side of the spectrum. What was the old saying? *If one doesn't know a freak in the family, then they are the freak in the family*, she thought.

Nell was the freak, lusting after teachers, the fathers of kids that she babysat for, or older neighbors. Nothing ever happened, no one even ever tried anything when she was younger. Her infatuations remained secret to all. The objects of her affections were of various moral persuasions, but none even returned a flirt to their credit. Once she hit eighteen, though, she hooked up with a member of a band in town for a concert.

At that same consequential age, she became the pursuer and hooked Colt early on. Hotels became cost prohibitive once she stopped sitting for his child (because his wife sensed something). Then he hired her for the construction company. Colt had been fighting that battle with his wife and winning so far. Nell had lasted over a year. Whatever good will Nell hoped to build back up with Colt's wife fell by the wayside when Colt stopped coming home on time. Nell just couldn't help herself around the man, big gut, and all.

There was also her own boyfriend. Despite Nell's age preference, her boyfriend Tim was her same age. It was for show. He was her boy toy. She got what she needed out of him, and it was mutual. She sensed the boy loved her, but it made no matter to Nell. There were rumors he cheated on her with Emma Maye, Nell's best friend. Nell did not care. Emma was super-hot, so she could not fault her boyfriend. She never asked either of them. Nell and Emma Maye made out plenty themselves. Now, if Emma scooped up Colt, then there would be a showdown.

Nell dialed her cell. "Okay, sorry. I was with boyfriend last night but only because you never answered my calls. Now I find out you didn't go home? Who is she, Colt? You don't spend nights with me. If you want to leave your wife, fine. But to ditch me for someone you just met?" She disconnected and tossed the phone again. It bounced from the seat onto the floor near the pedals. "Shit!"

She bent to reach for it, trying to monitor the road, but failed. As she lifted the device, she hit the brakes. The street sign nearly kissed her windshield. She navigated around it and drove up the length of road.

The sky appeared to grow darker the closer she got to the house. She wiped at the windshield once again, the entire sleeve covered in grime. Nell pulled into the driveway but saw no windows lit, so she killed the engine. Lightning offered brief glimpses through loosely closed drapes, revealing nothing of note.

Nell opened the glove compartment and yelped in glee at discovering an unopened bag of orange Circus Peanuts. She tore a hole in the plastic even though she did not know how long they were in there. They likely lasted forever. After the apocalypse, the sweet treats might even become currency, along with Twinkies and cockroaches. She popped one in her mouth and rolled her eyes to heaven.

Then she reached back into the glove compartment and pulled out the work order. She used it to double check the address. It matched. She considered blasting the horn. That would teach him. Make him come running naked out into the rain, trying to explain the other woman to his new one. She sat with the idea for a moment but never pressed the horn.

Rain thundered down atop the vehicle, plinking and plunking in time with the tics of the engine cooling. She tried to look to either side of the house with no luck in the heavy storm. There was no sign of a damaged window.

"No way you replaced a window by now. No orders came through. So where is the board up?" She rolled down a window and leaned her head out. "I'm going to drive across your lawn to check out the back. If you do not want me to do so, please flash a light inside!" More lighting was the only response. "I gave the owners a warning."

She rolled the window back up and started the truck, driving slowly across the yard toward the back of the house. The low speed ensured she felt every imperfection in the turf. She cursed every bump.

Nell frequently made deliveries to job sites. On one of her first, she took out flora without realizing. Replacing it cost Colt a pretty penny. He hired a landscaper to go fix her tire track error. She learned quickly how important it was to navigate a yard without damage, so that meant slow going. If she hydroplaned on turf, it would rip it through to mud.

Yes, she learned her lesson. She was all about being a careful Sally. It did not keep her from yelling in the cab. "I'm going to donut it out of here if I find out Colt's shacked up with some bitch!"

The boarded window finally came into view. She kept the truck running, headlights on, and sat there deciding what to do.

There was no other vehicle in the driveway. She arranged a tow for Colt's damaged truck. A call to Charlie confirmed the man hooked the vehicle but never spoke with Colt. Colt would have needed a ride. The fact Colt did not ask Charlie for one meant Colt remained at the house with the freaking female homeowner! Before driving out herself, Nell checked with Sergeant Taylor about whether he had seen Colt. The officer said he sent Colt to the board up job for a woman named Linda. The trooper did not even appear aware of the truck accident.

When the officer probed if there was an issue, Nell let it drop, because further conversation might reveal her affair with the married man. She thanked the trooper, hung up, and headed out onto the road. Now, as she sat in the yard, she needed to decide on a course of action. She popped another circus peanut, then two more, thinking maybe she didn't need men in her life, only the orange goodness.

Still, her mind wandered. *So, this Linda offered Colt a ride home and rode something else. The question was, where were they doing it?* Then it hit Nell. One of their backup spots.

Her anger grew as wild as the storm. She dialed her phone again. "Hello? Who is this? Harry, it's Nell. No, I don't want to book a room. I want to know if Colt already did. No? You're sure?" The man said something on the other end, setting Nell off. "What do you mean you wouldn't know if he checked in under an alias? You know what he looks like. If he calls himself Ryan Seacrest, he's still Colt, you idiot."

Nell pulled the phone away from her ear for a moment before placing it back as the young man ranted over her dis. The motel manager owed Colt something (probably for emergency repairs over the years) and for that, the man kept secrets when either she or Colt booked a room. She allowed the man to vent.

"Sorry. Came out wrong. I'm upset at him, not you. I meant to ask if you have seen him. You have not. Thank you. Now you keep that gun behind the counter just in case, correct? Then I am asking you to please use it on Colt if he arrives there with anyone other than myself. Okay? Yes, especially if he calls himself Ryan Seacrest."

Nell slowly backed down the yard, happy to see her tires left a minimal trail that would soon wash away in the rain. She eventually reached the dirt road, took one last look at the house, and drove on.

Then she hit the brakes.

A short distance past the home was a forest path wide enough for a vehicle. Probably created for deer hunters to get in and out with their bounty, or maybe loggers. Either way, it was the perfect spot to sit and wait. She backed the truck onto the narrow path. Trees scraped at the vehicle, but they were harmless. She bumped her head as she drove over the large hump leading from street level to forest level and she grabbed at her head, cursing Colt all over again.

She settled in with the bag of candy, leaving the engine running for heat. The house became mostly lost in the rain, but she was no longer looking for that. She was looking for a vehicle returning to the scene of the crime. She realized the folly of calling their motel, Colt would have thought about that, taken Linda elsewhere.

By the time the bag was half finished, Nell wondered whether it was worth waiting any longer. Colt would soon get an earful from both her and his wife whenever he answered his phone. She could just ignore his calls and leave him hanging. Yes, that would be enough punishment. That was the new plan. She prepared to drive back onto the main road when she noticed a light turn on in the house. Despite the storm, the light was visible. Nell fumed.

"Son of a bitch was banging in there all along. They probably fell asleep, and the bastard just woke up."

That was it. Plan set. Storm the castle and hit the headlight and horns. Except as Nell tried to drive up the steep incline, the truck glided to one side. She yelped and took her foot off the gas. Nell tried again, but the vehicle slid off to the side intent on making make acquaintance with a nearby tree. She heard the whiz of a tire losing traction. Hitting the gas made it worse. Mud ensured she was not going anywhere with the vehicle. She leaped out and slammed the door for good measure. There was no reason to examine the situation. There was nothing she could do. She would make Colt's cheating ass deal with it. She had only one thought: get to that lit window.

Nell crossed the street. She could hardly see a thing. The rain soaked through her coat immediately, causing the polyester shell to become heavy and cold. Her hair deflated on her head and plastered itself over her face. She finally reached the house and looked up.

"Show yourself, bitch."

Then someone did, but not who she expected. A child appeared in the window, maybe seven. Lightning flashed and the image of the girl grew stretched out, her face open in terror like the painting, *The Scream*. As the flash faded, the light in the room went dark.

"She's banging him in a motel somewhere and they left a kid here? Uh-uh!"

Nell's protective babysitter instincts kicked in. She wanted children someday when she was old, like twenty-five, but until then she was happy to babysit any critters. Boy, girl, did not matter. She was all in with the fine art of babysitting. A person leaving their kid alone was unacceptable.

This then would be her revenge on whoever this Linda woman was. Report the situation to child protective services. If Colt did not grovel enough after all this, maybe she would loop his name in, get his own kid caught up in things.

Drenched enough for ten people, she thought, Nell raced to the front door and knocked before yelling through the slab. "Hello? Anyone there? Little girl? It's okay. I'm a babysitter. Is your mom home?" The knob audibly unlatched, but the door remained closed. Nell pushed it open and leaned her head in. "Hello? Colt? Little girl?"

Nell stepped into the foyer to escape the rain. Eyeing the hardwood floor, she felt terrible about the puddles building at her feet. But Nell was too angry at Colt to care, and too worried about the kid to step back outside. The home was dry except where she walked, which meant no one else had been outside recently.

She glanced toward the window nearest the door and yelped in fright at the sight of a witch. No, not a witch but herself, with hair having given up the ghost and mascara pouring down her face like blood. If she was not careful, she would scare the kid. *Wow, they truly left a child behind*, Nell thought. If adults were present, they would have already answered or even confronted the intruder. The child appeared deathly frightened in the window. Nell did not wish to scare the child further, so she continued to announce her presence.

"Hello? I was here looking for my boss, but then I saw the little girl. I want to make sure she is okay. Hello? Anyone?"

Footsteps sounded overhead, strolling the length of the ceiling before racing back at a startling speed to the origin point. Nell spun in place, trying to follow, but found it impossible. Then it stopped. The world fell library silent other than the patter of rain outside.

Right when Nell adjusted to the silence, the footsteps started again, racing across the floor at an unfathomable speed. Everywhere at once. It was a kid all alone. Any adult would have screamed for the child to stop such foolishness. While Nell could not explain away the furious speed at which the child moved, it was still a child. Maybe one working off nervous energy, scared to know there is an intruder but not smart enough to act with stealth. It had been some time since Nell babysat. Kids were energetic and plenty fast. Nell decided to search for the child while she had an audible roadmap.

She stepped onto the first step. The floorboard squeaked, and the running ceased as if the child somehow alerted to her subtle noise. "Really?" Nell shook her head and continued climbing. At the top, she stopped to get her bearings in the unfamiliar space. A hallway with three rooms stretched ahead. She opened the first door. Nell looked inside but saw no one. The room was quaint, certainly large, but as for children, nothing.

Closing the door revealed Dead Sadie standing there. The little girl held fingers to her mouth, stifling a giggle as if engaged in hide and seek. Nell, unaware she was a player in such a game, continued down the hall and entered the second bedroom. Nell noticed the full-length mirror and walked past it to check the bathroom. As she did so, Dead Rose appeared in the mirror's frame, close to the surface of the glass. Nell failed to notice and exited the room.

One room left. The child had to be somewhere. Why had she gone silent? The third room had clothes strewn about, the place a bit of a mess. *Was this where Colt and Linda did it*? Still, no child though, even after calling out. Nell walked past the bed to look out the window. Behind her, Dead Sadie thrashed silently on the bed as if deep in seizure (or tethered like yesteryear).

Nell yanked the curtain open but while searching the yard she missed the reflection in the window, which showed Sadie freed from the invisible bonds. The child floated toward the ceiling. Nell searched the yard from on high, checking that there were no visible tire marks from her vehicle earlier. Washed away as planned. Nell dropped the curtains. The kid had to be nearby. It made no sense.

"Where are you, little girl?"

No answer. Nell turned and crossed her arms. (Had it grown colder?) Must have resulted from exposing the window. She retreated to the center of the room, unaware Sadie hovered against the ceiling. The floating child's hair dangled. Nell inadvertently walked through it, causing her to swipe her hand across her face as if clearing a web. Dead Sadie slowly reached for the woman. A child dashed past the doorway in the hall. Nell gave chase just as Sadie's fingers brushed Nell's coat.

Nell cried out to the fleeing child in the hallway. "I'm not here to hurt you."

Rounding the corner, Nell whipped out her phone, hoping to snap a picture, but the child was already gone, having vaulted down the stairs. Hurrying to catch up, Nell missed a step and caught the banister in time to save herself from a fall. She slowed down. There was only so much space in the home. She would find the child. The child had turned right at the bottom of the stairs. Nell followed and found herself in the kitchen housing the backside of Colt's handiwork. Then it hit her. Maybe she was wrong about her man. Maybe something happened to Colt. He boarded the place up and then, what?

Nell grew nervous. Already worried about the child, she worried suddenly about her lover. While the man's moral compass pointed nowhere near true north, he at least did his weasel best to juggle commitments. If he ran away with the Linda chick, he would have made up ridiculous excuses to her and his wife. It was unlike him to remain out of contact for so long. Something was wrong. She dialed his number.

"Pick up Colt, pick up."

Then she heard it, faint, before going to voicemail. She pulled the phone away from her ear and dialed again. The familiar ringtone rang somewhere below. A country tune she hated. Country music was *Devil's music,* where Nell was concerned. *Wasn't the world a sad enough place without all that added misery?*

The pair had set up different ring tones on all their phones, so they knew who was calling. Colt's ringtone for her was a song she despised because of its omnipresence. She dialed and sure enough, *Old Town Road* sounded somewhere below her feet.

The song led her to the basement door, which sat open. She called down.

"Colt? Honey? I forgive you. No apologies necessary if you cease scaring the shit out of me. Okay?"

She took the first step, dialing once more. Yep, Lil Nas X was ready to take his horse somewhere. She followed the song. Once the call went to voice mail again, she disconnected and used her flashlight app to descend the rest of the stairs.

With the phone no longer ringing, she heard another sound. (Scraping?) Whatever the source, it came from the same direction as Colt's ring tone. Her guts clenched. She expected Colt to leap out, scare her into forgetting about his tryst. If he ever had one. Was he okay? Was the kid's mother okay? The sound continued. Scrape, scrape, scrape. The noise came from a brick wall directly in front of her, yet no one was present.

Then movement. Subtle at first. A shift in a shadow drew her gaze. A brick low to the wall moved! The scraping the result of someone pushing a single brick from the inside out. But from the inside of where? What was on the other side of the wall? The brick pushed all the way through and fell to the ground near her foot. She danced away from it, then bent to look through the opening.

Darkness greeted her. She squinted, trying to adjust to the gloom when suddenly eyes opened on the other side! Nell rose and turned to run, coming to a hard stop when something pierced her abdomen. She gurgled as blood flooded in the wrong direction somewhere internally. She coughed and spit blood. Looking down, she found herself impaled on the Pointing Woman's outstretched arm. Nell's eyes glazed over, trying to understand.

Blood poured to the floor as she tried to call for Colt. Her words came out garbled, too frothed with red to pronounce his name. The Pointing Woman's arm remained fixed, straight, despite the weight of the soon to be corpse hanging from the limb. Nell's head bobbed until meeting the Pointing Woman's gaze. The woman smiled teeth that looked like half-chewed black licorice. The Pointing Woman's head maintained a crooked lilt the entire time, as if her neck were missing vertebrae.

The Pointing Woman grinned ever wider, inviting all her teeth to come out and play. With a tremendous burst of speed, her face snapped into Nell's. Nell finally dropped her phone. It would be of no use anymore.

CHAPTER 14

Andrew tried to hold back the runaway train that was Ruby. The train had fallen off the tracks after about the fourth time the hospital attendant (the badge read Halpern) refused the visitor's efforts to see their friend.

"If she came in as a Jane Doe, then we waltzed in and said we were family, you would let us in, correct?"

"Now you are making sense," the attendant said. "In such circumstances, we would gladly allow you in and be happy to identify the poor woman."

"But?" Ruby said, wondering whether she made a friendly break through.

"But that is not the case. We have the patient's name and medical history. She is sleeping and per doctor's orders, we are not to wake her. Only family can visit until the doctor says otherwise, and the doctor..."

"Isn't fucking here. You said that part a million times already."

Linda dropped her cell and joined the group. "Tried Tom again, left a message. He could get us in. And he should simply be here."

"He would be if he knew what was going on," Andrew said.

"I'm not so sure. Why isn't he responding to the voicemails?" Linda asked.

"Because he thinks we are trying to drag him back into patching things up with Heather. If I believed my friends were trying to trap me, I would ignore the calls too," Andrew said.

"Oh really? Is that how it will be when you and I call it a day?"

"Where did you get that from? Look, I understand you are angry, but Heather's doctor deserves a day off and is it so wrong to let Heather sleep? She was sick, freezing. There was more wrong than just a divorce."

"Sorry, sweetie. But hey, we know her room number. Let's just go up. Who will stop us?"

"Marcus?" Halpern called to a guard near the elevator bank.

Marcus, the size of a wall, looked over, hand on weapon. "Yeah?"

"Have your taser handy?"

"Right here. Used it recently. Every week, you know the drill, drugged out fool things he can take on the world."

"So, taking out these three?"

"No problem."

Andrew grabbed each woman by an arm and led them away. "We get it. We're leaving. Have the doctor call us when we can see our friend."

"That I can and will do. There are rules for a reason, folks."

"You know what you can do with your rules," Ruby yelled over her shoulder, threatening the fragile truce.

Linda mouthed a sorry to the staff as Andrew dragged Ruby out. Once outside, Ruby broke away from Andrew and grabbed her hair. Andrew turned on her, not angry, but concerned. They remained under the overhang as rain poured down.

"Honey, what the hell was that? We have day jobs. You want a parent coming at us like that?"

"Yes, because it would mean they care about their kid."

"You don't mean that, Ruby. You would never stand for someone talking to you that way. I am concerned about Heather too, even more now, but she is in the safest place, a hospital. So, what is this really about?"

"Tom is gone. Heather is in the hospital, and we thought she would be okay by the next day. Clearly, she is not. What happened to our summer? What happened to our trips? I knew we would have to stop traveling together someday, but not now, not like this."

Andrew and Linda exchanged sympathetic looks, and each touched one of Ruby's shoulders. Ruby extended arms around the two, battling tears.

"You know it only takes three to make things a party, isn't that right, Andrew?" Linda prodded.

"Right. And you know what makes a party? Shots."

"I LOVE shots!" Ruby cried, hugging her friends.

"Let's go then. Let's have some summer fun."

Andrew pulled out two small umbrellas from his coat. He opened one and handed it to Linda. The next, he opened and covered himself and Ruby. As they headed toward parking, Ruby grabbed his butt to get him moving. Linda smiled, happy to see some life return to her friends. Despite the urge, Linda did not look up at Heather's window.

S ERGEANT TAYLOR DID HIS best to ignore the moans and groans on the other side of the door. He knocked again and cleared his throat to boot.

"Aw, baby, don't stop," the female said.

The sound of rustling and stumbling suggested the man stopped. "It's the police. Christ!"

More rustling inside, followed by more protests from the woman, and then finally the door cracked open. The man had his lower half roughly wrapped in a blue sheet, but was otherwise nude. His hair reached for the sky, and he looked confused.

"Sergeant Taylor?"

"You going to let me out of this rain, Tim, or are you going to come outside?"

Taylor looked down at where the man's erection poked through the cracked door. Tim grumbled, reworked the sheets, and opened the door. The man scrambled back inside and sat on the edge of the foldout couch bed. Bottles and bongs occupied most of the room. A pert nude female leaped up and hugged the officer.

"Uncle Ronnie!"

"For love's sake, do not call me that when you aren't proper," Taylor said.

"Oh, I am proper, ain't I baby?" She said to her boy toy as she leaped onto him.

"To the man's point, maybe put some clothes on?" Tim grumbled.

"Aw, he's seen me buck naked plenty."

The trooper had seen her in such a state at one too many questionable locations. She was not family, not by a stretch, but was the daughter of an old lover for a very brief time when he made his own questionable choices. The girl was already at an age to get in trouble then and had since grown into it. She was an adult and could make her own choices, so he stayed out of it all the best he could.

She might have thought she was enticing him, but it only made him sad to see her that way whenever such situations arose. He would never tell her that though, let her live the fantasy that she was special, because she was in other ways. Emma Maye was her name, but Taylor was not there for her. He was there for the schmuck.

"Whatever it is, I didn't do it, officer."

"Yeah, I am certain you did. Normally I would let you confess to half a dozen crimes before getting to the actual one I was here for, but I am on a bit of a schedule. I am looking for your girlfriend."

"Shit! What did Nell do?"

Emma found her way to all fours, looking up excitedly, waiting for all the tea. Tim stripped the sheet off himself and draped it over her, leaving him naked and sitting on the edge of the bed, pointing up in all his glory.

Taylor rolled his eyes, but was otherwise unfazed.

"Why did you cover me up?" Emma asked, pouting.

"I get jealous," Tim said.

"That's sweet."

Taylor coughed. Then asked the question. "Now about Nell?"

"I haven't seen her. I assumed she's with her sugar daddy."

"One that pays for this classy place, huh?"

"Hey that game controller sticking out of that clothes pile over there belongs to an X-Box. There's plenty of fancy stuff here. We order out for food a lot too," Tim protested.

"If you can find a phone, you mind calling her for me?"

Tim rose and wandered through the room digging through domestic debris. Emma searched the mattress with no better luck. Taylor grew impatient.

"Christ, what's your number?" Taylor asked.

Tim told him, and Taylor dialed it on his own cell. Emma retrieved the ringing device from under one corner of the bed, dropping her sheet in the process. Taylor shook his head, giving up on seeing anyone even partially clothed. He listened as Tim made the call.

"Babe. Po-po is looking for you. Call me." He tossed the phone, which did its best to return to the same spot under the bed. "Nothing."

"Look, I assume she is doing the same thing with Colt that you two were doing when I showed up. Thing is, his wife is worried, says he never came home the other night. If she surfaces, then he probably surfaces. Do me a favor and call me if you hear anything. I would owe you one."

Emma leaped and hugged him again. "Come back anytime. I will be happy to help with your case."

"Yeah, I'll settle for that call." Taylor pried Emma's arms off and she returned to her other man. Taylor eyed Tim before exiting. "You staying hard the whole time I was here? Gas station penis pills?"

"Affirmative," Tim said.

Taylor nodded and let himself out. The couple were back at it before the trooper stepped out into the rain, thinking it might be worth stopping at the gas station. Once inside his cruiser, the officer decided the gas station would wait. He wouldn't want to buy them in town in uniform. No, he would go incognito to purchase some next time he hit the casinos out of town.

There was more business to attend to anyway, and he was on the clock. He called in his location. Regular updates were procedure, small town or not. Their cars had trackers nowadays, not like when he first started as an officer. Were the worst to happen, dispatch could at least call in the location of the missing vehicle. The thought creeped out the officer, so he tried to forget about that and focus on the case at hand.

The house. The lady's house. It still bristled his britches that all the time in Salem and he never noticed the dang place. Certainly no one lived there in the time he was on the force. Then there was the bird thing. Strange, but a one off. His bigger concern was the new homeowner. The woman had a nervous energy as if she was hiding something.

Linda was her name. He had resources to check her out, but check for what? Technically, the woman did nothing but move into a new place. Still, she was on edge the entire ride when he delivered her to Walter.

That man was a transplant, from across the pond, as they say. How had the two already connected? Were they shacking up? Was it as simple as they met at a bar first night in, celebrating the housewarming and hooked up?

Taylor rarely interacted with Walter since the man had arrived in town. And why would he? The outsider worked for the historical society and Taylor was more than over all the witch shit. The amount of dumbass calls that came through his switchboard as Halloween approached were off the charts. Still, the connection between the two newbies had to mean something.

Colt was a cheating crap-hound as far as the sergeant was concerned, but the man's wife was a pleasant woman who helped with many a school and social event in town. She had blinders on where her husband was concerned. It did not help that Colt lied with such conviction. Colt going silent for even a single night without returning with his tail or dick between his legs was reason enough for the wife to worry.

Failing to turn up any sign after shaking some trees about town left the trooper concerned as well. Deep down he had to admit it was possible Colt and Nell headed west and planned a Vegas wedding despite the man already being ringed up. Everyone in town knew Colt and Nell would end up together despite the age difference and despite their other *committed* relationships. Those two were fleas on a hound that liked to scratch, Taylor thought. There would be no separating the two. Nell never tried to hide much from her boyfriend, and based on the love fest in the apartment upstairs, the boyfriend cared little.

Yes, Taylor suspected the missing couple drove somewhere to elope. (Out of town, as Taylor already checked with the local justice of the peace.) Or as likely, they ran off to a hotel somewhere. Still, Linda's home was a start. He started up the cruiser and drove into the rain, going off memory on how to get to the place that was suddenly looking to be an issue in their little town.

L INDA DOWNED ANOTHER SHOT as Andrew and Ruby cheered her on before downing their own. They slammed the shot glasses upside down on the table alongside several others. Linda snorted and almost lost her drink, only to come back laughing. Ruby took another.

Ruby gulped. "To the summer of love!"

"Please, if you hang onto that idea, you will be sorely disappointed," Linda said.

"Dude, you're a catch. Such a catch. I'd do you," Ruby slurred.

"First. Dude? Rude," Linda said.

"Oh yeah, boobs, sorry…"

"And second Rubes, we've been friends all these years and you're just telling me this now? This changes everything. Our entire relationship could have been different. I can stop chasing men."

Ruby stiffened, her face registering confusion, slipping into a *what's happening* look. Andrew winked at Linda. A man in on the joke. Linda loved that about him.

"Really? Is that why you have stayed single? Are you really into women? Oh wait, you're playing me, aren't you?" Linda burst out laughing. "You're such a shit. My friend is a shit! A SINGLE shit!" Ruby yelled to the bar.

Several men looked in their direction, hope in their eyes. Linda turned away from the crowd. Ruby lifted another shot, only to get confused when it vanished before reaching her lips. Andrew held it high in victory after making the steal. He made a toast.

"To the best vacation ever." Andrew downed the shot.

Ruby tossed a napkin at him. Linda soured, rolling her eyes, drunk enough that it took a bit of effort to straighten them out. Andrew raised his hands and a defense.

"Hey, don't shoot the messenger," he said.

"Linda, there are cute guys everywhere. Pick one."

Linda instinctively looked at Andrew, who shared a sympathy smile. He rose and tried to drag Ruby to her feet. Ruby waved him off.

"If Tom were here, he would suggest we are all too old to still do shots. I am inclined to agree," Andrew said.

"Oh, Tom. I miss Tom," Ruby whined and pushed Andrew away. "Why don't you go find him?"

"Wait. What?" He noticed Ruby's look as she nodded clumsily for him to depart. Girl-talk time. Andrew took the hint. "I'm going to pretend to go search for Tom, but I'm actually going to go pay our tab." He looked at Linda and gestured to Ruby. "I apologize in advance for whatever scandalous garbage is about to come from my girlfriend's mouth."

Linda laughed and Ruby watched him go to make sure the coast was clear, then grabbed both of Linda's arms. They leaned heads into the table, almost forehead to forehead.

"Linda, what are we doing here?"

"In the bar?"

"No. Salem."

Linda stiffened, sobering up a bit. "We're looking for my family."

"Really? How's that working out so far? Because last I checked, your family is in CALIFORNIA! Us. The kids in the orphanage. All of it." Ruby shook her friend's arms.

Linda instinctively gripped the key dangling from her neck. "It's not that simple. There's a part of me that feels like I'm supposed to be here."

"Lin-Lin, come on. Here? I may be your biggest cheerleader, but I can't believe you are having any fun, that you're enjoying any of this. What are you thinking?"

"That I hate it here. That my new house gives me the creeps. But what do I have to go back to?" Ruby released her grip and crossed her arms, offended. Linda segued to damage control. "Look, I thought everything was okay with Heather and Tom, but I was wrong. I know less about them than I ever thought I did."

"Because they kept secrets from us."

"They wouldn't do that if we were as close as I thought we were. And what about you and Andrew?"

"What about us?"

"Are you hiding any secrets?"

Ruby recovered and grinned. She absentmindedly lifted each shot glass as if looking for a misfire, something more to swallow. Nothing. She turned away to check on Andrew's status. He remained at the bar.

"Only one. That despite how I give him such a hard time, I love him so much. It's the real thing. If you need at least one anchor in your life, we're it."

"I want to believe that. Want to believe in something."

"Believe it. We're going to get married and have two point four kids—the middle one won't be that bright. And you will be an auntie. What could be better than that?"

"Having my own?"

"Well, that's impossible because that would involve having sex."

The women stifled laughter as Andrew returned. Ruby rose and leaned into Andrew for support, legs rubber. Linda pushed away from the table and stood, only to come face to face with Walter. She leaped in surprised fright.

"Well, four for four. Something to be proud of in there somewhere, I suppose."

"In America, we call it sexual tension."

"Ruby!" Linda scolded.

The group left the bar to a night sky, the storm over. Streetlamps flickered dazzling displays off the wet cobblestones as if Christmas arrived early. The van sat parked nearby. Andrew supported Ruby the whole way.

"Is your car nearby?" Andrew asked Walter.

"No, my office is close so I walked."

"You mind driving our van? We're a little..." Andrew made a tipping drink motion. "We'll pay for your cab to get back after your life saving measure."

"There is something I need at the house."

"Linda has something she needs you to do in the house, too."

"Ruby, please."

"You'd be saving lives," Andrew said.

Walter took the keys, and they walked to the van. Walter opened the door for Linda. Andrew dumped the quickly fading Ruby into the back and then the guys got in and they drove away. Walter occasionally glanced Linda's way.

"Are you sure I am safe with you?" Linda asked Walter.

"What? Please ignore your friend. My intentions are of the best..."

"No. I mean, because you had an accident."

Walter nodded. "Ah, yes, that. Lesson learned, much more careful now."

An oncoming car flashed its lights. Walter realized the headlights were off. He fumbled to locate them in the unfamiliar vehicle. Andrew leaned in from the middle seat of the van and turned them on. He remained in their orbit, looking for company since Ruby passed out immediately after getting into the vehicle.

"What do you need from the house?" Andrew asked.

"Quite an exciting development, really. Facial recognition software which is linked to a historical database in England. Most of the earliest New England settlers had roots there."

"But private detectives already did DNA testing for Linda and found nothing."

"I gave Walter links on those reports," Linda said.

"It is trickier finding direct relatives through such a process than one might think. Easier to identify pathways, tracing someone's DNA back to Napoleon, for example. This system uses AI to scour an extremely dense database of stored historical paintings and photos. The program has been in development for ages back home. It matches over five hundred points on a person's face. From there, the program matches individuals until a pattern takes shape. It is shockingly effective. With those results, one can more easily use the same DNA tests that have proven elusive to date."

"Why use it now? Why didn't you do it earlier?"

Walter eyed Andrew in the rearview, then looked around as if trying to find someone watching. Andrew did a cursory check himself, while not aware of what to look for.

"Privacy issues. There was talk of the government using it to track the last of the Nazis. More talk of it being used to track terrorists. Some people fear a government overreach. Here is the thing. It is everything one might warn others about related to surveillance and privacy, but in the end, it is simply a tool. Whereas a plumber may use a wrench to fix a leak, a nefarious type might..." Walter mimed a whacking over a head and accidentally hit the horn, startling everyone.

Andrew grinned. "You got access."

"Quite so. My work here is history related, so the university signed off." Walter pulled into their driveway. "I need images for comparison, however, and there is one place that has a veritable treasure trove."

They looked to the house and then roused Ruby. The group left the van and entered the house. Andrew carried Ruby part way. She came to life before entering the home, kicking herself off Andrew's front long enough to jump on his back, piggy style.

Walter stepped right up to the pictures in the hall. "I'll be careful with them, I promise."

"That's the lamest excuse to get back in her house. Just ask her out already," Ruby said, still riding Andrew.

Walter appeared unfazed by the remark, too engrossed in his work, already at the end of the hall and carefully gathering the pictures. The others ascended the stairs. As they reached the second-floor hall, Ruby made an announcement.

"Lin-lin, you know I love you, right? But I think your boyfriend is a geek."

"Walter is not my boyfriend."

"Good, because he's a geek."

"At least yours is a geek. Mine's a drunk, Let's go."

Linda grinned in sympathy as Andrew carried the weight of his relationship down the hall. Linda entered her room and retrieved a cardboard box from her closet. Then she sat on the bed and dialed her cell.

"Hello? I was calling about my friend Heather Parson. I'm calling because it's late and they think she's been sleepwalking and..."

In the hospital's lobby, a night nurse cut Linda off with a smile in her voice. "Don't worry, it's not on my rounds, but it's slow tonight. I'll check in on her myself."

"Thank you so much. And please apologize whoever was in your position earlier in the day. I was there with friends and one of mine was, well, passionate about having her way with hospital policy."

"Ooh, I heard about that one. Do not worry, people behave irrationally when loved ones are facing health struggles. I will gladly check on your friend."

"Thank you."

Linda disconnected, happy for such a friendly conversation. It seemed unnatural for Heather to sleep for so long, but she was likely medicated. Knowing the nurse on duty was concerned and willing to check on Heather put Linda at ease. She got up, grabbed the box, stepped into the hall and into Andrew. The pair collided, their bodies pressed together and remained that way for a moment, a shared comfort with one another. Their eyes met, and they both excused themselves, stepping back.

Andrew threw a thumb over his shoulder. "She is out and getting the snore on."

"That will be me soon enough. I need to check on Walter. What are you doing?" Linda started down the stairs.

"Thought I would clean up."

They arrived at the foyer, where Walter balanced the trove of frames on a small table. Linda handed him the box. Walter packed them while Linda continued her conversation with Andrew.

"Cleanup what?" Linda asked.

"The basement. Heather's mess."

"No, Andrew, I will take care of that."

"Not this time. This kind of mess, I insist. Besides, just the creepiness of the basement is reason enough for me to do it."

"The basement? I could never open that door. May I?" Walter pleaded.

"See, I even have a helper."

Walter took over the mission, showing them where he stored the cleaning supplies. Andrew filled a bucket with steaming soapy water, then donned dishwashing gloves.

"What do I do?" Linda asked.

Andrew pulled a bottle of beer from the fridge, opened it, hustled Linda to the table and sat her down, plopping the brew before her.

"Drink."

"I'm still way too drunk."

"All the better."

The two men descended. Linda sipped away, looking around and feeling alone. The men's footsteps thudded loudly down the stairs.

"What are we washing?" Walter asked once they reached the basement floor.

"A blood trail our friend left when she was sleepwalking."

"Good heavens! Is she alright?"

"She's getting divorced."

Walter tilted his head with curiosity over the strange remark, but forgot about it as something drew his eye. A shaft of moonlight shone through a basement window, lighting one corner of the cellar. Walter approached the area while Andrew scrubbed.

"If you want to impress her, you need to loosen up," Andrew said.

"Excuse me?"

"How she has stayed single this long, I don't know. Fate decided for me, otherwise she and I, well, another time."

Walter ran his hand across the small window, which sat slightly above his head, and faced the side yard. Was the window painted? The moonlight seeped in through a spot where someone had scratched away the paint. Walter wondered why anyone would paint a window. He spoke over his shoulder. "My interest is in this house."

"That I believe. But I also see how you look at her. The thing is Linda is good people. She eventually will wish to settle down with someone stable, but the problem is, as much as she hides it, she is subject to the bad boy tax."

Walter turned from his window examination. "Bad boy tax?"

"Yes. One that most women must pay before they can invest in a stable relationship. She has remained so guarded for so long she needs someone to break through her wall," Andrew continued scrubbing. He lifted the sponge, a soapy red froth, and splashed it in the bucket to squeeze it out.

"One might find a brick wall out of place in such an old home. But Salem was a historic brick making town in the earliest days of colonies. They are even an anagram of sorts, with bricks being produced starting in 1629 while the witch trials occurred in 1692."

Andrew stopped scrubbing and looked at the alien next to him. "See? This is what I am talking about. You have no chance with her if you say things like that. She doesn't love Tom for a reason," he said before completing the sentence as a murmur to himself, "though he appeared fully ready to bang. Shocker."

Walter referred to the earlier part of the conversation. "To date her, I must be a bad boy tax?"

"She pays the tax; you just be a bad boy. Possibly drop the word date. My two cents. What do I know? I'm only one of her best friends."

Walter removed his tie. Andrew noticed, nodded his head.

"There you go."

Walter strode to Andrew and dipped his tie in the bucket. Andrew tried to warn him of the bloody mixture, but Walter was on a mission. He dipped the tie in the water, swirled it around, and then rushed to the window. He wiped the damp tie across the surface, but the window remained dark.

"Pitch black."

"It's dark outside, Walter."

"Yes. I understand. But the moon is here in the corner. See?"

Andrew shrugged, unable to see from a distance. When Andrew turned back to the wall, a fresh round of blood poured down, replacing that which he washed away. Andrew squinted, confused, but chalked it up to the water rivulets cascading down from the wash.

"Someone painted this from the inside. How strange."

Walter followed the narrow shaft of moonlight across the room, where it settled near a crevice in an opposing wall. Following its path, he discovered a crate nestled along a waist-high section of stone foundation. He waved away the inches of grime and reached inside the crate and pulled out the contents.

Wham!

The crate hit the floor. A frightening explosion of noise in the confined space. Andrew fell back, one arm overturning the bucket. He wrestled it back before losing all the liquid to the ground.

"What are you doing?"

Walter leaned into the wall and flipped through the stack of newspaper articles and photos in his hand. Off Andrew's complaint, he glanced at the fallen crate.

"Apologies. The newspaper articles Linda supplied only went back so far. These go further. More tragedy, I'm afraid. There are also more pictures. It was as someone wished me to find them."

Linda yelled down for the two men to hurry. They did, Walter carrying the box with him. Once they crested the stairs, Linda led the men directly to the living room window without saying a word. Walter dropped his box in the foyer on top of the first along the way.

Finally, she spoke as the two men looked out into the night. "Do you see it?"

"Walter's taxi?" Andrew asked, confused.

"I did not order the taxi yet because I didn't know how long you two would be. Why is there a car parked on our road outside?"

"Well, let's ask the driver why." Walter headed for the door.

Linda gasped, trying to stop him, but the man kept going. Andrew nodded, impressed. "Maybe Walter is more of a bad boy than we thought."

"What are you talking about?"

She followed Walter out the open door. Andrew followed along. Walter was quick, that much was for certain. The man was already at the end of the driveway and at the edge of the road. He waved the others down. Linda and Andrew arrived and looked across the street, able to see much better at such a short distance. The car was a state trooper cruiser. The window was down, and Sergeant Taylor waved.

"Good evening, folks," he said.

"The officer was asking about the gentleman who boarded up your home. It appears he is missing," Walter said.

"Missing?" Andrew asked.

"More like unaccounted for," Taylor said. "We have an idea who he may be with, but locating her has also proved difficult."

"We never met the man. We were all gone when he arrived and did the work. I am sorry to hear about that, but why are you here?"

"Curiosity. This was the last place we knew him to be. I was hoping I might find something here, and I did."

"What?" Linda asked, surprised.

"A friend of yours who needs a ride."

"I mentioned we confused him for the taxi. He agreed to give me a lift. I just need to get the boxes."

"Boxes?" Linda asked.

"A discovery in the basement. I will share more later, but it is perfect for what I am trying to do," Walter said.

"And what are you trying to do?" Taylor asked.

"That, I am afraid, is not to be shared with law enforcement," Walter said matter of fact as he rushed back to the house.

Andrew and Linda shared a look, aware of the approved technology. Andrew grinned at Linda over the man's reaction to law enforcement. "See? A bad boy."

"I don't understand," Linda said.

"Neither do I," the officer said. "I sense a conspiracy between these two. I will see if I can break the one on the ride home."

Walter returned and climbed into the backseat. When he realized he could not roll down the window to say goodbye, he simply waved. Linda waved back. The trooper tipped his cap and drove away, eager to grill his passenger. Andrew led Linda back.

High on the ridge behind the house, the dog growled, leaning toward the house. It sniffed wildly and appeared to pick up a scent. It would not be long now.

CHAPTER 15

N URSE FRAN WILLIAMS SAT behind the desk at the
entrance to the hospital on what had proven to be a
slow night. She admitted a drunk who, after losing his car keys,
used a fist to open the window. Never shattered the glass, but
shattered the bones in his hand. Then there was the poor food
poisoning patient for whom a late-night fast-food run turned
into something else. A few calls, of course, always the same
type. People getting their drink on and Googling symptoms
of something long bothering them. The internet was a solid
purveyor of worst-case scenarios, so she needed to talk many
people down from the ledge and urge them to visit their own
doctor during normal business hours.

The food poisoned woman's girlfriend had already picked the
vomit queen up. A doctor suggested an overnight stay and IV
to combat dehydration, but the young lady suggested she could
throw up just as well in the comfort of her own home. They
offered her a garbage bag to use for emergencies on the way home,
along with a cup of ice chips in place of the IV.

A simple garbage bag and ice chips would end up putting
the young couple out for almost a grand unless their insurance
picked it up. Such an expensive bill for minimal treatment, but
someone had to pay for all the uninsured who rolled through the

doors with emergencies of their own. Fran hated that part of her job, hated how what started as a health crisis could so quickly turn into a financial one. She could help with the first part, but was helpless with the second.

She did her best to never dwell on that, because she enjoyed helping people. It gave her great pleasure to receive annual holiday cards from various patients she assisted over the years. One such annual card that always arrived on April third had a special meaning. That was the day she stopped and assisted a woman and her daughter, who had crashed in a snowstorm. Their car was off the road crumpled against a tree, but the woman stood roadside holding her unconscious daughter. Blood dripped from the mother's skull as cars drove past, never slowing.

To see so many people ignore a woman in distress shocked Fran. She never learned whether her own call brought the ambulance or whether those passing by at least did that much. Either way, Fran rode to her own hospital in the back of the ambulance, keeping the mother calm while the paramedics did the work of saving the daughter.

A card arrived from the mother and daughter every year, filled with thanks. Both were doing well, each celebrating life, understanding what almost happened that day. Such a sweet child Darcy was. The youth was seven years old when it happened.

A child giggled down the hall.

Impossible. There were no children accompanying anyone during her shift. It was too late at night for children to be out on their own. A swing door down the hall sounded, flapping open and closed. Unmistakable. Someone was there for certain.

Professionals in her line of work used a term—overnight jitters. It happened to the best of employees. The abundance of silence placed the human body in a meditative state of calm. Introducing sudden noises to the environment could bring with it a sense of dread or fright not normally encountered when one worked a bustling busy day shift.

"A child did not just laugh in the distance," Fran said aloud with a chuckle.

The patter of feet sounded down the hall (from a child?). Then another swing of a door. Fran looked down the hall and noticed lights on. They ran on motion sensors. She had been behind the desk answering calls and working at Sudoku (hey some people still enjoyed it) for over twenty minutes. The corridor should have been dark.

"Hello?"

Fran stepped from behind the desk and moved cautiously down the hall. Silly, she thought. She understood overnight jitters, which meant she should have been able to avoid them, but they settled into her bones, giving her a chill, which made little sense given how she stood in a temperature-controlled wing. Only two of the rooms in the hall had swing doors, the others were all standard single doors.

She moved to the first pair and opened the door slowly. The motion lights jolted to life within the room and a face startled her. It was her own in a mirror. Looking scared as shit, she primped her hair for good measure before moving on, pretending to be nonchalant. She glanced in other rooms along the way, mostly supply rooms, but she had the keys. No one was getting in those without her knowledge, so she paid them short shrift.

Once she reached the second set of double doors, she leaned in. The auto lights did not come on. Disabled. Someone turned the switch off. She leaned further in, reached for the switch, then froze. The moon and stars leached into the room full of medical equipment, casting shadows with a strange mixture of sharp angles and curves. Then there in center room, bathed in moonlight, she saw it.

A body.

Under a sheet resting on a gurney. The morgue was in another wing. Her overnight jitters grew, causing her hand to shake as she reached for the light switch. She flipped it on. Incandescent lights burst to life, almost too bright. Sure enough, a body lay under a sheet.

It sat up (and groaned?). Mike Cook pulled the sheet away and grumbled at her through bed head hair, or more accurately, gurney head hair.

"Jesus Fran. Lights? Come on. Eighteen-hour shift. Can't a doctor rest in peace?"

"You mean intern."

"Semantics. Room for one more here if you'd like to join me."

"Funny how my husband frowns on that."

"Please, I meant non-sexual. Just offering you a nap."

"I'm wide awake, scared half to death, thanks to you. No, I promised to check on a patient. Answer the phones until I get back?"

"Not a chance." The intern pulled the sheet back again.

Fran switched out the lights and left the room.

"Voicemail it is then."

Fran rode the elevator up and got off on the designated floor. *Poor thing, this one*, she thought. Mental issues apparently. Fran entered the room. The patient, Heather, occupied a bisected room with each bed surrounded by a curtain. A lamp across the room remained lit, casting a shadow.

Spotting Heather standing in shadow behind the curtain surprised Fran. Possibly sleepwalking, like her friend on the phone suggested. The nurse approached the curtain carefully, remembering something about not abruptly waking sleepwalkers. Fran did not know why, despite having a medical background. Old wives' tale probably, but she would not take the chance. She stepped gingerly to the curtain and spoke in a soothing, calm voice.

"Heather? Let's get you back to bed."

Fran dragged the curtain slowly open, only to find the woman already in bed, fast asleep. Strange. Fran leaned down to check under the bed, just in case. She swore she saw someone standing and the woman's friend had been insistent on getting in earlier. Nothing. No misguided friend, or anyone. Fran rose only for her hair to tangle in a dangling hand. She yelped and pulled away. The hand dropped back down off the bed. Somehow, the patient remained asleep.

Lifting the hand gingerly, Fran placed the arm back onto the bed. It bothered Fran to think she saw a shadow in the room. But she also naively thought she heard a child earlier. Yep, overnight jitters for real. The patient appeared fine. Fran did her part, she looked in after the woman. Mission accomplished. She closed the curtain and exited.

Had she looked back, she might have seen the shadow of a sinewy child standing alongside Heather's bed. In shadow behind the curtain, the child grabbed Heather's arm. Heather's breath frosted immediately, solid enough to cast its own shadow. The nurse heard a fresh round of giggling as she stepped into the hall, but she refused to turn, chalking it up to the jitters.

CHAPTER 16

R OWS OF TREES TRACKED the progress of the police cruiser driving along a lonely, dark street. The foliage could be hypnotic, were one to stare out at them as Walter did from the backseat. The sergeant kept one eye on the road and one on his backseat guest.

"Must be my personality," Taylor said.

"Pardon?" Walter responded.

"You're a regular chatty Kathy around your friend back there, but since riding with me, bupkis."

Walter finally looked away from the passing foliage. "I won't pretend to understand everything you said, but I assume you are inquiring about my silence."

"Righto."

Their eyes met in the mirror. Taylor did not get a bad vibe from the guy. The man appeared clean, but the house had not. The officer knew because he watched for some time before the homeowner returned. No one seemed to notice his presence when they pulled up in the van. Walter even held the officers gaze under questioning, though Taylor figured it was time to get his eyes back on the road. He looked away from the passenger just as the man finally spoke.

"Chalk it up to previous problems with authority," Walter said.

"Any I should know about?"

"Certainly not."

"And the reference you made earlier. Nothing I should be worried about?"

"Not at all. Offhanded remark, really. Facial recognition. Using it to trace the previous owners of the home."

The trooper scrunched his face. "You don't know who passed it down to her?"

"Her mother, but it is a bit more complicated than that. The transfer is through an LLC and that has various stipulations about who the place goes to next. The best one could describe its bloodline requirements is—jagged."

"LLC?"

Walter nodded. "I have searched domain registries closely, matching the LLC name. All but one were unrelated and transparent. The company name that matched exactly has hidden ownership of the domain. I will continue digging through that mess, but can't even be sure anyone involved in the LLC would have any interest in running a website. My guess is they took the domain off the market to minimize the amount of people who might dig around in their business. Not sure how much time to spend there."

"And DBAs?" Taylor asked.

"Not required of an LLC, but of course, I did a cursory search. Nothing of note. In all of this, I believe the simplest answer, though a gamble, is to focus on Salem. The inherited home suggests someone from her family likely owned it. And given the estimated age of the home or at least portions of it, the family link could extend to the early days of Salem. Because of the dark history behind this town, tremendous amounts of paintings and drawings have captured the faces of people involved. Newspapers at the time even offered sketches of the trials themselves. Match a face to one of them and take it from there. A DNA profile would be easy to run with a name to chase after."

Taylor raised his eyebrows as he looked back at the man in the rearview mirror. "What is it you do around here? Because we sure could use a detective."

Walter smiled and returned to looking out the window. Taylor was long due to go home, his shift technically over, but he did not want his passenger to fall back into silence as he felt they were establishing rapport. If there was information to be had from the man, this was his time to get it. The thick runs of trees gave way to the more scattered greenery of the downtown area. He spotted a vehicle on the side of the road and made a play.

"I will drop you off as promised, wouldn't want you walking far with those boxes, but I am famished. You okay with me stopping at this food truck?"

Walter lit up. "I was trying to get food of my own in a pub earlier when I fortuitously ran into Linda and her companions. They were drunk so I offered to drive them home, before I had a chance to eat."

So, he was a good guy after all, Taylor thought. Not everyone steps up for designated driving. He pushed for an answer.

"That's a yes, then?"

"I am famished. Yes."

The sergeant had already driven past the stop, so hit his bar lights and u-turned back to the food truck. No one in the line bolted, so it seemed the criminal element in town was busy elsewhere. Taylor unlocked the back doors from the front so the man could let himself out. He did not want the man doing the yank the handle routine because it might make him feel trapped. They got out and stepped in line. A young couple ahead of them nodded to the officer, who nodded back. Taylor pointed to the menu board reading, *Taco Tuesday Every Day*.

"These aren't your regular tacos," Taylor said. "You pick the protein, then loosen your belt."

They reached the front and placed their orders. Taylor went for the lobster while Walter found himself intrigued by a fish and chips version. They took their numbers and had a seat. Not all food trucks had seating, but this one did, which was why Taylor chose it. Six-foot plastic banquet tables with flimsy plastic chairs lined the edge of a sidewalk along the truck. A few people ate nearby, but most took theirs to go. The two men fell back into silence as they waited for their order, but the sergeant was okay with that, did not want the man thinking the interrogation was anything other than free flowing conversation. A bit of silence would likely put the man at ease.

"Glorious," Walter said as he took a bite of his breaded fish taco, an opened vinegar packet resting in front of him. "Reminds me of home, with our fish and crisps." He looked at the basket in front of him. "They even put the crisps in newspaper."

"Well, no one reads papers anymore. We should use them for something. We call them fries. Food trucks are often the best food."

"Noted," Walter said, taking another bite.

Taylor lifted one of his. "You are the historian. Do you know about lobster?"

"Beyond being a delicacy and obscenely expensive? No."

"Our neighbors in Maine are famous for it, though we have our own too. Once lobsters were so abundant that they served it daily to prisoners. Inmates revolted in the seventeenth century, fighting to limit the amount of lobster on the menu. They considered it cruel and unusual punishment. Lobster. Can you imagine? Guess they prefer bologna sandwiches."

"Remarkable. I must investigate that. Societal norms at different points of history fascinate me. I imagine now many request it as a last meal. Yet they once considered it cruel? Perhaps societal dietary habits created stomach biomes unable to digest such food adequately during that era."

"Touché," Taylor said.

"Pardon?"

"Now I do not understand what you are talking about."

Walter smiled and finished his meal. Taylor did the same. His shoulder mic squawked a few times, with minor issues around town. Nothing significant. His officers would handle it all. Until an unfortunate call came through.

"Sergeant Taylor? Trooper Lambert is on a 10-34 waiting backup," a voice over the walkie responded.

"Have him stand down. I am on my way."

Taylor cursed internally. He was about to lose the opportunity to question a man warming to him. But one of his troopers discovered an open window where there should not be one and he was damn well sure not going to leave an officer to investigate the area alone. The sergeant rose and Walter followed suit. Taylor took a swing.

"Look, I was hoping to continue our conversation. Would you be willing to come by the station sometime to answer a few more questions?"

"No," Walter replied.

Taylor deflated. Swing and a miss. Well, he tried. Time to get out on the call. He headed for the cruiser and noticed his passenger was not at his side. Taylor looked back.

"But I will be more than happy to talk to you over tacos on a night of your choosing."

Taylor lit up. He knew he liked the guy. Strange egg, but good people. "That's wicked nice of you. I can drop you off at your car, but I need to get a run on."

"You go. You got me most of the way. I will gladly walk from here to work off the tacos."

On that skinny frame? Walter thought, but did not say. He opened the driver's door, then the passenger. "I'll tell you more when we reconnect, but I have some concerns about the Hunt place."

"Which is why you were sitting on the home," Walter said as he grabbed his crate from the backseat.

Taylor nodded. No sense hiding it. The man was sharp and picked it up. Walter knew what he was up to and was still willing to meet, which meant he likely had little to hide. At minimum, the historian was honest.

"Guilty. Just putting it out there. I am getting a weird vibe, and I have questions about previous occupants. I will pick up all that later with you. But the bigger vibe I get. You're sweet on her? This new resident?"

Walter stuttered, at a rare loss for words. After collecting himself, he simply pushed his glasses further up his face and supplied a non-answer. "I find Ms. Hunt most lovely."

Taylor nodded, slid into his seat, and pointed at his ears to warn Walter of the impending siren. Taylor hit the siren and lights then sped off. Once the vehicle departed, Walter turned to get his bearings.

"Quite lovely indeed," he said and started walking toward his office, whistling all the while.

THE DOG SAT ON its haunches, head hanging low, growling so deep the sound could have emanated from a rumbling earth rather than the beast. Its eyes burned red and focused on the house below, specifically the window where Linda stripped her clothes. Once Linda appeared fully nude in shadow through the curtains, the dog rose and trotted toward the house building speed as it went. As it neared the yard, it leaped. Shadows swallowed it whole before it hit the ground.

Linda stood naked in her darkened room. A flickering glow cascaded out into the bedroom from the bathroom. Linda grabbed her unfinished beer and followed the glow to the tub. Once there, she turned off the running water. Steam rose from the bath, warm, inviting. Candles placed strategically around the small room added a pleasant scent above that of her lavender bath bomb.

She placed her beer on a caddy holding the shampoo bottle and lifted a leg to slip into the water. Linda nearly slipped when her phone rang, startling her. She rushed back into the bedroom to the vanity. The phone danced across its surface. She answered.

"Hello? Oh, no, it is not too late. I would have let it go to voicemail if I was sleeping. Heather is fine? Thank you so much for checking on her. I cannot tell you the peace of mind that brings. Yes, thank you. You have a good night as well."

Linda disconnected and breathed deep. One less thing to worry about. Heather was fine. Linda returned to the bathroom, climbed in, and reached for her beer. She sipped while luxuriating in the bubbly water. After a sip, she dangled the bottle, the bottom of which came to rest against one of her breasts. She danced the glass tenderly along the contour of her curves, breathing, more of the pleasant scent, relaxing enough for her mind to wander to other thoughts.

Sliding the bottle lower, she traced the cool glass against skin even while her body warmed. She brought it back up, finished it off, and set it aside before using a hand to trace a path down her body. She did her best to bury any desires to share the candlelit space with someone. Her hand gently slid past her stomach. With a splash, she raised the hand before reaching a point of no return. She gripped both sides of the tub to keep from further stoking any flames, then closed her eyes and rested.

Andrew returned to the basement soon after Walter had departed. He was almost finished cleaning when he heard it. A boom, thunderous. And close. He set his cleaning supplies down and searched the room. Then he felt it. His hair lifted, as if someone brushed past him quickly. Then the smell hit.

Rain. He'd always been able to smell it in the air, always knew it was on its way. Some people had the gift of sensing it. He was one. His ability to sniff out rain's onset was, however, something he could only notice while outside. Smelling it in the basement meant there was a serious draft at play. It was an old building that likely needed plenty of work. Finding the source could help Linda save lots of money on heating the place in the winter.

He lifted his hand to his head to trace the breeze that lifted his hair. And there it was. Subtle but present. He followed the air across the room until arriving at a bulkhead atop a set of steps leading to the backyard. Only one of the two doors was visible. A gap filled the balance of the triangular structure. A door was open.

That was better than a crack in a foundation. Just close a door. Simple. Problem solved. He wondered how it came to be open. And when? If it had been open for any length of time, there should have been puddles on the floor. The steps leading inside were dry so far. That would change soon if he did not act. Already sprinkles flittered in through the opening, landing on his hands and face. Andrew climbed and stepped outside.

A heavy chain dangled from the handle of the closed door with an open lock nearby. Someone had to have opened it at some point, but he did not know if Linda even had a key. Probably Walter. The ever-present guy was all over the house. But Walter mentioned never having gone into the basement. If he did not open the lock, then who?

The whipping wind blew away Andrew's train of thought. He did not need his sense of smell to know a storm was brewing. The wind whipped violently and the clouds in the sky remained in motion, dashing past the moon high above. A flash of movement caught his eye. He squinted, noticing the swing. Strange. Of course, it would move under the current winds, but it surprised Andrew how it maintained a trajectory as if under control of a rider.

Something snapped in the other direction, followed by a growl. Monstrous, low snarling. Andrew loved the outdoors but lacked knowledge of local wildlife, so could not determine what might be out there. Lightning struck, as the rain fell, the latest storm in the cycle since they arrived. Thunderous rumbling hindered his ability to isolate whatever had him in its sights. He understood the night belonged to wildlife. How wild remained the question.

Andrew took one last look before retreating into the basement. He pulled the bulkhead closed and secured it from the inside with an old school wood piece that turned on a screw. He stepped back and looked for signs of the wind's ability to blow it open. It shuddered but held firm.

Then he shuddered. The growl from earlier sounded behind him. He turned around slowly. A large black dog (wolf?) snarled at him, drool dripping from large, bared canines. Its eyes appeared to blaze red, which Andrew took as a trick of the limited light. He raised his hands.

"Calm down, boy. I'm not here to hurt you. Good doggy."

The bulkhead suddenly exploded open with a tremendous roar. Wind and rain gusted into the basement. Andrew dashed for the fortuitous avenue of escape with the dog barking on his tail. Andrew made it up two steps before slipping on the suddenly slick surface. One foot flew out from underneath him, causing him to tumble face first, teeth clacking. He grunted, stunned, but turned in time to spot the beast in mid-leap. Then his world went black.

Linda startled awake from a light sleep in the tub. She scrambled to grab her terry-cloth robe, putting it on without stopping for a dry. A thunderous boom sounded somewhere below. Lightning danced outside her window and each flash came accompanied with its own thunder bumper. The explosive noise seemed separate from the storm.

She already found the home to have a unique voice, one with its own odd settling symphonies. *Christ, a house as old as this and it's still not settled?* Linda thought, the first night. Whatever sounded downstairs, she would file it in her home ownership discomfort menagerie. She raced for her bedroom door and stopped short of opening it.

Thump, kerthump. Strange footsteps ascended the stairs, heavy footfalls, lazy. Linda froze, listening. Thump, kerthump. The footsteps stopped at the top of the stairs, replaced by a strange wheezing. She feared opening the door.

The footsteps started again, still dragging. A thump sounded as something collided with a wall just outside her door. Wheezing again filled the space left behind by the halted footfalls. It was her house, and she refused to be cowed. Linda cracked the door for a peek. She furrowed her brow in confusion at the sight of someone leaned into the wall.

"Andrew?"

He turned, and she gasped. Blood coated his nose and tee. "I fought the steps, and the steps won," he said, tittering drunkenly.

"Oh my God, you're still drunk."

Andrew cringed at the word she spoke, but he quickly recovered, falling into the charm. "Guilty."

"Come in, I have a drawn bath. Let me fix you up."

She helped him to the bathroom and sat him on the edge of the tub. She ran a fresh stream of hot water to soak a washcloth.

Leaning in while doing so caused her robe to fall partially open. Andrew gazed at the view. She noticed and cinched the top tighter.

"What happened? There was such a loud noise." She placed the damp cloth against his nose, wiping the surface stains.

"I was cleaning, well this," he gestured to his own blood, speaking in between her swipes at his nose. "While I finished scrubbing the basement wall, the storm ripped open your bulkhead. The rain soaked the stairs, so when I attempted to close it, I fell on my face."

"Is that all?"

"Is that all? I could do a repeat, work on breaking a limb."

She laughed. His nose looked okay with the blood cleaned off. Realizing their proximity, she tried to hand him the cloth. He refused it.

"I only meant it was so loud I expected it to be more than that. It woke me up from my bath. You look good. Do you feel okay?"

"A little more water?"

She ran water to soak it again. Blood mixed with the water. She decided her bath time was officially over.

"Guess I should take this off." Andrew stripped his tee off, balling it and setting it aside.

His torso appeared bigger than before, muscles taught, tight, abs prominent. He watched Linda again as she soaked the cloth, creating the same gap in the robe. Linda rose and gasped involuntarily at his partial nakedness.

She handed him the cloth and stepped back. "Well, if you're okay, you should probably go."

"Is that what you want?"

He rose before her, growing visibly hard in his jeans. He did not hide it, even moved closer. Linda froze. Her robe hung low in the front. She did not try cinching it. She smiled awkwardly to laugh off the advance.

"You're drunk, can't even handle stairs. I'm drunk too."

"The alcohol has nothing to do with how much I want you. How long I've wanted you. It's easy. Just tell me to leave."

He reached a hand into her bathrobe. Linda closed her eyes at the electric and warm touch. She moaned as his hand found a breast. She opened her eyes, meeting his gaze. Her lips trembled on the verge of asking him to exit, but she found herself rooted in place, her breath quickening.

Andrew moved the hand to focus on her nipple, and her breath hitched. He leaned in, breathing heavily along her neck, whispering in her ear. "You only have to ask me to leave."

"We shouldn't," she offered half-heartedly.

Andrew answered by kissing her neck. Linda groaned in building pleasure. He lowered his hand to pull the tie open at her waist. The robe opened, exposing her body. He reached a hand lower still.

She groaned and fell forward. As she did, his mouth found hers. She moaned into the kiss as he probed with his fingers. She finally reached for his crotch, rubbing through his jeans, tugging at them, unzipping. They fell away easily. His trim waist released the denim the moment she tugged the zipper down, falling to the floor, leaving her to focus on touching him through his Calvin's.

They kissed and pressed together, groping frantically after years of foreplay. He slid her robe off altogether, then tore her panties off before lifting her nude body back into the bedroom. He stripped his own underwear and leaped atop her. They kissed again and rather than admit the mistake, Linda only moaned his name in between kisses.

He broke from the kiss and worked his way down her body, kissing her neck before moving on to her breasts. Soon he moved lower still. Linda cried out from a need too long denied. She gripped his hair as he explored her with his tongue. She cried out as lightning flashed and rain pelted the windows. With her eyes closed in passion, she failed to notice him glance up from his ministrations with blood-red eyes.

She continued to climax as he quickly rose above her and slid inside her. She moaned with renewed pleasure as he thrust wildly, animalistic. Her eyes still closed, she gripped him across his back, pulling him tighter even as his eyes grew deeper red. She cried out his name, but the only answer she received in return was thunder from the storm.

They moved in synchronicity. She met his thrusts, and the two continued with no sign of stopping. Too hungry for too long. Outside, the storm raged.

CHAPTER 17

A N IMAGE OF LINDA took up half the screen on Walter's largest monitor, while the other half remained black. Walter looked at the woman and inadvertently smiled. The smile was short-lived, slipping away into a yawn. Fatigue set in after a long night of digitizing the articles and pictures from Linda's residence. In all his years searching for artifacts, the box in the basement was the first time something almost literally fell into his lap. While he was grateful, researching the history of the home was only part of his job.

There were inspections throughout the town that still needed to be done, and articles to write for historical journals based on his time in Salem. Thankfully, Linda's residence was officially part of his duties, so he was not technically slacking on his job. The town expected him to determine the history of the home and its historical significance. Where lines blurred was in the exact job description, which meant he research the property, not the current owner's family history.

Walter hoped the dual investigations would converge and give him cover for why he proceeded in the fashion he did. Otherwise, at some point, they would discover his use of state and government (of Britain) resources to assist an unauthorized client. The sergeant pinpointed Walter's infatuation, and the two had barely interacted. His superiors would likely catch on much quicker. Walter decided on discretion for all things Linda. That was why he worked after hours while most of the world slept.

He wished he could sleep. Once he started the program, he could finally nap. First, he needed the files. Walter had arranged a small light box near the computer. One by one, he placed the articles and pictures inside the light box and snapped a picture from a mounted digital camera. The camera snapped images in high definition. Once he catalogued everything, there would be no need to handle the raw materials again. Digitization ensured historians could study materials well into the future without degrading source material any more than was necessary.

Removing pictures from the frames was part of the task, and that alone bore some fruit. A sticker on one frame insert showed a production code from the sixties while also naming the place of purchase. Woolworth's. Walter never heard of it, but he typed notes in a laptop as he went, part of the cataloging process.

The pictures were almost complete, and he took a moment to sip some tea before carefully packaging the whole thing back up and placing it in the crate. Next up was the plethora of newspaper articles, the theme of which intrigued him. It was difficult to say whether the articles had any relation to Linda or her home. True crime podcasts and TV shows were all the rage in both Britain and the US. There was every chance the articles were nothing more than a hobby of an individual from a time before the internet.

Only way to be certain was to lump them into the mix that he planned to run through the program. He changed the camera's memory chip. The plan was to maintain a separate file for the articles themselves. He was going to feed the images into a program that would crop them to the exact size he wanted.

Walter planned to study the articles a later date to see if there were connections between the people involved in the brutal slayings and accidents. The way someone cut the stories out sadly excised many of the dates and names of the newspapers, which would make it harder to connect dots. He read some as he placed them in the light box. One reported on a man drowning in less than a foot of water in a tub. Another was more dastardly, and intriguing. The headline read, *Woman Beheaded in Boston Hotel Room*. A caption under the image of the woman in her pre-headed days mentioned *Foul Play Suspected*.

"Understated," Walter blurted out.

It was time to stop reading and start scanning or he would be all night. He heard of people burning up time on TikTok and planned to study that app someday for its cultural implications but had avoided it so far for the same reason as the articles. Too much input.

Walter loaded one of a grim old woman. He noted the resemblance to Linda despite the photo's age. A yellowed silver black picture, before even modern day black and white.

He longed for an intern as it would make things go much faster. It occurred to him to follow up with the university soon. Walter started the program with what he already had on file. He would continue to work on the newspaper pictures in the meantime. After inserting a flash drive, the computer went to work sucking up the data.

Contained on the initial drive were images collected from the historical society. The data set included thousands of images dating back to the earliest days of the settlements, some prior to the trials. Images comprised multiple formats, whether oil, pen and ink, or pictures of sculptures. The face tracker did not discriminate between photographs and other mediums.

Even caricatures could match an individual if enough facial recognition points matched. There were multiple drives to load from the historical society, but it took mere moments to load each. Once finished, he inserted the memory card from the light box camera to a twin camera linked to the computer to feed that data in as well.

The second half of the screen displayed an image of a judge presiding over the witch trials, a high-def version of an image in a historical book. Walter hit some keys, and the images on the screen flashed by at a furious pace. They were not yet attempting matches, but were feeding into the master database to form a recognition set. While he waited for the images to populate in the program, he turned back to continue scanning articles.

As he turned away, the flashing images alongside Linda's stationary picture formed an image within the blurred data stream. An outline took shape within the morass of speeding images. A face of a child formed, its mouth opening wide.

A scream filled the room.

Steam from the teakettle. Walter turned toward it, never noticing the image within the images. The hidden image grew larger, as if the child were attempting to smash through the screen from the other side. The tea kettle continued screaming.

"I hear you," Walter said, and removed it from the heat source.

With practiced efficiency, he brewed a cup. Once finished, he returned and continued scanning articles, never glancing at the face which remained trapped inside but now watched him intently. With every article, Walter took time to add the names of victims into his notes. Reporters listed many victims as unknown male, or unknown female. He wondered how far back Linda's family began hiding their identity. One thing to hide a single generation, another to conceal multiple generations.

A child giggled behind him. He turned to the large monitor as the girl's image melted into the blurred motion. Walter rose and walked beyond the facial recognition setup, where he turned on the lights in the reading room adjacent.

"Hello?"

Nothing there. He turned away, and a thump echoed through the room. He leaped in fright, though quickly settled, noticing a volume had fallen to the floor from a bookshelf. Noticing the overhead fan turning, he pulled the chain to stop it. Walter found it curious how the slight breeze dislodged a book, but the evidence was on the floor. Walter picked up the book resting open on a page about the witch trials. A little girl pointed at someone on the street. The accused appeared terrified.

He carried the book back with him and set it alongside where he worked, never once glancing at the flashing images which formed another child's face. Despite the frantic movement on the screen, the image formed into one matching the child in the book. With one major difference. The one on-screen displayed an upturned cross on her forehead.

Walter went back to work cataloging tragic tales of the past.

CHAPTER 18

L INDA STRETCHED AWAKE, A smile of satisfaction spreading across her face until she remembered what had occurred during the night. She spun and noticed the space next to her empty, nothing but a tangle of sheets strewn halfway across the bed and onto the floor. Only a section of a comforter covered her. Enough destructive evidence to prove it all happened. Not to mention her nudity. She was a nightgown sleeper.

Not bothering to dress, she rose and made the bed, stopping midway to smell the sheets. His scent lingered. She fluffed out each piece of bedding as if hiding evidence. *Nothing to see here. Move along folks*, she thought. Except there had been plenty to see. So much. Blood rushed to her face as she thought of his abs, his ass, his face pressed into her neck.

It was wrong. What had she done?

Once she completed the bed, Linda sat on it and buried her head in her hands. Memories of their lovemaking filled her mind. It was what she wanted from Andrew for so long. She had denied it through years of friendship, but when the opportunity finally presented itself, she gave in to the temptation. Boy, did she give in.

Yet Andrew was not available. Linda had partaken in forbidden fruit. Despite growing up in a religious setting,

Linda considered herself progressive and not overtly spiritual. Something about a never-ending group of children at the orphanage receiving religious instruction but never parental, left her filled with doubt. Why did the very ones who prayed the most always end up alone?

There were a million reasons to doubt her faith. Her own isolation until finally finding her way as an adult. Her inability to move on from the very place she lived in and cursed at a as a child. Yet, no matter where she landed on the religious spectrum—wrong was wrong. She crossed a line with her actions.

Linda squeezed her eyes tighter, trying not to think of Ruby. Linda had been so foolish. If it were simply a need, Walter had presented himself. He was a package of all sorts. Kind, check. Handsome, check. Scholarly, check. Yet Andrew was her temptation, Andrew was her fantasy, and the man failed to disappoint. She hungered for him even now, resting on the same bed they spent hours in, discovering one another in ways she never expected from him.

Unlikely as it was, she had let go of everything when she slept with Andrew. Nervousness over her new place, sadness over her mother's death, anger at her friends' breakup. Everything went away when he touched her. Nothing needed to be in their proper places. All that mattered for a short time (well, not too short) was him and her. But all that could not change one damning fact. It. Was. Wrong.

She leaped from the bed, trying to put distance to the memory, trying to put things back in the correct place now that she was thinking clearly. A mistake. A one off. An error. They loved one another, sure. But wires crossed, they got mixed up was all. Andrew and Ruby were a thing. Not Andrew and...

Linda refused to think her own name, refused to turn the pairing of their names into a thing. If she said it out loud or thought it too clearly, it would make it all real. She was drunk.

Andrew was drunk. Things happened. It was time to move on. She needed to move on, but it would require her getting her mind off of the events.

Her vanity.

She moved to it, lifted the key that dangled from the mirror's frame, and placed it over her neck. Then she leaned palms down onto the desk and investigated the reflective glass, studying herself, looking for changes, anything different. A glow, perhaps? She considered anything she might notice would result from faulty attribution. How long had it been since she studied herself in a mirror? The last time she primped for a date? Cared how she looked to others?

This was a world of uncharted waters. Where it might go, she could not fathom, and the idea of cheating filled her with guilt. Yet the night itself had been glorious, filling a need she understood well but had long since buried as unattainable or hardly worth the effort to pursue. How her life had changed in such a short time. And changed for someone else as well.

Ruby.

Linda dropped into the chair, finally feeling the weight of the guilt. Heather was also Linda's friend for sure, but there was an age difference. Heather being married also kept some intimacy at bay. It was hard to talk about certain things when Tom was always around. But Ruby was one of Linda's earliest friends at the school, a firecracker who said and did all the things Linda never could.

Except Linda did, cheating with her best friend's man. Where did this new development fit into her life? It was messy at the very least, and Linda did not know how to clean up something like that. In the face of such uncertainty, she would normally turn to one of two people for advice. Andrew or Ruby.

She considered past advice from Ruby. "Would it feel good? Then do it," Ruby often said to Linda, regardless of the situation. But wouldn't this be different? Not even Ruby would suggest

Linda cheat on someone's boyfriend. The glow from the night before faded as reality set in.

Linda needed advice, needed to strategize how to proceed. There was always a bond between the two, an attraction. Linda wanted to be with Andrew since they met, but circumstances went another way. Maybe what they did the night before was inevitable and perhaps better now than after marriage.

That was the answer. It was a mistake, one that could not happen again, but there was more to consider. Stay silent or come clean? Ruby would understand, might even find some relief that the two got it out of the way. Had they? Were Andrew to show up at her door again, Linda could not guarantee she would find the strength to stand firm against another round.

If he still had it in him. They went all night; she had never made love to anyone for so long. They were both surprised by the hour when finished, and Andrew seemed to fall into a fog then, likely emerging from drunkenness to reality. Alcohol. That was it. That was their excuse if they confessed to Ruby. Linda needed Andrew. If not in the same way, then as the friend, the sounding board, the support to get through the colossal error the two made.

A crash. The kitchen. She had grown to know the house enough to isolate the locations, if not the reasons behind many odd noises. This sound was new and loud. She slipped on sweats and descended the stairs two at a time.

When Linda reached the kitchen, she found Andrew carrying Ruby piggyback. He leaned down to allow Ruby to collect a set of three metal mixing bowls which had crashed to the floor. Ruby raised the last one in victory, and Andrew spun her around so she could place them back on the counter.

That was when they noticed her. The couple carried on in lighthearted fashion, Andrew appearing as if nothing happened. Ruby spread her arms to recognize her friend and almost fell off her man, so grabbed his chest again.

"The dead have woken," Ruby said.

"Coffee for the lady, wench," Andrew announced and spun to place Ruby within reach of the coffee maker.

"Why is she the lady and I'm the wench?" Ruby poured a cup, then Andrew spun her back around for delivery.

Ruby noticed the cold shoulder emanating from her friend. "What's wrong Lin?"

"Is something wrong?" Andrew asked.

Ruby leaped off Andrew's back without spilling a drop from the cup. After setting it aside, Ruby approached her friend.

"Oh God, I was drunk last night. Did I do something beyond the normally offensive? I flashed my boobs again, didn't I?"

"YOU didn't do anything, Ruby," Linda replied, shooting a frigid glance at Andrew.

Andrew shook it off, oblivious. "Good timing with you waking up. We're going to go visit Heather. Do you want to get dressed or something? No offense, but you look like hell."

Linda winced, pained at the slam. Especially after the night prior. Ruby elbowed Andrew, then handed off the cup, placing it in Linda's shaky hands. Linda sipped.

"He didn't mean it like that. It's just that you look like you were up all night. Did you sleep okay?"

"I was up all night." Again, a look at Andrew, who remained seemingly oblivious.

"If it was worrying about Heather, then come with us. We will not rest this time until we see our friend. Check in station nurses be damned!"

"I'm not worried about Heather!" Linda shouted, startling her guests and herself. She pulled it back, fighting the rising anger at a man already pretending nothing ever happened. "Sorry. I am worried, but that's not it. It is better if I am alone for a bit. Think I'll take a run. I'm going for a run."

"You? A run? Since when?" Ruby asked.

"Since last night. A lot changed since last night." Linda dropped the coffee on the counter and raced up the stairs.

Andrew stopped Ruby from following her friend, suggesting she needed time alone. They cleaned up the place while Ruby grumbled about now having to worry about all her friends. With the place cleaned, they departed the house and drove away in the van.

H EATHER AWOKE WITH A start. And a shiver. *So cold*, she thought. The curtains designed to block light to allow patients to sleep uninterrupted did their work, but along the edges of the fabric sunlight showed. A sunny day. Time passed. There was a storm last she knew. If the sun had returned, how long had she slept? Heather could not recall the reason they admitted her to the hospital, but she remembered vaguely talking to a doctor and a nurse at some point. Then she remembered.

Exhaustion. Heather heard the term plenty, especially regarding musicians and rock stars who suddenly called off concerts or appearances. Prior to her blacking out only to wake up in a medical facility, she always assumed exhaustion a code for drug use. She herself never used them, well mostly never did, so exhaustion it was.

Nightmares fueled her sleep. That much she remembered, waking groggily many a time to the most horrific images. The things she witnessed in her mind were unlike any of the normal nightmares she occasionally suffered from. In her past, she dreamt about failing tests, appearing nude in strange places with people she did not know.

And then the nightmares about Tom. Not that something bad happened to him, but that the couple remained married but silent, bored, uninspired by one another. She knew they had problems for a long time. Like her nightmares visiting the waking world, Heather found herself increasingly bored in their marriage and she did not see change coming, especially since Tom thrived in the same environment that so unsettled her. To Heather, their life was becoming a nightmare of routine, while Tom lived the same as his dream.

That was all Tom ever seemed to want. Consistency. The same thing every day. But for Heather, she remembered growing up in an environment far different from that of California. In the South, families got together on Sundays after church with food and drink and the all-important word, fun. There were so many characters in her hometown. Not just relatives, but the locals. People would come and go whenever her parents hosted their weekend parties that ran long into the night. The grills would go all day and night and booze flowed eternally. Adults looked the other way when younger ones occasionally sipped a stray drink. The adults were often too busy laughing and dancing to even notice what all the kids were doing.

Life was a celebration. Or used to be. Somewhere it became so structured and uneventful. She had her shows and Tom had his. The couch at home was kind enough to cement grooves for their asses designed for each to drop into the exact same spots every night. No memory foam needed, repetition altered the furniture's surface. That was her waking nightmare, monotony.

But now, as she lay in the hospital bed, she shook her head, trying to rid herself of the lingering horrific images she experienced. Heather wanted change in her life, so perhaps irony visited her by inducing awful nighttime visions because of the unfamiliar environment. There were children involved in her dreams, that much she remembered from the dreadful dreams, but the memories vanished the moment she opened her eyes.

Children made sense as a dream manifestation. She wanted them, Tom did not. Argue over it, makeup, repeat. Hospital staff informed Heather that friends visited while she slept. When Heather first woke in the hospital, it freaked her out. A nurse informed her that her friends were worried but had gone home because the hospital only allowed family to visit patients in her condition. But what about Tom? His absence surprised her. Under normal circumstances, he would have sat at her bedside, awaiting her return to consciousness. The lone visitor chair in the room remained empty and free of any signs of use.

He was gone. Plain and simple. They discussed their relationship ad nauseam. They were two different people who failed to grow together. As time wore on, they brought out the worst in each other. They both fed the relationship with a toxin born of apathy and neglect. Heather hoped one last vacation would save things, but all the driving only made things worse. Far worse. They decided during the trip that they would divorce, but argued over when best to tell their friends. Heather had to believe it contributed to her exhaustion that landed her in a hospital bed instead of a hot tub for vacation.

A soft thud sounded across the room.

That was what initially woke her. When fluttering between the dream and waking worlds, Heather saw in her mind's eye a horrific pallid child playing the worst of games on her. She attributed the initial sound to a nightmare but had since had enough time to wake fully. What could be responsible?

Thud.

Someone at the door? Unlike all the other times she briefly woke, Linda could now see the room's door from her bed. Previously, a shower curtain style rod circling her bed had divided her from the balance of the room via a privacy curtain. Now someone had drawn the curtain open, allowing her to see the door in the distance. The door had a small wire mesh lined window at face height, but the angle was such she could not see through the glass from where she lay.

The thudding came from behind the door, like a hand slapping against it, not with fury but with a drunken lethargy. The slapped palm of an energy depleted individual, perhaps one leaning into the door and seeking entry might produce. Someone medicated? They were in a hospital.

"Hello? Are you okay? Do you have the right room?"

Heather rose from the bed on shaky legs, unaccustomed to extended rest. The thudding continued. Heather crossed the room and pressed her face to the glass. Nothing. She turned her head as far to either side as she could. Knowing it to be clear, she attempted to open the door, but it would not budge.

There appeared to be no lock, so she pulled harder. Heather yanked with such force that when the door failed to open, she fell against it. Her face rested near the window when suddenly someone looked through from the opposite side! A woman's jaundiced eyes stood out against the greyish-blue skin of her face. When the woman spotted Heather, she broke out into a black toothed grin.

Heather scrambled away as the glass exploded into the room. An arm shot through, making quick work of the underlying wire mesh. A hand grabbed Heather's hair as she attempted to flee. Heather screamed at the pressure on her skull, then cried out further when the attacker forcefully yanked Heather back against the door.

A second hand broke through and pawed at her face, then another, grabbing hold of hair, torso, arms, breasts. One pressed tightly against her mouth, muffling her screams. Heather fought back, pushing at the cold dead arms. She finally loosened their grip enough to scramble away. She fell to her knees, which cracked loudly against the hard surface of the floor. Grimacing in pain, Heather relied on adrenaline to keep moving. She grabbed the metal bed frame for support, but a frigid cold like an electric shock shot through her body.

Her breath crystalized. She yanked her hands free. They were red and damp from melting frost. She clenched them and turned back, checking on her pursuer. (Pursuers?) The window appeared intact. No face or limbs in sight.

CHAPTER 19

F RAN FINISHED HER SUDOKU and set it aside, mission complete. Some teens had arrived the night prior, having entered the woods searching for witches after ingesting a certain amount of psychedelics before doing so. One in their group did not fare so well, leading the larger group to drop the young man off before vanishing into the night. There was also a motorist who damn near sliced his palm to the bone while trying to change his own tire.

What may have felt busy overnight with skeleton crew staffing paled compared to the early morning activity flooding the hospital. For each staff member that arrived for the day, there was at least one new patient. Daylight was not a disinfectant (as the saying went) where hospitals were concerned. Despite all the late-night drunk shenanigans that occurred in any small town, daylight brought out the big guns where patients were concerned. The halls were brimming with activity, the main waiting room already half full.

Her coworker Charles finally arrived and took over the phones, so Fran packed her stuff, ready to vamoose and get some sleep before the next overnight. She had checked in on the young woman upstairs throughout the night. The woman slept the whole time, despite some occasional murmurs in her sleep. Nothing Fran paid attention to.

Fran was about to exit when she spotted the young woman. Heather fast-walked in bare feet, wearing nothing but the hospital gown, carrying her clothes in a wad. The nurse intercepted, grabbing Heather by the shoulders.

"What are you doing out of bed?" Fran asked.

Heather pulled away. "I need to go. You can't make me stay."

The nurse walked backward, tracking Heather's steps. "Fine. But at least let a doctor look at you."

Fran gripped a shoulder again, but Heather shook her off violently, almost causing a tumble. Heather darted out the door past an old man who shouted in protest over the near collision. Fran returned to the check in station and recovered Linda's number from the trash. She uncrumpled the Post It note and dialed the desk phone. The call went to voicemail. Fran left a detailed message relaying worry about the state of her friend. After logging the interaction, Fran finally left for the day.

LINDA STOOD IN LINE at the pharmacy. After her friends left, she set out on foot. Never much of a runner, Linda felt the need to do something, anything, to shake off her disappointment. For that was what it was more than anger. Andrew had always been a lifeline for her, a moor to a shore of stability.

The two of them had crossed a line, that was certain. The repercussions related to her friendship with Ruby might prove grave, yet a part of her expected Andrew to have an answer on how to navigate the uncertain waters. What she never expected was for him to act as if nothing had happened.

The two shared longing looks many times in the past, had danced with crossing lines before. They knew better all those times in the past. But their defenses mutually collapsed last night, so they... What? Slept together, sure. It was as exciting and satisfying as she dreamed it might be. Perhaps that was why the disappointment struck so hard.

The Andrew she knew from before would have pulled her aside. Thanked her for the passion, maybe joke about the two of them surviving such an endeavor. Bottom line, he would have put her at ease before suggesting they figure it out later, once alone, where they could talk. The new Andrew, the one who, after he got what he wanted from her, pretended nothing ever happened.

So, she ran. It helped to be out in the fresh air after a rain. As she ran, a destination came to mind. There was a stop she needed to make just to be safe, especially given the recent response from Andrew. She grabbed what she needed and stood in line when her phone rang.

"Are you going to answer that?" the pharmacy cashier asked Linda.

Linda wore an oversized hoody sweatshirt over yoga pants, the only things approximating running clothes she brought with her. She stuffed the phone into one of the large pockets and shook her head.

"No."

"Let one slip by, did you?" the cashier asked, ringing the Plan B product.

Linda added a bottle of water to the purchase, hoping to draw attention away from the first item. The effort failed. She looked around the store, self-conscious.

The cashier laughed it off. "An eighty-year-old woman bought one recently. Eighty. Can you believe it?" The young cashier scanned it several times, trying to get the barcode to work. When it did not, she started typing the numbers in one by one. "I didn't want to get into a biology discussion with her. Did want to ask how old the guy was, though. Lady might be a cougar. What's older than a cougar?"

"Not sure. Do you mind?"

Linda gestured to the cashier, who soured and placed the item in its own paper bag, lifting it for show. Then the cashier scanned the water. Despite the wait, Linda had forgotten to prep her wallet and searched the unfamiliar clothes for where she had placed it. She brought her cellphone back out.

"Can I pay with this?"

"Sure. Want a bag for this?" Linda shook her head. The cashier set the water bottle in front of her. "You know I bought this once, and the little one still showed up nine months later. What are you gonna do? Hopefully, your guy at least puts a ring on it."

Linda instinctively dropped her ring finger hand from view. With the other, she raised her phone and held it over the credit reader at the counter. It beeped on odd noise.

"Do it again. Haven't seen you around BTW (she spoke the letters of the acronym). You live around here?"

"I inherited the place on Gallows Way. Is it working now?"

"Go. Take your things and go."

Linda looked up, confused at the sudden turn in the all too friendly clerk. The woman's face burned red (had she stepped back a pace?). The card reader made the strange beep again.

"I don't know if I paid. Did it go through?"

"Leave now! Go! Get out of here!"

The level of the cashier's voice startled Linda, who looked around, all eyes on her. Accusatory one and all. Unfriendly.

"What is going on?" Linda asked.

"Please..."

The cashier asked so softly, so desperately, that Linda grabbed the water bottle and slinked away. She exited the store without looking back. Just outside the door alongside the entrance, a horse ride for a quarter bounced in motion with a little girl as a rider. The child giggled and pointed at Linda.

Linda took a few steps and tapped her pockets, realizing. "I forgot the bag."

She looked back, wondering whether to get it, but the girl kept giggling and the cashier stared at her through the glass. Her cell rang. She glimpsed the earlier missed call on her screen, which showed the hospital phone number. She furrowed her brow with concern and answered, assuming it was them calling back. It was not.

"Hello? Meet you where?" Linda asked, forgetting all about the bag and the missed call.

HEATHER SCRAMBLED, WAVING HER hand over her face to block the bright light. She spotted a row of taxis waiting curbside near the exit and dashed over. She jumped into the first. A man with greasy hair and greasy smile eyed her in the rearview.

"Where to?" he asked. She stated the address. "Gallows Way? Never heard of it."

The man typed into his GPS, but Heather barked at him to drive. She provided directions while changing in the backseat. The first thing she put on was a bra, sliding it on under the flimsy gown. Once she had it on, she lowered the gown, only to find the man leering in the mirror.

"Really?" she asked. He looked away but lifted his cell to snap a quick pic. She noticed and reached across the seat. "Give me that!"

"I wasn't..." the driver started.

Heather was too quick. She grabbed it from him and turned the screen toward the front. It showed a clear picture of her undressing. He shrugged, busted. She deleted it, then used the phone to make a call.

"Linda, where are you? I am getting my stuff and leaving. You should leave too. Leave Salem before it's too late."

She handed it back and tried to finish dressing, but found the backseat too small, so she asked the driver to pull over. As she gathered the rest of her clothes to step out and change, she failed to notice her friends' van drive past in the opposite direction. She stood alongside the taxi and changed. The driver adjusted his side mirror to watch.

D ERBY SQUARE STOOD NEAR the center of town. Quaint was how Linda thought of it upon arrival. She walked the few blocks from the pharmacy, following Walter's directions. The square comprised a large open courtyard of brick walkway leading into brick buildings overlooking the square. Walter stood in the open near the center of the square fully visible as promised, hoping not to catch her by surprise once again.

The historian appeared so kind over the phone that Linda reconsidered her thoughts on the man in the wake of disappointment over Andrew. She never gave Walter much of a chance. She didn't need Ruby's prodding to spot the man's interest. Maybe a spark was not the most essential thing to a romance. Kindness was underrated.

Her phone rang again, but she switched it off, too eager to learn why Walter bounced with such nervous energy as she approached. He appeared highly excited about something. She went in for a hug. Surprised by the gesture, Walter awkwardly placed his laptop in between them. After pulling apart, Linda addressed her clothing choice.

"Sorry for the sweats. I did not expect to meet with anyone today," she said.

"Casual suits you, but then anything does, I suppose," Walter said.

He flustered after saying it. There it was, Linda thought, one more signal from a man I all but ignored, chasing the shiny object. Walter dug into a pocket for keys, gesturing her to follow. They approached the largest building along the courtyard. He unlocked the door. They entered, passing a witch museum sign.

"Occupational courtesy. The museum is also part research center."

Walter closed the door behind them. Linda looked down at a large circle in the lobby. Names made up the circle. She read some aloud, assuming Walter would provide an answer.

"The victims of the trials." He pointed to a nearby sign offering showtimes. "They will start a show soon. We have very little time."

Linda followed him deeper into the building to a set of large mahogany doors. Walter thrust them open, and they stepped into an immense space where bookshelves lined every inch of the walls in the room. Glass display cases dotted throughout the center displayed historical relics.

Yellowed framed court transcripts hung from wire mounts on the ceiling, dangling displays draped in a specific order, designed to be read as one navigated through the area. Linda took in the sights. Walter set his laptop on a display case, booted it up, and started the facial recognition program. An old book sat on a riser in the glass case next to the one holding his laptop.

"There's one last thing I need to check. This book is one of the oldest known records of the trials. It covers the period in excruciating detail."

A lone window near the rear of the room, close to an exit, looked out into the belly of the museum. Lifelike figures stood at attention on the other side of the glass. The exhibit also housed a woman dangling from a gallows. The dummies were disturbingly lifelike. Linda leaned into the glass as she thought she saw one blink. Impossible, of course. Wait. Did it turn its head? Linda stiffened, trying to see further into the room.

She leaped as Walter's hand fell on her shoulder. For once, he failed to notice he startled her, too excited to share what he found. She glanced again, feeling foolish when she caught her face in the reflection. Surely the blinking eye was merely one of her own in the reflection. She felt silly and relieved as she followed Walter.

Walter made a show of opening a particular glass case holding a book parked open on a pedestal. The scene on its pages was that of a courthouse scene, a twisted variation of *The Last Supper*. Walter snapped a picture with his phone and then connected his cell to the laptop. The half screen with Linda came up again alongside the image. He tapped some keys to bring the new image up alongside her.

"You think my family had something to do with the witch trials?"

"I do, but I need to know for sure. Give me a moment, will you?"

As Walter worked with his laptop, Linda flipped through the ancient book, which offered an unflinching look at the past. She turned to a page of a little girl, malice in her eyes, pointing out as if straight at Linda. Much of the book was text only. Linda settled on a page and began reading.

CHAPTER 20

1692

A DOOR BURST OPEN. Reverend Ramses emerged with a bandaged ear. The flustered man leaned on Althea for support. Althea looked back sorrowfully toward the disturbing source of animalistic grunts. Somewhere in there, lost to darkness, was a child once her daughter. Goode emerged from the other room simultaneously.

"We have our first accused," Goode said.

In the presence of another church official, Ramses quickly distanced himself from Althea, rising back into sternness. Althea tilted her head, confused. Then, with a mere glance at the stairs, Althea and Ramses understood. Althea shook her head.

"Husband, please, I beg of thee. Was it not in the sermons where you deemed the vilest of creatures as the king of lies? How shall we know for certain the truth behind their words?"

"A trial. One that will show more mercy than shown your own children. Wouldst thou wish freedom for their hexers?"

"Not freedom, but certainly mercy."

"There will be no mercy. We shall confront devilish deeds with righteous fury and finality," Goode said.

Heavy breathing mixed with whimpering emanated from the open door at the end of the hall. Rose fell into a salacious nursery rhyme inside her room. The two girls fed off one another even while captive. That was enough to prompt the men into action. The religious leaders mounted the stairs. Althea intercepted and grabbed her husband's lapels.

"Husband, I beseech thee. Is she not family?"

Reverend Goode's face hardened. A nearby candle reflected flames in his eyes in such a way he could have been the devil himself. Althea shivered at the transition.

"I will stop at nothing to protect our children. Wise would thou be to do the same. One might consider whether such protests aid the enemy."

"The enemy? Long has she cared for this family!"

"And now she has succumbed to the wicked. There are two ways to clear my path. I urge you to consider stepping aside."

Althea searched his face. There would be no moving him, but he would move her. She stepped aside before he hurled her down the stairs. Her husband plodded down the steps. She looked to Ramses one last time, but he shook her off and descended as well.

The men stepped into the kitchen, where Haddy continued stirring fresh rags in the boiling pot. Steam and the orange glow of fire filled the room. Haddy looked up from her task, confused.

"Reverends?"

Reverend Goode glared at Haddy without saying a word. Off his look, Haddy checked her waistcoat to ensure she displayed no flesh. While her clothes were damp from the task, they proved to be cinched appropriately. Haddy squinted, confused at the dire demeanor displayed by her employer. The man's animalistic leer fit in with the growls overhead. Ramses finally broke the silence.

"The children have named their enchanter," Ramses said, his voice booming in the tight space.

"Who then? Who did they name?"

Reverend Goode's stare answered. Haddy shook her head. Althea emerged from the shadows, so small in the presence of the two men of God. Althea's sorrowful look supplied the definitive answer to Haddy's confused thoughts.

"No. Ms. Althea, I beg of thee! Never would I suffer the children. I treat them as if my own."

"And have none of your own. You are of a birthing age with nary a suitor in sight. Would not thou find herself envious whilst attending to a happy home?" Goode asked.

"Not envy, Reverend. I have long had a family. Thine. Have loved with such a heart, perhaps there was no more to give. I beseech thee to see through the ruse of lies."

"You dare call my children liars!"

Ramses reached out to hold back the fuming man. Althea gasped, frightened by the outburst, and shook her head at Haddy in warning.

"I call out the lies of the devil, in whatever form he takes. Were it not I who pleaded with thee to chase the demons from the child?" Haddy pleaded her case.

"As a ruse, to cover how thou called forth the very demons staining the innocence of children. Thou art one who could not conceive of her own, one with no flesh to carry on a namesake. Instead, thou would choose to bedevil that which she cannot possess by calling forth possession. A failed woman lusting for the abundance of others." Reverend Goode raged at the servant.

She raved back. "Lust? For sleep denied, for a back stooped, carrying the weight of tasks unfulfilled by the patriarch of the family? Who doth chase the rambunctiousness from thy children? Who doth challenge their excesses? I am a woman of faith, and all I lust for now is freedom."

"Denied!"

Reverend Goode stormed forward, grabbing the woman who slapped him in the face. He returned the strike, punching her. She faltered but rose back into the fight, screaming for Althea's help. Althea shrank into a corner, covering her ears. The children's laughter intensified overhead, loud enough to be heard over the kitchen fracas.

Ramses moved in, distracting Haddy long enough for Goode to get behind her and lift her into a bear hug. Ramses grabbed her legs. Haddy kicked, striking Ramses in the bandaged ear. He cried out in pain, grabbing at his wound. The ear bled anew.

Haddy kicked the boiling pot with significant force. The water splashed high, cascading across Ramses' body. The scalding liquid blistered his face. He screeched into his hands, dancing in place as if that could somehow erase the pain.

Goode shook the woman, trying to settle her down, tightening his bear grip from behind. She slammed her head back, cracking her skull against his eye socket. Reverend Goode cried out.

"Reverend!" Ramses shouted, with a slight slur from a blistered, fat lip.

Goode held the woman steady. Haddy's eyes grew wide when she spotted the object in Ramses' hands. The bucket. The one Althea carried from the brook. Haddy shook her head, begging the reverend off. The plea for humanity failed. Ramses swung the bucket. A massive cracking sound filled the room and Haddy collapsed in Goode's arms.

Goode looked up through soaked hair covering his face. He found his wife in the distance and offered her the warning. "There will be others."

The children continued giggling, in voices seemingly not their own.

T HE TOWN SQUARE BUSTLED with energy in the early morning hours. Families stretched in all directions along the cobblestone streets, the youngest ones rushed around greeting one another despite protests from parents eager to contain their herds. The pedestrian traffic flowed toward a distant field already full of townsfolk.

A hush suddenly descended over the crowd. Families parted to make room in the street for a certain entourage to pass. In doing so, parents moved protectively in front of their children. As the crowd hushed into whispers, the clack of formal shoes against cobblestone echoed. Reverend Goode strode down the center of the street, a daughter on each hand. Althea brought up the rear and averted her gaze from the townspeople as she passed. The girls stood tall, imposing despite their petite size. The red square on Rose's face and the scarred inverted cross on Sadie's forehead remained as proof of someone having bewitched them.

Children hid behind coats and frocks of their parents, frightened into submission by the Goode family's presence. Two young children, one with a lollypop, battled in the street, unaware of the intrusion. The boys' parents urged them to stop their shenanigans, but the boys were too far into the fight to notice until the Goode family descended upon them.

Both boys went rigid as they noticed the imposing reverend hovering over them. They looked away only to find themselves under scrutiny of the two daughters. Rose smiled at the boy closest to her. He offered his own crooked grin even as he broke out into a sweat. Rose raised her arm toward the boy.

The crowd collectively gasped. The boy cowered, waiting for the dreaded finger. Which never came. Rose reached out to free the lollypop stuck in the boy's hair. She returned it to the surprised kid.

Reverend Goode ruffled the boy' hair before turning to the crowd. "Such behavior is not necessarily of the Devil. Occasionally boys will be boys. Join us, will you? Where we vow to expose true sinners."

The crowd stepped back into the streets, following the family toward the field. The parents of the boys collected their children and apologized profusely to Reverend Goode. After waving off their sniveling, the reverend led his flock toward judgement.

Soon, the traveling group merged with others already assembled in a grassy field. Stones clacked against stones from somewhere behind a line of citizens. The Goode family headed toward the action. Goode worked his way over to where a frail old man lay atop a makeshift stone altar on. A pile of heavy stones covered the man's bare chest. The man's exposed skin bled in thin rivulets along his torso where rocks had cut skin.

The weight caused him to breathe in shallow, raspy gasps. A mountainous man with burly arms, Thomas Browning, stood between the trapped man and a cart full of rock. He held another large stone ready. Reverend Ramses, still scarred from his visit to the Goode home, oversaw the event. Ramses nodded to Reverend Goode, who stepped up and looked down upon Robert Carver, the man under stones.

"How goeth the trial?" Goode asked Ramses.

"The accused appears as short of confessions as he is of breath."

Ramses nodded, gesturing for Browning to drop another stone. Browning did and the old man gasped. Goode looked down at the man with curiosity. Althea and the children stood off to one side. Althea and Rose focused on the crowd while Sadie watched the man with great interest.

"Perhaps I should ask the accused. How goeth the trial?"

The man struggled to speak. "Please, I am an old man."

"Suggesting thou should be unafraid to face trial."

"A trial that seeks no truth!"

The man's ability to shout despite the weight on his chest ruffled Goode. Off a nod from Goode, Browning grabbed and dropped another stone. The added weight stole the fight from the man. Goode pressed the advantage.

"If thou be innocent, then worry not. Our trials identify the righteous as well as the wicked," Goode said to a collective murmur of approval from the crowd.

Goode grinned at the shift in the crowd's favor. Until laughter cut through the ceremony. The old man laughed heartily despite the abundance of stone.

Carver turned his head toward Goode, though the man's gaze remained unfocused. "I can see now. I understand."

"What doth thee portend to know?" Goode asked.

"I know what you are doing. I know what you are."

The crowd fell silent. Goode felt himself losing them. Another nod added another stone, but the added weight only drew further laughter from the old man. Hysterical, unnerving. Another stone. No difference. Laughter consumed the old man.

Goode gestured to one of two enormous stones at the cart's front, acting as counterweights to the load. Browning struggled but lifted the immense rock. He raised it as high as possible, then released it. Carver's bones snapped under the weight. The man's laughter and breathing ceased. His head drooped to the side, locked in an empty stare focused on Sadie. The child giggled with glee as the crowd roared.

"It appears the man was guilty," Goode exclaimed.

His words elicited a cheer from the crowd. Browning briefly flexed his tired arms, then grabbed a nearby black hood and pulled it over his face. A mere formality, everyone knew who the executioner was. The crowd roared anew, thirsty for more blood, feeling righteous. Goode waved the folks along as he followed the executioner towards the gallows on the nearby hill. They soon arrived at a boxy wooden structure designed to accommodate multiple simultaneous executions at once.

The roughshod structure comprised a twelve-by-twelve wooden base with support slats haphazardly hammered at random angles from base to the platform. Twin wooden beams rose from each side of the platform connected by a crosspiece matching the width of the stage. Two nooses hung from the crossbeam with room for a third. A lever jutted up from the platform's edge just shy of the small staircase leading down to ground level.

While the crowd maintained a social distance from the Goode family and other church officials, they jostled for prime viewing around the front of the gallows. The energy was palpable, and the eager crowd threatened to break out into a scrum over positioning. Occasional glances from Reverend Goode proved enough of a deterrent to stem brewing arguments between attendees.

No sooner had the crowd settled into place when two men wearing church garb wrestled a bound woman to the base of the stairs. The woman struggled with her captors, crying out to neighbors by name. Those called upon shied away, fearful of being associated with the accused.

Browning climbed the stairs ahead of the guards, who followed behind and handed the woman off once atop the platform. Browning easily corralled the woman and centered her on the stage before slipping the rope around her neck. He fastened it tight as tears streamed down the woman's face. Her hands remained tied behind her back. Her struggles produced choking, a sign of her inevitable demise. Browning grabbed the lever.

"The accused stands convicted of witchery. The punishment is hanging until dead," Ramses announced to the crowd from below the gallows.

The woman locked eyes with Sadie. "Dearest Sadie, please. Was not I your favorite teacher? Long have I shown kindness and respect in all your lessons. I beg of thee for release."

The crowd turned to the girl with the upturned cross. Sadie remained fixated on her former teacher. The girl shook her head, sealing the woman's fate. The woman then spit toward Sadie.

"You horrible child. How dare you judge me? You silly little bi..." the woman's words cut off when Browning pulled the lever.

The woman dropped. The crack of her neck was loud enough to reach the furthest edges of the crowd. She dangled wildly, settling into a spin that amped up an already excited crowd. They watched as every swing of the corpse, ignoring the smell of scat trapped somewhere in the woman's garb. Fresh cheers erupted when Ramses declared another witch defeated.

The Goode family departed, walking along almost empty streets, filled only with those uninterested in the ceremonies or morally outraged by them. Those who remained in the streets the entire time chose not to take part in such barbarism. One such woman was Livi Winslow, a woman of exquisite beauty. Clad in clothing of limited means, she hovered protectively over her child, trying to hide the little girl behind her tattered clothes. The little girl could see through the holes in her mother's dress.

Reverend Goode noticed Livi and gripped Sadie's shoulder. With no hesitation, Sadie pointed a finger at the girl's mother. The woman cried out in protest, shaking her head in disbelief and terror.

The same guards from earlier appeared as if from nowhere and grabbed the woman. Livi fought back but was no match for the two men. She screamed out as her daughter started crying.

"No, please. I am a widower, not a witch. I am only a mother. What of my child? What of my child?"

Reverend Goode stepped away from his family to sidebar with the two guards. He whispered to the men. "The town jail grows full. Take her to the other location."

The guards nodded and carried the woman away. Goode returned to his family, smiling at Sadie in recognition of a job well done. The girl beamed under her father's silent praise. The family departed as others distanced themselves from the abandoned and crying child. All too afraid to be seen as accomplices. The child stood alone on the street, wailing to passersby.

Darkness. Water dripped, plopping into an echo. A door burst open, slashing the darkness with a jagged ray of light. Footsteps thudded down steps. Livi protested as the guards dragged her along toward a dark space cold enough to turn her cries to steam. Each scream floating away, only to be replaced by another.

One guard lit the way with a lantern and pulled at what appeared to be a brick wall. A hidden door swung open to a space somehow darker than that she already found herself in.

Despite Livi's best attempts, they threw her inside. She stumbled and smacked her head against a distant wall, falling to the ground, bleeding from her brow. She cried out in panic as the door began closing.

Before the lantern light vanished, several sets of eyes opened in the darkness surrounding her. The eyes did not appear human, too bloodshot, too sunken into sockets, too filled with sorrow and pain. Hair fell in front of some eyes, none of which blinked. But there was not enough hair in the world to cover the hollow, faraway looks in the female prisoners' eyes. They reached out with hands gnarled and damaged from scratching at walls, grasping at Livi for something, anything. Fresh clothes. News of the outside. Livi wailed in terror as the door closed, encasing them all in darkness.

CHAPTER 21

L INDA LOOKED UP FROM the book, overcome with a chill. The page open before her showcased an artistic interpretation of Sadie pointing out an accused witch. Linda scanned the room, feeling it somehow darker than when they first entered. Walter continued fiddling with his laptop, but in a bout of multi-tasking, startled her by reaching over and turning a page.

"Shall I simply apologize in advance for all future discomforts I apparently cause?"

She smiled, despite everything. "Only if I can accept said apologies in advance."

Walter smiled back, then snapped a picture from the page with his cell phone. He tapped away until hearing a ding. Walter returned to his laptop and opened the image he sent himself. It was an ink drawing of Althea Goode. Linda examined the image, noticing some resemblance.

"Early drawings and sculptures are often eerily accurate interpretations of the subjects. Society celebrated artistic realism in those early centuries, so pre-film depictions from history are quite accurate. Artists made their fortunes capturing people of note. The Goodes were such a family. If the images of Althea are accurate, I would argue she is lovely," Walter said.

Linda noted a likeness without all the fancy computer equipment. Walter, being an "egg," never picked up on her awareness. Linda pondered Ruby's interpretation of the man and smiled. Walter had just awkwardly complimented her via the picture of a woman from hundreds of years ago. Apparently, that was how eggs flirted. It was working. Linda felt the brotherly feelings slipping away, especially now that she had some sense of who she was.

The light-hearted feelings slipped quickly away as Linda turned another page. Sadie appeared prominent on the page with the upturned cross visible. The child pointed in the image and Linda felt suddenly accused. The weight of what she did to Ruby weighed on her. She had enough of the book.

She stepped back, uncomfortable with the pictures. "Tom knows a bit about all this, the Salem trials. But he does not understand how people who knew one another intimately could allow this to happen."

"A mystery to this day. There is one mystery even greater. What eventually prompted it to stop? What made the last hanging the last hanging?" Walter's laptop dinged. A picture of Linda took up half the screen, the rendering of Althea Goode the other. A graph at the bottom showed a match of ninety percent. "This is what I have been waiting for. I know where to find your family."

Walter closed the laptop and gestured her to follow. They navigated through a wing of the museum depicting a hanging. Linda thought she saw the hanged body move. Then the flash of a face covered that of the figure on display. Just as quickly, it vanished, leaving a still scene just as unnerving. Linda bristled at the depictions of such a horrific moment in time.

Then movement for certain. A woman in torn clothing appeared, wearing a cloak that covered half her face. The remaining half revealed the woman to be withered. More motion caught Linda's eye as something twinkled in the light—buckles of a boot. The man wearing them stepped into the corridor, an imposing man dressed in clothing from another time. A child rushed by, almost dancing, spinning in a circle. (A cross on her forehead?) All stopped short when they spotted Linda.

The girl raised an arm and pointed. The man nodded in silent agreement before speaking.

"If you're looking for the auditorium, you can't get theyah from heah," he said in a Boston accent thick enough to confuse the words car keys with khakis.

"Duh. Then why am I pointing? The theater is that way, just past the restrooms," the girls said in a voice too seasoned to be an actual child.

Closer inspection showed a teen played the role of a girl. The old woman grumbled.

"What is going on? I can barely see in this thing."

"A civilian. Or an autograph hound," the fake reverend said.

Walter returned and gestured for Linda to follow. "Apologies, everyone," he said to the crew. Then to Linda, "the show I mentioned earlier."

Walter started off as the crew moved toward a curtain. Linda glanced back and saw the girl still standing there, staring. Linda squinted and swore the woman looked different, like an actual child. Before she could tell for certain, light blinded her as Walter burst through the crash bar of an exit door.

They walked a short distance to a large cemetery. Walter moved with purpose, bypassing dozens of headstones. Deep in the graveyard, he stopped and turned to Linda.

"We have a family name now to run a DNA profile against. I cannot say for certain, but based on preliminary evidence, we have likely identified your family."

He gestured to a series of headstones so old as to be almost unreadable. The first showed the interred as *Reverend Samuel Goode 1663-1693*. Althea Goode rested in the grave next to him. The dates on her headstone showed she outlived her husband. Buried alongside the parents were two children, Rose and Sadie.

Rose died very young. Sadie lived a little longer. Another stone named Belle anchored the family unit. Belle lived much longer than the others but was born in 1694.

Linda understood this was likely not her direct family. Her true surname depended on who married whom over the years, but this was a start. As morbid as it was, she felt connected for the first time in her adult life. She thought briefly of those underfoot walking on the same streets in Salem that she now walked on. There were many other names on headstones, and she wondered if any were her own. Unlikely. Interring extended families together was not common practice in America as far as she knew. Families begat other families, and the lines grew and eventually Linda was born.

But where? In Salem, or in California? Linda was less than a year old when dumped on the steps of the orphanage. There were still mysteries left to solve, but she was one step closer. She focused once again on the adult stones, touching Althea's marker.

"My name is Goode?"

"I believe so, yes. Descended from, of course. A little more work and we can get the exact name of your parents."

Linda walked, examining other nearby stones, and spotted a pattern. Many appeared to meet misfortune at abnormally young ages. The Goode name bled into rows of other surnames. Strangers buried alongside the Goode family or lineage through marriage.

"So many died young. What happened to them all?"

Walter grew somber. "It was the clippings which you provided that led me here. I was already aware of historical misfortune that befell the original Salem Goode family. The accidents in the clippings you gave me suggested relations to one another. I found information on a few of the victims in the articles which showed roots in New England. Now that we have identified the Goodes as a connection, we can trace the lineage of those in the articles as well. From there, we can determine how everyone and everything relates. Sadly, I believe there is a misfortune in your family bloodline."

"Misfortune? That's not a disease. That's not something contagious. There must be some other reason behind this. Some other explanation."

"Your family was a flash-point in history. I believe all the answers to what is happening lie here in Salem, but my resources have run dry. There is only one place left that may hold words and history never seen."

"Where?"

"A place where they have turned me away many times."

Linda followed Walter's gaze as he looked up toward an ancient church on the crest of a distant hill.

A COMPACT CAR WITH rental plates drove up a long, winding street, turning into a massive parking lot, the only car in the vast open space. Walter exited from the driver's side and rushed toward the passenger's side, but Linda had already gotten out. A church loomed high above them on an incline of lawn beyond the parking lot. The couple climbed the hill on foot as if ascending to heaven.

The pair walked in silence. Linda remained stunned by the recent revelations, instinctively grabbing the key at her neck. She wore it even during her run. The object was no less a mystery, despite her newfound knowledge. After cresting the hill, they climbed heavy steps leading to massive double doors fronting the ancient church. There was not enough paint in the town to disguise the weathered nature of the building. Linda checked her own exterior and felt self-conscious.

"Should I be wearing sweats?"

"No," Walter said truthfully. "But that is the least of our worries. I had an incident with the church back home."

"In England?"

"Okay, fine. In Rome. A bit of a kerfuffle. The incident has resulted in doors such as this remaining mostly closed for me. Word travels fast."

"What did you do?"

"Let us simply say I frightened them differently than I do you. Point is, your speaking to them might be helpful."

"But I do not even know what it is we are doing here."

Walter knocked before explaining anything more. The door opened too quickly. Someone knew they were there. Walter looked back and spotted camera domes in the parking lot atop light poles. Those inside did not need a miracle to know they had visitors, only a smartphone. Father Bergman appeared. The shriveled priest stood stooped over. The elderly man fixed a gaze on Walter that bordered on contempt. Not a good start. Walter opened his mouth, but Linda stepped forward.

"Father, I need your help." The priest did not speak but eyed her with concern, so she continued. "I am seeking information on my family, and I believe the church holds the answers."

"Her name is Goode, Father."

The priest stepped back, looking Linda over before turning and walking away. Walter called out after the man, stepping into the vestibule as he did so.

"Please, do not forsake us, father! I understand your reluctance with me, but at least speak to her. Answer her questions."

"Only our Lord can hear Father Bergman. He is mute from a stroke," a female voice boomed from an overhead balcony.

A nun in a habit, face hidden by shadows, stared down at the couple. Her size more than made up for the priest's lack of same. Linda looked toward the priest in the distance.

"I am sorry. I did not know," Linda said.

"We limit records here to church hierarchy or holders of a birthright key," the Nun replied.

Walter looked up, intrigued. "I have not heard of such a thing." He patted his chest for show, his hands coming up empty. "I have none, I'm afraid."

"Walter..." Linda began.

"But I am quite resourceful. If you supply me with more information, I am sure my research could..."

"Walter!"

He turned to Linda, who displayed the key on her neck. A grin overtook his face. "I bloody love you."

AFTER THE NUN EXAMINED the key and deemed it authentic with an annoyed grumble, she reconnected the visitors with the priest. The man led them to the rear of the church, where they descended darkened stone steps. The priest held a kerosene lantern aloft to light the way. Walter strode tall, proud, excited. He whispered to Linda as they went.

"If someone left you that key, it confirms our suspicions. You are a descendent of an original colonist in Salem. Likely the Goode family based on facial recognition. Our target DNA search will start there when we finish here. No reason not to assign that to your previous investigator. He already has your profile ready to go."

"Wonderful idea. I can't tell you how excited this makes me. When I saw the picture of Althea Goode, I felt a connection. I plan to Google her when I get home. The resemblance must mean something. Thank you, Walter, for all of this. I can't thank you enough. But as for now, what is this key giving us access to? Where are we going?" Linda asked.

"No fire shall these walls see," Walter said to a nod from the priest and a confused look from Linda. He explained. "Words of the church have outlasted the churches themselves by being kept away from houses of worship. Anything happens to the church and the works survive."

The priest thrust open a door. The trio stepped out into the bright afternoon sun. They stood in a massive cemetery with elaborate headstones and tombs. Metal fencing surrounded the vast lot, the burial spots for the more affluent and notable. They crossed half the cemetery before stopping at a large crypt.

Dousing the lantern, the priest hung it on a hook outside the crypt. He then wiped away foliage debris covering a recessed keypad and pressed a series of numbers. The crypt door hissed open, revealing a climate-controlled environment. Once inside, Father Bergman grabbed plastic tubes from a holder in the wall and handed one to each of them. The priest cracked his, which lit up brilliantly.

Walter and Linda followed suit. Father Bergman grabbed several more sticks, then closed the door behind them. Despite the door's tech, the balance of the space was that of an oversized tomb. Encountering a body was not out of the question. Linda searched the space for one, but the world remained too dark.

Father Bergman snapped the other sticks to life. Stone cups hung at intervals along the walls. Bergman dropped a lit stick in each one until the entire space glowed. The lighting revealed an open doorway which Bergman led them through. The group raised their lights to reveal a massive library somehow much larger than the space outside. Volumes of ancient text filled the entire cavern from floor to ceiling.

"Jesus Christ!" Linda cried out, shocked at the sight. The priest glared disapprovingly and made the sign of the cross. Linda blushed under the cover of darkness. "Apologies, Father."

Walter waded into the room and traced a hand over spines, lost in a world of wonder. He gasped occasionally as he recognized certain volumes. Linda eyed the same volumes but shook her head, overwhelmed.

She stepped back and bumped into a stone altar. Seven candle holders built into the altar lined its furthest edge. Bergman cracked each of seven sticks and placed them in the holders. The altar standing chest high stood ready as a reading desk.

"Where do we even start?" Linda asked.

Walter gestured to her neck. "A key. Your key. Father Bergman, does this place contain books of blood?"

The priest, eerily lit from below by the multiple sticks, nodded and looked toward a nearby bookcase. Walter's eyes went wide, and he rushed over, tracing fingers over spines in awe. The volumes varied in size, but most were inches thick.

"Blood?" Linda asked.

Walter gingerly walked a volume over and placed it on the reading altar. A raised lock stood out on the cover and fed into a steel band wrapped around the volume in a cross formation. Rust threatened to break the bond, the orange of which bled into the book's cover, a matter of time before history reclaimed itself.

"Not blood, per se. Acid. I believed these only to be the stuff of legend. They are a remarkable engineering feat for the time. Opened without the proper key and any such book releases an acid wash designed to destroy pages. These books are fabled to have recorded the most intimate and ugly details of history but remain locked to most of the world. They say the church hierarchy possesses keys and obviously your family was hierarchy and handed theirs down. There are stories of historians from long past attempting to breach such volumes to no avail, releasing the flood, destroying the books. No one has discovered any in modern times, so attempts to open them with better technology are nonexistent. Most chalked their existence up to fables, so stopped searching for them."

The priest nodded again, but tilted a hand back and forth, suggesting the information was mostly correct. Linda sidled up to Walter, and they looked down at the thick volume with wonder. She raised her key. The priest looked on concerned.

"The church bound such volumes based on their content. Some consider books of blood evil or sacrilegious. You may wish to brace yourself over the contents."

Linda inserted her key and turned it. With a click, the bands fell away. The book freed from its prison. It opened on an image of women hanged. Demons peered over the deceased women's shoulders.

Father Bergman grimaced at the image. The next page showed a demon with a large, erect penis jutting below a tight abdomen. As if posing for a picture, the beast smiled in the drawing. The Father stumbled back, unable to take in the sight. As he stepped away, he spotted something in the doorway leading out. A cloak fluttering past?

Something thumped outside the open doorway. Rhythmic, steady. Thump, thump, thump. The priest looked back at the others, lost in their volume, before raising his light and approaching the exit. He glanced through the open doorway into the hall. The thumping continued in a corner near the exit of the tomb. Something moving appeared to be the source of the gentle thumping.

The priest advanced on a corner hidden in darkness. Something rocked in the tight corner of the tomb's entrance. Black moving within blackness. He raised the light for a better view, then thrust a hand over his mouth to stifle a cry that he could not utter. A dead woman dangled by a noose. Her body thumped against the stone wall of the corner repeatedly. Thump, thump, thump.

Eyes thrust open, white in the darkness! Father Bergman looked toward the exit of the tomb and back toward the other room, calculating, deciding whether to warn the others or flee. The hanged woman thrust free of the shadows, or at least her head and a single pointing arm. The Pointing Woman. She reached toward the priest.

Bergman grabbed his chest (heart attack?) and stumbled, reaching toward the couple in the other room, mouthing the words for help. Nothing escaped save a tear from his eye. He looked back up at the Pointing Woman who swung with arm extended, still thumping, but the thumping grew increasingly loud, syncing to the thunderous beating of his racing heart.

A child's hands appeared, stretching from behind the adult, gripping the hem of the woman's dress, gathering the cloth in their grip. Pulling it away as if clearing free a well-covered hiding space. Father Bergman did not wait for the child to make an appearance. He bolted from the tomb out into the graveyard.

Bergman took a moment to adjust to the light despite the sudden cloud cover hovering over the church, threatening to swallow the sanctuary hole. A deep growl came from somewhere among the tombstones. Bergman found his feet and raced through the graveyard destination church. A dog kept pace with the man, black fur flashed between the grave markers.

The Father ignored the pain in his chest and continued running as fast as his elderly body allowed. Flashes of fur in between hungry growls danced in his mind in such a manner he could not tell whether he lived in a nightmare or reality. His target, the cross rising high above the church, vanished in a sudden onset of fog.

He refused to turn back, unwilling to face the beast at his rear. He neared the church, close to a haven. Finding a second wind, he dashed faster than he thought possible. He was almost there until the dog leaped from the priest's side, taking down the man quick, attacking with teeth and fury. The priest hit the ground, the darkest of dogs atop him. Through it all, the priest could not even scream.

I NSIDE THE TOMB, WALTER grew frustrated. "This is a rehash of the trials. Sickeningly detailed but offering nothing new. I thought. Well, who knows? Just more, I suppose."

Linda took over, shuffling through the volume until she stopped on an image and grunted in disgust. "Did they behead witches?"

"Not in America. Hanging and stoning only."

"Then you may wish to look."

Walter flipped through the next several pages. Horrific images of decapitated women filled the pages, artfully drawn. He jerked his head back, realizing.

"They wrote the book in reverse. This section pre-dates the witch trials. Women were turning up dead, beheaded. That is the answer. This is the missing link showing why citizens would turn on one another. There was a predator on the loose in Salem. Citizens likely would not attribute such attacks to evil spirits."

Linda read alongside of him, taking in the information. "So, if the church could not protect them, women turned to other means of protection."

"Exactly. Witches were not born in Salem, they were made."

CHAPTER 22

1691

Dozens of women surrounded Ramses and his personal guard, Anton, focusing their ire on the church elder. The assembled crowd raised fists in place of torches with an energy no less burning. Heavy cloud cover ensured the darkness of the sky matched the mood on the ground. Esther Willow, a striking woman with a hint of blonde hair dangling from her cap, led the charge, standing front and center.

"When will the church do its job and produce the monster in our midst?" Esther yelled, prompting a roar from the crowd.

"The job of the church? Brother Anton, dost such a demand fit within the purview of your job duties."

"Nay Reverend. My job as church guard is to protect the respected elders of the church and all those assembled in its pews. Any outside church walls are under God's care. I would also provide escorts for visiting men of the cloth."

"Men? Hence the problem. Perhaps if women wore the robes, the church might finally act on the predator who this very day surely considers his next prey."

"Women of the cloth? Fa! Thee doth dance with blasphemy sister Willow. I will follow the Lord's path and forgive thy trespass. In the spirit of community and communion, I would remind thee I am but merely a vessel of the Lord. What would thou have me do?"

The crowd launched into a chant, repeating the word 'confess.' The charge startled the priest, who exchanged a look with his guard. Anton reached for a dagger at his side, but the priest waved him off. Ramses locked eyes with Esther.

"Surely such a brute who relieves our sisters of their precious skulls must suffer fatigue from such acts, physically and spiritually. Such a burdened man would seek to unburden himself. Confess!"

Ramses reacted, suddenly understanding. The crowd fell silent, waiting for an answer. Ramses eyed them all before flashing a rare smile. A black line ran through one canine tooth. Not a gap from one missing, nor the full black of a dead tooth, but a thin line of rot stretched from gum to point. Ramses infrequently smiled because of the dental oddity, but looking down on the women, he allowed his teeth to come out to play.

"Confess? You wish for me to disclose the sacred confessions of my parishioners? To break the sanctity of God's forgiveness?"

"In place of protecting a murderer. Yay," someone in the crowd shouted to murmured agreement.

"Of course. Shall we start with confessions of those assembled before me? While the Lord shall never give me more than I can bear, it would relieve me to free the heavy secrets I carry. We can start with one I see before me who has defiled her marriage vows repeatedly with a lover. Shall I offer full details of such transgressions?"

The crowd murmured animatedly, eyeing one another before turning back to the priest, who grinned that black lined smile. Several women shied from meeting the man's gaze. (Guilty or worried about forthcoming accusations?)

"Shall I mention thee who lays with women? I spot one in this very crowd. Surely the Lord would forgive if I unburdened myself for the benefit of the community."

The crowd eyed one another again, seeking to determine who the accused might be. The sisterhood faltered, the crowd drifted further from one another, individuals distancing themselves from the group. Anton watched the priest with great interest, eager to learn the confessed secrets.

"Or the multitude of women who share impure thoughts and act upon them in a manner most unfitting for hands which clasp in prayer each Sunday?"

"Enough!" Esther yelled. "Hold thy scandalous tongue. Thou dost seek to splinter our resolve. Many here seek forgiveness within these walls. We ask again whether a madman has done the same?"

"Do the heathen indigenous not roam these lands? Might they not be suspect?" Ramses asked.

"Those of this land when we arrived have aided in our very survival. Wouldst thou suggest such a stranger eludes notice in our small town?" Esther said. "If the killer hides in plain sight, are we to believe the church is unaware? Doth not God see all?"

Ramses scoffed at the thought as his smile shifted to that of a scowl. "My position offers me awareness of a thread of brutishness coursing through this town. I witness boiling anger in those who struggle to tame our lands and tame their women. Yet in the course of my duties, I assure you, no neighbor has confessed such deeds as murder to me."

"What of Reverend Goode? Perhaps he has heard such confessions." Esther asked.

"Were the good reverend in possession of such knowledge, he would have sought my council. I assure thee, the predator is no man of God. One who commits such heinous acts would find himself struck down by the Lord were he to enter this house of worship."

"Amen," the crowd chanted.

Ramses examined the faces in the crowd, identifying those who questioned his authority. The sight of such defiance hardened him. "Despite circumstances, I would remind all of thee to revisit your own morality. How many here dance with thoughts of the Devil? How many strayed from their hearth into the night? For surely morals vanish with the sun. Why travel into the night? Such attacks occur only in the blackest of nights under the work of the blackest of heart. Doth not travel by night expose character?"

The crowd roared with disapproval. They shouted out reasons they needed to be out at night related to work. The assembled group hissed displeasure over suggestions of loose morals. As the fury of the crowd grew, night settled in. The priest raised his hands to shush the crowd.

"Were thee so worried about the cloak of darkness worn by the predator in our midst, perhaps all ye lasses should consider the current hour? I plan to retire for the evening, and as usual am available to any who wish to relieve themselves of their sins. All assembled have now borne witness that secrets shared shall remain so even when revealing them might benefit the church. And in moments such as this, myself personally."

Ramses flashed the black-lined tooth again before trotting up the steps, spry for his age. The guard followed. The sky had transitioned to full night, so the women broke into groups and began an exodus from the church steps. Haddy remained. Alone. Esther took note and the arm of the woman. They walked along the quickly darkening street.

"Did thou witness that smile? The blackened thread? As if Reverend Ramses dines on evil," Esther said.

Haddy gripped her Bible tight. "Careful, missus, talking such. God works through men such as he, no matter the constitution of the man."

"Therein lies the rub."

"Missus?"

"Always a man. Doomed are we who submit to the whims of patriarchy. Too few men stand for piety and true faith. Their weaknesses become our suffering. Even now, as we gathered, where were our brothers in arms?"

"Many watching children, I suppose."

"Or watching over their pints in the tavern. Free to walk about in the shadows, even in a vulnerable drunken state."

The two women broke from the street into a tree lined forest. The sky chased them with darkness until the moon finally broke through the clouds. Esther gestured to the glowing object in the sky.

"Sister Moon provides better security than our Lord sees fit to provide."

Haddy brought her Bible to her chest. "Careful with thy words lest the Lord take offense and guide the monster of the dark to our current path."

"More like paths." Esther gestured to the branch on the road. "Tell me, Miss Haddy, thou art employed by a high Reverend. What of his character?"

"The Reverend is a complicated man. His children I treat as my own. I treasure those girls, though Sadie most recently has suffered bouts of nightmares. Reverend Goode urges her into further prayer. I seek to help her find comfort where I may."

"Surely a good woman you are. Nary a word to praise your employer but besmirch him you did not, despite his allowing you to live so far and so poor while they have much room and warmth to accommodate you."

Haddy reacted, the words stinging in their truth. "Were it that simple. Areas of the home are off limits to all. I suppose the work of the Lord requires more privacy than less pious occupations. The basement in which the reverend seeks privacy is the very space that concerns the bothered child. I have considered informing the master how the mystery of his privacy in the bowels of his home stokes a fire of imagination in his oldest."

"Always thinking of others, but it is time someone thinks of you. As you follow this dark path this night, I beg thee to carry protection greater than the church provides us in our hour of need."

Esther pulled open a bundle tied at her waist, revealing an object constructed of twine and tiny branches—a stick figure. The string wrapped elaborately over the assembled pieces. Repeated wrapping over the chest area implied a woman's breasts. Haddy searched the vicinity, fearful of observance.

"Take it, sister, for protection on the last of your journey. It will protect you where the patriarch has failed," Esther said.

"And what of you, Missus?"

"Sister Soule's home stands along my path. It is she who fashions such protections for the mothers of this earth. Seldom does sister Soule leave her homestead, as she understands the nature of the hunter in our midst. I deem she will be home and will fashion me a new totem of protection to replace that which I gift to thee."

Haddy accepted the object. The servant stuffed it quickly in a pocket and walked off with a nod of thanks. Esther studied the darkness ahead, searching for hints of movement in the pools of moonlight looming ahead along the otherwise dark path. The hoot of an owl prompted Esther forward.

Esther moved quickly from one light puddle to another. Illumination from the town and residences glowed at her back but faded the further she ventured into the woods. The less affluent and women of limited means and stature lived in shacks spread across the forest landscape. In the far distance, a shack stood out against the shadows of the night. Something snapped. Esther turned around. Nothing.

Picking up the pace, the woman headed toward the ramshackle shed. Even the dark of night failed to hide the crooked shape of the makeshift home. Smoke from a tiny chimney puffed into the night sky. Something snapped again. Esther turned. Then another snap. Nearby. Esther bolted toward the home, which remained perilously far away.

Thick forest encroached onto the path from both sides, plenty of places for wildlife to hunt from. Or predators of another sort. Esther looked back while running. When she turned back toward her destination, something sprang from the shadows too fast to avoid. A tree branch, used as a club, striking her face with a thunderous crack. Esther dropped immediately, unconscious. A dark figure dragged the woman by her feet off the path into the trees.

VERITY SOULE HELD COUNSEL with herself while nude and prostrate on the floor in the tiniest of living spaces. A small stone fireplace burned along one wall. Smoke flooded into the house in equal measure to that escaping through the chimney.

The woman meditated atop an animal fur spread across an uneven floor. The woman's forehead rested against the ground, with her hair splayed out above her head. Her arms stretched out on either side.

Verity pressed her head against the floor and breathed deep. Her back rose and fell with each breath. A small table occupied a corner of the room, on which sat a bundle of twine and a bowl of twigs. Totems in the making. An owl screeched outside. The woman tilted her head slightly toward the source. The shack contained no windows, only a loose-fitting front door.

The owl cried again, so the woman finally rose. Her long hair fell across her front, covering her face and breasts. She parted the hairy curtain enough to reveal a beautiful youthful face, one familiar. Verity Soule's face was that of the Pointing Woman.

Verity yanked open the door and looked outside. The woman stood proud, showing no signs of shame over her nakedness, a woman comfortable in her skin and home. Spotting nothing worthy of an owl's cry, she retreated inside.

From the edge of the forest, a dark figure watched Verity, grunting in hunger at the sight of the woman. When the woman retreated into her home, the dark figure returned to his task involving a blade. Hands wet with blood, the figure carried Esther further into the woods.

An owl hooted again. Just another night in the forest.

CHAPTER 23

THE CAB DRIVER KEPT one eye on the road and one on the woman in the backseat that he had seen partially undressed. Heather rolled her eyes. One day on the dating market and a photo-snapping, leering man was what she got. The beaming driver suddenly soured as their destination came into view. Heather noticed the visible change in his demeanor.

"What? What is it?" Heather asked.

"I have driven by here many times. I do not like this home."

"Join the club."

He stopped on the road, refusing to use the driveway. Heather shook her head over the lack of service, but handed off her credit card. Exiting the vehicle, she approached the driver's window, waiting for the return of her card. Heather eyed the house nervously. She leaped when she turned back to the cab, finding the driver's face almost pressed against her body as he leaned out the window. He handed over the card with a grin.

"Anything else I can do for you, Heather?" The man stretched out the name as if discovering a secret.

Heather looked again from the creepy man to the even creepier house. She decided on the lesser of two evils. "Yes. If you can please wait, I just need to gather my things."

The man's eyes went wide. She followed his gaze, which looked past her and toward the windows. He burned rubber. Heather leaped back, frightened by the gunned engine, squealing tires, and proximity to the fleeing vehicle. She approximated where he was looking and saw a curtain moving in the living room window. What had the man seen?

With long strides, Heather rushed up the driveway. The front door stood ajar. She stepped into the foyer, her footsteps the only sound in the place.

"Linda? Ruby?'

No answer. She looked around nervously, then rushed up the stairs to her room where she threw a suitcase on the bed, opened it, then attacked the closet. She grabbed clothes in bunches and started stuffing. Upon returning to the closet for round two, she noticed more clothes. His not hers.

His clothes should not have been there. Heather woke several times in the hospital, shocked Tom was absent. They had argued, decided the divorce would happen, but she thought he would still be there in her time of need. She was wrong. She woke each time alone. Her friends made an appearance even though she never saw them. One nurse spoke of an abusive friend. Ruby, no question.

Heather was certain Tom would be far away by now, already course correcting his vacation, jetting off to some nerdy spot, an oasis for the man. Heather grew up around southern gentleman and never expected to end up with such a scholarly and serious man, but it happened, and it worked. For a time. Then it did not.

The pain of not finding him there at the foot of her bed when she woke was unexpected and fierce. She was ready to move on, was ready to find a country bumpkin like herself. Heather was not planning on waiting for the next fella, she was ready to sign papers and have another go. Life was too short. So why did it hurt to discover Tom was not there?

Except maybe he was. Heather's heart fluttered, remembering his smile, often accompanied by a sliding of glasses up a nose. She ran her fingers along the arm of a sport coat, following its line to the floor. Men's shoes. The clothes meant one thing. A break for sure, but he remained somewhere in town, probably exploring witchy things. Maybe he was unaware of her being in the hospital.

"Tom is still here. He didn't leave me."

Mist floated through the air as she spoke. Heather exhaled to test the air, knowing full well what to expect. The chill overtook her quickly, cold enough to hurt her lungs when she breathed. Dimples rose all over her skin. The unnatural temperature prodded her back into action. She grabbed more of her things and stuffed them in the bag. Somewhere a child giggled.

"Ruby?"

No, not Ruby. Foolish to even consider it. Heather taught class long enough to recognize a child's laughter. The patter of tiny feet down the hall confirmed it. Heather stepped toward the door. A child ran past, brushing Heather back. The girl raced down the stairs. A giggle sounded somewhere below. Heather exited the room and slowly descended the stairs.

"Who are you?"

The house fell silent. Heather reached the bottom and spotted movement in the living room. The child lay huddled in front of the fireplace, her back turned. (Warming herself?) The place was cold. So cold. Heather's breath continued to steam in the frigid air. The child moved slightly and giggled again.

As Heather moved closer, the child bolted, holding something in her hands. The girl moved so fast Heather failed to get a good look. The girl raced into the kitchen. Heather followed. Despite running herself, she arrived too late to intercept the child. The door to the basement stood open, frost lining the door frame's molding. Heather looked through and peered into darkness.

Eyeing the exit, Heather considered her options. The laughter of the child rose from below. A chill greater than the temperature drop gripped her chest. Something was wrong. She turned to go when suddenly the laughter changed to murmured voices.

"Linda? Ruby?" Another voice joined the chorus, mournful. Male? "Tom?"

That might be an answer. Maybe Tom could not be there for her. Maybe something happened to him. She descended the stairs. The whispers and cries appeared to come from everywhere. A cone of sound circling her ears, trailing her every step. Midway down the stairs, the voices ceased.

She reached the bottom and heard it. A scratch. She sought the source and noticed a brick wall in the distance. One brick missing near the floor. For a moment she was overcome with memory. Had she been here before? It was the brick wall as much as the scratching which flooded her mind with memories. She looked at her fingers and remembered the questions from the doctor which made no sense at the time. Had she been the one scratching? And if so, who was doing it now?

"Tom?"

The scratching ceased. Heather moved forward on trembling legs and leaned her head onto the brick, listening.

"Tom," Heather whispered, stroking the wall as if it contained her husband.

A hand shot out through the hole in the wall and gripped her leg. Heather cried out and tried to kick it away but could not free herself. She fell back against the wall, her leg twisting painfully. Then several bricks exploded out higher and an arm shot out, grabbing her across her chest.

More bricks exploded, more arms emerged, all dull, grey, grabbing torso, hair, arms, all combining to trap Heather in place. They held her in a position where she could only look straight ahead. Dead Verity, the Pointing Woman, emerged from the shadows in the distance.

In a flash the Pointing woman was upon her, the extended finger touching Heather's forehead which frosted over, a different kind of brain freeze. Ice spread down Heather's face, forcing one eye partially closed, the lashes stuck together by frost.

The Pointing Woman grinned at the trapped woman. Heather ceased fighting against her human bonds, the arms too strong. The frigid temperatures caused Heather's motor skills to slow. Her chilled breaths came in shallow gulps. Then the Pointing Woman swung her arm, pointing elsewhere in the room.

Heather turned her head in the same direction. Dead Rose stepped forward, cupping something in outstretched hands. The red square on the girl's face seemed to spread with every step the child took. Was it melting? It was. The red square drooped, spreading down the girl's cheeks as the child stepped forward, destination Heather. The Pointing Woman vanished somewhere in the dark.

With every step Rose took, her face changed. Step. Her face suddenly mutilated beyond recognition. Step. An exposed skull. Step. A screaming child. Step. Back to before, but the square dripping down her face as if made of wax.

The girl finally reached Heather and spread her hands open to reveal a burning coal. It ignited in the girl's hands and quickly spread to her nightgown. Rose erupted in flames and her face fully melted. Rose screamed, wailing in terror while Heather did the same. The child embraced Heather, who burst into flames as well. All the frost covering Heather sizzled to steam and the arms holding her receded into the wall.

Flames burned both woman and child to black until, with no more fuel left to burn, the fire finally went out. Acrid smoke danced through the air, carrying memories of lost lives. The couple remained in an embrace, leaning against the wall like the aftermath of Pompei. The child turned to ash and fluttered to the floor, leaving Heather's corpse entirely alone.

Dead grey legs trudged through the ashes and plodded up the stairs. The arms behind the wall re-emerged and grasped at Heather, grabbing her in chunks, pulling bones and burned flesh through the tiny openings until nothing remained.

From atop the stairs, a child giggled.

CHAPTER 24

They drove the van along an isolated road filled with twists and turns. The winding pavement forced Andrew to drive at a cautious pace. Ruby's bare feet dangled out the open passenger window. Inside the van, Ruby breathed in the fresh air coursing through the vehicle. Andrew focused on driving but appeared at ease. Country living slowly took hold of the couple as they enjoyed a rare moment of silence. Rounding a curve, Ruby's feet brushed against roadside foliage. She yanked her feet inside with a gale of laughter. Andrew grinned.

"I warned you," Andrew said.

"You drove into it on purpose."

"I drove into poison ivy on purpose?"

"Poison ivy? Oh my God, was that poison ivy?"

Andrew nodded stoically before bursting into laughter. Ruby slapped his shoulder.

"You turd."

"It could have been. I'm a city guy, not a country guy, in case you hadn't noticed." She leaned against him, and he mock panicked. "Hey, don't give me the ivy!"

She laughed but suddenly bounced away into the passenger door as Andrew swerved to avoid an oncoming pickup. The truck blared its horn long into the distance.

"Narrow roads. How about I pay attention, huh?" Andrew settled back in.

Ruby pulled herself back up and noticed the sun gleaming through breaks in the trees. "It's beautiful. Why aren't we seeing more of this?"

"Seeing plenty now."

"Yes. But Linda hasn't. Why is she so moody when this new place is so stunning? This is as beautiful as any of our other excursions. Prettier than Vegas, for certain."

"Hey, don't knock Vegas. We almost got married there, remember?"

She slid over again and caressed his chest. "How could I forget? Tom was going to be the best man. Then Heather and Linda fought over who would be the bridesmaid. What happened to that group of knuckleheads?"

"We done grew up, missy."

"Yeah. I wish things could be so simple again. It doesn't make sense why Linda is so on edge lately."

The van pulled free of the forest and onto a town street. A large sign with a painted witch on it greeted them. They merged into traffic, heavy for such a small town.

Ruby noticed the sign. "Okay, fine. The camping vibe is gone. This whole witch vibe is a weird thing. Maybe that is her reason."

"I think I see the hospital." Andrew squinted, making out their destination.

"What did Linda mean by I did nothing wrong?"

"What are you talking about?"

"Earlier. Before she went on her run." Ruby mimed air quotes while saying the word run. "Linda said I did nothing wrong. There were only three of us there."

Andrew turned the wheel and used the moment to look away from his girlfriend. She grabbed his arm.

"Andrew?"

"Hey, I'm trying to park."

"What aren't you telling me?"

Andrew parked and leaned into the steering wheel. "I don't know what she's talking about."

"She was clearly upset."

"And has been since we got here. I swear I don't know who she is anymore. This whole place, this whole vibe. What are we doing?"

"Helping our friend."

"Really? Because Tom was our friend too, was he not? Where is he now? Now we're visiting our other friend in a hospital. When does that happen?"

"Andrew..."

"No. I'm not done. We zipline, party, white-water raft, surf, mountain climb. Have any of us ever suffered anything more than a hangover?" He noticed Ruby open her mouth and interceded. "The answer is no. Maybe I told her she should give us all a break. Maybe I told her to lighten up."

"Andrew, how could you?"

"You were just saying the same thing. Besides, I can't be certain what I said since I was drunk. Everything is fuzzy. It's like I'm gaining clarity now only because we are out of that damn house."

"Her house."

"Yeah. Is she staying here? Because if so, this is my first and last visit. We did our part. We played the good friends. I don't remember fully, but likely said something along those lines to her last night. Drunk or not, maybe it's how I feel."

"Then it is not just me. Feeling the creeps. I'm trying for her. Really trying, but something is off about this whole town."

They exited the vehicle and stepped into the shadow of the hospital as the world grew dark. They climbed the driveway. The double doors slid open silently before them. The couple entered the hospital into an empty corridor. No one sat at the check-in desk. The waiting room sat empty. Not even crickets chirped. Ruby leaned over the admission desk. The chair remained empty.

A cup of tea rested next to a computer. The drink appeared cold, not a drop of steam left, only condensation on the lip of the cup.

"What the hell?" Ruby asked.

"Small town. This is not a big city ER. They probably do not receive a lot of patients."

"Bullshit. A hospital is a hospital. You think some kid isn't falling out of a tree as we speak?"

"Yes. But that kid's parent can't afford insurance, so they will tear up a sheet and fashion a sling."

Ruby looked at him sadly. "Like the kids we care for?"

"Not all orphans are without parents."

Ruby shook her head to shake off the melancholy. She postured, placing hands on hips. Defiant. "When we tried to visit Heather proper, they sicked security on us. And now nothing? Be consistent people! We're going to visit a patient, bitches!"

The couple approached the nearest elevator, which opened on the button push. They entered. The elevator delivered them to a dark floor, pitch black, other than the elevator lights and exit signs on either end of the hall.

"They ever hear of windows?"

Andrew stepped forward and motion lights kicked in. He spread his arms along with a grin. The goofiness relaxed Ruby. They moved down the hall.

A hissing sounded from behind the door ahead. Ruby stopped and gestured for Andrew to do the same. *Whoosh, click, shhhh. Whoosh, click, shhhh.*

"Do you hear that?"

Andrew nodded. They moved closer to Heather's room, where the volume increased. A ventilator breathing for someone. Ruby reached for the door.

"Did she get worse? Why is there no doctor around?"

They pushed the door open and saw a curtain pulled around Heather's bed. An outline of a female showed through the plastic. The ventilator stood outside the curtained section, its tubes extended through a gap in the fabric, attached to the patient. Ruby and Andrew approached. Ruby yanked the curtain and screamed.

An ancient woman occupied the bed, one eye wide open, almost out of the socket. The single eye glared at the intruders. Ruby stumbled back, pulling the curtain with her. Andrew reached out and caught Ruby. A man appeared and yanked the curtain away.

"What the hell are you doing?" The man yelled. He appeared as grizzled as the patient. "My wife had a stroke! Why are you bothering her? Are you trying to steal from her? You vultures! Hasn't she suffered enough?"

"No, I..." Ruby raised her hands, confused. "We are in the wrong room. So sorry."

Ruby bolted for the door and screamed as she ran into someone. A nurse.

"Jesus! Fuck! Christ!" Ruby yelled.

"What are you doing here? You are not Linda's family."

"What did you say?" Ruby recovered, glaring at the woman.

"I said you are not family."

"Damn, right they aren't family. Vultures, the lot of them!" the old man yelled.

Andrew escorted Ruby around the woman who gave them room to exit. Ruby turned back to the nurse.

"Where is our friend, Heather?"

"Your friend created quite the stir earlier, not unlike you now. She left Salem."

"You mean left the hospital?"

"She insisted she was leaving Salem," the nurse reiterated.

"Why wasn't someone at the desk to tell us all this?"

"Small town. This is not a big city ER."

Andrew shrugged at Ruby. Told you. Ruby fumed, ready to lash out again until noticing the old man. Adrenaline gone, he sat in a chair alongside his wife, sobbing. The old woman continued glaring at Ruby, the eye unblinking, looking through her into another place and time. Ruby deflated.

Steering clear of Ruby as they exited the hospital, Andrew gave her plenty of room. Ruby spun as she walked, looking up toward the upper floors of the hospital. As they reached the van, Ruby shook her head.

"She said I wasn't part of Linda's family."

"What? She said we weren't family."

"No. I heard her. She said Linda's family. You were there."

"She's right. We're not."

Ruby shoved Andrew in the chest. "How can you say that?" Ruby walked away from him and opened the passenger door.

Andrew grabbed her shoulder. "I did not hear the nurse mention Linda. But if she did, who am I to argue? We are not her family. You heard Tom. He would sleep with her if he had the chance."

"Tom's a pig."

"Way to talk about my best man."

"Former. He walked out on us, remember?"

"And now it looks like your bridesmaid did as well. Or one of them. Lucky you have a backup."

Ruby fell back through the open door and fell onto the seat. "Wow. We're not in Vegas anymore, are we?"

"We could be."

"What are you saying?"

"It's my van. There is still some summer left."

"They have pools, margaritas."

"Wedding chapels," Andrew added.

Ruby brightened, the sparkle returning to her eyes. She reached out and clasped her arms around Andrew's neck, pulling him into the van and a kiss.

"Maybe Heather and Tom had the right idea."

"Well, the leaving part, not so much the divorce part."

The couple kissed. Ruby pulled away and stared into Andrew's face. They kissed again, growing excited. They grabbed at one another, hungry, passionate. Ruby moaned, her eyes closing, but something caught her eye. She yelped, alerting Andrew, who turned and spotted an elderly couple outside their door on their way to the hospital.

The two people were similar in age to those in the room above. Andrew laughed and issued a quick apology. He closed the door for Ruby. The old man wore shorts displaying stick legs with veins crisscrossing his skin like a wrinkled road map. He used a walker to remain upright and his wife helped him along. Andrew waited for them to pass.

The old woman turned to her husband. "Why don't you do that to me anymore?"

"Because I can't," he replied.

The old woman shook her head and moved him along. Andrew smiled and climbed into the driver's seat. He and Ruby drove away, their faces beaming with hope.

CHAPTER 25

WALTER FLIPPED THROUGH A series of pages depicting the early beheadings. Something fell from the book and hit the floor, vanishing into the shadows at their feet. Walter looked about frantically, worried about angering the priest. Had they broken the spine? Had a section fallen out from the ancient, valuable tome? It quickly became clear the priest was nowhere nearby.

"Father?" Walter asked quietly. Upon receiving no response, he breathed in relief. "Thank goodness the man did not see that. Normally, I am careful, but I admit finding myself lost in the new information."

Linda searched the dark floor with her glo-stick. She rose slowly, inspecting her find. "It appears to be a book all its own."

She showed the thin volume to Walter. Linda opened the blank cover to find the sloppy handwriting of a child. The scholar lit up. Linda flipped through a few pages, not reading but checking out the strange drawings on every other page. The pictures were crude but disturbing. Walter could not hide his excitement.

"A child's journal! Cannot get more intimate details about events from the time than that. This must be what you Americans feel like at Christmas."

"Minus the creeped-out part, sure. I wonder where the priest ventured to."

"There is much history here. He is likely exploring another section of books. Fine by me. The longer he keeps busy, the more time we have. I assumed they would have long ago moved historical records to a larger city like Boston. Scholars would normally begin hunting there for these types of documents. That would explain how these have gone unnoticed for so long."

"Except they never left Salem."

"Exactly. And your inherited key eliminated bureaucracy, allowing us this unprecedented access. Before investigating the words of a child, I wish to finish my current course of study."

Walter returned to the original book, snapping pictures with his phone every time he turned a page. Linda set the child's journal down alongside the larger volume. A shadow passed across the open door behind them. Linda approached the open space and peered through.

"Father?" No answer.

Walter turned pages excitedly until stopping at a disturbing painting. "Here is the proof."

A pebble tumbled in through the doorway, landing at Linda's feet. Linda eyed it curiously, but returned to Walter. She grimaced at the image on the open page.

"This was when Catholicism butted heads with emerging Protestantism. The best way to make people return to the flock is to find a common enemy. Christianity also pushed back against paganism. Many of America's celebrated holidays grew out of pagan rituals. The most religious of holidays, Christmas, as I mentioned moments ago, actually..."

"Walter, focus. Can we keep this on the trials and the links to my family?"

"Yes, sorry. Child in a candy store here."

"Kid. The term is kid."

"Yes, well, this image provides some answers. Women were desperate. They were being hunted, but not by native Americans in the area. In fact, the indigenous people appeared to have cemented a trade relationship with the settlers in Salem. A truce, one might say. Within such small communities, citizens would have noticed outsiders, which meant the attacks came from someone local. Having women go missing only to end up beheaded left them vulnerable, with no one to trust. For protection, they appear to have gone well beyond paganism. Someone in the community turned to darker arts." Walter turned a page which displayed an ink drawing resembling the totem in Haddy's possession.

Linda looked at the totem and felt a shiver run through her body. Walter waved the light stick over pages like a wand, turning pages quickly, searching. Despite the grim nature of the book, he proceeded with glee. Walter gasped at several passages. Linda looked to the man for explanation, but he gave none, too absorbed in the words.

Linda traced her hand over the child's journal before opening it to the first page where she saw the name Sadie Goode written. Goode, her name, Linda's identity. This was a relative as a child. The sloppy writing brought Linda back to her days as a child. In an instant, she felt herself back in the school. Not as an instructor, but as a student sitting at a desk so large her feet did not touch the ground. She wrote in a journal of her own with an oversized flat pencil. She practiced her letters over and over on the lined yellow page.

All the other children did the same. Silence filled the classroom as a nun walked the rows, making *tch*, *tch*, *tch* sounds at every inspected page. Not good enough, never good enough. The nun neared young Linda, who started sweating. Linda scribbled, trying to stay within the lines, but her hand grew tight. She gripped the pencil, pressing too hard. The page threatened to tear.

The nun drew closer. Linda's letters were too messy. Too sloppy. She would receive the scorn of the nun in front of the class. The nun would embarrass Linda and make an example of her. So close now. The woman's feet stopped alongside Linda's desk. Linda looked up and saw only darkness underneath the habit. A black void. Until the woman opened her eyes. They burned red. Young Linda screamed.

Linda jerked in fright, slamming the journal closed. Normally cognizant of her fright, Walter, for a second time, was too engaged in work to notice. Linda tried to shake it off. Her past just mingled with her present in her mind. There were too many dreams (visions?), too much discomfort since arriving in Salem.

Despite finally discovering a potential name, or at least a thread to her past, something she searched her whole life for, she could not hold on to the happiness of discovery. Initially, she felt the charge and excitement of the discovery. But now, mere moments later, the unease returned. She could not shake the sense that something was not right.

Walter continued flipping through pages, reacting animatedly with every turn. With a gasp, he turned to face her. "This is it. This explains not just the quest for protection from the dark arts, but the event that led to the end of it all."

"The end of what?"

"The last hanging. This written account purports to explain away the very last hanging."

CHAPTER 26

1693

H ANDS TWISTED BRANCHES WITH practiced precision. After several twists and turns, the form took shape. The tightly spun twine held the sticks together. Once completed, the stick figure joined several others atop a small table. Verity stepped back and examined her handiwork. There were several totems now, though she wondered whether it would ever be enough. Ethel Jenkins was the latest, her head discovered in a field, staring up at the sky with maggots blocking whatever view the poor woman might have had.

The local newspaper refused to report on such butchery. They deemed the material too sensitive for their readers. That left herself and others in the town to share the information of who and when women disappeared. There was frequently a gap between a woman's sudden disappearance and her reappearance split in two. What happened to the women in the interim?

Ethel was a highly attractive individual, as were many of the missing. While the law and church (one and the same) in town appeared clueless, the circumstances did not go unnoticed by Verity. *Crime now to walk in the form in which we were born,* Verity thought with disdain.

The hunter had stolen more than women's last breaths. The monster caused the purest of individuals to question their own piety. Was it no longer enough to act subservient to forces around them both in home and the church? Was the glimpse of an ankle enough to draw attention from the beast? For that certainly was the correct designation for such a killer.

Verity returned to her tasks. Not proud to be nude, but free to be. She refused to wear a disguise in her own home. Verity was a child of Mother Earth. Her body was a gift, so to wrap it until unrecognizable was blasphemous in her eyes. Ceremony required honesty, and truth. But ceremony also required tradition so she retrieved a folded garment and shook it open.

The garment was an amalgamation of robe and dress. With no hood, it scooped open at the neck, designed for an easy slip over the body. No buttons or lace adorned the thin, sheer, white muslin material. She pulled it over her head. Unlike the daily societal demands to dress modestly, the ceremonial outfit barely disguised her true form. Her breasts stood out prominently under the fabric and draped as comfortable as skin. She did not mind the need for ceremonial clothing because she considered the outward facing garment a representation of her inward spirit.

Ready to begin, she pulled the animal skin rug off the floor, revealing a large, painted pentagram. Heavy layers of wax covered each of the pentagram's points, remnants of past ceremonies. She opened a drawer in her end table and retrieved five black candles. She lit them and placed one on each point of the pentagram. Next, Verity collected a bowl and knife. She sliced open her palm and allowed the blood to fill the vessel.

Once partially filled, she retrieved a nearby strip of cloth to wrap her wound. She used her teeth to cinch the knot. Verity moved with grace about the small enclosure, petite enough to move unencumbered. She remained silent the entire time, never even grunting when she bled herself.

Grabbing the totems, she placed them in a line along the center of the pentagram. She dropped to her knees and bowed her head to the floor while lifting the bowl up in offering. Lifting her head, she poured blood from the bowl over the totems. Her white outfit absorbed a stray splash of blood. The small red dot bloomed over the surface near her stomach. She paid it no mind, focusing on the task at hand.

With a thunderous clop, the door burst open. Three church guardsmen burst into the room. Verity rose, leaping for her blade. She swiped, slicing the cheek of the first through the door. She recognized him, Joseph Milton, a braggart, and ruffian. Milton yelped and grabbed at his face as the other two advanced on her. She swung wildly. The men leaped aside. Hugh Brooks caught fire from a candle which spread over his leg. He danced around, trying to put it out.

The remaining guard, Thomas Cromwell, grabbed her wrists, fighting for control of the dagger. She released it, surprising the man, but she did so to free her own hands with which she punched him in the face. Cromwell dropped the blade. Milton rejoined the fight, and the two went after Verity at once. Unaccustomed to such a tight space in which to battle, the men slammed walls with elbows each time they pulled back an arm to strike. Their own size was a hindrance.

Verity moved deftly through the space, gouging eyes and striking successfully while avoiding the men's grip. Brooks finally extinguished the fire, making it three on one. Verity bent for the blade when a knee struck her in the face. She grunted and fell back. Then a boot kicked her face. Blood spurted from a busted lip, and she grunted again, fading from consciousness.

Reverend Goode stood over her. From the ground, she reached for the blade. Goode kicked her ribs, and something snapped. She cried out and involuntarily twisted to protect the damaged area. Goode retrieved the knife from the floor and held the handle by fingertips, dangling it loosely over her face so it could fall at any moment. He surveyed the home.

The reverend's features hardened as he took in the blasphemous image at their feet. He eyed the stack of totems dripping with blood, looked from candle to candle. The blade dangled over Verity's face. She moved her head from side to side, trying to avoid the knife if it her captor released it.

"There is wickedness at work here," Goode said.

"Aye. We agree," Verity said. Verity turned her head to look straight at him. The two locked eyes. "We tried your God. A foolish effort that cost many a woman her head."

"And your efforts here are the reason it cost many a neck," Goode replied.

"We needed protection from the likes of you!"

"I am but the messenger. The Lord speaks through my children, and they identify the wicked. However, in your case, my servant revealed where she received her blasphemous totem. That led us here. And not a moment too soon. No need for a trial with all this evidence."

"Curse your false trials. Curse your false righteousness."

Goode smiled and dropped the blade. It barely missed the woman's face. A mistake. She moved quickly, rising onto all fours, and grabbed the knife, jabbing it into Milton's leg. He went down screaming, grabbing the wound. Before she could stand, Goode kicked Verity so hard she flew into the wall. She crumpled to the ground, out of breath. The remaining guards lifted her to her feet.

The reverend backhanded her face, and she fell limp in the guards' arms, barely conscious. Goode grabbed her hair and lifted her face. She prepped to spit, but he thrust a hand over her mouth.

"Save your spittle. Every drop of water is precious where you shall be going." Then he leaned into her ear, whispering. "Beautiful in your fury. I shall make private time with you when the guards are scarce. Make it worth my while. I will take my time with you, even if it delays the gallows. Though neck shall meet rope imminently, the town demands their sacrifices."

Milton removed the blade and rose to his feet, battling a limp. Sweat dripped over his brow, brought on by pain from the leg and facial cuts. He pressed the blade against the woman's throat. Goode placed his hand in between.

"Why slice that which shall hang soon enough? In the meantime, apply your discontent on her belongings. This place is unclean. Unholy. Burn it. Burn it all."

The guard handed the blade to Goode. The reverend used the hilt to strike Verity in the face. She fell unconscious. Goode took one side of the woman, Cromwell the other, and led her to the doorway. The remaining guards kicked over the candles on the floor. The flames quickly spread, but only within the space of the pentagram, racing across the star and taking on the shape of the symbol.

Nothing else burned except for the pentagram. The flames shot high into the air, creating a wall of flame but refused to spread. The men shared confused looks. Goode finally kicked over the table, which quickly went up in flames and spread the blaze. Goode then exited with his prize. The other guards added more fuel.

On their initial approach, the men staged the horses at a distance to keep from alerting the woman. Such stealth required them to carry Verity a significant distance to transport. By the time they reached their rides, the fire had spread. Unknown to her, Verity's world burned.

Verity woke to darkness, uncertain of her surroundings while bouncing in motion and groaning awake to a world still blurry. Steps. She heard footsteps on creaky wooden stairs. Then she felt the descent. She struggled not to slip back into darkness.

Smoke. She smelled its heavy odor. In the coat of a captor, in her own hair. Had they burned her cabin? It would account for the smell. Verity realized she was nude at the same time she realized her plight. She dangled over the shoulder of a captor.

The woman tried to rise but found herself bound, and still groggy. Keys slid loudly into a metal lock. A door opened into darkness. Cries of despair streamed from the shadows inside. Goode threw the woman in. A guard stood behind the man holding a lantern, the light of which landed on Verity's bruised face. Verity backed away until hitting something hard. She turned and noticed a stone altar center of the room. Chains led from the floor to the stone temple. Verity gasped upon spotting hands in the chains near her head.

A nude woman stood bent over the temple, much like in a stock. Chains held the woman in place atop the rock and she appeared unconscious. Verity sought to help the woman until hands reached out from the shadows, grasping at the new prisoner, touching Verity all over as they reached for a humanity lost. Various eyes caught the light, all open in fear, standing out obscenely white against their soot covered faces. All whimpered in misery, lost.

They tugged at Verity's hair, at her body. She stifled a cry, unwilling to reward her captor. He noticed the slight, and with a harrumph, closed the iron gate. Instinctively, she leaped for the bars, grasping them, and pressing her face. Goode only smiled as he closed a false brick wall beyond the bars, stealing the last of the light from the captors.

CHAPTER 27
1693

R EVEREND GOODE LOOKED OUT on the assembled crowd from behind a pew as formidable as a cemetery gate. His family sat in the front row. The only townspeople brave enough to sit behind them were several elderly people, too close to a grave to worry about accusations. Goode slammed his hands on the pew. The noise startled the rapt crowd.

"On this day, God rested. After creating all that we hold dear, wouldst thou deny our heavenly Father a heavenly nap?"

The crowd chuckled at the sentiment. One of the old men behind the children mentioned how he, too, needed a nap. More chuckling from the crowd accompanied by a few *amens*. Sadie looked around the room and people fell silent. Goode met his daughter's gaze and nodded gently. An unspoken language. *Let it be child, let the cattle have their fun.*

"Amen indeed. Surely, we shall not question the wisdom of the almighty who, in his desire to nap, understands that on this day, the holiest of holy, that He leaves gates unguarded. Who shall stand watch while the one who sees all slumbers? We know He rests on this holy day, and that is why we assemble. Are we not the eyes of a God who sleeps? Are we not His righteous arm of justice ready to strike down those who would sin in the absence of our Lord?"

The crowd murmured, agreeing. Sadie grinned, taking it in herself, smiling at her father's cries of justice. Rose fiddled with her hair and studied her shoes. Althea pulled her daughter's hand away and forced her to sit up straight.

"Righteousness never sleeps! Righteousness beats in the hearts of God's true creations. Ask those who stray from the Lord's path. Are they righteous? Nay. They walk in the footsteps of the devil himself. Quite a trick marching in time to tiny hooved prints."

The crowd laughed once again until noticing the intensity overcoming the reverend's face. Goode stepped away from the lectern and reached toward Sadie, who stood and joined her father. Goode patted her head as the girl looked out on the crowd.

"Through the mouths of babes. Thank the Lord for our children, for we too slept on this Holy Day. Perhaps not in our beds, not in our homes, but in our hearts. We grew complacent while evil brewed. We napped while sins of flesh spread through our community. Evil thrives under the averted eye. So, who did not sleep? Who never sleeps? Our children."

Sadie beamed with pride at her father's praise. Goode took one of his daughter's hands. Sadie raised her free one, drawing gasps from the crowd. False alarm. The child merely pulled a strand of hair away from her face. Goode observed with fascination the power his daughter held over the masses.

"Worry not. The accused hide from these walls, not in them." The crowd laughed nervously. Goode continued. "I praise you Father, Lord of Heaven, because you have hidden these things from the wise and learned and revealed them to little children. Blessed are the children, for they see through the masks we wear. They are free of the deepest and darkest of desires beating in the hearts of adults. It is through their eyes we shall find our salvation by ridding the land of those who would defile it. Are we not better off freed from the wretched wicked women who flaunt their desires for all to see, the heathens who lift their skirts to tempt the virtuous? Are not we a better society for removing those who would question the hierarchy sent down from the Lord himself? The wanton lust of the accused would live forever unabated, if not for our children. Isn't that right, dearest Sadie?"

Sadie raised her arm and pointed at her father. "I accuse thee of being correct, dearest father."

The crowd laughed at the turn.

"See how the innocent shall pass? Well done, my daughter, well done. Now onto the fields everyone, a hanging awaits!"

The crowd cheered and rose, flooding the exit. Ramses stood nearby, more morose than normal. Goode gestured his daughter to join the rest of the family, then waved his wife off. Althea melded with the crowd, taking her children along, the congregants giving the children wide berth.

"Ramses."

"We are down to a single accused," Ramses said.

"How can that be?"

"Many reasons. Your daughters growing timid, losing their nerve. The courts in Boston demanded we release some of the accused into their care. I fear they are questioning our motives."

"Boston? Bah! Pigs at a trough eager to feed on that which we have procured. Foul goods they will find in the prisoners they keep."

"Is that all they shall find?"

Goode stared down Ramses. "Discretion in all things proper and more discretion in all things less so. My assistants are few. One of the best is family. Sadie takes part with a glee bordering on excess. The daughters you fear are losing resolve strike fear into the hearts of the imprisoned as well as the accused."

"Are they not the same?" Ramses asked.

"If it helps you sleep at night. Fewer hangings in the meantime until we restock the stocks," Goode said.

"And when the masses, hungry for their shows, find none? Will they not question the number of citizens they know to be missing versus those on the ropes?"

Goode eyed the nearby crowds. "Were an inventory taken, then yes, that could prove problematic. But even if my daughters cast more fingers today, trials must go on. Even this bloodthirsty crowd insists on the guise of justice."

"Too true. The Lord himself could not have arrived at such a conclusion," Ramses said.

"Flattery is not required, reverend. It was thee who led me to such a conclusion. What is it thou seeketh from me?"

Ramses fluffed his garb, making a show of the formality of the church. "As the church is prone to visitors, it serves clergy well to know when to serve a house wine and when to proffer a bottle of a more private nature." Ramses spread his hands and tilted his head, seeking recognition behind his request. Open the private cell.

"I supply counsel. Give the accused a chance to repent by informing on their peers," Goode protested.

"And where from remains a mystery to the church, never mind the populace."

"Not a mystery to myself or the Lord."

"I would be more comfortable if the church had a say in the condition of the convicted."

"You question my methods?"

"And if so, shall I find myself at the end of the arm of a child? I am not so foolish to challenge your authority, but a hungry crowd left unfed will soon seek sustenance elsewhere."

"A single rope today?"

"As I stated, yes. The crowd is quite large. The spectacle draws more than any sermon. Until your kin identify more guilty, perhaps it is time to dip into your private stock? If they have failed to repent by now, what more purpose could they serve?"

"They fulfill a certain... need. But what am I but one man against a crowd? I ask you to stall and prepare two ropes more."

Ramses flashed the dead toothed smile and exited. Goode gestured to Milton and Brooks, the very two injured in the abduction of Verity. Milton still wore a bandage over his leg.

"You wanted your revenge? The time has come."

W ITH A LOUD CLACK, the brick façade opened, revealing a cell. Goode entered with Milton and Brooks. A stone altar filled the center of the prison. A nude woman lay across it, chained in place, partially standing, not even allowed to lie down, though it would have been possible. Piles of clothes surrounded the stone temple, garbs removed from so many victims. Goode pulled a torn black dress from the pile and tossed it at the woman after the guards unfastened her bonds. The woman fell on rubber legs after holding position too long. It was Verity, aged well beyond the time of her incarceration. She swiped ineffectively toward her captors, who easily avoided her effort.

"Cover thyself lest the world see you as I do. I had other plans for thee, but fortune insists they change."

While the woman struggled to pull the gown on, Goode gestured to another woman, the mother who lost her child on the street. Her fingers were raw from using them to write the same message repeatedly on the walls in her own blood. Lantern light revealed her work. The words '*my child*' covered every inch of the wall within her reach. The defeated woman's features bled into the shadows as if she were part of the darkness. As the guards unlocked her chains and dragged her away, the mother's fingers continued moving, still trying to write the words, always writing, her hands moving on muscle memory.

As the group departed, more eyes opened in the darkness accompanied by moans hidden in corners of the tight space. Some eyes opened like twins, as if one person's face held two sets of eyes so close were some prisoners. Huddled too tight, a mystery of bodily configuration, the answers to their positioning hidden by shadows as dark as evil. A slamming of metal bars closed the door on a world of misery.

A MASSIVE CROWD CHEERED in the field around the festive atmosphere of the gallows. A single woman dangled from a noose, one leg occasionally kicking. Finally, the leg went still and with a loud squish, the woman's bowels vacated, soiling the ground beneath her feet. The crowd fell silent for a moment, then cheered, roaring with satisfaction. Many yelled, "Huzzah!" Others emulated flatulence sounds to the glee of the masses.

The hangman climbed down the stairs and chased away a pair of boys poking at the corpse with a stick. The hangman whistled and two ditchdiggers stopped digging nearby and wheeled their wooden cart into a position below the dangling woman.

Ramses looked over the crowd and declared it good. But he also understood how quickly they could turn. The hangman cut the rope and went about resetting the trap door. The body flopped into the cart and the ditch diggers used their shovels to scoop up the dirt containing the woman's foul. They dumped the shovels atop the woman and rolled her away as looky-loos eyed the body, covering their faces from the odor.

The dead woman's face remained frozen in a twist, her neck at an odd angle, the rope still attached to her throat. The woman's tongue dangled long, thick, in a deep purple matching the color of her face. Her eyes jutted out as if startled.

While the ditch diggers went about burying their charge, the crowd grew restless. A rumble of discontent flooded the crowd, who were unhappy to see the hangman finished after one turn. Sensing the shift in the atmosphere, the burly hooded man turned to Ramses in the distance. The reverend discreetly raised two fingers. After a quick nod of understanding, the hangman made a show of assembling a fresh noose. The crowd cheered as the man set the rope into position, checking the trap door. When the man started a second noose, the crowd went wild.

By the time the hangman finished, the crowd parted at its center. Horses clopped through, the guards each riding a horse with the accused at their rear. Hair eclipsed the face of the mother, her head lolled as if already dead, though she searched the crowd through her tangle of hair for her child. Too weak to lift her head, she smiled at each girl she passed as if it might be her own. Eventually, she succumbed to laughter, which unsettled her rider, Brooks.

"Settle down, you," the guard said.

"They are all my children," the woman whispered in a rasp, her throat damaged from too much screaming.

"Crazy witch," Brooks said.

On the second horse, Verity looked out upon the crowd as she passed, meeting the gaze of various people who shirked away in unease at the forceful stare. Verity finally turned her attention to the horseman, Milton.

"How is the leg?"

"Been fighting infection and fever, you evil wench. But my time for revenge is soon at hand.," he replied discreetly as he waved to the crowd drawing cheers. "Those cries are for your end. Consider them all speaking for me."

"I will take that into consideration when the moment arrives. Worry not about your leg falling as useless as the space between. Your misery shall soon expire."

Milton growled and considered throwing a backhand off from his wave, but recognized the number of witnesses at play. In the distance, Goode descended from his own horse and took place alongside his assembled family, positioned near Ramses. Sadie looked up at her father with glee.

Brooks climbed from his horse and handed the woman to the hangman, who dragged her up the stairs. The woman ceased laughing and cried out for her child, asking who had seen her. Citizens looked away when she looked in their direction, the first signs of guilt. Wincing in pain at the at the movement of his horse, Milton tried to steady his restless animal. Brooks walked over and retrieved Verity from her perch. Milton remained on his steed.

Verity eyed the throngs of people as the hangman took her arm. The woman stood firm, surprising Browning. Before making a show of dragging her away, Browning noticed a murmur in the crowd, accompanied by shouts of surprise and concern. Citizens on the outer perimeters looked back and forth from the two events. One a woman on her way to the gallows and the other a disturbance in the crowd. Verity eyed the commotion in the distance with curiosity. The hangman shoved her toward the stairs. Verity climbed slowly, and that was when she noticed the red eyes in the distance.

Browning ignored the disturbance, pushing Verity along. "Get a move on."

"Don't worry, no hurry. Thou shall die before me," Verity replied.

"Unlikely. You will die soon enough, witch! Move along."

Verity no longer fought as the man positioned her atop the trapdoor. The woman was too busy searching the landscape. The hangman looped the noose over the woman's neck and spotted something. *Is that a dog?*

Closer to a wolf. The massive animal made its way through the crowd. People parted, distancing themselves from the huffing animal with thick, black fur. Its eyes danced between jaundice yellow and blazing red, shifting with every movement, possibly reflecting the waning sun. Goode and Ramses failed to spot the cause of the commotion. With nooses firmly in place, most of the crowd chanted for the hanging to begin. Verity turned her head and gazed at the hangman. Browning gripped the lever and pulled.

Crack!

With a loud snap, the lever snapped. The hangman windmilled his arms along the edge of the platform, but too late. He caught Verity's smile before falling to the ground below, where his neck snapped louder than the pull handle. Screams filled the crowd, accompanied by cries of witchcraft.

A growl drew the crowd's attention as the dog arched its back, then leaped toward the injured guard's horse. Rearing up on two legs, the horse threw Milton off his mount, trapping the man's legs in the gear. The horse kicked up, causing the man's head to strike the ground, drawing blood. The dog moved in, glaring at the man. Milton covered his face, expecting a bite, but the dog only barked, causing the horse to sprint. Milton cried out in pain until encountering the ditch digger cart. The man's head smacked sickeningly into the cart's side, opening like a melon. He left gore in his wake as the horse ran off with its dragged corpse.

Brooks raced up the stairs and grabbed what remained of the handle. Both accused dropped when the platform opened. Twin necks snapped simultaneously. The mother fell still immediately, dangling in place. Verity kicked briefly before going still. The crowd fell silent, stunned at the turn of events. Then it happened.

Verity opened her eyes!

A collective scream filled the crowd. Impossibly, Verity lifted her head at a twisted angle and then lifted an arm and pointed at the crowd, waving her finger across the gathering until stopping at Reverend Goode and his family.

"I swear by my lover Satan a curse upon my accusers. A curse upon their children, and their children's children."

Her head finally drooped to stillness, twisting even further at an angle, and her hand remained extended, accusing the crowd. Verity had, in death, become the Pointing Woman.

CHAPTER 28

WALTER GESTURED TO AN image which showed the Pointing Woman dangling from the gallows. Terror filled the faces of the townsfolk in the background, many of whom pointed back at the frightening display. Walter appeared ecstatic despite the horrific image.

"Verity Soule. This woman was the last hanged. The aftermath of her demise ended the practice. Fear brought the community into the hunt for witches and fear removed them from the same," Walter said.

"It is too horrible to imagine."

"The writing suggests Soule cursed her accusers with her last breath. That would include your family. Based on the news articles you provided, it appears things did not go well for your family after that day. Nor for many others in Salem. Many homes burned in the aftermath of the trials, lost to history in a relatively moderate climate, not prone to uncontrollable fires."

"You believe that? Misfortune spread because of one woman?"

"More likely because of what the town did to that poor woman. Some studies suggest the most horrific events in history record themselves in time, like a skip in a record. It might be a little woo-woo, but people believe quartz rocks record events as well, at least the energy of certain events. In Ireland, many have seen the image of a young girl holding a pet bunny moments before a bomb destroyed the building behind her. She did not survive, but her image did, as if burned in time. At least according to locals."

"So are there records of anyone seeing this hanged woman after her death?"

"Good Lord, I would hope not. A pants pisser that would be one could suppose. But what they did to the woman could have lingered in Salem. The collective sacrifice of innocents doomed the town to suffer through a reckoning. No matter how far they might strive to move past the events, if the record skipped, it would keep those filled with guilt trapped under the shadow of past transgressions. I do not believe in curses, but I believe in mental health issues brought on by collective or individual misdeeds. Those involved in such misery would likely attribute every future tragedy to sins of the past. It would explain why someone would try to hide you if they believed you to be in danger."

"My mother dumped me on a doorstep. Am I to believe my mother was being altruistic? Get rid of me fine, but don't burn the bridge to my past."

Linda breathed deep, trying to quell the anger. There, always there, somewhere in the background, anger at her parents for what they did. Each time she comforted a crying child at the orphanage who wished to know why she or he was unwanted, Linda did her best to console them, knowing no words would ever be good enough. She and her students were all peers in one way, in that they belonged to the same club. The Unwanted Society. That was the name she and the other orphans named it. If they could not form a family, they could form a society. It helped then, but not as Linda grew older. She started disliking all adults for their willingness to steal innocence in others.

"However misguided, if they believed they were protecting you..." Walter started.

"From what? What did they expect to happen to me that was worse than being alone for my whole life?" Linda leaped as a voice sounded from the darkness.

"Something horrible." The nun stepped into view, her face underlit by a glo-stick, highlighting the worst of her features. The nun scanned the room. "Where is Father Bergman?"

"I don't know," Linda said.

"Then we are done here."

"There is an undiscovered children's journal here. It likely holds more information about the actual events than any history book. We need more time. You people have history locked in a cage. It is not right," Walter said.

"I agree it is not right. We should not preserve the words of such evil children, but should burn the pages."

"I am just looking for answers to who I am. Why are you so hostile?" Linda asked.

"Your kind has brought nothing but misery to these hallowed grounds. We thought the curse over, but someone always returns."

"The curse?"

"Your bloodline. Other bloodlines in Salem died out. Yours has remained stubbornly defiant, but death will find you and yours. It always does."

"Yours? I have no family. What do you mean, yours?"

"Those close to you."

"How can you threaten my friends? I thought you were a person of God."

"My position demands me not to lie. Your friends are not immune. No one around you is. God is merciful to his children when he knows they exist. Your family somehow found God's blind spot. Have mercy on your souls. I fear even for Father Bergman for assisting you at all. Much praying it will take to ensure he remains a son of God."

"You think something will happen to him simply for helping us?" Walter asked.

"What if I performed only a cursory search and accidentally locked a man inside who cannot speak? Who cannot cry for help? Would that not prove the gravity of his assisting you? It is time we search for him and leave. Now!"

Walter protested, but the nun slammed the book closed. A snap sounded as the locks reengaged. Linda yanked her key from the podium. Walter continued to protest as the nun led them through every inch of the space, searching for Bergman. Walter gasped at the sight of unexplored volumes; books likely closed since first being written.

Conversely, Linda seemed hurried, rushing the nun through her paces, eager to leave. Walter threw her a confused look and Linda simply gestured toward the exit. Once clear, they exited the tomb. The nun reengaged the security door.

Without the priest in tow, they hurried back through the graveyard, into the church and out. The nun tried to make a show of slamming the door on them on the way out, but it proved too heavy, so she showed her displeasure in slow motion, using both hands to close the large oak doors.

WALTER WATCHED THE DOORS close on his chances of finally understanding certain missing pieces of the Salem puzzle. Church doors had closed on him before, once upon a time decades ago. That unfortunate event led a bishop to yell, "accipere sicco!" Latin for *get out*. A similar sized door closed on him back then. Ever since, Walter found himself unwelcome in many churches, no matter the denomination or location, as if he remained on a list. Like a doctor who red-penned difficult patients, Walter found himself red-penned in the religious community.

It should not have happened. The Vatican expected him that day. Walter was a rising star in scholar circles after publishing many papers of acclaim. Universities sought Walter out for lectures despite his only recently graduating from one himself. Podcasts were not yet prominent, so speaking circuits thrived then, attended by history geeks as much as academics.

The only problem was that embellishment drew larger crowds, so Walter quickly learned to twist a tale. What was more important to know about Rome's Marcus Antonius? (Marc Anthony to the Yanks) That he formed a cabal of leaders loyal to the deceased Caesar called the Second Triumvirate to forge a dictatorship? Or the man's bedroom antics with Cleopatra?

Walter's own bedroom antics were far removed from the bodacious tales he shared about historical figures. Walter developed a following through such stories, a pre-social media version of friends. It humbled him too much to consider them fans. One such person was an academic herself. Maja Kallis.

Maja was a tall, regal looking woman in her twenties working toward her PHD in history at Edinburgh. Walter had many contacts at Maja's university, so found reason to visit often. Their departments were indeed a grand resource for his research, but there was the added benefit of tea with a certain student. Maja introduced herself after one of his famed lectures.

They went for a pint that night and Walter embarrassed himself by calling her the best. She eyed him questioningly, forcing him to explain her name meant exactly that. Maja meant best. The name of Greek origin. His reference to the surname led her to speak of disdain for a family long on issues but short on support. Maja moved in with an aunt at an early age and forged her own path. The young woman cared nothing about her lineage. She had no interest in where she was from, only where she was going.

The pair dug up history like old bones that night, closing the place down. When the time came, Walter pondered a kiss but feared the scandal of her student status despite both being adults with only a three-year age difference. Rather than indulge his desires, he wished her well and the two parted.

That night set the tone. They were always together when one chanced upon the other but remained apart in matters of the heart. With a slim age difference between them, he still took on the role of mentor versus lover. Walter regularly tried to change their relationship status to no avail.

Until one lecture, where everything changed. Walter drank a pint before a lecture and the juice loosened his caboose. A lightweight, his condition revealed itself not as a sloppy demeanor but through an overly explicit accounting of a frequent target, Marcus Antonius. Walter shared Antonius' rumored affair with one of his male generals. The crowd ate it up, with one exception. Maja, seated in the front row, frowned. Her look held the rest of the evening.

Walter understood the error immediately. Maja had no issues with anyone's orientation or sexuality, as he knew her to have had lovers of both sexes. No, it was simpler. Many considered those who trafficked in gossip to have a lack of character. That was a truism for everyday society. Doing the same as a historian was akin to medical malpractice within the health industry.

She did not wait for him after the lecture as she normally did. Walter made small talk with attendees gushing over his lecture in the college version of a green room. But Walter's mind wandered, wondering where a certain old friend was.

A lovely friend. One he should have chanced making his feelings known to. Unsaid words played in his head. *When I met you, when I called you the best? That was a lie. Since I have gotten to know you, truly know you, now I can say with confidence you are indeed the best. What do you say we give this thing a push? See where it goes?*

Walter excused himself and slipped out the rear of the hall. What began as light rain earlier in the evening had since turned heavy. He was without an umbrella. Ignoring the downpour, Walter raced to the street and saw her, drenched herself, sitting on a bench. A cab passed by, splashing Maja, who failed to respond. It was then Walter realized she was a woman used to disappointment.

When he gestured to take a seat alongside her, she failed to respond. Walter sat anyway. The two stared ahead, suddenly old beyond their years. "Drier inside, I suspect."

"That goes without saying. Factually, it is dry inside," she said in a tone Walter had never heard from her before.

"And warmer. Tea might be in order."

"More and more your stories, they grow. I have watched you for so long. Your lectures once inspired me in my own studies."

"Once?" Walter asked.

"Yes. As in upon a time."

"No longer?"

"I consider Monty Python brilliant."

"What are we talking about?" Walter was confused. And wet.

"Monty Python had a way of pointing out the absurd nature of events, current and historical. At least when they were a group."

"Not much for TV and film myself," Walter left it there, feeling it unnecessary to highlight his propensity toward books above all else.

"Nor am I. My current boyfriend has a fondness for Monty Python, so we watch the movies regularly."

Current. Walter knew of her past. They had shared many intimate details together. But she never mentioned a current lover. Walter searched himself, wondering how he allowed himself the notion she waited for him. Foolhardy thought. She noticed his look.

"If I have led you on, I apologize. You are a lovely man, handsome. I find myself alarmingly attracted to fellows of a more blue-collar variety. It was never that with you, which is why I find myself so disappointed."

"I never considered us anything beyond..." Walter started and stuttered.

"Stop. Walter. Stop. That is a lie. Had you asked, yes, I would have slept with you, given it a go. But love? No. Unnecessary. What I find necessary, that which I demand, is truth. In all things, in all people. Not just lovers, but friends. Professors for certain, and mentors most of all. I have watched you deteriorate until there is nothing but show on the stage."

"The audience. They enjoy such a show. Never have I had such crowds."

"Of non-academics, of students hungry for entertainment but absorbing nothing. At the start of your career as a lecturer, I would look left and right and find myself surrounded by academics of stunning pedigree. Now, it might as well be a rock concert. And when have you last published?"

"Critique my performances if you will. Allowed, I suppose, as a fan. But my publishing schedule is not of your concern."

"It is when you are part of my studies. When I use your papers as references. As far as being a fan? Never. A friend, Walter. You have been a friend."

"That sounds despairingly final."

"It is. We will correspond no more. Truth Walter. I require it, demand it, deserve it. Trust has broken between us." Then she laughed, sitting there in the rain.

"What?" Walter asked.

"I guess you could say we are history."

Maja walked away. Walter sat there until a vehicle splashed him as well. Then he had enough. It was time to move on. He spent too long pining for a woman he could have had, but never did. The whole thing confounded him, but he had little time to consider it, for something else gnawed at him.

Shame.

Her words hurt. Not her involvement with another man. That stung, but her critique of his recent professional excesses truly hurt. Not only because they were true, but because they came from her. He wished to be a rock star, something other than the nerd, to draw attention to himself to win the affections of not just someone like her but Maja herself. Walter wanted Maja from the moment he met her, and he changed to what he thought she desired. How wrong. How foolish. Now Walter was alone in the rain. Just as well, he thought, as it made it difficult to show whether he was crying.

He knew in his heart his recent foray into sensationalism was a folly. It took a woman of exceptional means and honesty to remind him of the fact. He would not contact her again, would leave her to her studies. She deserved that. But he also vowed to make her proud by making himself proud again. She was correct. It was time to move on.

M OVE ON, HE DID. Walter cancelled several upcoming lectures and instead went to work planning his next area of study. He settled on the Plague, known as the black death. After a year of studying and research, a nugget of unexplored history made it onto Walter's radar involving the Vatican, a notoriously private corporation. A corporation is what he considered the Vatican, but kept that to himself when he prodded contacts to set up a visit to Vatican City.

Walter's reputation preceded him and resulted in a surprising amount of access. They assigned deacon Orsi as his guide, a man who always remained within view. The name Orsi meant either bear or strong, neither of which represented the deacon who approximated a walking skeleton, one wearing a paper mâché version of skin. Something inside the reed-thin man clicked when he walked. Walter feared sneezing lest he blow away the man's tender flesh, leaving only the bony underpinnings.

The man was immensely helpful to start until the true nature of Walter's inquiries became clear. When Walter first asked about the Vatican's formation and its relation to the black plague, the deacon appeared eager to remind Walter how the church did not create Vatican City until 1929, a date much closer to the 1918 influenza outbreak in the US. There could be no connection to the black plague, as that occurred between 1346-1353.

At least the deacon knew his history, Walter thought to himself. Things went south when Walter confronted the deacon. "Well, they donated the land we stand on now to the church in the fourth century. 313AD to be exact."

"Sono affair mieie," the deacon said, stiffening.

The man's movement created another creak somewhere inside the bony frame. His skin pulled back across his face in surprise, resulting in a face Walter had only ever seen at a funeral, or a museum which housed mummies.

"We agreed on English. Though I believe you are saying this line of questioning is none of my business," Walter said.

"Scuse. English, yes. Real estate inquiries related to Vatican City were not on the approved list of topics."

"Aha, there is a list," Walter said.

"Submitted yourself in advance as required. The resources here are vast. To enable a particular line of study requires advanced planning. Our researchers have prepared proper texts designed to accommodate your line of inquiry. Horrible years, the plague, but the Vatican was yet to form."

"I speak of a time when Christians began overcoming persecution from the Romans. Churches of all types thrived, and they ruled not only spiritually but politically and collected monies from a desperately poor populace."

"Wars were abundant in early centuries. Surely, you Brits understand the cost of war," Orsi said. Brits came out as *Britssa*.

The deacon grew more animated, leaving Walter to fear the man might collapse into a pile. He took his chances and continued. "When the plague struck, priests fell as quickly as paupers. Religious leaders, once thought of as the hands of God, proved to be all too human. I mean, a priest lying in a pile of his own soil, how would that look to the devoted?"

"Come ti permetti!" The skeleton shook with all the vigor of a Halloween lawn ornament in an October wind. A bony finger found its way to Walter's face.

Unfazed, Walter continued. "In such an environment, people did not lose faith in God. Oh, no. Many more found God as they prayed for the invisible enemy to pass them by. But events enlightened the population. They saw the light, but not a religious one. The masses came to understand religious leaders did not have a direct line to God or protection from on high. That was when people went rogue with their beliefs, abandoning the church. The black plague threatened to kill more than people. It threatened to kill Christianity."

"I believe you have misrepresented yourself in coming here, professor."

Walter thought of that day in the rain, where he lost a woman who meant a great deal to him over the concept of truth. No, his days of lying were over. "I submitted this exact line of questioning to the church. They informed me of limitations on what I could access and which lines of inquiry I could pursue."

"Denied means denied," Orsi said.

"Denied because they knew of what I speak. Obviously, you are unaware of the history and the denial of my request. If they have hidden knowledge from you, then obviously it remains hidden from the world. For that reason, I ask you to provide clarity to the world. I ask you to give me access. Eliminate bureaucracy."

"I am certain the church, in its wisdom, has reasons for their actions."

"Yes, to deny the truth. In 1377 Popes lived on this land. Only about twenty years after the plague. They built fortified structures designed to minimize rat infestation so that they could ride out a second wave were one to occur. In the meantime, they spent decades bringing people back into their fold, using the fear of future outbreaks to influence citizens. I believe in this very building there are records of such plans, including how the church intended to regain power. The Pope is infallible. Is not that the doctrine? Never again shall anyone contradict the leader and he will pass power before he passes his mortal coil so as not to show weakness, so as not to show his very humanity. Is not that admission of humanity and humility what religion should represent?"

Orsi breathed deep, and the skin along his chest fluttered. Without another word, Orsi left the room. Walter yelled after the man.

"Not even God can hide the truth!"

Walter thought for the briefest of moments that his guide left him alone on purpose, to discover and explore without a witness. Plausible deniability from the staff until two mountainous men, who lived up to the name Orsi, arrived and helped him to the exit. Walter's feet never touched the ground, but his hands and knees did when they tossed him onto the street outside the Vatican gates.

From then on, Walter was an outsider, learning that the Vatican's reach was long and vengeful. Even a Satanic temple once denied him access at the urging of the Vatican. Strange bedfellows. That connection intrigued Walter further, but he let that mystery lie.

Walter intended to come on strong with the Vatican on the initial visit, to stir the pot. He expected to be escorted out but thought a second invite would follow, one where, after conversations behind closed doors, the church hierarchy would agree to greater access to quiet the demanding man. Except there was no second visit.

WALTER MISCALCULATED BACK THEN. Doors closed on him everywhere he turned. Now, while visiting Salem, he found an ambassador to unlock doors for him. For a moment he was inside once again, exploring long hidden truths. Then, with swift finality, a nun closed the doors again.

While disappointed in himself, and his inability to navigate the complex niceties of church-speak, Walter was more disappointed in failing a woman for a second time. One who somehow meant as much to him as any in his lifetime. Walter rarely noticed beauty until encountering the intelligence behind a smile. Only then did he normally notice the woman in front of him as something other than a friend, coworker, or stranger.

He suffered several failed relationships over the years, too dedicated to his work, too aloof in commitment to a partner. But the very first look at Linda stirred something within him. Falling for physicality so suddenly was uncharacteristic for the man, and he struggled to make sense of it. The investigative part of his brain failed to identify environmental conditions responsible for causing him to react in such a way. In the end, he settled on the reality that the woman was bloody lovely.

But he had possibly lost Linda when the book closed in the mausoleum. Truth was now buried among the dead. He let her down, much like letting Maja down. He eventually sent correspondence to Maja, who was a highly successful scholar herself. But the message came too late to change anything between them. He wished not to fail Linda similarly.

Since they returned to the car, Walter refused to look at Linda, too ashamed over one more holy roadblock. The nun had given him quite the bollicking. Also, he wished to delay admitting defeat to a woman who... *Who what?* What was she to him other than a client? Despite his fancying of the American, he still had a job to do.

Walter took his frustration out on the car horn, honking it with the punch of a fist. The lackadaisical effort produced a sad honk shy of a goose. Not enough even to startle himself or his passenger.

"They gave us mere minutes to catch up on hundreds of years of history. We need to petition the church for more time."

"Walter."

"Probably a waste, but certainly we can write to local politicians, urge them to consider..."

"Walter!"

Linda caught his attention. He turned to her in the passenger seat, ready to apologize. Then she did the most wonderful thing. Linda pulled a book from underneath her hoodie. The child's journal.

Walter melted in his seat as he gazed longingly at her. "Have I mentioned I bloody love you?"

CHAPTER 29

A FLOCK OF BIRDS fluttered wildly from a tree growth along the Salem thoroughfare. Delivery vehicles roaring past at unsafe speeds never fazed the flock. But in the presence of the strange man, they took flight. The mean wearing torn and dirtied clothes stumbled along the road's edge as if drunk. The birds might have ignored such a passerby if he were no less disturbing than the massive vehicles roaring past, but the man was not so subtle.

His hands moved faster than his feet, gesturing in herky-jerky motions. The man rambled, holding a conversation with someone not there. Sensing danger, the birds had enough. They clouded the sky in flight, their fluttering wings temporarily drowned out the noise of passing traffic. Soon they faded to dots and descended into a section of forest far from the madness of man.

The man struggled to remain on the shoulder as the wind created by passing vehicles threatened to spin him in circles. Honks filled the stretch of road while drivers made their displeasure known over the man's proximity to traffic. His unsteady gait threatened to propel him from the relative safety of the shoulder into the road itself. The man's hands moved faster and faster, trying to catch up to the traffic. His words came out unintelligible, garbled, spouting things which made no sense. The road cleared temporarily.

Sudden quiet caught the man's attention, and he looked back from where he came. His eyes tearing up as he grew lucid, if only for a moment. He clenched his fists and screamed until unable to breathe. The man wished it would be his last breath, but he sucked in air, involuntary, a survival instinct. He whimpered in realization that he lived. Drool spilled from his mouth. A truck blared its horn to warn him off the road's edge. The wind whipped his clothes and sent the man stumbling back. He followed the momentum and kept going, walking somewhere, anywhere, knowing he could never return to where he came from.

WALTER PULLED OUT OF the church lot, excited at the recent development. He drove the long driveway while steeling glances at the prize in Linda's grasp. He veered toward a ditch.

"Walter!"

"Sorry. It appears my lot in life is to frighten you."

"The others startled me. I prefer not to have to worry about your driving. Eyes on the road, please."

Walter checked his mirrors, searching for religious authorities of some type. There were no bears of men to be found, not even a stern nun with a ruler. They were clear.

"Perhaps that book is best placed in the boot until we arrive back. Its pages have not had exposure to sunlight for centuries."

They reached the end of the drive. Vehicles passed by along the stretch of road used by trucking companies delivering goods throughout Salem. Eventually, the trucks would head back to the turnpike to return to Boston or Connecticut. Linda opened the glove compartment and placed the journal inside. Walter bristled. Linda raised her hands as if waiting for a better idea.

"What? It's as good as the trunk."

"Never thought I would traffic in stolen artifacts in the glove-box of a rental car."

"I am sorry if this goes against your ethics."

"The church locking up history has always gone against my ethics." He looked at Linda before glancing at the glove compartment. "But yes, stealing such an artifact also rubs up against my ethics. I find myself caught in a conundrum with this one."

"I'll spare you the consequences if they catch us," Linda said. "This is on me. You have never touched the property. I took it for several reasons. First, I agree with your views on the church obstructing history, having just witnessed it myself. Is that why they have banned you? For raising such issues?"

"Too long a story for too short a drive." Walter waited to see if she would push, hoping he did not have to tell stories of a lost love, one that never fully blossomed.

Linda did not push. "The bigger reason, however, is I need answers. With a name behind me now, I can reconnect with private investigators and get at the heart of my parent's history. Did my mother marry into the Goode family or was she born into it?"

"Your lineage ties directly to the events in Salem all those years ago. I am more than willing to research further myself."

"I appreciate that, Walter. I really do. Without you, I wouldn't know my birth name. But I am concerned with the line of tragedies befallen my family. The nun warned my friends were in danger."

"Are you saying you believe in a curse? I would have approached the information from the book differently had I known it frightens you."

"Not so much belief but worry. Aren't there stories of curses to those who opened mummy tombs in Egypt?"

The blast of a horn caused them both to leap. Walter looked back. A semi sat on their tale. The driver remained too high in his seat to be in view, but the grill of the vehicle seemed plenty angry. Walter steered onto the shoulder. The semi blasted a quick double as thanks. Walter merged back onto the asphalt.

"I swear, the way they drive on this stretch." He noticed Linda awaiting an answer. It would have taken several semis to divert her attention, he supposed. A strong-willed woman, that one. He nodded. "Well, technically, yes, tragic fates befell many an archeologist of the region. The term originally was mummia. It became mummy only a few decades before the Salem trials."

"Are you stalling, Walter?"

The man was, but he refused to admit it. "Explaining. My point being that the unique decay in the human body that we now call mummies has existed since the dawn of man. Yet the name mummy began in early sixteen hundred."

"Meaning?"

"Meaning that while some archeologists suffered what could be strange demises, one must look at the bigger picture. Statistically, if one looks at the deaths of those who disturbed a sarcophagus versus general population death rates, the numbers do not support an actual curse."

"That argument is based on a false premise."

"How so?"

"From my understanding, grave robbers have disturbed more sarcophagi over the centuries than archeologists. I heard it from my friend Tom, the history nerd."

"History nerd?"

Linda kept going before Walter could find himself offended. "Wooden coffins have been much more in use and many societies burn their dead. Grave robbers would never confess to their spoils so we cannot know their ultimate fates, and besides, lifestyle choices could skew those results even if we had them. The only sample of comparison that we should use is how many legitimate archeologists, diggers, financiers for digs, students, interns, anyone involved in legitimate digs. How many of those people perished untimely versus the public? That is the only way to see if there is something more to this whole thing."

Walter liked her more and more. The woman was as intelligent as beautiful. He sighed involuntarily, a gasp of attraction. He covered quickly by posturing. "Bad data for my previous argument. I will admit the goal was to put you at ease."

"I caught that, thank you. But I am looking for facts right now. These curses? Did they affect others? People in the family of those who disturbed sacred tombs."

Walter gripped the wheel. His silence answered the question. From what Walter knew of such things, there were unfortunate circumstances for many a good historian in Egypt, in particular. A few other countries as well, but Walter had only studied so much. He felt no need to share such information. Linda looked out the window, contemplating.

"That is why I took the book. The child writing in it is one generation closer to me than Reverend Goode and Althea Goode. I can learn more about the family lineage from her own words. But more than that, I hope to learn why her grave marker showed her dying so young. If something can really reach that far into a family line, then my friends could be in danger."

"But your friends are not your family lineage."

"Wrong, Walter. They are my family, and it took me too long to realize that. I've been searching when I had them all along." She thought of her tryst, could not help but flush with excitement at the sight of Andrew nude, sharing her bed. But guilt extinguished the budding flame of excitement. "I messed things up with them. Either I am a horrible person, or this curse has influenced some of my recent decisions. Some I will have to live with."

Walter turned to her. "You are far from a horrible person. If that means I must attribute a curse to something you appear ashamed of, then a curse it is. There is no way you could do anything dastardly. When I look at you..."

Linda turned to him. Walter checked her face, searching for signs of a street sign, anything that might make him stop. But no, it was time. She had a name. He helped her find it. That meant his professional time with her was mostly over. Linda did not need to be involved in his search for the home's history. It would be goodbye unless he did something about it. She was also alone. Her friends made that clear, had no one in her life and ever since he met her. Perhaps she was as ready as he.

He cleared his throat. "Since I met you, when I look at you, I..."

"Walter!"

She saw it, but he did not until it was almost too late. A man on foot strayed into their lane. Walter swerved but over-corrected and shot back toward the side of the road. Tires squealed. Linda never even screamed, only placed one hand against the dash and one pressed against the ceiling, bracing for the inevitable.

Walter braced himself against the steering wheel, arms stretched out tight, pressing on it as if it served as an additional brake. It did not. The car swerved again and spun, finally coming to a stop facing the opposite way on the lane they started in. The man continued walking, unfazed by the near miss.

Inside the car, Linda gasped when she identified the man. She wanted to get out and help him, but something else took precedence.

"Truck," Linda said.

"On it."

Walter backed up, pulling onto the shoulder, still facing the wrong way but safe from oncoming traffic. A lumber truck loaded to the gills with sheetrock passed by, never slowing despite a car facing the wrong way. Once the danger passed, both passengers refocused on the man. Walter backed up, moving them further away.

"What are you doing?" Linda asked.

"Turning around. Feels like home, but I understand we are facing the wrong way. It is not safe to do so here. The curb widens back there."

"Let me out first."

Walter hit the brakes and Linda leaped out. She rushed toward the man while Walter took advantage of the empty road, turned around, then got out and checked to make certain he was on the shoulder safely. Meanwhile, Linda made contact.

It shocked Linda to see the man in such a state, his appearance resembled someone homeless, but she knew that not to be true about him. His hands jerked about frantically in some sort of repetitive motion. She had deaf students before but never fully learned sign language. He kept signing part of the Lord's prayer, repeating the part, *our Father who art in...*

"Father Bergman? What happened? What are you doing out here?"

"My soul for my voice, a promise of my soul for my voice," he said through spittle.

"Good Lord, Father, you can talk?"

Bergman cowered under the utterance of the holy name. He finally completed the hand signaled prayer. It took a moment for Linda to realize the variant. Bergman signed, *our Father who art in... Hell*!

"Linda? Is everything alright?" Walter asked from a distance as he approached.

Linda shook her head. It was not. She looked at the priest. "Father, please, you are hurt. Allow us to help. We can take you to a doctor."

Bergman grinned and grabbed her. "I want to hurt you. I wish to defile you!"

"Let me go, you are hurting me!"

Walter rushed over and shoved the priest. The priest's collar hit the ground as the man stumbled back only to lift his head, eyes burning red beyond bloodshot, tongue licking his lips, ready to go two on one. Then Bergman caught sight of the collar on the ground and his eyes cleared. He looked around at his surroundings and spoke again.

"Listen to the children," Bergman said.

"What children?" Linda asked.

"Listen to the children. The secret lies in the children. From the mouths of babes, listen to the children."

Without another word, Bergman raced into the street too late for an oncoming semi to stop. The impact vanished the man, standing there one second, then gone. Something caught up in the violent impact bounced around until settling near Linda and Walter's feet. One of the priest's shoes.

Further down the road, the brakes of the truck finally screamed. And when Linda, like the priest, finally found her voice, she screamed too.

CHAPTER 30

TAYLOR LOOKED AT A debris field in the front yard of an elegant two-story colonial. Sections of grass on an otherwise well-maintained lawn were browned to dirt under the wheels of a convoy of toy trucks, mostly dump style. There was an earth mover, a semi, two monster trucks, and several pickups in the bunch. *If the kid isn't being groomed to take over the family business, he could at least open a car dealership someday*, Taylor thought.

A young boy about six sat in the center of the dirt mound, crashing the group of vehicles into one another. The boy noticed Taylor and leaped to his feet, excited, pointing a finger toward the officer. Taylor glanced down at the object of the boy's exuberance. His gun. Taylor smiled.

"You're Billy, right?" The boy remained mum in a way Taylor understood. "Do not talk to strangers?"

The boy nodded before piping up. "Or cops."

"Is that right? Well, my name is Sargent Taylor, and I am a friend of your father, Colt. And as for being a cop, I am more of a detective. I know your mother never mentioned talking to cops. That would be from your father. But did your father say not to speak to sergeants?"

"No. Only strangers and cops."

"Then what do you know? We can have a conversation. I see you looking at my gun."

"Is it real, or like ones on TV?"

"It is real, but don't you worry, this one only shoots bad guys."

"Cool!"

"I suppose it is. Do you know where your dad is?"

"He is out whoring around," the boy said, with eyes as wide as a Disney animal.

Taylor was glad not to have a beverage in hand because the spit take would have wet his uniform. "Is that so? That is what your mother said? Do you know what that means?"

The kid nodded. "Out having fun. Hanging out with his buddies. Golfing and things like that."

"Oh, horsing around."

"That's what I said," the kid replied, unaware of the gaffe.

"Well, I aim to hear more about it from your mom. Good thing I am moving on too because I see at least half a dozen traffic violations in progress there." Taylor nodded his head toward the toys.

"Cool!"

Billy returned to his trucks with newfound enthusiasm while Taylor made his way to the front door and rang the bell. The telltale clop of heels crossed a wooden floor inside. Taylor wondered why someone would dress so formally in the middle of the day, but figured it was none of his business. Fashion was not his friend.

The woman who opened the door indeed wore elegant clothes. A khaki skirt with a white button down top and a mid-size heel that matched her skirt. Trudy Warren was the total package, Taylor thought, which was why he never understood Colt's dalliances.

"Hello Wonder Woman," Taylor said.

"Oh Ron, please. Don't start."

Trudy Warren held a striking resemblance to the original Wonder Woman Linda Carter, right down to height and build, so Taylor often greeted her that way. Trudy at least pretended never to tire of it.

"Do you mind following me into the kitchen? I'm making my lunch smoothie."

"I figured you must be hard at work, dressed down as you are," he teased.

Trudy smiled and led the way through an immaculate home. Taylor had visited the home several times in the past, attending barbecues in the generous backyard. Taylor wasn't the only cop who threw work Colt's way. As morally bankrupt as the man's personal life was, it did not carry over into the man's work life. There was good reason to recommend Colt's services.

To ensure there were no ethic violations, Taylor cleared his RSVP through a lieutenant. Colt hosted the barbecues to thank clients. Many people attended and Taylor felt it was a good way to get to know the neighborhood he worked in. The event leaned alcohol heavy, so it was an adult only situation. Nell likely babysat Billy during the get-togethers, which was why Taylor had never met the kid before.

As Trudy led Taylor through the large home, the woman kept one eye on her phone. Once they reached the kitchen, she docked the device, which displayed her small screen onto a nearby monitor. The image was the front yard. Billy continued making a mockery of traffic laws. *Good mom*, Taylor thought.

On the marble countertop sat a compost paper bag holding the detritus of chopped veggies and fruit. A whole concoction of ingredients filled a blender that looked like it was from the future. Trudy secured the top and hit a button. The ingredients became one in an instant, blazingly fast, and quiet. The technology turned Taylor's stomach, but he waited for her to finish the task at hand.

She poured the green contents into a glass and took a sip. She gestured to the leftover in the blender. "Can I get you a cup?"

"Nah, my liver would surely revolt."

Trudy shrugged and sipped again, somehow avoiding a green moustache. "Is this visit official?"

"No, but it should be. That's the problem."

"How so?"

"Staying out of the relationship part for a moment. Colt's good people. We would have many resources available to search for him if you officially declared him missing."

Trudy set her green stuff down. "Can I speak frankly, Ron?"

She was one of the few who regularly use his first name. Her beauty struck him immediately when he first met her years ago during his bad choices in life phase. The two made an instant connection that suggested they could be more than friends in different circumstances. Taylor was less charming than he believed himself to be when he drank, so he quickly ruined a world of possibilities and ended up in the friend zone. Since then, he treated the woman like a sister, despite her attractiveness. He nodded.

"I insist."

"There is no proposition hidden in what I am about to tell you. I regularly cheat on my husband."

Boy, second spit take of the day moment, Taylor thought. "Okay."

"As you know, my job is in philanthropy. I meet many men and women along the way who I am attracted to in a spiritual manner. Their presence brings me joy and so I sometimes invite them into my life in a more intimate way than I do others. It fills a need."

"I understand."

"You're patronizing me now. You do not understand. I am certain you understand the physical needs and why I would cheat, especially since my husband does, but you do not understand why I stay with the man."

"Look at me, I'm a book." Taylor made jazz hands celebrating her reading him so well.

"I get physical release, but that is not why I have affairs. It fills other needs for me, things I know I will never get from my husband. But none of that changes that I am married. We built a life, a home, and a child. I want more children. My own parents divorced and went through so many partners I lost track. Some were kind, most not. I swore I would never live that lifestyle. I believed my parents gave up too easily."

"They failed."

She nodded. "They folded. I do not require things to be perfect in my marriage, I only require that it remain a marriage. I would never leave Colt despite my being fully aware of his cheating ways."

"I get it, I am not your type, and you are worried I would leap on this new knowledge to hit on you?" Her turn to nod. "You are a few years too late for that. I consider myself more respectable these days. Where does this fit in with whether he is missing?"

"He truly loves that young girl, and the poor thing loves him back. Colt does not have the same past I do. He is more open to leaving everything behind for a fresh, pretty face than I am. If they are both missing, I believe they ran off together for good."

Taylor was not so sure. He wanted to mention the strange feeling he had that something bigger was going on. Something about the house and the recent visitors in town, how it all kept him on edge ever since their arrival. But logically, the couple ran off together. The sergeant had nothing to go on, which was why he had yet to update the squad.

It was Trudy herself who called Taylor to check on her husband, but when he called her back after learning Nell was MIA also, Trudy said she understood and hung up. Taylor did his due diligence before meeting Trudy in person. He would not inform her of his worries, but he could do nothing official unless she filed a report. Taylor looked at the boy on the screen.

"It would devastate the kid, huh?"

Trudy shrugged matter of fact. "Who knows? Billy loves Nell too. Maybe we could make it work."

"I believe you are right. I believe they likely ran off together. But if there is one thing that makes you doubt it. One thing. What would it be?"

"That Nell has yet to brag about it all over her social media. I follow several of her accounts. She was my babysitter once upon a time. Trust me. Were they to run away, she would brag. And second, they cannot marry while he is married to me. Trust me, that child will not settle for anything less," Trudy said.

"Which means you have some doubts."

"Yes. But if he has vanished, I become suspect number one. He was cheating. I am the aware spouse. So, if I declare him missing, then I become the suspect should anything have happened to him. Is that correct?"

"You are a smart woman. Yes. They would assign certain detectives to look at you hard. Everything you told me makes sense, but they may read it another way. It will be uncomfortable for you, but eventually the case will move forward with or without your help, so you may as well get the process started. Like you said, the knucklehead probably shacked up in a hotel in Vegas, making promises of a bright future for his passenger along the way. But in the off chance something bad happened..."

"Okay. I would like to file a missing person report."

"Thank you. Consider it done. Now that things are official, would you like to take any of the private conversation back, or can I use it all in the report?"

"Like you, I am an open book. Use whatever you need to speed things along. Billy's birthday is coming up soon. I'd like to make sure Colt attends."

Taylor showed himself out and stood over the boy along the way. The officer waved to Trudy in the camera positioned near the eaves of the house. Then he promised the boy a treat. Walter blooped his siren twice, to the boy's delight. Billy clapped and jumped. Taylor believed if something happened to Colt and Nell, it had nothing to do with Trudy and everything to do with the new kids in town and their strange house.

But just in case, the whooping siren would alert the neighbors to his presence, and they would talk. If one of them knew anything, they would spill it to the detectives soon to be assigned to the case.

The day was looking to be a busy one. Then a call came over his radio, guaranteeing a long day. He hit the sirens for real and sped off. Billy screamed in delight while all the neighbors pressed their faces to the windows. The new call related to a dead body.

T HE BODY WAS ALREADY under the sheet by the time Taylor arrived. It was not his case, at least yet. It could be if foul play was involved. (And when wasn't it where a dead body was concerned?) Normally he would get a briefing from the lieutenant, except in this case, those who found the body asked for him specifically.

The street was closed off and he flashed his badge to navigate the mess. A distraught truck driver talked to an officer near the sheet in the road that lay below his bloodied grill. In the distance, he saw those who asked for him.

The new kids. Walter greeted the officer as soon as he pulled up. The officer got out and asked what happened. The foreigner told the tale while occasionally using words that Taylor did not understand, but he got the gist.

"Jesus, stepped in front of the truck?"

"Quite so, yes," Walter said.

"But you said he was speaking. The priest can't talk, not sure if you know that."

"I am aware, but I assure you, the man spoke succinctly."

"How about you tone down the encyclopedia words? We need to write this stuff up. We would appreciate clear and concise language. Regular English, not all your proper stuff. You say Linda was there also?"

"Indeed."

Taylor looked over to where the woman sat in a vehicle. She could have been a ghost, so white she was. Taylor called another officer over. The woman exchanged greetings with him. Her badge read Stanton.

"What is it, sergeant?" Stanton asked.

"Has someone already taken the woman's statement?"

"I did. Yeah."

"General idea being truck met a moment of a man's poor judgement."

"Leaped in front of it. Driver statement matches."

"Anything weird?"

"Like the mute priest talking?"

"Exactly like that."

"Stories match up. His, hers, his again." Officer Stanton gestured between Walter and the driver and Linda. "Except the driver never interacted with the deceased, only contact he had was the splatter. The driver confirmed no one pushed the priest, he went willingly. Curious that a man of his age got off the blocks like that."

"Divine timing, I suppose."

Stanton laughed and then strode off, checking in with some other officers. Taylor turned back to Walter. "Reason I asked is your friend appears fragile right now. Nervous."

"She did just witness a person expire," Walter said, careful to leave out the part of them being nervous about trafficking stolen artifacts.

A ruckus rose in the distance as cops yelled for someone to stop. Ruby made it clear she would not, while Andrew did his best to intervene with the cop on her tail. An officer had his hand on the butt of his gun and looked happy to use it. Taylor nodded for the rookie to let them pass.

"Where is she?" Ruby asked Walter.

Walter pointed to the car parked nearby. Ruby rushed over and Linda launched herself from the vehicle to hug her friend. They held one another.

Andrew turned to Walter. "How is she?"

"Distraught with good reason."

"And you?" Andrew asked.

Walter jerked his head back, surprised to be considered in the equation. He took a moment to determine his status. "I will admit to missing England a bit more. Until today, I was unaware trauma could induce homesickness."

"As pleasant as all this is..." Taylor started.

"Pleasant?" Walter gasped.

"Sarcasm, Walter," Andrew said.

"Sorry. What I meant is this is a simple traffic accident or suicide and is not my case. I am not sure why you asked for me, especially when officers already took your statements."

Walter looked back toward the two friends hugging and chose not to engage the women. He turned back to the detective. "Sergeant, you seek information on the missing people."

"What missing people?" Andrew asked.

People, he said people, Taylor noted. The historian never said *couple*, meaning Walter did not know the background of the individuals and likely had nothing to do with the disappearance. But he had information of some sort. Taylor's gut told him the outsiders were involved, but now he had doubts. Doubts were good. It meant Colt likely shacked up with his babysitter.

"I do not know how much stock you wish to put into this as Linda suffered a shocking tragedy today, but she insists this has something to do with her house," Walter said.

"What?" Andrew and Taylor replied in unison.

"I know how it sounds," Walter said.

Crazy, but only because I think the same thing, Taylor thought. He was suddenly very interested and eager to learn more, but he did not want to push. His gut feelings were back in play. Taylor stood silent.

"Linda moved cross-country to search for family. Then our friends chose this place of all places to get divorced. Linda would think bad things about her home for good reason. You can't believe any of it, can you?" Andrew asked Walter.

"No. Not at all. I climb through ancient structures for a living. I feel nothing other than excitement in such places. But she does, and she wished for me to tell you officer Taylor. She is concerned for the missing people and thinks something happened because the man visited her home."

"For a board up! Are you listening to yourself?" Andrew bordered on rage.

Taylor looked at the young stranger with fresh eyes. Genteel was a word that Taylor did not know the exact meaning of, but it was how he felt about Andrew when first they met. Genteel. No more. There was anger in the man. One more surprise on a surprising day. Let the two mouthpieces for Linda hash it out, Taylor figured. He was all too happy to observe and listen.

"Not saying it is rational, but she mentioned it. And then there is our deceased friend nearby. The priest helped us with confirming Linda's identity. She is of the Goode family, one with long tragic ties to the town."

"Please. That's my cue to get her home. Clearly Linda is in shock and doesn't know what she is saying. Is there any reason we can't take her home now, officer?" Andrew asked.

Andrew squared off with Taylor as if less a question than a challenge. Taylor instinctively placed his hand on his hip. Andrew's eyes followed. A challenge for sure, all with a turd-like smile on Andrew's face.

"One of you should stay, just to wrap up any loose ends. Maybe I have a few questions. Namely, how the priest helped you. One thing you drive up on the scene, another knowing there is familiarity."

"I will gladly stay. I would be equally glad if you allowed Linda to leave."

"Yeah, well, asking nice like that worked. See how that goes?" Taylor answered Walter while staring down Andrew.

Andrew didn't linger. He turned and beelined for his friends. Taylor watched with curiosity. There was something he did not like about the house and something he did not like about the young man. There would be time for that. As it was, he had some fresh questions for the Brit.

"Hey," Andrew greeted the women.

Despite everything, Linda pulled away from Ruby and hugged Andrew. "I'm ready to go home."

"It took a horrific event like this to make you finally call Salem home?" Ruby asked.

"I wasn't talking about Salem. I meant California," Linda said.

"Well, that's a big ask. Let's go back to the house for now and figure everything out. The detective says you can leave. Walter is going to stay and answer questions." Andrew said.

Linda nodded through red eyes, past crying. The couple made space and supported Linda between them. Ruby apologized for the van being parked so far away because it had to remain outside the police perimeter. They had not walked far when Linda stopped.

"Wait. I left something in the car."

"Walter's car?" Ruby asked, intrigued. "What the hell do you have in Walter's car?"

"Nothing. Really."

"Then let's go," Ruby said, gesturing further down the road.

Linda shook her head. "I can't. just a minute."

"Panties. Did you leave panties in Walter's car?"

"Ruby, please," Linda rushed away to open the door to the vehicle. Looking around for police, she quickly opened the glove compartment, grabbed the journal, and slid it into the large hand warmer sleeve fronting her hoodie. She turned to leave when a voice called out from behind her.

"Stop!"

Linda froze. Busted. What would the penalty be, and worse, would they think she and Walter killed the man to get away with the artifact? Despite the harrowing events of earlier, Linda's heart threatened to beat through her chest. She turned slowly, trying not to dislodge the volume. Stanton stood at the ready.

"Officer?" Linda asked.

"Stanton. Officer Stanton. Just wanted to give you a card. We have contacts with counseling services. Our own officers use them regularly. No shame in admitting one needs help after witnessing such an event."

"Oh. Wow. Thank you." Linda said, genuinely touched but also relieved not to be busted for what she had hidden in her hoodie pouch.

Stanton nodded and moved on as an officer called her name. Linda backtracked to make certain she was clear before rushing over to her friends. Linda and Andrew looked for what she might have retrieved, but Linda urged them on. They walked toward the van in the distance. Linda was never so glad to see it, even though she was deathly frightened of their destination.

Linda insisted on the rear rather than the front. Andrew shrugged and got in the driver's seat. Ruby slid the side door open and got in the second seat, waiting for Linda to follow. She would not let her friend sit alone. Before getting in, Linda stopped and looked back. The number of people on the scene surprised her despite having been in the middle of it all.

Then she spotted someone in the crowd. Impossible. Father Bergman stared at her, his face mostly gone, fused red with gore from the truck grill. Bergman stood in one spot but continued listing in the drunken manner she witnessed upon first encountering him on the street. He finally straightened ramrod straight, and then it began.

Blood dripped from the top of his skull. Even from far away, she saw it soak his face and pour down like a waterfall. Too much too fast. The blood covered the man completely, soaking his clothes. It kept gushing, pulsing out in thick spurts until taking on the form of a liquid red blood sack shaped like a man.

With a splash, Bergman collapsed in a flood of liquid red. A river of blood soaked the asphalt, running down the street as if a flashflood overflowed a nearby river. Linda froze, too shocked to move, or even scream. She blinked when Ruby grabbed her wrist.

Linda looked at her friend, then back to the street, only to find a fire crew spraying the road with water. No flood of blood, only a hose clearing the gore from the pavement. Ruby pulled Linda into the van with her.

The vehicle drove away under a fading sun.

CHAPTER 31

WIND RATTLED THE TREES as the van navigated the winding road toward Linda's house. Andrew took in the scenery, leaning into the windshield. He tilted his head occasionally, like a child seeing the world for the first time, or a dog trying to understand human speech. In the rear, Ruby leaned against the far side of the seat with Linda resting atop her. Unlike Andrew, Linda stared off into space, oblivious to the world passing by. Ruby, who earlier could not help but probe about Linda's trip to Walter's car, had since met the moment, falling silent for her friend. Occasionally, Linda touched her hoodie to ensure the journal remained in place. She caressed it through the clothes like a baby bump.

Then they hit a real bump. The violent motion lifted the women into the air before bouncing back onto the seat. Andrew laughed behind the wheel.

"Whoa. That was a good one!"

"Andrew," Ruby scolded.

"What? Too soon?" He replied, looking back in the mirror where he met and held Linda's gaze.

Ruby only shook her head and adjusted to make sure Linda remained comfortable. Linda looked at Andrew, searching the eyes of a man she once knew. In his gaze, she spotted someone who appeared the same, yet somehow unfamiliar.

Linda looked away, overcome with guilt. She unexpectedly welcomed the guilt because it helped drive the thoughts of the accident from her mind. It was not until they left the scene that Linda realized how horrible the odors at the scene were. Burnt rubber mixed with spilled oil, and another scent. Blood and ruptured flesh sitting in the sun.

The tragedy threatened to consume her, so Linda fought to focus on the guilt. She was so angry at Andrew the day after their encounter, but it was anger displaced, a panacea for the true target. Herself.

Linda loved Andrew. She had desired the man for so long and still felt a rush of excitement when revisiting their liaison in her mind. Yet there was Ruby. It was easy to believe Ruby would eventually cheat on Andrew or leave him as she had with so many men in her past, but that was Ruby's choice to make. Linda took such a choice away by cheating on Ruby with Andrew. Worse, her friends, knowing how eternally single Linda was, offered several awkward attempts over the years to invite her into their coupling. Linda could have partaken of forbidden fruit without it being forbidden.

Whether charity or desire for fresh adventures, her friends clumsily invited Linda along for the ride known as their relationship. Except Linda cut the line, leaping past one of the most important people in the equation. Ruby. Ruby was Linda's best friend, the closest thing she ever had to a sister, and yet she betrayed that trust.

Linda thought back to a recent recess at school where the kids snuck up on Andrew, pelting him with game balls. She distracted Andrew with an offer to rendezvous, but it was all show. Linda never considered an actual hookup during the playful goof. Further, Andrew declined outright. Even when Andrew winked while taking the barrage from the kids, his eyes were those of a kind man, one she treasured well beyond the physical. Linda never crossed that line with them when invited nor solo with Andrew because their friendships were too strong, too important to upset. Andrew was her friend, and Ruby was her friend, and Heather was her friend, as was Tom.

And now? The man at the wheel appeared aloof, unconcerned with the trauma Linda had just experienced. Only her friend Ruby remained strong for Linda, consoling her in silence, a feat for a woman who loved nothing more than to speak. There was a reason Ruby was such a wonderful teacher. And a good friend.

Why? Why had Linda crossed such a line? Or Andrew? The answer loomed through the window as they neared it. The house. She had defiantly called it her own before when they searched the basement, only to find Heather inexplicably scratching at a wall. Linda had not taken the time to consider how such a thing could have happened. She was too busy sleeping with her best friend's boyfriend. Too busy searching for her parents. Too busy ignoring that which she knew all along.

Something was wrong with her house. Was it not only a house? Made of wood, nails, sheetrock, paint? The answer was a resounding no. Linda grappled with the aftermath of having cheated and took responsibility. It was her fault. Yet she also recognized that she never acted on anything before, never even came close. Perhaps something in Salem nudged her along. There was no hesitancy the night she slept with Andrew. Linda willingly partook of her friend's body.

Then there were her married friends. The only thing surprising about their divorce announcement was the timing and the way it happened. Heather was a good friend. Their age gap was the only thing keeping Heather from competing for the title of bestie that belonged to Ruby. Heather made it known for some time that the polish was off the diamond, that Tom's aloofness had elevated to a nuclear level, one where divorce was imminent.

But couldn't it have waited? Linda asked herself. Why do it in the place where Linda searched for her lineage? Was it the house or the town? Could a house carry with it sins of the past? She understood well the horrific nature of the town, the entire world did, but how did it all tie to her house?

Then there were the secrets. She hid a journal under her clothes, keeping it hidden from her friends. Why? She did the same with the key that opened a mysterious book of blood. Linda never kept secrets from her friends before, but did now. That was unlike her. So much was unlike her since Salem.

It was the house. It held secrets as well. The secret to why she crossed a line with Andrew, the secret to why her friends finally split, the secrets about why her mother kept articles about tragic events, and the secret to why birds fly into freaking windows!

As she rode in the back cradled in the arms of her one genuine friend, Linda decided it was time she stopped going along for the ride. It was time to stop dancing to the invisible tune of the structure as it guided her along in a dance of uncharacteristic behaviors. She thought back to her original instincts. It was HER house. She owned it, not the other way around, though the home did its best to dispel her of such a notion when its shadow swallowed their vehicle upon pulling into the driveway.

Despite having grown accustomed to Salem weather, a chill trickled along Linda's neck as she exited the van. She looked up, searching, uncertain of what set off her nerves. Then it hit her. She had not heard from Heather since speaking to the kind nurse.

"Did you guys check on Heather?"

"Yes. Check is the right word. She was gone," Ruby said.

"What do you mean, gone?" Linda asked.

"Heather checked herself out," Andrew said, as cold as the weather.

"What do you mean? So, is she here?"

"I don't think so," Ruby said.

"What are you talking about?" Linda turned on her friend, stunned at the revelation.

"The staff said she checked out, very upset, said she was leaving Salem," Ruby said.

"Did she? Leave?"

"I don't know. We tried her phone several times, but she never answered," Ruby said.

"She might be here then? Except wouldn't she have called us to see where we were?"

"I don't know," Ruby answered, bordering on a stutter, growing anxious under interrogation.

"What do you mean, you don't know?" Linda barked.

"I, well, uh..." Ruby started.

Andrew intervened. "In case you have forgotten, we have been taking care of you, so how about you back off, huh? Heather said she was leaving, then she was leaving. I might do the same if this is how you treat your friends," Andrew said.

"Andrew!" Ruby looked at her boyfriend, shocked.

"No. He's right. But so am I. Check the house or get her on a phone, please."

Linda stormed off toward the backyard. Ruby pulled out her phone. Andrew looked back and forth between the two women, left in no-man's-land. He finally settled on the one closest to him.

"What are you doing?"

"Calling Heather. Linda's freaking me out. Come on, let's go inside and see if she came back." The couple made their way inside, but not before Andrew glanced back at Linda plodding toward the backyard.

Water wicked away with every step Linda took. Then a squish. Mud. Linda eyed her foot and spotted something off. She examined the ground. Tire marks? She saw only a few feet of tire tread. The rest would have washed away in all the rain. Linda eyed the van tires in the distance and understood right away that those tires were too thin. The track was wider. A construction vehicle, a pickup truck at the least. The contractor?

He boarded up the kitchen, but why would he drive on the lawn without getting permission from a homeowner? He could easily carry a single sheet of plywood from the driveway. Linda considered asking Walter to check in with the man except the man was missing. After driving on her lawn?

The answer lies with the children. Linda considered the words of the priest. How the words of a child could answer why tire tracks were on a lawn and why she felt influenced, Linda could not fathom. But maybe it was time to go read the journal. She intended to do just that until spotting the swing moving as if under control of a rider. The sky darkened as clouds rolled in. The onset of a storm could have moved the swing. She approached and reached through the ropes where a rider would sit. It stopped moving.

Linda dropped into the seat and gently rocked, watching her house, taking in the view that the children would have had. She noticed for the first-time basement windows almost flush to the ground. She had seen them from inside, but they were too busy with Heather to explore the cellar further. From where she sat, the windows appeared unnaturally dark. She rose from the swing to investigate and yelped as her cell phone rang.

The ringing startled her, causing her to bobble the device and drop it in the wet grass. As she bent to retrieve it, Dead Sadie came into view behind her, sitting on the swing. The dead child sat motionless.

Wet grass covered the phone case and screen. She wiped it away and answered. "Ruby? Why are you calling me? I'm right outside."

"I couldn't wait because I have good news," Ruby said over the phone. "Heather's stuff is still here."

"Which makes no sense if she was leaving Salem," Linda replied.

"Right. That means she did not leave. I think she has rendezvoused with Tom at whatever hotel he is staying at. They reunited and are not answering because they are finally having vacation sex."

Linda's breath caught in her throat. Such a thought made her smile. Except the relief proved short-lived as she considered the circumstances. "Heather would have called us."

"During make-up sex? Could be a couple of days before we hear anything. Wait. It is Tom. Okay, fine, a couple of hours. Any minute now."

Linda turned back to find the swing empty but moving again. She walked toward the basement window. Rain sprinkled, readying the world for another downpour.

"They are such good friends, the two of them, but they were more than that to me."

"What do you mean?" Ruby's voice broke up over the phone.

Linda looked up as the drizzle grew heavier. "Because they were older, I thought of them as my parents in some ways. I know it is twisted, but my point is they are responsible. One of them would have called."

"Not if they are having a mid-life crisis. They are older, like you said." The phone squealed with static. "Are we really doing this over a phone? Come inside."

Linda hung up. "I'm on my way."

She walked to the nearest basement window, crouched, and examined its surface. Scratches revealed translucent glass in thin stripes, but someone had otherwise painted the pane black. She ran her fingers over the surface but felt no texture, meaning someone painted from the inside. Before she could study it further, the sky burst open as a downpour began. Something thudded nearby.

The bulkhead.

Its doors rattled in the wind. It was the closest entrance to get away from the storm and she needed to keep the journal dry, so she yanked the door open and stepped inside. A mistake. The basement light was not on, so the world was dark. She stood on the small steps leading down from the bulkhead, but did not know where the next step was. She needed the light. One could turn on the single light fixture from a switch atop the stairs or by a pull chain attached to the light fixture.

Linda turned her phone's flashlight app on to step down the small series of steps. It relieved her to find her feet on solid ground. It would be hard to find the bulb even with her phone, so she needed to orient herself. She knew where everything was based on the brick wall they discovered Heather at. Linda followed the wall off the bulkhead over to the workbench and from there she followed the next section of wall until feeling brick.

Upon reaching the brick section, a hand shot through an opening in the wall, followed by another hand and another. Linda kept a pace ahead of the grasping arms, oblivious to their presence. Reoriented from where she knew the brick wall to be, Linda turned, reaching into the shadows where her light barely illuminated the immediate area surrounding her. As her hand vanished into darkness, eyes opened, caught in the cellphone's light. The Pointing Woman! Linda failed to see the ghastly face when she reached for the light's pull cord. Her fingers tangled in it and she pulled. The room came to life with light, Pointing Woman nowhere to be seen.

She turned and bumped into a body standing solid, unmoving. Linda pushed to get away, but the figure gripped her arms. A face came into view.

"Andrew?"

The man looked down at her with a grin held partially in check, studying her as if a foreign species. "What are you doing, Linda?"

"Trying to get dry. Trying to protect..."

More secrets. She declined to tell him about the book in her pouch. Off his look, she realized he was not truly listening anyway.

"No, I do not mean that. What are you doing? Really?" Andrew asked.

It was all too much. She decided she had enough of secrets, of tiptoeing around her friends. This was Andrew, the one she talked to when things were tough. She opened the floodgates by opening her mouth, spilling to one of her oldest friends.

"I'm trying to figure out what's going on. There are tire tracks outside on the lawn. Was that you?" When he shook his head, she continued, her words flowing faster than she could think. "I didn't think so. And then there is a man and woman missing. Plus, the priest. Oh God, the priest," Linda said.

Any semblance of a grin vanished when Linda spoke the word God. Andrew grimaced as if struck. Linda continued, too involved in the moment to notice.

"And Heather and Tom vanish. They left without saying goodbye. Something is wrong with the house."

Andrew chuckled. "You have not figured it out yet, have you?"

Linda's silence was the answer. She had not. Andrew's grin came back, stronger, wider. He continued.

"It is not the house, but you. Your friends do not want to be around you. They abandoned you like your mother did."

Linda staggered under the blow of the words. "No, it's the house. It's..."

"Do not be so naïve. If Heather and Tom cared about you, they would have made things work while they were here. But we know they did not care, otherwise they would not have kept their marriage issues secret. They told me. Ruby as well. We knew everything. I guess we are their real friends, their actual family."

"Andrew, stop. This isn't you."

"Oh sweetheart, it is. You just have this deluded sense of who people are, but I guess you would with your condition."

"My condition?"

"Sure. Delusional. Thinking you have any real friends. Tom wanted to fuck you. Hell, I did fuck you. Hang around the lonely chick long enough and BOOM! You get to stick it in there. That was the only reason the two of us stuck around."

Andrew thrust his groin at her. Linda slapped him, but his face never moved, holding firm under the powerful strike. His eyes flashed with anger when she struck him, but Andrew held his gaze. Water dripped down Linda's face, an equal mix of the earlier rain and tears that started flowing. He continued, not even acknowledging the blow.

"No one wants you. No one. Not even your mother. It is a mother's DNA to protect newborns, but not in your case. Left you on a doorstep. Wow. How pathetic that your own mother wanted nothing to do with you!"

Andrew's words cut Linda cleaner than a blade. She had the same thoughts so many times over the years and went to dark places when such thoughts overtook her. Linda shook her head, not in disagreement but because she could not bear hearing more.

"Stop, just stop!"

"If it makes you feel better, you still have one thing I want. Or want more of."

Andrew stepped closer. Not sexy anymore, never sexy again. He reached out and cupped one of her breasts. Matter of fact, no gentleness, just a firm grip. Linda pulled away and caught a flash of red in his eyes. He grabbed her by the waist with one hand and took one of her arms in the other. His grip was powerful.

"Stop. Andrew, you're hurting me!"

He groped her as he attempted to position her to take her. Linda broke free and punched his face, drawing blood from his nose. He licked the overflow and smiled. She raced for the stairs, scrambling up, falling on the way, but kept moving.

"Do not tell me you did not love every second of what we did!" Andrew yelled from the darkness in the basement, but he did not follow.

Linda burst into the kitchen and screamed as someone grabbed her. (How did he move so fast?) No, not Andrew, Ruby.

"Hey, slow down. What is going on Lin-Lin?"

"Did you try Heather again?"

"No, I left a voicemail earlier. Some of my best work, she'll call back."

"I don't think she will. Ruby, you must leave before it's too late. It's the curse, it's..."

"What are you talking about?"

From somewhere in the house the music box sounded, playing warped. The song slowed, stretched out. "Do you hear that?"

"Hear what? Linda, you're scaring me."

"Good, use it to leave. You must leave. The woman in the pharmacy knew. She tried to warn me." Linda's head danced around, seeking the source of the tune, speaking as much to herself as Ruby. "As well as the child on the ride."

"Pharmacy? Child on a ride? Something is seriously wrong with you. Let me get Andrew and..."

"No!"

The volume behind the demand startled Ruby, who stepped back. Breathing deep, Linda steeled herself and looked directly at her friend. It was time to talk.

"Ruby, Andrew is not who you think he is. Stay away from him."

"From Andrew? The guy I'm going to marry?"

Linda cringed. Where were the fissures in the relationship? Where were the similar relationship issues Tom and Heather shared? Had Linda been so blind to her own needs that she never considered the strength of Ruby's relationship? It was too late now to worry about that, but it wasn't too late to warn her friend about the beast her man had become. (Or always been?)

"I slept with Andrew."

Ruby staggered, then searched Linda's face, waiting for the crack of a smile. Surely, Linda was joking. Except Linda never faltered. The shorthand of their friendship meant they could read one another easily and Ruby saw it. Truth in the damning words.

Ruby let out air, less a gasp than a mortal blow. The last breath of someone formerly untainted by betrayal. Ruby tilted her head, begging for answers, though she could not find the words. Linda found them for her.

"It was here. In my bedroom." Linda's eyes drifted skyward, the song, the twisted song. Of course, go to the source. The music box in her room. Though how could it be so loud?

"No!" Ruby shouted, shoving Linda, who stumbled but remained on her feet. "No!" she shoved Linda again. "Why?"

The shove forced Linda into the wall. Ruby eyed her 'friend' as if for the first time, then threw punches wildly, too angry to focus, too stunned to land properly. Linda raised her arms, absorbing the body blows, the much-deserved blows.

"No! No! No!" Ruby cried out before crying.

Ruby breathed in between stifled sobs, trying to catch her breath from the sudden activity. Linda recomposed herself and looked at her friend through mussed hair fallen across her face in such a way she could be the Pointing Woman.

"So, you're angry now? You hate me?" Linda asked. Ruby nodded without hesitation. "Good. Then get the hell out of my house while you still can!" Linda brushed past Ruby and exited the kitchen.

Ruby did not stop Linda, instead she staggered under the weight of heartbreak to the threshold of the basement door and looked down on a relationship that used to be while searching for a man she once loved. And still did, so much that she thought she might not survive the heartache. Staring into the abyss, she did not spot her lover, only darkness. *Like my heart*, Ruby thought. *Like my motherfucking heart.*

Linda stepped into the foyer, chasing the warped song floating in the air, following the twisted notes. As she climbed the stairs, it became clear it came from the actual music box in her room, though how it played so loud she could not understand.

She burst into her room. *The room*, she corrected in her mind. She no longer thought of the place as her own. The entire home was a trap. A place of misery, a place designed to punish. It tore apart Heather and Tom as easily as paper, and with substantially more effort, did the same to Ruby and Andrew. It even separated Andrew from his own personality. Or she hoped it had. If the home merely removed his mask, then it sickened her to think of all the years she spent pining over him.

The song demanded attention, throbbing in her mind as much as it played on the device. She wished to silence it. The notes muddled her thoughts, kept her in a fog. Walter. He was always there. He would help. Why had she not called him yet? *Because he doesn't want you, he never wanted you, no one wants you*. Linda's thoughts answered.

It was the song. The twisted song. (Had she heard it in her sleep? In dreams?) The box was closed, which made little sense. When open it struggled with the tune, closed it should have muffled the notes or not played at all. She picked it up and launched it across the room. It made a mark on a distant wall and hit the floor, landing on its side. That did the trick. The music stopped.

The world fell silent. Too silent. Linda cleared her throat to determine if she could still hear. She could, but her own throat clearing sounded like someone else. Someone far away. Linda felt herself falling, going somewhere distant. Drifting into sleep, or drifting back in time? Then she looked in the mirror and froze.

Father Bergman appeared in the glass. Not the living version, but the truck smashed version. Half his face was missing, along with one eye. The blood covered flesh half held bits of grit and asphalt from the street, while the other half was skeletal. A section of his brain made a show of it, the spongy organ rising like a bubble through a hole along one side of the man's head. His torso was mostly bare, exposing bloody, twisted carnage. Exposed ribs showed how severely the accident transformed the poor man's bone structure. The ribs overlapped one another like a gore filled hair clip. Like a car crash, she could not look away.

Though the mirror rose above the vanity and normally showed her own reflection from the waist up, the dead priest stood far enough away in the reflection that she could see his entire body. She glanced behind herself, and did not find him there, only in the reflection. His legs were the most impacted. More accurately, his waist and hips. The bottom half of the man faced the wrong way. Only one shoeless leg held the man up. The other leg twisted at a forty-five-degree angle away from the knee.

Bergman pointed as best he could with a gnarled hand. Each finger jutted in different, unnatural directions. One bony finger jabbed in Linda's direction. Linda calculated the angle of his finger and looked down at her stomach.

The man in the mirror mouthed the word *child*. Wherever the old priest ended up, it appeared he returned to being a mute. Then Linda remembered. The diary stuffed into her hoodie. She had forgotten after confronting Andrew. She thought of the priest's words back on the road, back when the man could talk and before he appeared as a vision in a mirror. *The answer lies with the children.* She pulled out the diary, relieved to find it was barely damp. The hoodie absorbed most of the rain. When she looked back, the man of the (torn) cloth was gone. Linda understood he had never been there at all, his image brought on by traumatic memory.

Walter had discovered why the trials ended and mentioned a curse on the Goode bloodline. Tragedy followed members in her family, but it would take time to match those up with the people in the newspaper clips. Could a curse be real? Linda thought of all the hurricanes, tsunamis, earthquakes, and other natural disasters that sadly took so many lives without warning in most cases.

Were those people suffering such fates of nature also cursed? Then it hit her, the difference. The disasters she dreamed up were natural. They happened over the globe, a byproduct of living on Earth. The incidents in her mother's files were much different. The random beheadings, drownings, fires, and other incidents in her mother's files were unnatural.

Unnatural.

That was the key. Did curses exist? Could her house, her bloodline, be subject to such a curse? She looked around the room and decided the answer was yes. The mirror had released the priest for now. She found herself alone and unprepared for the truth. Linda set the journal down on the vanity desk and moved to her closet, where she stripped off the wet clothes. She wished not to further damage the journal with water, and she did not feel herself in the casual wear, anyway. She changed into khakis and a blouse, then stepped into a pair of flats. Everything in its place.

She sought normalcy, trying to get to a place of curiosity, not fear. It was not working. There was no going back to such a thing as normal after all that happened. Dressing a certain way did not change events. Resigned to forging ahead into whatever her new life might look like, Linda sat at her desk and read the words from a child.

As Linda read the journal, she imagined the events as they happened, filling in blanks of the child's words with the information gleaned from the book of blood. A horrible tale came to life in her mind.

CHAPTER 32

JOURNAL OF SADIE GOODE—DATES OMITTED

FATHER HAS BEEN VERY busy these days. Though a stern man, mother makes it known that father loves us. As well as he can with our precociousness, mother clarified. Even while I swing, one of my most favorite of things, I cannot help but notice my father's comings and goings.

Sadie sat at a petite desk in her room, writing in her journal with a pencil thicker than her fingers. The upturned cross was nowhere to be seen. While writing, the child conjured images in her mind of events as they happened, choosing which words to put on the page.

Suddenly she was not at her desk but on the swing, swinging lazily. She did not bother to put much effort into it, too occupied with watching movement flash behind the cellar windows. The very presence of such windows denoted wealth and high societal standing.

My father frowns on pride during his sermons. I do not listen to him in church, for I hear the sermons at home every day as he practices the words of the Lord. I have asked him if the words come from God, why must he work so hard to remember them? There was no supper that night and I never asked again. I learned the Lord works in ways beyond my understanding.

Despite father's lectures on pride, I understand well that such niceties as a basement (with windows no less!) make us better than many of our neighbors. Many are petty folk, always begging my father for a blessing, or scraps of food, or both. Father calls them his flock. I find the masses without character, and I often wish they would go away. I once told my father about such feelings and worried it might deny me a meal once again, but my father honored me with a smile and a rub of my head.

I enjoyed it so. Receiving praise from my father feels different from that of my mother. It is as if I am receiving praise from the Lord on high. Blessed be I that day. Father, in his good graces, blessed me with an extra serving. I took it to mean my father would feel as I did were it not his job to suffer the indignities of entertaining such peasants.

Haddy tucked Sadie in, hugging the girl. Haddy, despite appearing haggard from a hard day's work, lit up while performing the act. Althea stood in the doorway, watching with a smile. Haddy plinked Sadie's nose, producing a giggle from the girl. Then Haddy left the room, bidding good night to mother and daughter.

Althea entered to perform a tucked in check and declared it good. Sadie asked her mother what preoccupied father so much in the basement, only to receive a shush for her troubles. The line of questioning seemed to hasten her mother's exit. Althea suggested she heard Rose in need of help, but Sadie heard no such thing, and listening was one of her most excellent skills. Sadie turned to her side to chase sleep while listening for sounds from the basement.

Father used to spend all his time in the church, but in recent months found more comfort in our family home. The basement, to be exact. Even at night, I hear my father make his way down. He tries to be quiet as not to wake us, but I hear him anyway and can only wonder why he visits there so often at such a late hour.

My sister Rose confided in me how the noises disturb her slumber. I am not so susceptible to such discomfort. The sounds intrigue me, and each night I seek the courage to ask my father what type of Lord's work can prompt such horrendous but interesting sounds.

Heavy boots tromped down the basement stairs, a burning lantern guiding the way. Despite the slow pace, the footfalls boomed against the thin planks. Reverend Goode walked to the center of the basement to where a stock rose from the floor. The poorly constructed device served its purpose, with holes for wrists and head. Chains and metal cuffs dangled on one side, tools designed to keep someone in place. He lifted the top of the device.

Scratching sounded from behind the brick wall at his rear. He yanked open a door built flush into the wall, difficult to see, especially in the basement's darkness. Beyond the open brick door rose bars, a prison built with far more skill than whomever constructed the pillory. The lantern illuminated only the front of the tight cell, its flicker catching a pair of eyes scrambling toward the rear of the cell.

Goode hung the lantern on a hook and entered. The woman fought furiously but lacked the energy to overcome the powerful man, too hungry, muscles too atrophied from the cramped cell. He dragged her from the prison. The dirty thin fabric covering her fell away in the struggle. Once in the open basement, she stood nude, unable to cover herself, too busy raising her arms to cover eyes blinded by long denied light.

Dragging her to the center of the room, Good placed her in the stock and slid the top back down, quickly fastening metal collars around her neck and wrists. She struggled anew and pulled at the chains, to no avail. The woman could not scream with a throat so parched, but she managed a haunting moan.

She tried to kick, but it caused her to fall against the thin board at her neck, producing immense pain and choking her. She stopped using her legs, but she struggled all the same, finding some strength in a desire to escape. The rattling of the metal at her hands blended with the clinking of more metal as Goode unfastened his belt. His pants dropped to the floor, and he moved in on the woman from behind. He produced a cane from the shadows and raised it to strike. The woman bit down on the rag, screaming with every blow.

In Hope's room, she pulled her pillow over her head, unable to make sense of the chaotic sounds below. In Sadie's room, the girl remained on her back under covers, blankets pulled to her chin. She slept with a smile on her face.

Never did my mother seem to wake, nor did she ever inquire about my father's tasks. My sister and I remained curious. Day and night my father spent time below, in the dark. The demons he battled must have been powerful, for it required much of his time. Father grew increasingly private about his work affairs. It was as if he deemed the demands of his job were not for the eyes of even his own flesh and blood.

Sadie pushed Rose on the swing. Bored, Sadie looked around as she pushed. The normal scenes greeted her. The wood pile along the house, being prepped for winter, an axe stuck in one log. She scanned the forest nearby. Then something out of place caught her attention.

A hand slapped against the glass from inside the basement. The hand scratched frantically. A stronger hand pulled that one away. Sadie ran to the window and dropped onto her stomach. Once the swing slowed, Rose leaped off to join her sister, where they both peered through the glass. Unable to see any people, they spotted only shadows cast along one wall, blending in a manner which made little sense. The life-size figures performed like a life-sized puppet show. The actual events remained out of view.

The moving shadows stilled and suddenly Goode's face filled the pane, his hair uncharacteristically out of place. A scratch lined his face. The man lifted a finger to his lips, swearing his girls to silence. Then he vanished, only to reappear with a rag and bowl. He dipped the yellowed cloth into the substance of the bowl and the rag came out black. Pine tar. He wiped it across each of the windows from the inside, making them opaque. The girls raced from one window to another as he did so, trying to spot the source of the earlier commotion, but their father was too quick.

Mother suffered from consumption that father attributed to lack of faith. My mother prayed daily, so I failed to understand how he could say such a thing. Still, my mother could afford a second set of hair, another sign of our status. That mother could remain beautiful even in the face of health struggles was one more way I knew we were special. Chosen.

One of my favorite things was to brush mother's hair in her absence. Father would often watch as I did so, proud of my skills. I could only dress the hair while mother slept, which she did more frequently in the days my father spent time in the basement.

At night, Sadie brushed out the wig resting atop the wooden dummy's head. She brushed with great flair, not worrying about hurting a non-existent scalp. Goode watched from the doorway, smiling at his child, who occasionally smiled back.

Goode eventually entered and took the hair from her, praising her work. Then her father left her to pray.

Women in Salem had been vanishing only to reappear as corpses relieved of the weight of their own heads. Father claimed the victims were sinners who never prayed enough. That made me pray harder each night. I prayed for the safety of my family, prayed for my head to remain attached, and prayed to better understand what demons lived in our basement.

Father never allowed us to speak of his work to anyone inside or outside of the house, lest doubters of faith weaken his efforts. I remember the words of a sermon my father once gave. 'Look away from evil, for it will never look away from you.'

A day came where my sister and I failed to heed those words. We did not look away. In fact, we sought to witness all we could.

Sadie and Rose held hands, spinning in a circle until eventually letting go and falling into the grass, laughing. Sadie rose first, trying not to tip over. She noticed something in the distance and wondered if her dizzy spell had her confused. Once she felt stable, she checked again. Her initial thought proved true. The axe was missing from the woodpile. It never left its station as far as she could remember.

Then she heard it. Skritch, skritch, skritch. The basement window nearest her came to life with activity as someone scraped lines in the painted window from within by fingernails. Only a small section cleared, but it became a window into their father's world.

Sadie gathered her sister, and they flopped to their bellies on the grass, looking in. Darkness filled the small, exposed piece of glass until an eye opened, blinking frantically, catching Sadie's gaze.

From the moment I learned my father's secret, I understood he was battling the Devil. The devil was a cunning foe who took on many forms. Including the faces of some of the most beautiful women in town.

That night, Sadie slept soundly with a smile on her face. Meanwhile, Rose tossed and turned, as did Althea Goode, minus her wig, her scalp bare and weeping blood. The wooden head on the vanity wore Althea's wig. Reverend Goode was not sleeping next to his wife. Instead, he led a different woman into the basement pillory and raised his cane.

Father allowed me to enter the basement once he recognized my ability to remain quiet in the face of such evil. Understanding my love of brushing, he allowed me to service the women in his care. Rose grew jealous of my closeness with father. She was too young to understand the evil he sought to vanquish. The situation drove us apart.

Rose often tried to catch my ear, stressing how she needed me during such a confusing time, and with mother sleeping more often. But I had little time for games when such evil grew underfoot. I understood Rose would eventually succumb to curiosity, and she did one day, peeking inside the window as I serviced the hair of those under my father's care. It did not go well.

Rose approached the window and at first her legs stood there as the child looked around, searching for witnesses. Soon, the pull proved too great. Rose dropped to her belly and pressed her face to the glass. Her eyes went wide. At the workbench, Sadie brushed the blonde locks of a woman, tugging at tangles. The brushing took great effort, not like the thin strands of her mother's artificial hair. Sadie grinned at Rose, fully aware of her sister's presence.

As if for show and bragging rights, Sadie rose and moved to the next woman in line, one with shorter locks. Sadie started brushing, but by shifting over in her seat, Rose got a better view of the basement situation.

Tears filled Rose's eyes as she stared in disbelief and shock. When she had enough, the child ran away screaming into the woods behind the home. Sadie yelled for her father as her sister sprinted away.

I alerted father to my sister's flight, forcing us to abandon our battle against evil. Father was quick and powerful and easily caught up to my little sister. Despite father's best efforts, Rose fell into a fit of hysterics. Unfortunately, my sister could not understand how my father's actions protected us against those who would do us harm. Strict measures were called for.

Althea and Sadie looked over at Rose, now tethered to her bed, the same as during the exorcism. The girl fought against her bonds and screamed to her mother, who fell to weeping and left the room. Reverend Goode finished the knots and shooed Sadie away. Once they all stepped into the hallway, Goode closed the door on the younger's cries for mercy.

In the weeks that followed, Rose proved stubborn with eating, and had long since stopped talking in a manner that made any sense. I did my best to regale my sister with tales of our father battling demons in our home, but she did not appear to understand all his methods. Nor could I. There were times father excised me from his company during certain work. That did not keep me from spying.

Sadie sat on her stomach, looking through the gap in the window as her father dragged a woman from a cell. Sadie could only see so much. The limited view kept Sadie from identifying the exact nature of her father's interactions. Mostly, Sadie watched the prisoners struggle while being moved from the cell to the basement. She could see nothing after that, as events happened in a section of the basement beyond her range of view.

I promised Rose that she too could join me in brushing such glorious hair. If there was one thing that the demons had in common, it was luxurious hair that I could never find in my mother. At least not in recent years. Promising Rose a hand at brushing was one of the rare moments I noticed her show interest.

Rose, now gaunt, so small, remained tethered on the bed, a bedpan nearby. At the mention of brushing hair, Rose's eyes blinked off an omnipresent fugue and opened wide to gaze into her sister's eyes.

Sadie smiled, thinking they achieved a breakthrough, until a commotion sounded below. Something different from the strangled noises and moans in the basement. Sadie rushed from the room and looked down the stairs to find a mob bursting into the foyer.

It appeared the townspeople, already weary of losing women in their midst, had noted my sister's sudden absence. The crowd raged toward my father and inquired about the whereabouts of Rose. They failed to notice me until I staked a position atop the stairs and announced the bewitching of my sister.

I will forever remember the proud look on my father's face as he beamed at me as if I stood in Heaven itself. Momentarily freed from the crowd's wrath, my father raced to my side. We entered the room where my father quickly undid restraints. The mouthpieces of the crowd soon made their way into my sister's room and cried out at the sight.

My sister, freed from her bonds for the first time in weeks, fell from the bed, a bird of a girl, so frail. Perhaps because of the burst of excitement or merely the lack of food visited upon her in recent days, Rose fell into a seizure, jerking and writhing for all to see. The timing could not have been better planned and, for a moment, I believed my sister was finally ready to protect our father's mission. Her efforts proved fruitful.

Though mother cried out for someone to help the girl, father cut her to the quick and allowed the seizure to play out. The entire crowd watched minus old man Carver in the foyer. Unable to navigate the stairs, he remained below.

I was grateful for the commotion of footsteps on stairs and the thunk of my sister banging her head on the floor, for I hoped it would drown out that which I heard the moment the crowd arrived. The demons in the basement cried out for the visitors, likely hoping to influence those in attendance. Or to entice an escape from those who might not understand the true nature of the women below.

My father stood before the crowd and announced there were witches loose in Salem, and he vowed to seek them out. He promised to build a prison beyond the small jail in the town center. (Not informing them that such a place already existed.)

Then the unthinkable happened. Old man Carver heard the cries at his feet, him being the closest to their source. The old man dared quiz my father. For the first time in ages, I bore witness to a seed of doubt in my father's demeanor until my sister performed an anatomically odd twist on the floor. She performed wonderfully for the crowd. I wished her spine would remain intact, though based on her positioning, that remained in doubt.

My father took advantage of the crowd's renewed shock by declaring old man Carver a warlock for hearing the same voices that raged inside Rose's head. The crowd reacted accordingly and confronted the old man, rushing down the stairs. The sounds of so many footfalls drowned out the cries of those imprisoned, and as they dragged the old man away, normalcy returned to our household.

Word quickly spread to the church. Rose survived her acrobatics, but father repurposed the knots, leaving her back in bed where she would once again be safe. When Ramses arrived to investigate, he could not deny Rose's fragile state, yet he could not bring himself to believe in bewitching. Faced with such a lack of faith, I dropped to the floor and writhed in a manner matching my sister's seizure.

The twists and turns suffered me great discomfort but oh what I performance I gave! By the time I rolled my eyes into my head, Ramses was eager to perform an exorcism on the spot. My mother knew not what to think, herself haunted by the cries of disembodied voices somewhere deep in her own home.

Caretaker Haddy tried to revive me, explaining the danger that was forthcoming from the reverends. I bit her arm as an answer. It proved enough for the woman to agree that desperate measures were in order.

Had I known the pain, the genuine pain that was about to be visited upon me, perhaps I would have changed course, but things had progressed too far. My actions that day led to my own tethering and eventual exorcism.

When the cross burned my forehead, I spoke in true gibberish. The pain was unlike anything I ever felt, but a part of me quite enjoyed it. The scarring my sister suffered caused her to beg for mercy. After that, we freed Rose from her bonds, certain she would remain silent about all she witnessed that day at the window. Ramses left determined to aid my father in his quest for witchery.

The scar I bore became a badge of honor as I roamed the town, helping my father identify heathens in our midst. My father provided me with the knowledge and wisdom that if the devil took human form, it would be as that of an enticing, comely woman more often than not. Still, his firm hand guided me. Sometimes too strong.

Goode and his daughters roamed the Salem streets. Upon spotting a ragged peasant woman resting alongside the road,

Sadie raised a finger. Goode gripped his daughter's shoulder tight enough to draw a grunt of pain from her. Sadie adjusted and swung her pointing arm toward a beautiful woman nearby.

The woman bolted, but Goode's personal guards quickly caught up to the woman and rendered her unconscious before dragging her away. Other citizens in the streets averted their eyes, happy not to be chosen.

One day, the true nature of what my father battled showed itself to the world. A woman, once striking, a beauty who I admired despite her isolationist tendencies, crossed our path. Verity Soule was her name. She outraced my father and his guards the day I pointed her out, but my father reassured me he knew where to find her.

I never witnessed someone escape before and part of me cheered the woman on. Maybe my aim had not been true. I often doubted my mission, but each capture steadied my hand, made me believe I was doing right. When Verity escaped, I found renewed doubt. Until that day on the field.

My father did indeed find her anew. For how long she remained in the prison, I was uncertain as many women came and went. I never got the chance to brush her hair like I had so many others. I wished I had, for perhaps she would have spared me the curse.

In the field, Verity pointed at the Goode's while dangling with a crooked neck. Sadie and Rose could not look away despite the fleeing crowd trampling through the surrounding grass.

Not long after, the curse struck close to home. Exactly in our home. That day at the window (oh, that day in the window!) changed my sister. When Rose lost her voice, she lost something more. And when she found her voice once again, she came to enjoy our new standing as much as me.

There came a period where we were sisters again. Luxuriating in the glow of companionship forged by the most unusual of circumstances. Father never trusted Rose the way he did me, so he forbid Rose from visiting the basement, which I frequented more and more often.

After days of pointing out women on the streets, (always women, Father made sure of that, and his tastes became increasingly known to Rose and me) dear father allowed me to brush the hair of those in his keep more frequently. Rose often watched from the window.

That access allowed me to visit the basement even while my father was around town. Mother remained oblivious to the world below her feet, too worried over the ever-growing clods of sputum that thrived and rattled in her chest. Unless mother returned to town, she never much bothered to wear her wig, leaving it to sit on the dummy head atop her vanity. (I sometimes brushed that while she slept, but it was not the same as the luxurious hair afforded me in the basement.) On the days of my father's absence and when mother slept, I left the basement door unlocked, allowing my sister to find her way down.

Rose explored with great vigor, though avoided my brushing station. I was the elder sister, so Rose knew enough not to invade my space, lest I revoke her privileges. Still, it pained me to watch her wander while I gleefully made braids with efficiency and skill. I longed to show them off but would never tell Rose that. With her respecting my space, and me too proud to invite her over, we remained at a standstill.

My sister invested most of her time talking to the witches hidden behind the bars, themselves hidden behind a door of brick, a tricky mechanism hidden in shadows as it was. In those moments, when the annoying screams subsided (so loud they were when not muffled by a layer of brick) the witches would offer my sister riches galore to set them free. More than once I had to lecture my sister on the folly of such thoughts and though father trusted me in the cellar, he was wise in always keeping the keys on his person.

For that reason, my sister could not free a soul (not that a witch had one). Rose suffered bouts of consciousness that emulated my mother's consumption symptoms. Oh, how she wailed in her sleep. Rose often questioned me about morals. I reminded her that the Lord's work remained above us, and we were merely a guiding hand in the mission of the men in charge. Our father being one.

It all changed on the day in the field where Verity pointed back at us. The protection my father offered against all the witches traveling through our town somehow faltered. The pointing woman on the gallows cursed those in attendance, and I noticed how her hand landed on me.

The witch raged and spit and cried out a curse through vocal cords snapped at the neck. It would have been quite the show were it not so unsettling, and accurate. Crops and livestock suffered the brunt of the curse at first. Then, people in the church suffered in unimaginable ways. One town metal worker, a dear friend of father's, fell under a molten spill in his shop. There was no casket available to hold the weight of the molten man. How horrific a statue he made, rotting from the waist down while a perfectly formed statue from the waist above.

The man's horrific death was not to be the town's last. My own dear sister decided, considering the tragedies, to revisit her worries about the path we tread. The town's appetite for hanging ceased when the pointing woman lived for an uncomfortable duration in her noose. Our own pointing ceased as well under threats of townsfolk suggesting our own family suffer a noose were we to continue identifying the cursed in our midst. Can thee imagine? How ungrateful.

It took dozens to find the true one in our midst. Was that a reason to stop? The crowds thought so. I had pointed out Ms. Willoughby, a recent widow, when the crowd descended upon us. They took out their rage on my father's guards, one of whom died of infection brought on by the twenty strikes of a knife supplied by the crowd that day. Shame they could not understand how in the end we were protecting them.

That day likely was the catalyst that brought my sister to our cellar with a new light. (New light, such a phrase now brings me shivers.) The cellar burned cold in all but the warmest days of summer and that day was a cold one, such that I interrupted my brushing often, my hands seizing up under the frigid air, forcing me to leave occasionally to seek the comfort of our fire in the hearth upstairs.

One day, my sister listened to the pleas of the imprisoned. With father gone, my sister used the unlocked door of the basement to her advantage. Having grown to think of the beasts in our basement as people, she took an ember from our fireplace. There were many a lantern she could have used instead, but she was too young to understand that all flames meant heat. In her mind, only a fireplace gave warmth.

Rose pulled on heavy wool gloves, then removed a nearby candleholder and discarded the candle. She set the base near the fireplace and used tongs to lift a burning chunk of wood, placing it atop the wide base of the candleholder. She headed for the kitchen.

The child descended the stairs. Sadie sat at the workbench, combing a woman's hair. Sadie turned and watched as Rose opened the brick façade to expose the prison. Rose moved closer to the cell where soiled arms reached out, seeking the warmth. They cried out in joy at the development, with voices damaged from too much screaming. The commotion drew Sadie's attention.

My sister meant well, but I considered it cruel to supply hope to those already condemned. I yelled at my sister to leave the heathens be. Then it happened. Oh, so quickly it happened. Rose turned to me. Whether startled at my command or pushed by a witch in the cell, the ember dropped into her gown.

The flames made quick work of the fabric, igniting my poor sister, who danced in a manner I would have considered comical under different circumstances. Her voice, seldom used since the days of being exorcised, found new heights as her screams rose to the heavens. Possibly seeking warmth (for I could not entertain any other reasons they might do such a thing) the prisoners reached out for my sister. They, too, ignited. Flames lit the dungeon.

Maybe celebrating the introduction of light so long denied, the prisoners joined my sister in her dance, and all waltzed gleefully through the flames, pirouetting as chunks of black fell from their bodies. Soon, all tired of the dance and fell into stillness, embracing one another as if accepting Rose into their sisterhood.

I found my own lungs, forced to cough as smoke flourished in the tight confines. A smell I could only attribute to pure evil sought me out. I hacked and tried to clear my lungs. My eyes watered as much from the acrid smoke as from the memory of my poor sister. The whole incident caused me to stop brushing, my most favorite thing, but I found I could not let go of the brush. It brought me comfort, the sluicing of the bristles through a stranger's locks.

I remained frozen in place, awaiting the same fate as my sister, when flames threatened to overtake my position at the workbench. Then, as if God himself noticed my plight, the door to the outside burst open. Rain poured in and my father appeared, scuttling me from my spot on the floor. His remaining guards, growing more skeletal by the day, suffering their own maladies, were there as well, and brought buckets from outside already filled with rain.

They formed a brigade from the creek, and soon they had the fire under control. They saved the house with help from the rainy season we long suffered through. Dark smoke poured from the basement as they battled the flames. At one point I thought I saw a black dog form from the very smoke itself and run toward the ridge. Shouts arose from the distance. The smoke would surely bring townsfolk.

While the additional help would normally be welcome, my father still battled evil while hiding such efforts from the masses.

Father stepped up to me in the rain and looked down. I saw no emotion on his face regarding my poor sister, and I realized then, perhaps he, like me, felt—nothing. Somehow, I found myself numb to any thoughts of Rose's passing, as if it were God's will.

Nor did my father attempt to comfort me. Instead, he reached down to retrieve that which I still held in my hand. There would be no more brushing, not for some time. This head of hair was one of my favorites, as it did not fall out in clumps like so many did when I brushed. Mrs. Winston, a widower whom my father appreciated from afar. He relieved Mrs. Winston's decapitated head from my grip.

Reverend Goode buckled his pants, his face flush with sweat, an overworked man. He exited through the bulkhead and discreetly retrieved the axe from the woodpile as his daughters spun in circles on the lawn. He smiled at their antics as they fell to the ground, dizzy and laughing. The girls eventually rose from the ground and sought out the basement window.

Inside, Reverend Goode raised the axe high above a woman in the stock, then swung with authority. With a sickening thunk, the Widow Winston's head rolled across the basement floor. He grabbed the woman's hair and added the decapitated head to two others standing upright on the workbench. Goode winked at his oldest, who vanished from the window.

Sadie eventually visited the basement with glee and brushed the aligned heads which served as warnings to the other prisoners. The chains always kept the balance of the body standing up in the stock, so he would wrap it in a tarpaulin before unlocking the chains and allowing the corpse to visit the floor. Once there, he went to work with the axe to make the sizing more manageable to carry away.

Later, as the fire roared in the basement, Sadie stood on the lawn, still holding the brush, which remained tangled in the head of widow Winston. The woman had sat long enough that only her partial face remained in place. The balance was only skull. All that remained of the decapitated head dangled at Sadie's side.

Goode approached his daughter and retrieved the brush (and therefore the head) and walked it toward the last remnants of the fire as townspeople appeared in the distance, eager to help. Goode tossed the woman's skull into the flames and gathered the other decomposing heads on the workbench as well, tossing them into the flames which found new life under renewed fuel.

The home survived, but the respect our family earned did not. Mother has found herself once again with child, causing a row with my father, who claimed it to be a bastard child unless somehow the Lord immaculately conceived it. Mother spoke of matching father's indiscretions. I could not understand their arguments nor find the strength to care.

I will probably write no more after today. I have grown tired, and oh so weary. The doctor claims it is a blood disease I suffer. The man suggested an aggressive treatment to which my parents agreed, something about appeasing the citizens in town.

The therapy leaves me so exhausted. I wonder less how I shall continue to write and more how I will ever be able to identify my tormentors again.

Sadie rested on the bed, covered in sheets from chest to groin, the balance of her skin exposed. Leeches covered every inch of her legs, arms, and shoulders. A stout doctor lifted a bed pan and reached into it with tongs, retrieving another leech and placing it on her open eye. He repeated the same with the other, covering both Sadie's eyes with black bloodsuckers.

Sadie lay still, the leeches breathing for her, drinking her blood. Her body grew pale as she stared into the nothingness of the ceiling above her bed.

CHAPTER 33

L INDA PUSHED AWAY FROM her vanity, stunned at the revelations in a child's scrawl. While reading, she filled in the details of what she learned from the church. She also filled in details that she understood would be beyond a girl's understanding with good reason. Absolutely horrible what happened and under the noses of his own family, a supposed man of God. Pure carnality and abuse.

Unthinkable that the child wallowed in the aftermath of the corpses. Young Sadie was a child suffering from a troubled mind and spirit. Rose, the more innocent of the sisters, (still no means innocent) suffered the worse fate. At least Linda assumed she did. Linda never learned Sadie's ultimate fate. The child ceased writing in the journal after sharing her diagnosis and treatment. The writing at the end of the journal was nearly unreadable, suggesting Sadie suffered debilitating eyesight issues from the induced leeches. And there was the matter of the grave marker verifying Sadie died young. Sarah was pregnant, however, but Linda did not remember a third child headstone. Though she was not taking notes in a graveyard.

Curse or no curse, Linda's descendants committed atrocities upon an unsuspecting populace. Rooted in darkness, the witch trials had nothing to do with the cleansing of evil. *Could a curse be real?* Linda wondered. All the evidence left behind by her mother suggested as much. Her mother must have believed in it, otherwise why keep such mementos?

And what of the house and its influence? Did it trap evil within the walls? Was it contagious even after all those years? Linda committed a cardinal sin of cheating. While not as outwardly evil as the events in the journal, was it no less a sin? She never crossed a line like that until the house in Salem. When it happened, she felt the full pleasure of the experience, lost herself in a haze of satisfaction. Yet she never once considered the consequences.

Was she influenced? Did the same influence cause her to confess to Ruby in such a callous manner? Linda was panicking when she blurted it out and feared for her missing friend. But why be so cruel? Then it struck Linda. Tom and heather. Were they also influenced? And what happened to Heather? There was still no word. Linda grabbed her cell and dialed Heather's number. Voicemail. Linda dropped the phone and exited the room.

Immediately upon entering Heather's room, Linda spotted the partially packed suitcase. It was not there before. Or was it? Did Tom attempt to pack a bag for Heather's trip to the hospital? Linda could not remember. And where had Tom gone? She wanted to dial him too, make sure he was okay, but his last words kept her from doing so. Tom said he would sleep with Linda. Never had Tom raised such thoughts before. Only in the house. Only in the walls born of sin.

Sure, she blocked some awkward passes, but that was Tom. He was an awkward guy, if nothing else. And innocent. They all spent plenty of drunk times together, relieving the stress of teaching. There were bound to be moments where lines blurred and fantasies surfaced, but nothing more came of it until Salem.

The contents of the suitcase provided clues. Undergarments, makeup bag, essentials. Heather must have packed it. Tom would have thrown in a bathrobe and some pajamas, but never cosmetics for a hospital stay. The question was, when had Heather packed? And where did she go?

Linda checked the closet. Tom's clothes were still there, including his shoes. (Did he pack multiple pairs?) Tom was a simple man with clothing. It felt unlikely he would have packed more than one pair for what originally was to be a week's stay.

Then Linda heard something. Voices. She craned her neck and looked down. A vent. The small screen rested at almost floor level between the bed and the exterior wall. Linda crouched down, barely fitting in the space, and listened. Rage. She heard rage. And hurt. Ruby confronting Andrew.

What had Linda done?

Unleashed misery on her friends. It was all Linda's fault. Tom and Heather needed a romantic getaway to resolve their issues, but Linda took them to rain-soaked Salem. Then she slept with one of her best friends. Ruby and Andrew were her family before she knew she had family. They were the two most important people in her life, and she had pitted them against one another. Would Linda end up being involved with either when the dust settled? Would either of them ever wish to speak to her again? Had Linda orphaned herself?

For it was Linda who did it all. Curse or no curse, she acted in bad faith and caused the issues. How could she think for even a moment the house could somehow cause such misery?

She spotted legs underneath the bed on the opposite side! Bare feet with cracked toenails cracked and grimy, the legs corpse grey. Linda leaped back up to find no one there. She bent back down and looked under the bed again. The legs were there and ran out into the hall. Linda scrambled back to her own feet.

The answer lies in the children. Was it a child that ran past? Linda gave chase, running to the end of the hall. From the top of the stairs, she could hear her friends fighting, clearer than before. They were really going at it. Linda could not intercede in the argument while something was loose in her house. (A child?) It had to be a trick of the light, but she needed to know for certain.

She sensed more than saw movement behind her again. Her room. She entered and looked around. Nothing. Then the temperature dropped. The air changed, becoming oppressive, heavy, like a weight pressing on her.

Boom!

The bedroom door slammed closed with thunderous force. The shock of such an inexplicable event had no time to register before another horror revealed itself. She looked at the vanity and screamed. The wooden wig stand took on a human face. A single eye darted about within the crack on its surface. Chunks of hair covered the top of the previously bare wood and a face hung slack over its front, like a mask made of human skin.

Linda instinctively struck out, sending the object flying. It landed on the floor and rolled. No more hair, no more skin. The eye remained for a moment before blinking out of existence. Humming sounded outside. Linda raced to the window and looked down. A young child with an upturned cross on her forehead rocked on the swing, staring directly at Linda.

It was Salem! It was the house. Everything. That meant Andrew was not himself either. Linda needed to warn her friends. She raced to the door and yanked. The door refused to budge. She pounded at the slab, yelling for her friends. She could only hope the pair had ceased arguing long enough to hear her cries. They needed to get out, all of them, before it was too late.

As she pounded on the door, the outdoor swing rocked into view, entering from the bathroom before vanishing back within. Linda did not notice, not even when Dead Sadie leaped off the swing and landed in the bedroom. The girl's face shook violently into a blur. Then the dead girl found her footing. The child walked toward the unsuspecting Linda, who continued pounding out a warning.

CHAPTER 34

R UBY WATCHED THE DISEMBODIED head float up the stairs. It was not until Andrew stepped into the light of the kitchen that he appeared whole. And the same. Ruby eyed the man who looked—normal. If it were not for her friend's (former friend?) confession, Ruby would have no clue something was amiss in their relationship. She tried to form words, thoughts, a way to articulate her feelings. Eventually, she articulated by slapping Andrew's face. Once, twice, three times. He absorbed the blows, never moving, accepting the punishment.

Once she stopped, Andrew looked down at her. "Are you done?"

"Don't you mean aren't we done?" She squinted, peering into his eyes, searching for something to signal he was different.

Andrew shook his head. "Please, Rubes, I'm sorry..."

"No, don't! Sorry is when you leave the toilet seat up or arrive late for a date without texting to say you're on the way. This is way beyond a sorry moment. Tell me you didn't fuck our best friend!"

"What do you want me to say?"

"That you didn't. It's easy. Here, let me help you. Rubes, the love of my life, I never banged Linda. I would never think of such a thing because I love you."

"I do love you."

Thunder rumbled overhead. Rain pelted the side of the house, echoing off the plywood covered window. The lights flickered.

"Then say it. Say you didn't do it."

A growl rose from the basement. Ruby approached the stairs to investigate, but Andrew pulled her into an embrace, spinning her around until her back faced the open cellar. Andrew had a clear view into the dark abyss, where a set of red eyes watched from the base of the stairs.

"No, don't. Andrew, don't do this, please." She tried to fight him off, but he held tight.

"It's not me, don't you see? Thomas, Heather, and now us. It's this place. Don't you see what this place has done to us all?" Andrew pleaded.

Ruby faltered, breaking down in his arms. She sobbed while tears rolled down her face, vanishing into the folds of Andrew's shirt.

"Why? Why is this happening? I want this to stop," Ruby said and sniffled, trying to pull back on the tears.

Andrew gripped her shoulders and pushed her back, looking down, gentle. "I understand. I have disappointed you. Hurt you. You want to get back to a point where we are driving down the road, only the two of us. Your feet dangling out a window in a cool breeze with no cares in the world."

Ruby nodded again and broke free of his grip to wipe her tears away. She kept some distance but looked up at him and nodded, lost in the memory of simpler times.

"Well, no cares until you get poison ivy from the brush."

Andrew smiled a contagious smile and Ruby went along for the ride, grinning despite herself. "It wasn't poison ivy."

Then she deflated. There was a different poison in their relationship and the couple were no longer in a van. No road of endless possibilities stretching before them. They sat parked at a crossroads. Ruby could not decide which direction to turn. Lean into the hate or try to understand.

"Regardless. I know what to do. I know what can make this all go away/"

She met his gaze, waiting for an answer. Waiting for something she longed to hear. Andrew remained silent. She wished to speak, yet words escaped her. Her thoughts were butterflies of which she had little chance of catching any. Ruby's heart hurt, her stomach ached. Sick. She felt sick and near tears again. Whatever resolve she possessed slipped away. The two people she needed the most caused her pain.

Andrew saw her lips move and placed a finger over her lips. "Trust me. I know you are hurting, but I can make it all go away."

She shoved his hand away instead of biting it. She stood tall, defiant, shifting into the anger stage of grief.

"No, you can't make it go away, Andrew. You betrayed me! And what now with Linda, huh? Is it marriage for you two? Because she has always loved you. I know that. I thought you knew that. Are you going to hurt her, too? Do you love her?"

"Nah, Linda was simply a fuck."

Ruby flinched. There it was, the something different. She wondered who the man standing before her was. She did not know him. (Did his eyes flash red?) More growling down below. Ruby scrunched her face, concerned with the noise, but too angry to turn and look.

"What did you say?"

"I was ready for some strange. What can I say? Time with you was so boring. You did not think I would remain faithful. Tell me you were not that stupid."

Ruby covered her ears and shook her head. "This can't be happening. This can't be real."

Andrew reached over and lifted her chin. She looked up at the strange man.

"Oh, my bad. Did I hurt the princess's feelings? Here, I told you I knew how to make the pain go away."

Andrew kicked Ruby's stomach with enough force to launch her off her feet. She flew backward, arms pinwheeling, never touching the stairs. She hit the bottom of the basement with a loud crack, landing on her back.

She blinked, trying to regain her senses, but could not breathe. She grabbed at her throat, struggling for the air knocked from her lungs. Survival kicked in and she sucked a breath. The simple effort brought with it immense pain. She breathed again out of necessity but did not want to. It hurt, simply breathing hurt. Tears flooded her eyes, obscuring her vision. Tears formed through an unfamiliar pain, more physical than the earlier anguish.

From her position on the floor, she saw Andrew leering from atop the stairs. The ultimate betrayal. She reached toward him for help despite his being the perpetrator. Her arms flailed, the only thing she could move while she struggled to breathe regularly again.

Sucking in another breath of sweet oxygen, her exhale formed into frigid mist. The world grew cold. She lifted an arm to her face and watched it turn blue before her eyes. She was beyond shivering, still too intent on finding her breath.

Then she heard them. Footsteps. She turned her head, wincing in pain, and focused on the area producing the footfalls. A dark shadowed corner from which two figures emerged. Both children. Ruby tried to call to them for help, but only a wheeze escaped her throat.

Too stunned at first to question the children's presence, she grew concerned when their features became apparent. A cross on one girl's face. Was it placed at an odd angle or was it Ruby's position on the floor? Then the younger stepped closer with a mark of her own, a red square blotch. Something had disfigured both children.

The two giggled as they approached. Ruby's arms continued dancing in the cold air of their own accord, her body trying its best to do a factory reset. (Was she in shock?) The children looked down at Ruby, pointing. Accusing her?

Ruby shook her head, relieved to rediscover movement in other parts of her body. The children shifted their arms and pointed in the distance. The girls ceased giggling. Brick sliding across brick sounded from the area where the girls pointed.

The brick wall. Where they found Heather scraping until her fingers bled. Ruby shifted her head. It was still too hard to move her body. She spotted a brick sliding out of the wall. (Being pushed out?)

The brick slid until falling to the ground with a thud. Ruby jerked instinctively as the brick landed somewhere over her head. Another brick moved, and another. She could not see them all from her vantage point but could hear them. She focused on what part of the wall she could see. An arm thrust out from within. Its fingers touched her hair.

Ruby groaned and rolled onto her side. The activity by the wall came into better view. Multiple bricks thrust out until falling free. Each one became a hole through which arms stretched, hands grasping for freedom. Ruby glanced back up the stairs and glimpsed Andrew standing in the doorway watching (eyes red for certain now) with a huge grin on his face.

Another brick closer to the ground dropped free. The hand that thrust out gripped Ruby's hair, quickly tangling in it. The arm pulled her closer to the wall. Once within reach, more hands grabbed at her, catching her shoulder, neck, an arm, a breast. They pulled Ruby toward an ever-larger opening in the wall. More arms appeared. So many, too many.

Ruby twisted, trying to break free. Whispers and murmured cries filled the air. The limbs dragged Ruby painfully over the pile of fallen bricks. Ruby grabbed at the wall, to no avail. With a sudden forceful tug, they yanked Ruby into darkness, where she finally found her voice. The remaining brick wall partially muffled her screams.

From the kitchen, Andrew slammed the basement door closed, opened a drawer, and retrieved a chef's knife. Humming the song from the music box, he left the room.

CHAPTER 35

"WHAT HAVE YOU GOTTEN me into, Walter?" Professor Hopkins screamed the question through Walter's laptop. The man's face pressed close to the camera, filling the screen.

"I am sorry, Robert. I do not understand," Walter said. Moving the laptop from his lap to the dash.

Rain pelted down and lightning flashed, but it was the cascade of police vehicles still on scene that lit the cabin of Walter's vehicle. Moving the computer failed to help. The man's face still filled the screen, giving an up-close view of stray nose hairs.

"Who is this person you asked me to track down? Jack the Ripper, American style?"

"Uncertain if you are aware, but you appear to be too close in the frame," Walter responded.

"It's the only way I know how to rid myself of the cat's ears. I am in no mood for them to display because this is not funny."

"Understood. The cat ear part, but nothing else you mentioned so far."

"I did my search, as requested, and linked the family of the woman back well into British territory. The first connection with America occurs in Salem. No surprise there, since that is where you sourced information from." The man stopped for a moment, pulling back. The cat ears made an appearance but vanished when he pressed his face back to the screen. "She has connections to the Goode family who are central to the Salem witch trials."

Walter lit up. He was hesitant to inform Robert that they had presumably cracked the code, with the aid of the poor gentleman recently taken away in a coroner's van. (Plenty of police remained on scene investigating though.) Walter had yet to confirm the Goode family was the source of Linda's inherited key, but Robert's research confirmed it.

"Thank you. I will not say how we learned her name was Goode, but we got that far."

"Did your efforts result in a visit from Scotland Yard?"

Walter sat up, intrigued. "I cannot say that it did."

"Of course not, with you not being in England. But they were not alone. They brought with them a woman from the FBI."

"I'm sorry," Walter said, not understanding.

"You should be. I told you using this software would cause eyes to check on it. What I did not expect was the number of fatalities involved with the woman you work for."

"I do not work for her."

"She is not paying you?" Walter shook his head. Robert banged his head on the camera, increasing the size of his visible nose hairs. "Then what in the Queen's name are you... Wait. Are you smitten?"

Walter stopped himself short of an answer. Was he smitten? He was uncertain how to address his friend's question. She was lovely. Lovely is all. Otherwise, things were professional. *My, how lovely she was,* Walter thought. A police siren blooped, announcing its departure. One by one, the emergency vehicles left the scene of the accident.

Walter planned to leave earlier himself until receiving an urgent text from Robert. Rather than drive back to the office, Walter pulled over. Another storm front rolled in, so he figured he would wait out the rain while connecting with his friend online.

"It is not like that."

"I have her pictures, Walter, and I know your type. Do not insult me," Robert said.

"Can we get back to the FBI, please?"

"Oh, yes, that. Are you aware there are many deaths related to your friend?"

"I am aware. Yes."

"Well, there are adjacent deaths as well."

"Adjacent deaths?" Walter asked.

"Yes. It appears there are several deaths going back decades that are unrelated to the family itself but happened within proximity of certain family members, which makes said family members suspects. Many cases have gone cold, as they say in America. Once I started poking around in the family timeline, it earned me a visit from the authorities."

Walter had many questions, but his concern for his friend overrode those. "Are you okay? Did they accuse you of anything?"

"They tried. They would have loved to solve a case or two at my expense, but once I explained everything, they understood. It would not surprise me if they reached out to you or your friend, however."

"Robert, I have learned a great deal. We accessed church records that filled in so many gaps in history that..."

"Tut, tut. Write it up, have it peer reviewed, and then I will look at it. You know my standards. I refuse to traffic in hearsay. Enough of that with the churches on our side of the pond."

Walter deflated. He wanted to share his recent excursion with someone who could understand the gravity of the information uncovered but understood Robert's skepticism. Possession of the child's journal might change his friend's mind. Yet he was unwilling to bring it up while there were so many police still lingering. History had remained hidden for this long. Walter figured it could wait a little longer to see the light of day.

"I have learned of a curse," Walter said.

"Oh, well, that explains everything. Excuse me while I call the authorities back and explain all the unsolved murders were simply from a curse." The mere suggestion prompted Robert to pull away from the camera and thrust his hands in the air. The new view revealed another shot of cat ears.

The combination of cat ears and the topic caused even Walter to smile. "Please, I know how it sounds, but Linda has reason to believe there is some truth to it."

"And related to her how?"

"Actions related to Salem. Related to her bloodline."

"Well, she needn't worry much longer," Robert said.

"How so?"

"Because there are no curses! You know better." The professor raised his hands and ears, giving up on the tight framing. "Next, you will talk about Egyptian mummies and the aftermath of disturbing those tombs."

Walter thought back to just such a conversation with Linda earlier but refused to mention it. What Walter kept from Linda was that there were seemingly unexplainable events in numbers that made no sense where tomb raiders were concerned. Lore. It was all lore. Walter knew better, but the rain and current events had him leaning slightly into conspiracies. He was glad he had his friend on the line to set him straight.

"Time is the leading contributor to death. I firmly believe that all death certificates should list time as a contributing factor. With each day that passes, all living beings are closer to expiring. From the day one digs up a corpse, they themselves are closer to becoming one. Curses? Bah! But if it puts your friend at ease, she appears with the death of her mother to be the last in her family line. There was an older sister with a ten-year age difference. It was her death that prompted the visits from the authorities."

"I'm sorry," Walter offered, mind reeling at the thought of a sister that Linda would never know.

"They understood the depth of my ignorance about your adventures almost immediately. Do not worry about me. They are far more interested in the lot of you raising a ruckus in America. They took copies of my files, however. I will send the same to you. History has not been kind to your friend. And please do not attribute that information to a curse. My point is whatever bad choices her family members made along the way to result in such horrible events, she can now chart her own path. She is a lone survivor."

Walter beamed. Not at the knowledge she was the last in her line, but because he had new information to share. Walter thanked his friend. Robert said goodbye before walking away from the screen. In the distance, Walter saw the man making tea, cat ears and all. The professor did not know how to end the call, so Walter disconnected.

Tea. That was what Walter needed. He was eager to see Linda. (Why? Was she more than a friend?) Walter wished to share all the new information with her and get his hands on her... journal. Yes, that was why he was excited.

It had been a long day, and the poor woman was probably resting. Walter decided he could use a rest as well after answering questions for a long time before the local police (and his recent lunch buddy) decided he could go on his merry way. Before leaving the scene of the accident, Walter received the call from Robert, which led to more questions. He was ready for a break. It was time for tea so he could clear his head.

There were no curses. Linda would be fine. She did not need nor want anything from him now that she had her answers. (Well, answers to her name. He had some new info to be shared.) His time with Linda had ended. She did not need him any more than he needed her. He started the car and drove away, destination tea. Linda would be fine on her own.

CHAPTER 36

L INDA GRUNTED WHILE YANKING the door handle. The door refused to budge no matter how hard she pulled, which made little sense as it worked fine moments earlier. She realized something else was at play. One more puzzle piece to verify the house or its history influenced the world around it. Why else had she seen such strange things? There was no human head in place of the wig holder. The smooth faux surface remained on the floor in a position that would stare at her if it still had a face. It did not.

And a child? No, she simply had thoughts of them in her mind from reading the journal. The history was distressing and creeped her out. Even shadows could have taken on shapes in such a state of mind. Or at least she tried to tell herself that. Everything had seemed real. But no matter, the one thing she believed in fully was the influence of the house itself. She worried about her friends because they remained unaware.

Andrew appeared more influenced than the others, or at least she hoped so. The alternative was to take his cutting remarks at face value. There was no way she could handle thinking of him as a monster any longer. She loved him, loved Ruby, and it was time to get them out. Time to fix the mistake of ever inviting them to Salem. She planned an immediate dis-invite, planned to check them into a hotel, but that required getting out first. The door still would not open.

She looked back to the window, but that was a two-story drop. No, her friends would hear the pounding, eventually. Maybe it would even break up their fight. Then she realized she did not hear them any longer. Linda pressed her ear against the door, listening for her arguing friends, but heard something else. Soft footsteps. Too soft. Ruby? She almost cried out for help, but it sank in that Ruby was nothing if not a traveling noise machine. Unless heartbreak had broken her best friend, the steps were too soft even for Ruby. Padded steps intermingled with clicks in between. Paws? Whatever approached it crested the stairs and navigated the hall. Quick snuffing sounds gave further credence to an animal's presence.

Sniff. Sniff. Sniff.

The old door did not sit fully flush with the floor, so Linda crouched down on her hands and knees and lowered her head to the cold floorboards. She stifled a cry. Andrew! It was Andrew, but his face peered through the same opening she did with one insane difference. His head looked through the gap from an upside down position. She saw no signs of the rest of his body, which would have suggested he looked in from a twisted, crouched position. No, his face was simply upside down, as if he balanced on the very top of his head.

Linda attempted to flee but her hands slipped, causing her face to fall onto the floorboards, her body weight locking her in place, which left her momentarily unable to look away from the horrific sight. Andrew pounded on the door with unnatural force. She could not imagine how he could strike so hard from a pretzel position. Linda righted herself and scrambled away until finding herself backed against the bed.

With a thunderous boom, the door burst open. Andrew raced in, yielding a knife. Linda leaped to the side as he stabbed into the mattress, barely missing her. She fled, but quickly hit the wall alongside the window. Turning to face him with no escape route, she raised her hands as if it could ward him off.

"Andrew, please. This isn't you."

"Precisely."

He freed the blade from the bed and in a flash was upon her. She gasped not from the hand at her throat but at the impossible speed at which he moved. He tilted his head, taking her in.

"You look so much like her," Andrew snarled.

Linda could not ask who, too busy struggling for air. She struck him with her fists, but he absorbed the blows without flinching. He raised the blade and sliced, so quickly Linda could not register what happened. She felt release along her skull like someone unzipping a too tight coat. *Did he cut me?* The answer presented itself as a curtain of blood that poured over her forehead into her face. He had cut her!

Andrew pressed the blade against her forehead again. Slowly this time, (ever so slowly) he drew the blade across, digging deep. The slower slicing amplified the pain. The throbbing, sharp ache of the first cut joined the party, and she grimaced in agony and went pale with shock as he performed the gruesome carving.

Finished with the slicing, Andrew loosened his grip but still held her firmly by the throat. Blood poured into her face, the tributaries of red split off and ran between her eyes and down each side of her nose, sparing her eyes. Strangely, the pain settled into her shoulders and through her back. Fire as bad as the throbbing pulse above her face.

Linda glanced at the distant mirror and saw an upturned cross carved into her forehead like the girl in the pictures. She felt a tightness as the blood began clotting, tightening around her cheeks and nose. She hoped it meant the cuts were less deep than they felt.

Something moved in the mirror. A blob, out of focus at first but quickly taking shape as it moved closer to the frame. A girl. The one with the cross, pressing her face against the mirror from the other side. Dead Sadie moved her face until her cross matched up with Linda's own in the reflection. The child put her fingers to her lips and giggled.

Andrew raised the knife again. The weapon glimmered in the light, poised to end her. She turned to face him in her last moments, searching for the man she once knew. What was he waiting for?

"Andrew, please. I want to go home."

"You are home!"

Wrong choice. If Andrew was in there somewhere battling, if that was what kept him from striking, she just removed any hesitancy. She saw the switch. It was the way his hand gripped the knife tighter. The way his eyes shifted (to red?). No hesitancy left. The tip of the knife poised to strike her chest.

Linda inexplicably moved in on him, closer to the man, but by default, the blade as well. She pressed her hands against his chest, soothing the same spot she pummeled moments before. She gazed into his eyes. The cold, dead eyes.

"Stop! What about one last time, you and me? Are you going to do it with me only once when I am right here?"

Andrew faltered, looking down at her hungrily and licking his lips. Then she smiled. His eyes widened in recognition.

"Wait. You are setting me up, aren't you?"

Something swung perilously fast. with a loud crack, Andrew crumpled to the ground, unconscious. Walter stood over him with a fire poker. Linda launched herself at Walter, hugging him. Walter warmed to the hold despite fumbling with the poker in one hand and struggling to fix his glasses with the other.

She pulled away and looked at him. "Thank you!"

"Almost went for a tea. Rather glad I did not. Saw you in the window. It was all quite alarming. Oh, good Lord!"

As he straightened his glasses, he noticed the state of her injuries. He reached toward the cut with one hand, but she touched it herself, wincing. Hurt, but okay. She shook him off. Bad move, the motion of her head made the injury throb.

"It's the curse Walter, it is real. I read the journal. Reverend Goode, my ancestor, killed those women in Salem. He beheaded them. He tortured them, did horrible things, I..." She stopped when she noticed his focus elsewhere.

"Tell me I did not misread this situation?" Walter asked, looking at the unconscious man at their feet.

Linda looked down sadly and shook her head. "You did not. A part of me wants nothing more than to help him but that's not Andrew. I don't know who that is."

"Then what say you tell me more of what you discovered over a cup of tea, far from here?" Walter pointed the tip of the poker at the downed man's head. "If you do not mind, I have seen enough American scary movies. Can you please take the knife?"

Linda retrieved the blade. "Something happened to him. I don't understand what forces are at work here. All of this, since I first learned of my mother, it was as if a shadow cast itself over me and followed me wherever I went. I feel responsible for what happened to him. If that isn't a curse, then what is?"

Walter looked around at the destruction in the room. The damage to such a historic home weighed heavy on him, but Walter also understood some monuments crumbled. Maybe this was one. He had information he originally planned to share later but thought sharing it right away might put Linda at ease.

"I do not pretend to follow the full nature of your concerns. But if you believe in bloodline curses, this one ends with you."

She turned to him. "What do you mean?"

"Early on, I submitted your DNA results from your PI, along with all the information I gathered so far, to my friend Robert. A splendid chap. Despite giving me some access to software, he had better tools available. According to his research, after your mother's death, that leaves you as the last in your family line."

At the mention of family, a realization settled over Linda. "Ruby! We have to find her. What if Andrew hurt her too?"

Linda rushed into the hall, knife at the ready. Walter followed. She headed toward the stairs when suddenly Rose ran from the last room to the middle across the hall and slammed the door. Walter's eyes widened, shocked at the sight.

"A child? Where did a child come from?"

"She is not real, Walter. We must find Ruby."

"Not real? We both saw her. She is in that room. I heard a child when I had my car accident." Walter started toward the door, leaving Linda on the top step, pleading.

"She is from the past. She means to distract you," Linda said.

Walter continued, stunned. "The past? She was right here. I saw her!"

"I know it makes little sense, but it is the evil trapped in this house. She is nothing but an echo, Walter. Someone else needs help. Today. We can't help those in the past, can't change history. We can only affect the present. I'm going to help Ruby with you or without you."

Walter reached for the doorknob. A world of wondering, of searching for truth, searching for history. The answers to so much he sought hid behind a simple door inches away. He looked toward Linda, then at the door. Just the twist of a knob would reveal secrets. The child existed for certain because she hummed a haunting melody inside the room. Walter eyed Linda again and remembered when he last disappointed a woman who meant so much to him. History or now. The choice was simple. He left the door closed.

Walter understood he made the correct choice when a smile overtook Linda's face. He moved toward her, ready to help her with her search for her genuine family. But then her face inexplicably changed. Was she raising the knife? Linda cried out. What was she saying? A warning? Was it a warning? By the time he understood, it was already too late.

"Walter, look out!"

Linda raised the blade as if she could stab Andrew when he leaped from her bedroom. Fast, oh so fast. The moment Walter stepped in front of the open door, Andrew leaped at the unsuspecting man. Their momentum carried them both through the stair railing, which exploded in shards of splinters. The world transitioned to slow motion as Linda witnessed Walter's legs vanish from beneath him. Walter never took his eyes off her, watching her until disappearing over the side of the stairs. The poor man never had time to even yell as he dropped to the first-floor hallway. The floorboards collapsed on impact. Splinters, dust, and timber exploded as a hole ripped open, swallowing the men whole. The pair tumbled into the dark basement below.

"Walter!" Linda screamed until rising dust and particulates forced her into a cough. She closed her eyes to block the floating debris.

When she opened them again, Walter's glasses rested at her feet. The cloud dissipated, falling back into the hole from where it originated. Linda remained frozen in place, still trapped in a world moving so slow. Time returned when Rose burst from the room and barreled down the stairs, passing Linda. Startled, Linda almost tumbled over the edge herself. She dropped the blade, which landed upright in the floorboards.

Linda found her feet and raced down the stairs. The child had already vanished from view, gone somewhere downstairs. Linda stopped to look down into the hole and scream for Walter, but received no answer. Humming sounded in the living room. Linda looked over to where Rose crouched before the fireplace. The child used tongs to lift something glowing. A large ember of wood. It smoked even as she set it into a wide candle holder.

The child stepped into the foyer alongside Linda, and suddenly the hole in the hallway vanished. The floor looked pristine, not even a sign of the defective floorboard she stumbled on the day she met Walter. Linda considered whether the events that had just happened were nothing more than a nightmare. Perhaps Walter was fine, had never fallen through. Until she noticed the change in the surroundings.

The photos in the hall were absent, though a few paintings hung in their place. A coat rack stood alongside the base of the stairs, with a family's worth of coats hanging from its hooks. Everything appeared new. Rose passed by, oblivious to Linda's presence. And why would she be? Linda did not exist then. The child blew on the ember, keeping it aglow. Linda smelled the smoke from the burning piece as it passed.

When the child disappeared into the kitchen, the pristine surroundings disappeared with her. The hole in the floor reappeared. The sight drew Linda into action. Linda raced to the kitchen and saw Rose descend into the basement. Linda could not concern herself with the girl's fate. She had friends to find. She yelled down the basement stairs.

"Hang on Walter!"

A quick search of cabinets turned up a large flashlight of a type they often used when camping together. The thought saddened Linda, making her wish they went camping rather than visiting Salem. Once turned on, the bright halogen beam even cut through the well-lit kitchen. It would help navigate the basement.

Except after descending the stairs, the basement turned out to be already relatively bright. Not from the lone bulb she knew to be at the base of the stairs, but from candles and lanterns flickering throughout the open space. Linda froze, stunned at the unexpected sight.

It was one thing to think she saw a child earlier. Another to think the hallway reverted to its original time. But now as she looked about the basement, she smelled the strange scent of burning oil from the lanterns, a sweet bordering on offensive odor. And warmth. The cellar itself was cold, distressingly so, but she felt zones of warmth from the burning candles nearby. They burned in wall mounted metal holders at regular intervals around the space.

A soft swishing drew her attention. It came from an area awash in shadows despite the lights filling out much of the space. Linda aimed her flashlight and captured the sight of a girl's back sitting at a workbench. The child diligently brushed the hair of someone out of view.

Linda already knew what to expect but could not look away. Linda lifted the light higher, focusing on the workbench itself. She gasped. A face stared back. Not any face, but that of a woman decapitated. The head balanced on its neck atop the workstation.

The victim appeared eternally surprised, with her mouth slack-jaw open, one eye missing, the other white. Skin sagged, partially sloughed off. The child caught a tangle. Sadie tugged and a chunk of hair and scalp came away in the hairbrush's spokes.

Linda covered her mouth, trying not to gag. In doing so, the flashlight shifted onto the young girl. Sadie turned and half her face fell under the light of the flashlight. The half face in the beam and the half in the shadow were completely different. One side showed a girl long deceased with grey skin, a glossed over eye, and scraggly hair. The other half revealed a vibrant young girl. The dead half opened its side of a mouth and hissed.

Despite the fright, Linda turned away. Past versus present. She needed to find Walter. She aimed her light at the ceiling. There was no hole. It had to be further along in the basement, somewhere behind the brick wall. She never realized at the time how small the basement appeared compared to the actual size of the house. There was missing real estate, blocked off by the same brick wall that Heather inexplicably clawed at.

"Walter!" she cried out again.

There was no answer other than more noise nearby. She turned and lit the area, revealing a pillory rising from the floor (wasn't that what Tom called it?). Linda screamed at the sight of a woman trapped within it. The woman's head dangled low, showing nothing more than a mop of hair. Movement caught her eye, and she shifted the light to where a nude man stood behind the woman,

Father Goode. She recognized him from the book of blood. He stepped away from the woman and further into the light, confused. Goode was fully erect, like the demon in the pictures from the same book. Linda shook her head; it could not be real. Not the vision, but the acts. She fought her instinct to intercede. If there was a way, if she could change the nature of a monster so long ago, she would, but for now, she needed to save someone in the present.

Goode reached into shadows and produced a cane, a wicked looking object capable of significant damage. He raised it and started toward Linda. She pointed the light away from the man and he vanished. She understood a light could not have such power, could not transport one in time. Echoes. Like she and Walter talked about. Wounds of a time so horrific that their energy bled into the land, the walls, the property. Her property. Did she condemn everyone to a similar fate?

"Ruby! Walter! Please, where are you?"

"Here," Walter said, weakly.

The man sounded so far away, but Linda locked on the position. Behind the wall for certain. She aimed the light at the brick, and it became clear, a gap in the center. A door designed to appear flush with the wall. She gripped her fingers in the groove of a damaged brick and the wall opened!

"Linda?" Walter cried out again, wheezing.

Linda rushed forward, trying to forget the past, desperate to reach her friend. A small corridor opened before her. Just beyond the corridor rose bars. A cell! The area was dark and cold. So cold, which made no sense. It was summer break. Salem did not appear to recognize that. A chill, like the coldest of winters, filled the space. Something sounded immediately to the left. She aimed the flashlight and stifled a scream as the beam revealed a woman chained to a wall. Or something approximating a woman. The captive was black with grime, unwashed, unfed, almost too thin for the chains holding her in place. The woman dangled nude, though her long unkempt hair covered her breasts.

When the light landed on the prisoner's face, the woman pulled against the chains, reaching out for help. Linda instinctively reached out, but as her light shifted, the women vanished like the ghost she was. More chains rattle. Linda lifted the beam mere inches further along the wall to where a woman crouched, chained by one leg to the wall. The leash was so short there would be no room for the woman to reposition herself. She sat nude, crouched in an upright fetal position.

One of her hands scrawled words across the wall in something wet. (Blood?) The wall read 'my child' over and over within the woman's reach. The woman's voice clicked and clacked like a language not human. Linda waved the flashlight back and forth over the prisoner. There, then not there. Wherever the light landed showed Linda a different time. She wanted to help but needed to find Walter first.

"It can't be," Walter said before his astonished outcry turned into a coughing jag.

She aimed the light and found Walter atop a stone pedestal in the center of the prison. Shackles sat on the floor next to the large ceremonial structure designed to accommodate a person. While not bound to the top of the stone temple, he could not move. Debris covered sections of his body. Absent his glasses, he looked vulnerable and was in poor shape. Blood-soaked various parts of his clothing and his clothes were dust covered and torn where visible. A large section of his torso lay buried under debris. One shoe vanished somewhere during the descent.

Linda held the flashlight at her side, pointing down, not wishing to blind the man. She rushed to his side and dropped the light. It gave off enough light from the ground for her to make out the extent of the damage surrounding him and covering him. Linda pushed debris off the man. A piece of wood rose high into the air laying atop him. She grabbed it and Walter screamed.

She felt the wood meet resistance and suddenly realized. A portion of staircase rail punctured Walter's chest. Its pointed end jutted up where it impaled Walter in the fall. The movement caused Walter to spasm and scream in agony. Blood poured from the wound and spread further across the chest, bleeding into the material of his shirt before the pool of blood vanished somewhere underneath more debris covering the man.

"I'm sorry. Walter, oh my God. Let me get the rest of this off, then we need to get you to the hospital," Linda said.

Walter breathed and a hiss sounded as air leaked from somewhere. Every breath brought with it agony, but he did his best to hide it from her. He shook his head gently, drawing fresh pain. He just needed to lie down, that was all. Maybe a nap and a cup of tea.

A cup of tea would be quite nice, he thought, but there was something more. He squinted toward the distant wall of the prison. Nothing but blackness from where they stood. He tried to look. Lifting his head hurt immensely, but he had to see.

"Is it my condition, or did I see something?"

"Yes, Walter, you did, but that doesn't matter right now. We need to get you help," she said.

He smiled at her, grateful for the worry, but he needed to know. "Show me. Please. I need to see."

Blood poured from somewhere along his hairline. A track of red rolled down and pooled into one eye. Walter was so far gone he only blinked, almost oblivious to the warm liquid. Linda reached down and wiped the eye clear. He nodded again gently, too tired to say thank you. She gazed at him and saw his eyes flutter. Her own eyes blurred as they filled with tears.

She touched his hair, caressed it, but as much to shift the direction of the bleeding as to provide comfort. Linda offered a tight, pained smile and nodded to the man. She bent and retrieved the flashlight. Picking it up and aiming back at the initial section of the prison wall. The same chained woman appeared.

It pained Linda to witness the woman's predicament, but this was not for her any longer. Walter's eyes widened as he stared in amazement. He lifted his head, coughing but actively viewing the impossible. History revealed itself. Next, the crouched woman. Linda continued passing the light over the wall where so many women struggled against bonds holding them tethered to a world of torture, pain, and death.

The light fell onto a dark corner where eyes shot open from a darkness so grave not even the beam could cut through. Multiple pairs of eyes danced in the dark as if floating. Linda thought maybe they did float. Maybe some broke free of their bodies that men stole from them. Perhaps some women had discovered freedom by escaping not metal bars but their own vessels of skin, which served as prisons themselves in that they housed hearts within cages of ribs. Had some women found a way to no longer exist when darkness struck, when frigid cold stole breath away, when torture visited itself upon skin?

Linda averted the light, unable to take more. Walter remained agog. No amount of misery and evil could dampen the curiosity of a man learning the truth of that which he could only study. He looked up at Linda and coughed again.

"Walter please. Let me free you of this wreckage so we can get you out."

"Wreckage?" As if he could not feel the debris atop him, Walter found the strength in his neck and looked at Linda, pleading. "Show me more. Please."

He could have been a child were he not turning so frightfully pale. His breaths came in sharp gasps, and a section of ceiling covering his waist that formerly rose with each breath had stilled, the breathing too shallow to move it. The only thing that rose in time with each exhale was the wooden obstruction rising like a sword through his chest. It rose and fell with the flow of blood, which seemed never ending.

Linda complied and lifted the light. She aimed it directly at him to see if there was any way to free him. She placed the light on his chest and shoved the debris away. The man was not in his right mind, unable to understand his condition. Linda removed the largest objects, wood, and plaster, hoping not to grab anything else that could hurt him. She would deal with the chest wound last.

Walter's eyes lit up when he saw the light shining in his face. He blinked, blinded momentarily until his eyes adjusted and he realized he looked directly at the sun. He tilted his head toward an overwhelming cacophony.

He turned to his left and witnessed a crowd in a field jeering and crying out. Those in the crowd wore righteous anger on their faces like Halloween masks. Hands raised with fists held high, as if they wished to partake in that which they cheered on.

Walter found he could not move and looked back, finally understanding why. A pile of rocks rose high atop his chest. He was in a field, chained to a rock. A man of imposing size stood over him, as did another man, one who smiled with a black streak running through one tooth.

Someone spoke near his ear, but it was hard to hear over the crowd. Another man, religious. Goode. The man was Goode. He knew him from the pictures. Walter had done it. He had found Linda's family in a way he never could have imagined.

Despite the weight on his chest, Walter breathed deep and smiled, which upset those overseeing his torture. The world smelled different in the days before the industrial revolution. The grass smelled so fresh and would normally terrorize him with allergies, but he was too far gone for that. Walter laughed uncontrollably at the wonderful world around him.

"I know. I understand who you are. Why did you do it? Why did you harm those women?" Walter asked of Goode, Walter's voice too strained to reach any other ears but his intended target.

Goode went white and nodded to the burly man who raised an impossibly large rock and dropped it. Walter braced for the blow, but suddenly found himself in darkness once again. A fresh pain overcame him. Was there something in his chest? He looked at the object jutting through his chest, and he tried not to move for the pain it caused him. Linda stood over him now, looking far more lovely than the trio he was recently with.

She held the light near his feet, pushing something away. With a crash, she shoved a beam off his waist and onto the floor. That felt better, he thought.

"I understand. I understand now..." he said weakly.

"Understand what?" Linda asked.

"The past and my unfortunate present," he said.

"Let's get you out. I can share with you the contents of the child's journal."

"No need to tell me. I understand. I see it all now."

Walter looked past Linda to where the light had inadvertently pointed. Walter saw the women, so many tied up in various positions, all ragged, tortured, a single breath away from death. Tears formed in Walter's eyes as he viewed the horrific sight. Actual history not filtered through the lens of nostalgia. He winced at either the thought of his sensationalistic speeches before packed houses or from the pain in his chest. He was fading.

"You don't have to tell me what was in the child's journal. I see it all now," Walter said.

Linda watched as the color drained from his face. "Stay with me. You're a historian. You can write all about this."

"They will not let us go. The sins of the fathers..."

"Don't talk like that. You're scaring me," Linda said.

Linda grabbed his hand to lift him, but he cried out in agony. She quickly let him fall back into place, then raced into the basement and turned on the lightbulb. She extinguished the lantern to stay focused on the present. The light guided her to the workbench, which contained no visible heads, only boxes of clutter. She found rags and grabbed them before rushing back into the prison. She had no choice but to use the light there, but she kept it aimed low, toward the floor.

"Walter. This is going to hurt, but we need to remove the obstruction to move you. We need to get you help soon." He did not answer. His face was sickeningly pale. "Walter, please answer. You're scaring me!"

He looked up at her and smiled before finding his voice once again. "That is five for five. Something to be proud of in there somewhere."

Linda set the light back on his waist and nodded. "That's right. You're going to be fine and scare me aplenty in the future. I will forgive all if you just be okay. You need to be okay. I'm going to pull this out and then press the cloth into the wound. It might hurt, but I don't know what else to do," Linda said.

She grabbed the board with both hands and pulled. She was relieved to find it slid easily, but worried about what the result might be. He grimaced but did not cry out. As the obstruction came part way out of his body, Linda felt a tug. Linda checked but failed to identify an obstruction. Yet it became harder to pull. She put her strength into it and yanked the board free.

Then screamed!

The pointing woman's hand gripped the end of the board, her arm rising through the same wound that penetrated Walter's body. She held the wood in a tug-of-war with Linda. The woman's arm rose out of Walter's body up to an elbow.

The woman somehow rested below Walter, her face grinned over his shoulder. Rivulets of blood poured down the woman's arm, spilling across Walter's chest. Linda dropped her end of the board, as did the Pointing Woman. It dropped to the ground, freed from Walter's torso, but he remained impaled on her arm, which continued rising, taking Walter's body with it. Walter started lifting off the pedestal, coughing through the pain, gagging as blood filled his mouth.

Linda stepped back and watched as Walter all but levitated, lifting off the pedestal as a relentless arm threatened to push all the way through his body. His torso lifted while his arms and legs dangled lifelessly. Linda grabbed the flashlight and aimed it directly in the Pointing Woman's face!

Verity Soule stood on the gallows looking out at the crowd, a noose around her neck. Linda stood in the field, watching in shock as the woman dropped. A loud crack filled the air. Another woman fell as well, but Linda could not avert her gaze from the striking woman looking peaceful in death until she opened her eyes.

The woman's head tilted on a broken neck and her arm raised. Throngs of assembled people fled as the hanging woman sought individuals in the crowd until her finger found its target. Linda? Linda glanced to her side and spotted the young children and their parents. They stood next to her.

Linda gripped the flashlight in one hand but felt a small hand take her other. She looked down at a concerned young Rose. The poor thing had a red blotch over most of her face, a deformity that would likely have followed her into adulthood were she ever to reach it.

"I'm scared," the little girl said to the stranger whose hand she held.

"I am too," Linda said truthfully.

Verity continued spouting a curse as Linda turned off the flashlight.

Darkness. Linda waited and turned it on again. Walter lay there, no pointing woman in sight, but his wound bled liberally.

She grabbed the assembled rags and pressed them to his wounds. They turned red so quickly, so wet under her hands. It was not working. All color had left Walter's face. He still smiled at her.

"Walter, please hang on. I'll get help," she said. "Ruby! Heather! Tom! Somebody!"

"Do not fret. You showed me. This is history. I am not studying it. I am living it. This is real. This is my evidence. I am living history now. I'm living..." Then he spoke no more.

Linda took his face in her hands. "Walter. No. Please, Walter. Please come back."

It was too late. Walter was gone, smiling at her even in death.

CHAPTER 37

L INDA CLOSED HER EYES and listened. She searched for a sign that the nightmares experienced in the new environment had taken hold, that she really had not lost someone dear to her. The first genuine friend in such a long time. She had opened herself up to a man who could not seem to find his way around her. Linda smiled despite everything, almost bursting into laughter at the awkwardness on display that was Walter. Then she thought about him further and choked back a sob.

Gone. He was gone. She opened her eyes to confirm. It was a nightmare, but a waking one. She lost her friend. Then she realized she still had not seen others. Footsteps sounded in the distance from outside the cell. The footsteps were soft enough to be those of her missing friend. Loathe to leave Walter, Linda cried out from where she stood.

"Ruby? Ruby, please, I need you!" Linda wondered if her friend would even respond. After all that Linda had done.

A humming rose above the footfalls. Did Ruby know the song from the music box? And the voice did not match. Linda raised the flashlight, aiming it toward the cell entrance. The cell door was no longer open. Linda had never illuminated the entire room and therefore missed the prisoner chained near the entrance on the opposite side of the door from the wall-chained woman.

This new prisoner was a frail bird wrapped in filthy rags. Only a single ankle chain kept her tied down and she had decent mobility. The woman rushed to the bars and hummed the song back.

"Kind one. What do you bring?"

Rose appeared at the cell door, looking nervously over her shoulder. Linda glimpsed Sadie at the workbench in the distance. Sadie appeared to scold her sister, but Linda could not hear the words. Rose turned to the woman in the cell and displayed the burning ember that already leaned toward burning out. Rose blew on it and a small trail of smoke swirled into the cell, chasing one of many frigid drafts inside.

The woman smiled at the child. "You have brought us freedom."

"Freedom? I am afraid not. I wished to bring food, but after the last time, they punished me with none of my own. Instead, I brought warmth," Rose said, displaying the candleholder and its contents.

"Were I not aware of the suffering your actions have caused us all, I would think you were a mere innocent child. Perhaps you are only naïve if you cannot see freedom in your hands."

The child looked down, and Sadie appeared to understand. Linda watched the older sister cry out a warning too late. The old woman shoved the candleholder into the girl's gown, which ignited immediately.

Rose screamed as the fire quickly claimed her body. She turned to run away, but the old woman grabbed the burning child through the bars and her own clothes ignited! The woman burst into flames but did not cry out. Instead, the woman raised her hands to the sky and waved them back and forth slowly, as if dancing.

Linda screamed as the woman finally lowered a finger and pointed like the accusers of yore. The woman's fingertip and arm, burning brightly, illuminated the prison, revealing the next woman in the cell. The woman reached out and took the burning woman's hand.

That prisoner burned. The woman, blonde, bruised over much of her body, swiped her hand down as if sluicing it through water, lighting a pile of rags near the floor, igniting remnants of torn clothes. She grabbed a pile of the rags and threw them toward the next woman in line who remained out of reach. Chained tight to a wall like the initial prisoner in the room.

The woman lit up, burning in place, unable to move, but a smile of relief overtook the woman. Tears rolled down her face and quickly turned to steam. The second prisoner kicked a clot of across the room within reach of those huddled in the deepest shadows. They emerged, blinking at the brightness of freedom rising before them. Each grabbed portions, enough to ensure their way out of the cell.

The women acted in unison, never crying out in pain. They danced together, partaking in the deadly escape route until one by one they ceased moving, leaving behind bodies no longer controlled by the whims of man.

Linda wept over the stunning display of humanity. Outside the cell, Sadie screamed for her father's help, though Rose had already lost her life to the curse of her own making. If the child felt guilt over her actions, at least she, too, was free. Rose fell away from the bars while fire spread in and out of the cell.

Caught between two times, Linda could only watch, could not intercede, could not change the past. She never even felt the heat of the prisoners closest to her. But then, something strange happened. She smelled smoke. Close. Scanning with the flashlight, Linda sought the source, but her beam showed fire everywhere. She raced for the cell bars only to find them locked!

She felt heat at the closed cell door and douse the flashlight. Orange flames lit up the dark cellar. It was Rose. The child burned in both times, except the current one wore a sickening skull for a face before her face shifted back to that of a child. The girl giggled as she sat there burning just outside the cell doors.

Smoke billowed in, filling the space with a different darkness, one born of smoke and ash. Linda fought through tears as the particulates stung her eyes and tickled her lungs. The cell remained locked, even in the present. There was no way out.

Then a growl. Close by from inside the cell. Ferocious. The animalistic sound swept the room, and Linda understood it was no echo. Something hunted. It barked and through a rising cloud of smoke she saw a flash of black fur. The beast used the smoke as camouflage, taking its time stalking trapped prey.

Red eyes danced in the gloom, flashing occasionally so quickly after repositioning repeatedly. It knew it had the upper hand. Linda turned the light back on, set it on the floor aimed at a spot in the distance. She recognized the eyes as those which filled Andrew with cold cruelty. Linda made a stand.

"Where are you? What are you? You took my friend from me. Are you too frightened to take me? Are you so scared you need to hide in the shadows? Come out, you pathetic coward!"

It revealed itself, a dog of monstrous proportions, fangs bared, the drool spilling down its fangs which glittered orange while reflecting the flames outside the cell. If beasts could grin, this one did, hungry to take new flesh. Linda searched the red eyes. In them she thought she glimpsed women at the ends of ropes dangling before crowds of wicked men. When it narrowed its eyes, she knew it was about to attack.

Following the path of the flashlight beam, Linda raced further into the cell. The beast matched her trajectory, repositioning itself and leaping through the air. Linda grabbed the wooden stake that had killed Walter and dropped onto her back, raising the stick high.

The beast landed on the wooden spike, impaling it near its heart. Linda felt her arms ready to collapse under the weight. Locking her arms, Linda kept her grip even while the beast soared over her head, following its initial momentum interrupted by the piercing of flesh mid-flight. It howled as it flew past. Once it hit the ground, Linda scrambled to her feet, not waiting for the thing to gain an advantage.

With so much smoke in the room, she isolated its location by watching for its blazing red eyes. The wild thing thrashed, trying to dislodge the deadly point, but the stick wedged too deep into the heart of evil. Given up on ridding itself of the wood, the creature faced off with Linda. The growling was as ferocious as earlier but rattled with air escaping from the wound.

It barked ferociously at Linda before fleeing by crashing through the cell doors. The beast burst into flames when it leaped over the burning child at the entrance, howling through fresh pain as it sought an exit. It found one by smashing through the bulkhead and slipping into the night.

There was a heavy storm and Linda wondered if the rain would be enough to stop the spread of flames? It did not. A new line of fire spread straight out in the distance, following the animal's escape route. Sizzling heat reached Linda through a smothering blanket of smoke. Flames sizzled as the tinderbox home fed the flames. Linda struggled to breathe.

Linda approached the open cell door, but the child stood blocking the door, burning still. Rose spotted Linda and extended the candle holder and ember. The child smiled at Linda with a face that flickered back and forth between innocence and a flaming skull.

"I am sorry. They punished me for sharing food before, so the only thing I could sneak this time was warmth," Rose said.

There was no way out. Even if Linda could get past the child, more flames filled the space beyond and grew. Linda returned to the prison. She choked, searching for a way out, but like the prisoners before her, Linda was trapped.

Then she spotted Walter, smiling as ever. Her heart ached, but she understood his resting place was the way out. Linda climbed up on the side of the altar and reached for the hole in the ceiling. The ceiling was too far. She leaped, touched the edge, and fell back into the wall of smoke. She readied to jump again when something grabbed her. Linda screamed and lashed out until she saw him.

"Andrew?"

Andrew's face was pale, matching Walter's pallor at the end. Or even that of the dead girls. The look of someone on borrowed time, but he was alive. And ready to attack? She raised her arms, but he shook his head and tried to lock into a smile but grimaced in pain instead.

"Don't worry. It's me. The real me," he said. "Let's go. I'll lift you, then you help me up."

She nodded and they approached the altar. Linda turned to him, one thought on her mind. "Ruby?"

He shook his head as an answer. The smoke already filled Linda's eyes with tears, so there was room for no more. Before she could climb back up, he grabbed her and spun her to face him. She did not fight back this time. Andrew finally found his smile.

"I wanted you to know you always had family. Always. You were never alone. I'm sorry for everything I said."

"Andrew, right now, fuck apologies. Let's go," she said.

Linda climbed up onto the altar and her leg bumped Walter's torso. She shuddered but found her footing. Andrew followed and lifted her at the waist, high enough for her to catch the edge of the floor above. The floor had broken clean, and the edge felt solid. She struggled to pull herself up.

Andrew released her waist and grabbed her kicking legs, giving a second push which allowed her to make it to the solid ground above. Smoke billowed up through the opening, but no flames were visible in the main part of the home beyond the nearby burning fireplace in the living room. The formerly cozy spot felt menacing while the world burned below. The fire would eventually spread but had not yet, giving her time.

Linda rose to her feet to regain feeling and strength in her limbs. Looking down into the abyss, she saw nothing but thick, dark smoke. Linda hoped she had the strength to lift Andrew. She dropped to the floor on her stomach, leaning over the edge, feeling solid in the position. If nothing else, he could climb over her to get back up. Still, she reached out.

"I'm in place!" Linda yelled down.

She felt his hand waving in the dark and brushed against hers before falling away. She could not see him for the thick wall of smoke. Both coughed, giving them some sense of the other's location.

"I can't see. No way to get your hand. Back up. I'll leap for the ledge, and you can help me up," Andrew said.

Linda stepped away from the ledge and waited. She could easily see the edge of the hole in the floor. It was the space above the hole where the curtain of smoke made it impossible to see. The smoke rose straight toward the second floor in a column. The balance of the house remained clear. With a grunt, Andrew caught the ledge and dangled, swinging wildly from the motion but holding firm from the chest up.

Dropping back down onto her stomach, Linda grabbed Andrew's arms and pulled as he struggled to lift himself up. It was working. He rose until his arms extended straight from the floor, bringing his body along for the ride. Linda fell back, still gripping his shirt even after he began lifting himself. Then he jerked to a stop.

Andrew looked down into the darkness, confused, trying to see what snagged his legs. He pulled again, unable to rise any further. "I'm stuck on something," he said, then screamed.

The crackle of fire was distressingly loud below. The fury of the flames provided a soundtrack, a coda to the home, an announcement that the structure's end was imminent. Yet a disturbing sound dwarfed that of the flames.

Snap!

Loud. Unnatural. Sickening. Already pale, Andrew's face lost another shade. His eyes shot wide, and his arms faltered. Linda gripped his shirt tighter, understanding he might fall. She yanked but encountered resistance greater than simply his weight.

Snap!

Andrew screamed again, his arms collapsing, causing his upper body to smack into the hallway floor. The face plant drew blood from his nose. Stunned, he glanced up at Linda, who lost her grip on him.

"I'm sorry," Andrew said.

Then he vanished, yanked obscenely quick back into the darkness. Linda screamed and scrambled to the edge of the hole, looking down, trying to spot him.

"Andrew!"

Snap! Snap! Snap!

Linda blinked with every horrific sound. Andrew ceased screaming the moment he vanished back down the hole. Linda searched for movement, but it was too dark. With a whoosh, the smoke spiraled into a twister as something disrupted the flow. An object shot up through the hole, flying over Linda's head from where she sat crouched near the gaping hole. She followed the object's flight.

Object it was. She had to think of it that way. Merely an object because it resembled nothing human, even though it once was. The thing that used to be Andrew landed in a heap just inside the living room. The legs were bent at forty-five-degree angles jutting sideways at the knees. His arms were in a similar state, twisted in unnatural angles which made no sense, dangling so loose it was as if the shell of skin held detached limbs inside the body.

And finally, the worst. Though Andrew landed on his stomach, his face was visible, the head turned all the way around on the neck. Unlike Walter, Andrew did not die smiling. The twisted limbs provided an answer for the source of the horrendous snaps.

Linda shoved a fist against her mouth and screamed into her hand, biting down, unable to process what lay nearby. Then more smoke swirled as something else broke through. A rope rose rapidly into the air in a form as solid as a pole. It kept rising, shooting past Linda, going higher and higher, moving so quickly. Like a magician's ribbon trick, it seemed never ending and the length should have long ago reached the ceiling above. Yet it never stopped, disappearing somewhere in a cloud of smoke which caressed the upper ceiling.

Soon a thread of black intertwined in the rope as it passed. The black strands ran the length of the rope, continuous, growing larger, more prominent, until black hair came into view, flowing as if weightless or underwater. A face followed, locked in a noose at the neck. The pointing woman. She grinned blackened teeth as she swung like a pendulum, her eyes locked with Linda's.

Linda ran toward the stairs, taking them two at a time. The Pointing Woman rose as well, riding the rope up to the second floor. Linda reached the landing and grabbed the knife from earlier, which remained stuck in the hallway floorboard. She sliced into the air. The arc of the blade cut clean through the rope. The Pointing Woman dropped, vanishing into the inferno below. Linda lowered the knife to her side and rushed back down the stairs to the living room. Once there, she opened the front door, a step away from freedom.

Even the howling storm seemed welcoming after the events inside. Linda felt rain pelt her face. Never had it felt so good. Fresh air cascaded around her, mixing with the scent of rain-soaked grass. The van sat parked in the driveway, a reminder of happier times, a reminder of the freedom of the road. A reminder of her friends. Her family.

Linda slammed the door on the outside world, then turned back to the home where the far end of the hall caught fire. Linda stormed into the living room, avoiding looking at her long gone friend. She raised the knife and sliced into the couch, dragging the blade along its length, loosening tufts of cotton filler. She tore at the exposed fabric of the couch and ripped strips free of the furniture.

Smoke billowed into the living room, using the fireplace as an escape. Fire crackled at her rear, an inferno growing. Linda wrapped the strips of fabric over the end of a fireplace poker then reached it into the fireplace. The makeshift torch ignited. Keeping the flame at arm's length she touched it to the couch which went up in flames. She touched it to the curtains which did the same. Tears filled her eyes, but she kept her coughing in check, trying not to breathe too deep.

It was HER home. And she was the last. Linda remembered the brave women in the cell and their quest for freedom. Linda vowed to partake of the same escape to make certain the curse harmed no one again. If ghosts of the past could perish, she would take them with her. In her home on her terms.

Linda dragged the poker of flame behind as she stepped into the foyer and ascended the stairs. Once on the second floor, she entered the room at the end of the hall and opened the closet, lighting Heather's and Tom's things on fire. The closet quickly went up. She then moved to Ruby's bedroom and lit the bed and curtains.

Behind her, a window exploded from Heather's room. The place was quickly going up. The smoke made it hard to breathe, but Linda did not mind. She counted on it as she tossed the poker off to one side and entered her room, where she laid on the bed and closed her eyes.

Then they shot open. Linda leaped off the bed, grabbed the music box and stepped into the burning hallway and dropped the thing into the hole in the floor below. Everything in its place.

She returned to her bedroom and closed the door. She got on the bed again and crossed her arms, waiting.

When Linda closed her eyes, she smiled, hearing the laughter of the orphans so dear to her. She thought of her friends and the wonderful times, the wining and dining, and even occasionally crying. They took so much from her, but she would never allow them to take the memories. Linda would take them with her wherever she was going.

Linda opened her eyes, not surprised at the sight waiting for her at the foot of the bed. The Pointing Woman stood alongside Dead Sadie, and Dead Rose. Somehow, the accusers had joined with the accused, all trapped in a loop, unable to escape the events that culminated in such terror and sorrow. They all pointed at Linda's face. Guilty by bloodline.

"Take me! I'm the last one. There are no more after me. Take me so you can finally burn in Hell!"

Linda's eyes faltered; the smoke would take her before the flames. Her breath faltered as she used up her oxygen to rail at her accusers. As her head drooped, she thought she saw the trio's arms point lower, somewhere else. Until no one pointed at her anymore. She left on her terms as the world went black.

CHAPTER 38

A MURMURING VOICE BROUGHT Linda around. Remembering the fire, she jerked upright and regretted it. She felt woozy, so gripped the nearest thing she could for support. The metal rails of a bed? Was she in a hospital? She blinked, trying to emerge from her fugue. The voice continued, whispering as if keeping secrets from her. She struggled to make out the words.

"Sorry, I have to call you back."

Linda turned toward the voice and screamed. Reverend Goode stood at the end of her bed, naked once again, dripping with sweat. He swung the cane. Linda raised her arms in defense, only for someone to pull them away. Gently.

"Hey. Hey. It's okay. You're okay." Then doubt. "Are you okay?"

It was not Reverend Goode. A different authority figure stood at the end of her bed, fully dressed. He looked haggard and held a cellphone which explained the talking that woke her. Officer Taylor looked at her with concern.

"You're back with us," Taylor said.

"My friends? Why are you here? Where are my friends?"

The man's face shifted, a little too practiced. But she could read his face. Linda figured he practiced on many people over the years. Now it was her turn. Surely, someone had to be okay. He would have led with that. The fact Taylor did not soften the blow struck her gut and her heart.

"Oh no, no, no." She dropped back into the bed, struggling to remain conscious, trying not to think about it. She failed. Tears bubbled in her eyes.

Her head turned and fell on the nearby chair covered in snacks galore, a bit of a mess. Taylor moved in closer to remain in view as she reclined. He slid over to block her view of the unkempt area.

"Sorry. Someone on our team has been sitting on you for weeks."

"Weeks?"

"First week you were unconscious. Doctors could not understand why, but it gave them time to work on superficial burns and the cuts on your forehead. You woke occasionally, screaming. Asking for your friends each time. Doctors have kept you mostly sedated. There's a clarity in your eyes now. First time I've seen it."

"Ruby..." Linda bit her lip, lost in thought.

"Look. The reason we have sat with you is to make certain no one is after you. We will need some questions answered soon so we can determine what happened. They have instructed me to get a doctor as soon as you wake, but if you can tell me anything about why someone targeted you. Walter called me..."

"Walter?"

Taylor nodded, but Linda was not asking a question. She remembered. Her heart ached even more. Taylor continued; unaware she was on a different train of thought than he was.

"He called and said it appeared someone was attacking you in your bedroom window."

She nodded. "Andrew."

"Your friend? Was he behind this?"

"Oh, poor Andrew. He wasn't himself," Linda said.

He wasn't even a person, or much of one at the end, Taylor thought. He searched her face. There was so much she held back. How else to explain the pretzel that was Andrew? One of the worst corpses Taylor had ever seen. But the call from Walter suggested it was Andrew as well, and Taylor had a bad vibe about the man. But what? Andrew killed everyone, then committed suicide by playing an aggressive game of Twister? No, something else was going on. He wanted answers, but would wait. He already had waited six weeks.

And now she was awake. "Before I get the doctor, when did you last hear from Tom?"

The question threw Linda. She attempted to figure out what the officer meant while trying not to think about what happened to her friends. Maybe Thomas was okay. Hopefully, he ran away, but if he did, it meant things were not over. The sins of the fathers would visit them all. She answered the officer. "I haven't seen him since he left."

"He left without his things?" Taylor asked.

Linda nodded. Then a thought struck her. "How do you know he left without his things?"

"We found his clothes in a closet."

Linda's eyes shot open wide. *A closet I burned*, she thought. Then another thing registered. Superficial burns? She glanced at her gown covered body. Skinnier than when everything started, she clearly had not been eating regular food for some time, but she remained burn free.

"Didn't the house burn?" Linda asked through a cotton mouth.

"What? No. Some smoke damage, but the place is intact. How else did you think we found all the bodies?"

"Bodies?" Plural. Oh, no. The dizziness grew. She found it hard to focus on his words. The house burned. She burned it.

"The fire was extinguished by the time I arrived. Maybe it was the rain, maybe something else."

"Something else for sure," Linda said.

"Tom is unaccounted for," Taylor said.

He searched Linda's face again, seeing if that meant anything. At the least, it did not instill terror in her. Maybe he did not attack Linda, but all the others. The man could have partnered up with Andrew and together they offed everyone. After it was done, to make sure there were no witnesses, Tom killed Andrew.

Everything was falling into place. Five minutes with Linda back in the world and Taylor had a good idea of everything that happened. Eager to put out a fresh BOLO on Tom, Taylor left the room and sought a doctor.

Linda fidgeted. Why did she allow the man to suspect Tom? And where was Tom? Deep down, she knew. Tom was likely gone, along with the others. All Linda had to do now was to live a hermit life, or not live at all. She was the last. It ended with her. She could not figure everything out as the medication kept her woozy.

The doctor entered, the same woman who treated Heather. "Well, look who is awake," the doctor said, lifting the chart like a prop. She did not appear to read anything but got to the point. "Have you always suffered from night terrors?"

"Always? Never. Do I now?"

The doctor harrumphed and wrote something on the chart. Maybe there was something to it. The doctor examined Linda's face. She squinted, then futzed with the tubes and equipment connected to Linda, who did not ask what any of it was or what any of it did. Too fuzzy.

"I was concerned about how long you have been out. It made little sense with your friend who visited us before either. Sorry for your loss."

Heather? Heather was gone? They found her? Nothing made sense to Linda.

"Your injuries, while not inconsequential, were not life threatening. For severe burns, we sometimes induce a coma to allow time for a patient to get through skin grafts and such. You never needed that and have completely healed in the six weeks since you arrived."

Linda twitched, imagining the fire again. Then she saw Andrew fly overhead. She saw Walter on the altar designed as a torture device. She saw in her mind the women dancing in flames. The doctor wrote something else on the chart.

"We offer counseling."

"I'm fine Linda said," while thinking she was anything but. All she wanted was to leave Salem, to get as far away as possible. There was no one left for the curse to hurt besides her, not even Tom. Sadly, she no longer believed he left. Authorities would likely find his body, eventually.

Walter, poor Walter, informed her she was the last. She would take Walter at his word that she was the last in the bloodline. The doctor went on about treatments and next steps, but Linda only wanted the woman to leave. Once in the clear, Linda planned to test her ability to walk (though currently it seemed unlikely). She asked the doctor to cut back on the meds. The doctor nodded and wrote something else on the chart.

The cop glanced in. Linda vowed not to drag him in any further. She would test her legs once everyone left her alone and she would slip off into the night, as far away from Salem as she could get.

She thought of how her friends pushed hard for her to find someone, anyone, to start a family of her own. Now, more than ever, she understood she would remain forever alone. Never would she get close to anyone again. Never would she allow anyone in. She would decide at some point whether to even keep teaching. All that mattered now was dealing with arrangements for her friends and getting out of Salem. She was the last. It was over. The Pointing Woman and the children could take her, Linda would not mind. She suffered too much pain. Too much loss.

Linda nodded occasionally as the doctor kept talking, but Linda was miles away, visiting memories in her mind. The doctor finally made her way to the door. Before exiting, the doctor stopped and looked back.

"Oh. I almost forgot. The good news is that your baby is fine. Congratulations." The doctor exited with a smile.

Any remaining color on Linda's face drained. Then she remembered the bedroom. The Pointing Woman, along with the children, had initially pointed at her. Linda assumed judgement. Like the witches in Salem, the trio found Linda guilty.

But they lowered their arms. Why? She finally understood. Their lowered hands pointed at her stomach. They knew! It was not over. There would be more. Unless Linda could hide her child, make him or her vanish in the eyes of the world, ghosts would continue to walk the halls of a house in Salem, reliving the sins of the past.

Linda closed her eyes, trying to decide how to protect a child not yet born. But it was hers. And Andrew's, the real Andrew, the one she would forever love. Linda would finally have her own family. And in doing so, she understood for the first time how much her own mother had loved her.

THE LITTLE COFFEE SHOP OF HORRORS ANTHOLOGY VOLUME 2 PREVIEW

THE BIG GUY

I DIDN'T NEED A badge to navigate the police tape. The assembled officers were expecting me. Most did not like me. That's fine, I'm not a fan of myself either. Still, I had a job to do, and I was good at what I did. Very good. Too good sometimes. My doggedness drove many a person from my life, usually those of the female persuasion. There was one I missed more than others. Unlike some that I pissed off along the way, I understood Amy would not be coming back any time soon.

Amy was a simple name for a complicated woman. Things began badly between her and me and ended worse. Despite my desire to make things work, she made clear her intention to never see me again. Circumstances worked in her favor. The fact I was thinking about Amy instead of whatever I was walking into shows how routine murders had become in the city. Sad but more of the same.

Until I saw the crime scene. Amy vanished from my thoughts along with other women whose names I could not remember to begin with. This murder was big. Literally. Though I'd been a PI for half my lifetime, I understood this would be no ordinary case. The evidence before me differed from any I had ever seen. Starting with the color of chalk on the ground.

"Blue?" I asked, referring to the outline of the deceased on the pavement.

"Right out of white we were. My partner Toomie had blue carpenter chalk in her trunk, so we went with that," Hector said.

Hector was a good bloke. I call him bloke because he speaks with a British accent. He is Latino but suffered through a nasty car accident a few years back and came out talking that way. He made up plenty of words as well, but coworkers and friends never corrected the mistakes. We mostly figured out what he was trying to say. He was great at what he did, though. Like I said, a good bloke. Hector shook his head at the scene.

"Blimey," Hector said.

"Blimey indeed," I repeated. "Took a lot of chalk for this one. Big guy."

"The biggest," Hector said.

I circled the spot where they found the body, which they had already removed. "Strange spot for an ambush of a guy so large," I mused.

Hector nodded in agreement. "Took six right toughers to get him in the coroner's van."

While circling the outline, I noticed damage to a brick wall in the alley. A shopkeeper looked out through the fresh hole in his establishment, watching the ruckus. I waved at the weasel of a man. Who says I'm not nice? The shopkeeper twiddled his fingers back at me. From what I could see through the hole in the wall, the damaged business was a bookstore. There were no bricks on the outside of the hole, meaning they all fell inward.

"What do you suppose caused the damage?" I asked Hector.

"The noggin' I suppose."

"Speaking of. Did you run out of chalk?"

"No, Toomie did not run out. Her outline is right exact it is."

I let go a long overdue harrumph. That was curious. The chalk outline rounded closed atop the massively broad shoulders, meaning someone made off with the big guy's head. There was no mistaking the outline. I never even asked who the victim was. Only one guy that size around town and everyone knew him. Love or hate the big guy (and most hated him) there was no mistaking that someone had just offed Frankenstein's Monster.

And they did it by means other than fire and pitchfork brigade. No matter how it went down, the big guy tumbled and his head struck the wall, breaking through. From there he bounced back and landed lengthwise in the alley, otherwise he might not have even fit. The kicker was that someone made off with his head.

There were plenty who would have liked to off the big lug after that whole thing with the young girl some years back. Say what you will. The guy did his time. He had been a mostly solid citizen since his release from prison. But why take the head?

Solve that and I'd solve the case. I knew it wouldn't be easy, though. These things rarely were. Something crunched underfoot. I looked down and spotted some broken glass. There would be plenty of that in an alley. I needed to look for things that did not belong to learn what happened. A cursory glance revealed nothing telling. No smoking guns. When I got a minute, I would check what business was opposite the bookstore. I failed to notice when I arrived. Whatever business it was, it had no wall issues. They got lucky over which way the big guy fell.

The worker watching us was a potential witness. I threw a thumb toward the shopkeeper. "Whole thing must have caused a ruckus. Did our guy over here hear anything?"

"Nutter," Hector said.

"Nothing?" I asked, assuming Hector had misused the word.

"No. Nutter," Hector reiterated by waving a finger around his temple. "Says he was unlocking his shop after lunch when he heard the noise. By the time he got inside and looked through the hole, someone was racing down the alley. Says it was an alien."

"An alien? Like from space?"

"Aye."

It was Hector that started it. He snickered, and that got me started and soon we were grabbing our sides laughing so much. Never in my life had I heard anything as ridiculous as aliens. My eyes were tearing up from the type of laughter that you can't stop once it starts. Something hit me mid-guffaw, though.

"Maybe he saw a werewolf?" I asked through a gale of laughter.

"No. Says some of his customers are werewolves. Knows them right well he does. No, this here fella is seeing aliens. Little green men," Hector answered, wiping his eyes.

I laughed some more, thinking about little green men while looking at the chalk outline of the former big green man. The laughter finally died as sure as the victim did.

"Is Frankenstein's Monster the name on the death certificate?" I asked.

"Toomie!" Hector waved his partner over.

Toomie was a pro body builder when she wasn't busy being a cop. She was whip smart and would soon be in the role of detective. She was quick to take to me, figuring we'd work together someday. Her biggest muscle was her heart, though. She cared a lot about people. Maybe too much.

"Hello, Dalton," she said.

"Toomie."

"What did they tag him as?" Hector asked.

"Frank Jr." Toomie kicked the ground.

Rocks flew, plural. The woman could have given the big guy a run for his money where few others could. But someone managed. Taking off with the head as a trophy, no less.

"Frank Jr. it is," I said.

"Shame what happened to that little girl," Toomie said, looking straight into my eyes since she matched my six-one height.

"My thoughts exactly," I replied.

That made her smile, which I liked plenty. That warm heart showed through whenever she flashed those teeth. Word was she had a thing for werewolves, both his and hers, but I did not traffic in rumour. And if that was her thing, they were lucky to have her. Get this woman her detective badge. By mentioning the little girl, Toomie forecast who I should look into first and she was right.

"I'll be in touch. See ya Toomie, Hector."

Toomie nodded.

"Cheerio," Hector said.

I tipped an imaginary cap and went in search of my Mustang, parked somewhere outside the perimeter of the police tape. It was time to find out what happened to the sometimes gentle-giant. Originally born of dead bodies, Frank Jr. was dead again, and it was my job to find the monster who did it. Human or otherwise.

F OR UPDATES ON THIS and other new releases visit: paulca
rrohorror.com or scan below:

ABOUT THE AUTHOR

Paul Carro is a Windham, Maine native who left the delightful winters of New England to pursue a film/TV career in Los Angeles. After years writing and producing in film and television, Paul returned to his literary roots and his love of horror. A lifelong horror nerd, Paul has finally started crafting work in the genre he loves, starting with his debut horror novel The House. When not watching horror movies, reading horror books, or listening to horror podcasts, Paul can be found traveling and hiking all over the state. He continues living in Santa Monica, CA to this day.

PAUL CARRO

ALSO BY PAUL CARRO

For those who like their coffee dark and their stories darker. The Little Coffee Shop of Horrors Anthology is the highly rated debut horror anthology by Paul Carro and Joseph Carro. If you love crazy hill people, evil witches, creatures from the deep, and coffee, you will love these twelve terrifying tales!

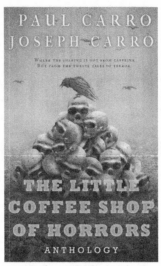

*For updates on this and other
projects, visit:
paulcarrohorror.com*

ALSO BY PAUL CARRO

THE HOUSE

Horror has found a home! Nine strangers with nine secrets so dark they plan to take them to their graves. One house is willing to accommodate them all. The House is now open. Enter if you dare! See why *Comic Book Resources* named ***The House*** as one of their top ten horror novels!

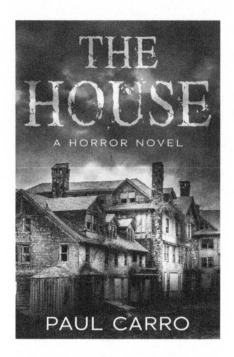

ALSO BY PAUL CARRO

ROOTS OF ALL EVIL

A cult murder. A missing wife. A deadly secret. Two families must travel to the ends of the earth to find their missing loved one. When terror strikes the idyllic farm town they learn that it only takes one bad seed to raise a little Hell!

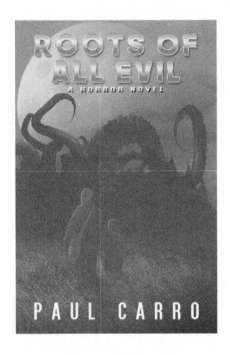

Made in the USA
Monee, IL
14 May 2022